UNDER OBSERVATION

Amalie Skram

UNDER
OBSERVATION

❧

Translated from the Norwegian
by
Katherine Hanson
&
Judith Messick

WOMEN IN TRANSLATION
SEATTLE
1992

Originally published as two novels, *Professor Hieronimus* and *Paa St. Jørgen*, in 1895.

Publication of this book was made possible in part with support from the National Endowment for the Arts and from NORLA (Norwegian Literature Abroad).

Text and cover design by John D. Berry.

The cover painting is *Interiør. Strandgade 30 (Interior with sitting woman)*, 1908, Vilhelm Hammershøi (1864–1916). Oil on canvas, 79 × 66 cm. Reproduced with permission from the Aarhus Kunstmuseum, Aarhus, Denmark.

Skram, Amalie, 1846–1905.
[Professor Hieronimus. English]
Under observation / by Amalie Skram ; translated from the
Norwegian by Katherine Hanson and Judith Messick.
p.   cm.
Contents: Professor Hieronimus — St. Jørgen's.
ISBN 1-879679-03-5 (pbk.: acid-free)
1. Skram, Amalie, 1846–1905—Translations into English.
I. Skram, Amalie, 1846–1905. Paa St. Jørgen. English. 1992.
II. Title.
PT8928.P713 1992
839.8'236—DC20   92-14129
CIP

Printed in the United States of America
First edition, October 1992

Women in Translation
3131 Western Avenue #410
Seattle WA 98121

Contents

Translators' Note

UNDER OBSERVATION originally appeared as two novels: *Professor Hieronimus*, in February of 1895, and *Paa St. Jørgen*, in November of the same year. In 1899, the London publisher John Lane issued an English edition of *Professor Hieronimus*, translated by Alice Stronach and G. B. Jacoby. Our translation restores a number of the lines and words that Stronach and Jacoby chose to omit. Over the years the novels have appeared in a number of Norwegian editions. As we worked on *Under Observation* we noticed a number of discrepancies between the Pax edition of 1984 and the 1976 Gyldendal edition of the collected works. In resolving these problems with texts we have used Gyldendal's Danish edition of 1906. We have retained proper names in their original form but normalized spelling and punctuation.

Introduction

Elaine Showalter

AMALIE SKRAM'S *Under Observation* (1895) is both a feminist *Künstlerroman* and a *fin-de-siècle* protest novel about the psychiatric abuse of women. Skram's narrative meditations about the problems women face in art, both in terms of overcoming internalized stereotypes of feminine prettiness and niceness, and in combining family life with the demands of a vocation, have much in common with the questions being raised by women writers in other countries, such as Mona Caird's *The Daughters of Danaus* (1894) in England, and Elizabeth Stuart Phelps's *The Story of Avis* (1877) in the United States.

Her anger towards the treatment of women at the hands of a male psychiatric profession, particularly the incarceration of women in asylums controlled by men, is also part of an emergent international chorus of women's voices. In England in the 1870s and 1880s there had been considerable discussion of the wrongful confinement of women in lunatic asylums. Georgiana Weldon's *How I Escaped the Mad-Doctors* (1878) and Rosina Bulwer-Lytton's *A Blighted Life* (1880) followed the American tradition of Elizabeth Ware Packard in exposing the power of husbands over rebellious or independent wives. In *The Bastilles of England; or, the Lunacy Laws at Work* (1883), Louisa Lowe criticized the male monopoly of Victorian psychiatry, and argued that the presence of women doctors and asylum superintendents would better meet women's needs, since they would be "better able to enter into their feelings, and detect the border-line between sanity and insanity than those of an opposite sex, and consequently, different habit of mind."* Only a few years before Skram wrote her book, Charlotte Perkins Gilman's "The Yellow Wallpaper" (1892) had combined in fiction an indictment of psychiatric power and a critique of marriage as another patriarchal institution.

Although Else Kant, the artist-heroine of *Under Observation*, is initially presented to us as happily married, Skram is in line with tradition in making connections between the perfidy of the psychiatrist and the husband. A gifted painter, Else is tormented by the efforts to continue with her work after having a child. She becomes obsessed with an unfinished painting, is unable to sleep, and even threatens suicide. In desperation, her husband Knut proposes that she go for a brief stay to the clinic of the well-known psychiatrist Professor Hieronimus, and Else readily agrees. As we later learn, she had been helped once before by a restful sojourn in a clinic with a kindly doctor and is optimistic about psychiatry.

But Professor Hieronimus proves to be an implacable tyrant, who will not listen to her requests, and who will not allow visits from her husband and child. In his hospital Else undergoes a contest like the taming of the shrew. She is given an ugly and empty room, is kept awake all night by the howlings and shrieks of the other lunatics, and is forced to eat food she dislikes. Although she makes common cause with the nurses, Else is unable to get messages to her husband about her distress. Gradually she comes to see him not just as a dupe but also as a conspirator in the plots against her sanity. A woman writes Else an "anonymous letter filled with the most poisonous insinuations about her husband's relationship with her," but by this time Else has apparently lost interest in maintaining her marriage.

When Professor Hieronimus allows Else to go from his private clinic to the state mental asylum, St. Jørgen's, she is pleased. Here she hopes to persuade the staff of her sanity, and in the hospital's more benevolent atmosphere, she succeeds. Here too she forms strong friendships and alliances with the nurses, and although she disagrees strongly with the super-

---

*See Elaine Showalter, *The Female Malady: Women, Madness, and English Culture 1830–1980* (New York: Penguin, 1985), pp. 126–27.

intendent, she comes to respect his fairness. By the novel's end, Else has regained her freedom, but thoughts of her husband and child – even of her painting – have receded into the background. She no longer dreams of reunion, but only of revenge: to tell the story of her treatment by Hieronimus. "Only death," she swears,"can keep me from doing it."

Skram's determination and uncompromising anger are impressive, but the modern reader must also ask questions about the reliability of Else as a narrator. At the beginning of the novel, she is in a severe depressivespiral, unable to control her self-destructive impulses. Skram presents Else's behavior as that of the driven artist. She is struggling with a "gloomy paint-streaked canvas," which shows a symbolic figure with "tacked-on black wings," a "character from a masquerade."

Else's life, which also seems like a masquerade, is obviously being represented in her art. As a woman, she is expected to paint "sweet, charming pictures of smiling landscapes and pretty people," while she yearns to portray "the agony of life." In her role as artist, she is unable to realize her vision, a failure she blames on her domestic obligations. As Skram explains, "the battle between what she wanted to paint and what she actually painted left her in a confused state of misery that gnawed at her brain." She is unable to take a rest from her painting, and to allow herself emotional renewal: "She hovered over it constantly, because it attracted her irresistibly and because the mental torment caused by her fruitless labor increased if she fled from the work."

Yet Else also tortures herself with guilt about her failures as housekeeper, employer, wife and mother, overcompensating by obsessive anxiety about her son's health. Unlike the narrator of Gilman's "The Yellow Wallpaper," who cannot bear to be with her child, Else cannot bear to be separated from him, and indeed her constant hovering worry about him, much like her compulsive painting, interferes with his development and health. When he asks for a nursery song, Else responds with a dismal tune about the pussycat with a headache who "howls and howls about his fate/ and thinks he'll soon be dead." Her inability to find a balance of the two sides of her life has taken her to a point where she can only think of suicide: "To die was the only thing left."

Else's lack of insight into herself makes the novel both puzzling and compelling. Can we depend on her account of things? Her narrative seems confirmed by the occasional shifts of point of view to her husband Knut, who reinforces her interpretation. Yet Else's moments of insight and self-criticism are rare. At one point she seems to admire the courage and resilience of the lunatic Miss Hall: "In spite of all the misery connected with being at an insane asylum, she welcomed all the little things life offered with enthusiasm and joy. Her delight over the first blossom of spring, her exuberant happiness at feeding the birds, her intense emotions which found expression in lyrical creations, the satisfaction she derived from her 'child's' company, and now her proud joy over having controlled herself at night for Else's sake. It was as if she were revived by all this, and every day found her more and more contented and normal."

At St. Jørgen's, however, Else only sustains herself with the promise to wreak revenge on Hieronimus. The superintendent of St. Jørgen's remonstrates with her: "What do tales like that accomplish? ... The author becomes the butt of ridicule, or, in the best case, the object of pity ... For Hieronimus and all the rest of us it will just be entertaining reading, but for you the consequences will be deadly serious."

But Else is unmoved. She is clearly an autobiographical projection of her creator. In 1877, Skram had a nervous breakdown brought on by the stresses of a difficult divorce. She spent three months in Gaustad mental hospital, a helpful and curative experience. After leaving the hospital, she obtained her divorce and the custody of her children, and began for the first time to write. In 1884 she married the Danish writer Erik Skram, and moved to Copenhagen. The stresses of combining her roles as writer, wife and mother led to another breakdown, and less successful treatment. *Under Observation* is the story of that experience, and the vehicle of Skram's revenge. Her account, according to Katherine Hanson, "gave rise to a heated debate in Copenhagen and resulted in improved conditions for psychiatric patients." Yet the outcome was not so happy for Amalie Skram. In 1899 she and Erik Skram were divorced, and the remaining six years of her life were marked by poor health and only sporadic writing. Revenge without compassion proved an obsessive but not a healthy muse.

PROFESSOR HIERONIMUS

Chapter 1

OH GOD – SHE COULDN'T GET IT RIGHT – she couldn't get it right! It was evening in the studio, the lamps burning brightly.

Else Kant stood despondently in front of an easel that held a gloomy paint-streaked canvas. She had been working night and day for over a year, tearing the soul out of her body trying to portray what was in her heart. But the longer she worked the worse it became. This figure in the corner who was supposed to symbolize the agony of life – ha! – a miserable fool with tacked-on black wings – a character from a masquerade.

Oh God, God, what should she do? She had been capable of something once, had aroused such delightful outrage among the "respectable" public. But now that had stopped. Suddenly stopped.

Well, she could always start painting sweet, charming pictures of smiling landscapes and pretty people. But that was something she couldn't do.

If only she could lay the painting completely aside, never touch a brush again. What peace would come over her. Live her life absorbed by habitual, everyday duties whose fulfillment brought contentment to her and comfort to her loved ones. Free of this intolerable burden that lay upon her day and night like an evil spirit. If she had just been able to do one thing – been able to give herself entirely to her work and let tomorrow take care of itself. But when the household failed to run as it should – the child, the meals, the housekeeping, the maids – she suffered torments, reproaching herself for being negligent and careless.

No, it took tremendous strength to perform well in so many areas. St. Paul was right when he forbade women to go out in public. Married women, he should have said – although no, those who weren't married might still marry.

How pathetic! The sight of that amateurish daubing seared her soul like a flaming torch. To feel so clearly and vividly the way it should be and then . . .

This battle between what she wanted to paint and what she actually painted left her in a confused state of misery that gnawed at her brain, colored everything she heard and experienced, paralyzed her spirit and destroyed her will. Made her, moreover, unreasonable and difficult to live with. Her poor husband – seeing how upset and desperate she was – yes, desperate to the point of death, because she had to, simply had to finish her work, and her incapacity was becoming more frightening and inescapable with every day that passed.

Sinking down on a hassock, she propped her elbows on her knees, buried her face in her hands and wept, rocking back and forth, her muffled sobs broken occasionally by a violent cough.

And what good would it do if she went away for a while, as she and her husband had discussed on occasion? She would just take her troubles with her, her pain and sorrow over the unfinished work, her longing for her husband and child, that adorable little boy from whom she couldn't be parted for a day without a nagging sense of loss. And she couldn't afford to travel, either, couldn't afford a thing in the world, since she hadn't finished or sold anything for so long.

She felt a nervous twinge in the back of her head, and sat up with a start. She slid her hand slowly up the back of her neck and squeezed her eyes shut.

Well, it wasn't really so surprising when she considered that she hadn't been able to sleep for almost a year. All summer in Switzerland with the child she had not really slept a single night. Often she would not get a wink of sleep from the moment she lay down at night until she rose in the morning, because the little one, who had to sleep in her room because the nursemaid was undependable, was a restless sleeper, and every time he tossed and turned the little iron bed creaked. So she would read by lamplight all through the long night, and in the morning when the boy had been bathed, dressed, and taken out by the nursemaid, she would lie down again and try to sleep, though the noises of the day usually prevented it. And then there was the terrible strain of the large painting, which of course she had taken with her, on which she never made progress, couldn't make progress. She hovered over it constantly, because it attracted her irresistibly and because the mental torment caused by her fruitless labor just increased if she fled from the work. And her insomnia had continued all through the winter at home. Not sleeping had almost become routine, and sleep for her had always been so necessary. Without sleep at night nobody could manage very long. Even the strongest person would go under. That's why she was in this state. Oh God, these spasms that nearly split her head in two – sometimes she wanted to wrap a cloth band around it. And no change, no way to escape. Living life nailed fast to the martyr's stake that her work had increasingly become to her.

She dried her face and sat motionless, her expression stiff with anguish. Then the coughing fit came again, so prolonged and exhausting that her eyes filled with tears.

What a wreck she had become.

And she had the gall to play judge and accuse other people. Kirsten, the maid she had dismissed for stealing, was ruined for life, because now she had started drinking to dull her sorrows. Her heart-rending sobs when she learned she'd been found out ... The sound rang in her ears and she saw the girl's white, stricken face. And she hadn't found another position. What would become of her? She would come to a bad end, of course, and it was her fault. Oh poor, poor Kirsten ... I beg you to forgive me, forgive me ...

Yes, wherever she turned, whatever she thought about, everything seemed difficult and depressing. She couldn't get the boy to eat properly and he lay for hours at night without sleeping. Other people's children ate and slept, but of course she handled him all wrong. It was that way with everything. There was no bright spot – not one, not one. And things kept getting worse and worse. She never had time to regain her strength, because this nervous cough that was so terrible at night made her so exhausted she could hardly manage to get up in the morning. Her mind got no rest. Always churning with the same obsessive thoughts. To die was the only thing left. Give up the struggle. Disappear from a life that was filled with pain, that she also filled with pain for others. It was immoral to go on living when you couldn't manage to accomplish a thing, when you knew you were a burden and a plague to the people you wanted most to please, and knew, also, that it would never be otherwise.

Still it was strange how long a human being, no matter how miserable and racked with pain, could hesitate when it came to casting off the burden and removing oneself from the ranks of the living. The dread of slipping into the eternal darkness of oblivion must be deeply rooted, since she still kept dragging herself on, day after night, day after night.

Well, this last way out would always be there.

She stood up hurriedly, walked to the easel, and began to paint, her brows contracted, her lips tightly compressed. Suddenly she had to suppress a cough. Her chest and shoulders ached and her knees felt weak. But she paid no attention – just kept on painting.

All of a sudden her face cleared, her eyes took on a joyful expression and she smiled radiantly. Now she had it – finally – finally! Putting the palette aside, she took a step backwards and contemplated the painting.

Suddenly she jumped. Wasn't that the boy? She listened for a moment and hurried into the nursery where a night lamp was burning. The nursemaid was lying there snoring through her open mouth, and in the little bed against the other wall the boy was sitting up, his arms flailing.

"My sweet little Tage ..." Else bent over and in an instant kissed him wide awake. "What is it, my sweet little boy? Shall I sing to you?"

"The one about the pussycat, Mama."

Else settled the boy down on the pillow and pulled up the covers. Then she sang a languid little tune:

> *Pussycat's under the cook stove*
> *With such a pain in his head.*
> *He howls and howls about his fate*
> *And thinks he'll soon be dead.*

"What is 'dead,' Mama?"

"That's what Grandpapa is."

"You don't go to bed at night any more and drink cocoa in the morning, Mama?"

"Not when you're dead."

"It's pretty nice when you're dead, Mama. It is, Mama."

"Now you mustn't talk any more, just hurry and go to sleep. Remember it's the middle of the night."

"What's night, Mama?"

All the mousies laugh and play
For the pussycat is dead.
Now they run to the cupboard
And eat the buttered bread.

"Did they put cheese on it, Mama?"

"No. But now you're talking again."

The dining room door opened and in walked a tall, broad-shouldered man, with a dark complexion and a bald head.

"Papa!" the boy shouted, suddenly sitting up in bed. "Tage's hungry. Two pieces of bread with liverwurst, and one with beef, and one with cheese."

Kant walked over to the bed, bent over the child and said tenderly, "So you're hungry, little fellow."

"Go in and go to bed," he turned imploringly to Else. "You're in here again – you don't give the boy a chance to sleep."

"How can you say that, Knut? I'm desperate when he won't sleep."

Tage was standing up in bed, his arms around his father's neck. "Let me come with you to the dining room, Papa," he coaxed.

"Don't do it," Else begged.

"Perhaps it's just as well to tire him out. He'll sleep better afterwards." Knut wrapped the boy in a blanket, picked him up and carried him into the dining room. He sat down at the table, the child on his lap, and gave him some food.

Else followed and also sat down at the table.

Tage was in high spirits. He tugged on Knut's beard, chattering inces-

santly, occasionally biting off a piece of bread only to pop it into his father's mouth. He had freed one foot from the blanket and suddenly held
it up to Knut's face; the father looked just as delighted as the child.

Else smiled anxiously and shook her head.

"You see, he doesn't eat a thing," she said. But Tage immediately seized
a piece of bread and declared he was very, very hungry and he was going
to eat all of it.

"Won't you go to bed, Else?" Knut asked again. "You don't realize how
you look."

"Go to bed – what's the point of that? I can't sleep anyhow. Especially
now that you're sitting there with the boy!"

"Why is Mama crying?"

"Well, Mama is sick. Poor little Mama."

Else went back to the studio and started to work again, stepping back
every few moments to stare at her painting with a troubled, questioning
gaze.

God knows, she thought dubiously, it's not any better after all. She was
so exhausted that her hands were shaking. And there was her cough. But
she had to go on. Had to. Tomorrow when she got up she would be even
more exhausted, and the entire day would be the same.

And Knut still hadn't come back! He was sitting in there waiting for the
child to fall asleep, instead of calmly going his way or waking up the
nursemaid, at least. Knut talked about *her*, and her excessive concern for
the child – but he wasn't any better himself, if anything, worse.

Oh, the expression around the mouth – that terrible rebellious expression around the mouth! She shaded her eyes with her hand and looked at
what she had painted. Now she had made it look like the mask on a mummy. With brush and palette in hand she walked slowly and despondently
back and forth. Then she began to paint again, her head burning, sweat
beading up on her forehead.

"Oh now really, Else..." Knut had come in. He looked at her, ap-
palled, then walked over and tried to take the brush from her hand.

"I need to use the few moments when I feel I can work, whether it's
night or day." She wrenched her wrist out of his fingers. "Is Tage asleep?"

8

Knut paced slowly back and forth a few times, his head bowed. Then he stopped behind Else, who was painting steadily. He lifted his head as if to say something, but abandoned the idea and again started pacing back and forth.

"It's half past one, Else. You know this energy at night always comes when you are worse. Stop, for heaven's sake. I beg you, Else."

"Go on to bed, and let me take care of myself. Besides, I'm not sick. Tage is much worse – he won't eat or sleep. Won't you speak seriously to Tvede about it?"

"Now be good, Else." With gentle force, Knut took the palette away from her. "You're destroying yourself and you're destroying me, too." He spoke softly and his furrowed brow expressed deep concern.

"Come on, now, " he persisted, as Else stared blankly, without making a reply. "You must get some sleep – I'll bring you a sleeping powder."

"Oh, the powders don't do any good," Else muttered, "Not if you gave me a hundred. Won't you talk seriously with Tvede about the child?"

Knut turned away and again began pacing the floor. Else repeated her question.

"There's nothing wrong with the child," Knut said in a pained voice.

"So you won't talk to him?"

"Yes, of course I will. Just calm down."

"Tomorrow, first thing in the morning?"

"Yes. Will you go to bed now?"

Else walked over and sat down on the chaise longue.

Knut watched her, then sat down a short distance away.

Suddenly Else got up and started painting again.

Knut rose and left the studio. He would try going to bed himself. It was unbearable to see her standing there, driving herself to exhaustion.

A half hour later he slipped back into the room in a robe and slippers. Else was still painting.

"Oh, you frightened me," she exclaimed, turning with a start. "Do you want to drive me completely distracted, wandering around at night as if I'm the one who's keeping you from getting any sleep?"

Knut shook his head helplessly.

9

"Look at what I've painted tonight," Else said, "and tell me what you think."

"Not now. I have to feel well and alert to be able to look at it properly, and I'm dead tired."

"I implore you – I'll go to bed right afterwards."

"That's just what you won't do," Knut sighed. He went over and scrutinized the painting with narrowed eyes. Else waited expectantly.

"Well, I don't know, Else. I tell you, I really can't see it at this time of night. What you've painted is good, I suppose."

" 'I suppose' – do you think I don't know you? You really ought to say what you mean. Oh God, oh God, then it's all in vain, and it always will be," she wept, wandering aimlessly around the studio. Knut followed her, talking, beseeching, but she didn't listen to him.

"Well, I'll go to bed now," she said finally, drying her face. "Now that I no longer have any work. It was good of you to say what you felt. Thank you for that." She took a little bottle out of the table drawer.

"What are you doing with that?" asked Knut, who had been watching her intently.

"Nothing. Just leave me alone."

"No, Else! Give me that bottle this instant. I know what you're thinking."

Else looked at him fixedly. He stood quietly with his hand outstretched, with a look that was filled with sorrow, but was also tired and hopeless.

A strange man, Knut. He shared her view that suicide was permissible. They had talked about it often. Once when a young relative of his was floundering on the verge of ruin, she had said she was afraid he would end by shooting himself. Knut had answered calmly, "There are worse things than that." But when really put to the test, as he was right now with her, he behaved like a common policeman. He had done that once before, a few years back, when she had felt there was nothing left for her but death.

Was it because he loved her so much?

Yes, he loved her, but not enough to willingly grant her death. Nor did he have the courage to be a passive observer where this final step was concerned. "I must take measures," he was thinking. "I won't have a moment's peace night or day!"

As if measures could do anything – as if she could again be the way she was in the old days – able to sleep, work, finish something – be happy. But Knut didn't believe that, and she didn't either. No, no, no! She could look at him and see he didn't believe it. But it was utterly contemptible of him not to shut his eyes and ears and let her do what she wanted.

"This is despicable of you," she said.

"Give me the bottle," Knut answered firmly.

"But why? Afterwards, wouldn't you feel in your deepest heart: Sad that it had to end this way, but nevertheless inevitable and for the best."

"No," Knut said.

His "no" startled Else. There was so much pain and love, such absolute certainty in his face and voice. Was it possible that he didn't think it was best for her to die? She felt the hard lump in her chest begin to melt.

"Then I won't do it," she said softly. "But you must show enough faith in me not to take the bottle away."

"I can't do that. Remember how many nights I've been here, virtually battling with you for your life. How do I know, how do you know, what fancy will strike you next?"

"But you must believe me," Else burst out passionately. "I can't bear it if you don't believe me!" She threw herself face down on the floor and burst into loud sobs.

"All right, Else. In God's name, I believe you."

Else rose and composed herself. She put the bottle back in the drawer and locked it.

"Will you go to bed now, Else?"

Else wanted to answer but her cough started again. She felt as if she were being torn to pieces.

"You mustn't look so sad, Knut."

"I don't see much reason to feel otherwise," Knut mumbled, running his hand over his forehead.

"No, poor thing."

Finally Knut managed to get her to bed. She undressed with a frightened expression, looking around every few moments, listening anxiously. Knut gave her the sleeping powder and went to his room.

But as soon as Else got into bed she was seized by a fit of coughing. She sat up in bed finally, coughing in great hiccoughing spasms.

Here came those stamping hoofbeats, up the stairs, in through the hall door, which sprang open of its own accord. Swiftly, in step, they came. The bedroom door slid open and in swept the stately procession of beautiful brown horses – Else had seen them often recently. The horses' heads and upper bodies were stiff and lifeless, and instead of eyes they had large black holes, but the graceful, slender legs stretched and lifted, conducting the procession on through the dining room and studio, out through the hall, and into the bedroom again – rhythmic, ghostly, imperturbable. Again and yet again. And Else sat in bed, coughing and staring, wondering, but unafraid.

Then suddenly Knut was there, and the procession of horses had sunk into the ground.

"You must take your opium drops," he said. "This is getting worse and worse."

But Else refused. She had taken some the previous night and was afraid to take too much.

"Didn't you see the horses?" Else asked. "The room was full of them when you came in. It's really a pity you can't see or hear them."

"Just go away," Else went on when Knut made no reply. "I'm used to this."

"Yes, I must," Knut answered. "I'm so tired I'm ready to drop, and I have so much to do tomorrow."

"The promise I made not to use the bottle – that only holds for tonight," Else called after him. "Just so you know."

Like a sleepwalker, Knut groped his way into his bedroom and lay down. He wrapped himself tightly in a blanket, turned toward the wall, and instantly fell into a sleep, through which the sound of Else's cough pressed like a weight on his chest.

Suddenly he started up in terror, sprang out of his bed, and opened the door to the hall. Else was standing there, putting on her long coat.

"Now what are you doing?" Knut asked roughly, gripping her by the shoulders.

"I can't get any peace," Else complained. "I keep thinking all the time about Kirsten, the maid we dismissed. I'm going over to her mother's house to ask about her."

"At this hour?"

"It's the middle of the day."

"Not another word. Right this minute, get into bed."

Else went on, "I keep hearing these words in my ears: 'Oh thou wicked servant, I forgave thee all that debt because thou besoughtest me. Shouldest not thou ...'"

Knut took off her coat and at last got her to bed.

And at last she fell asleep.

Chapter 2

AT TEN THE NEXT MORNING, Knut was with Dr. Tvede, their family doctor and friend.

"Now you must say what ought to be done," Knut said. They had been talking back and forth about Else's condition.

Dr. Tvede did not answer immediately, just looked at Knut mildly, a philosophical expression in his deep-set eyes.

"For the time being, there's only one thing to do. We have to get her some peace and quiet. She's got to leave home and go to a hospital. In any other place she won't get the rest she needs."

"In some private clinic?"

"Do you think your wife would put up with a bunch of hysterical women?"

"Oh no – naturally..."

"We have Professor Hieronimus, of course. He's the best in the field, and she respects him. She's read one of his articles and talked to me about him a number of times."

"So she could go into the hospital under his care?"

"Yes. When he's calmed her down and had her there eight to ten days, he'll tell you what ought to be done. I don't think there's any other advice I can give you. I'll write a note – take it to Hieronimus at the hospital. You'll find him there now. Talk to him, and then talk to your wife. Naturally, she must want this herself."

Knut stuck the note in his pocket and went out.

Then there was hope, after all.

Chapter 3

THE KANTS WERE SEATED at lunch.

"I don't want to eat now, Mama," declared Tage, who was sitting across the table from Else with a large bib around his neck, poking at the fried egg and chopped meat on his plate. "I won't do it, no matter what. I won't."

"If you won't eat, you can leave the table," Knut said, with a movement as if he were just waking up. He rang the bell, and when the nursemaid came in, directed her to take Tage for a walk.

"I've talked to Tvede today," Knut said. "Do you have any objection to going into the hospital under Professor Hieronimus's care?"

"Did Tvede really come up with that on his own?" Else asked, an almost hostile expression coming into her eyes.

"Yes, he did. Now the only issue is whether you're willing."

"Yes, I'm willing," Else replied, her eyes slowly filling with tears. "I've got to be torn away from my picture by force, before everything goes wrong. Because I'm certainly not normal."

"Stay there a few days," Knut went on, "a week and a half at the most. You can put up with that, surely."

"I can put up with anything, as long as I have peace and quiet. I could take some odds and ends of work with me. The sketches for the *Children's Christmas Book*,[1] don't you think?"

"Of course. Then we can get his opinion about whether you should take a trip to Switzerland or go to the country for a while."

"It will be good to talk to a man like Hieronimus. To explain all my thoughts and feelings to him. You must go see him today."

"I've already been there."

Else's cheeks grew a little paler.

"What did he say?"

"He didn't have time then, but he asked me to come back at three o'clock and bring you with me. He made an excellent impression – calm and thoughtful. Actually, he looks like a country preacher in his shabby coat. But those were his hospital clothes, I suppose. Be ready promptly at half past two."

Else went into the studio and looked at her large picture. All wrong, impossible, now and forever. She shrank under the consuming pain of her own helplessness, which filled her heart and robbed her of her power every time she stood before the picture. Insignificant, lifeless, meaningless. She felt as if a large, cold hand had seized her heart and she could only breathe with difficulty.

If she tried just one more time, now at the last moment, when she had given up everything and was about to run away from it all ... What if she succeeded! She thought she had read or heard about such cases. If she could just get *something* right – the expression in the eyes, for instance. She would gain hope and courage and new strength.

Hurriedly she began to paint, but before long she tossed the palette aside and turned away. This was what always happened. How many times in a mad desire to push away the pain and gain new hope had she not thought that *this* was the moment when inspiration would strike – but always her efforts had been in vain. No, she had to get away, away from everything – her work, the memory of poor Kirsten, the sight of Tage's sickliness. It would really be good to go stay with Hieronimus.

If she could just get the picture out of her mind so she wouldn't sit in the hospital painting and painting, seeing before her eyes an image of the way it should be, burning to start all over again. She would do anything to push those thoughts away, sleep herself to health and strength in the hospital's peace and quiet. Eight to ten nights' sleep would work miracles.

She lifted the large canvas off the easel and turned its face against the wall. Then she went into the child's bedroom and looked at Tage's clothes. She had been working on a shirt that needed snaps and ties. She finished it, gathered a pile of socks and underclothes for the nursemaid to mend, and after tidying his things, sat down by the table and rested her heavy head in her hands. Her eyes burned from the long lack of sleep, her head buzzed, and she felt a sudden dizziness. Involuntarily she reached for support. Faint and overcome by drowsiness, she let her arms fall to the table and her face drop onto her folded hands.

There were strange noises around her, heavy breathing and a dull whimpering mixed with the rustling of dead leaves. She wanted to lift her head to see what it was, but she couldn't do it, no matter how hard she tried. Finally she succeeded. "What is this?" she thought. There was so much space around her, the ceilings were so high, and the light was as bleak and grey as the haze of distant moonlight. And along the walls stood rows of beds with white sheets and tucked-in blankets, under which people were lying stretched out and rigid, moaning. Occasionally they lifted their heads and begged in heart-rending voices that the tight blankets be loosened, but no one answered. Beside the tall narrow door directly opposite, a figure with bound hands and a long dazzling white coat was standing tied to the wall by a thick dark rope looped around the waist. The upturned eyes had no pupils, and the whites were large and bulging. A long, pitch-black tongue hung out of the mouth. Else wanted to stand up, but she couldn't move a limb. Rigid with terror, she stared at the door. In a couple of leaps she could reach it. But suppose it was locked and the key wasn't in the door ... Yes, it was locked and there was no key, she could see that distinctly. Then she felt her body become a paralyzed mass and she started slipping down out of the chair, just as the door soundlessly opened and four men entered quietly, carrying between them a long pale casket, its lid arched at the head. The front opening of the arch was covered with a pane of glass through which Else saw a human head lying at an angle, its face sunken and vacant, lead-black against the white sheet of the casket. At that instant, she knew it was Knut and that he was dead. Struggling to make a sound, she let out a shriek, fell face down on the floor and woke up.

She bounded from the chair to the middle of the room and stood there, looking around in confusion.

The dining room door opened quietly, and her husband poked in his head. Beside herself, Else held out her arms and ran to him, sobbing loudly. She threw the door wide open and flung herself on his chest.

Knut had difficulty calming her. He wanted her to lie down on the chaise longue in the studio – there was still an hour and a quarter before they had to leave, but Else clung to him, trembling, and begged him not to leave her alone for a second. At last he got her settled on the chaise longue, where she lay with wide-open eyes, staring fixedly at the vision from her dream, feeling all around her a world of terror and misery. She had often thought that she was the most wretched person on earth. Now the realization rose in her that for the children of humanity there were sufferings and torments of a different and more terrible nature than her own. At the slightest sound she started and reached out her hand for Knut, who was sitting with a book in an easy chair close by.

Chapter 4

WHEN THEY ARRIVED AT THE HOSPITAL it was only a quarter to three, so they walked up and down the side streets, too nervous and excited to talk any further.

"What time is it now?" Else asked.

"It's only been seven minutes."

"Is that possible?"

They walked on, the silence only broken by Else's repeated questions about the time. Knut kept saying the same thing, that only a few minutes had gone by.

"I've never known how long a quarter of an hour could be," Else burst out. "Don't you think your watch has stopped?"

Knut shook his head, and Else started counting to herself. Every time she got to 60 a minute should have gone by, and so she started from the beginning.

"Now I know it's three o'clock," she said suddenly, coming to a halt.

There were still four minutes left, but now Knut thought they could go in.

They walked through the hospital gate, passing a number of large graveled courtyards and fenced-off gardens with beds of black earth and trees left brown and naked by winter. When they reached the innermost courtyard, Knut pointed to a small two-story stone house lying a little way from the other long buildings, and said, "There it is."

Else glanced at Knut as if to ask him if he didn't think her very brave, then walked quickly up the little stairway into an entrance hall, where written on a door to the right was a verse from the Bible, which Else studied carefully.

"Shall we knock?"

Knut knocked on the door and when no one answered, pushed it open, letting Else precede him.

The room was long and gloomy, with a bare floor, yellow benches against the walls, and a large, conspicuously-placed spittoon. There were two men in the room, a farmer who was slouched forward with his hands between his knees and his head deeply bowed, and a younger fellow who looked like an artisan or teacher, with a grimy, jaundiced face and a mass of unkempt, lifeless hair.

Knut and Else sat down on the bench across from the artisan, who seemed deeply absorbed in the open newspaper he held in his hands. A few minutes later, he glanced shyly up from the paper, and when he encountered Else's scrutiny, gave her a somewhat embarrassed, yet superior smile, as if to say: "You realize, of course, that I'm not sitting here on my own account."

It was quiet in the room. The only sounds were the deep sighs of the slouching farmer whenever he spat, which he did frequently, always hitting the center of the spittoon several feet away, though he never lifted his head or changed his posture in the slightest.

The hall door opened and a tall man entered, wearing a home-made linsey coat; his head was narrow and closely cropped, and he had a wool scarf wrapped around his neck. Else's heart started to pound and she looked questioningly at Knut, but realized at once that this was not Hieronimus. The man paused for a second and looked around, then he tiptoed slowly to the farthest corner of the room, where he seated himself with his back wedged into the corner.

A few minutes passed. The artisan read the newspaper, the farmer sighed and spat, and the man in the corner sat as stiff and motionless as a statue.

Then light, swift steps were heard on the stairs outside, continuing into the entrance hall. The door flew open, and in came a thin, bustling gentleman with a cold, pale, beardless face and smoothly slicked-down hair.

He walked across the room, looking neither to the left or right, making a sign as he passed the slouching farmer, who had straightened up, and now rose and followed the bustling gentleman into a side room.

"So that's how he looks," Else whispered. "But I don't think his clothes are shabby."

Knut smiled and whispered, "Not these."

Shortly afterward, the farmer emerged from the side room and Hieronimus appeared on the threshold. He directed a quick, sharp glance at Else, and nodded almost imperceptibly at Knut, who rose and went into his office.

Hieronimus's glance reminded Else of someone – who was it? She pondered, and then a man appeared before her mind's eye, a sad man, speaking earnestly – then, moments later, a white necktie under a pointed chin, and hair slicked down with water – then finally, a pulpit... A pulpit? Now she had it! That young theology student she had met many years ago in her uncle's parsonage, who had preached once when Uncle had a cold. Yes, that's who it was – that pious, fanatical being, whose eyes seemed filled with lamentation at the sins of the world, and not just lamentation, but also zeal and wrath on behalf of the Lord. She had often talked with him about religious matters and had grown fond of him because he was so honest and his mind was so pure. Thank God Hieronimus didn't remind her of an unsympathetic person, for he wasn't a bit like what she had expected. And thank God, she had found out who he resembled, so she didn't have to brood about that.

Knut came back and then Else went in to see Hieronimus. He was sitting sideways at a desk, leaning back in his chair, one leg crossed over the other. He was holding a small object in his hands, turning it over and over. With a slight movement of his head, he signaled Else to sit down in the chair by the corner of the desk.

"You're not very well, I gather," Hieronimus began in a sharp, colorless voice; he regarded her intently.

"No," Else managed to get out.

"You suffer from insomnia," the professor went on, then paused for a moment. "Your state of mind is very depressed." Another pause. "Your husband tells me ... Well, in short, you're not well. Is that right?"

Else wanted to answer, but she could only weep, bending her face over her muff, pressing it to her eyes.

"Your family doctor thinks you should stay here in the hospital for a while. You have no objection to that, I presume?" The last sentence came rapidly, as he straightened up in his chair.

Else shook her head.

The professor rose, opened the door, and beckoned to Knut.

"Your wife can come here this afternoon. In an hour, let's say."

"Oh no, not until this evening," Else begged.

"Hospital rules don't permit anyone to come in after six o'clock."

"Well, all right, six o'clock then."

"She can bring a valise with the necessary toilet articles and some underclothing," Hieronimus said to Knut. "Nothing else. You can find out at the office about the deposit required and the fee for a private room."

Else had a number of things she was eager to ask him about, but Hieronimus had already opened the waiting-room door, and they said good-bye.

"Oh dear," Knut sighed as they walked through the courtyard, "I just hope we're doing the right thing."

"Why wouldn't it be right?" Else replied bravely, yet the sight of Knut's doubtful, anguished face made her strangely uneasy.

"Well, let's hope so," Knut sighed again.

When they had finished dinner, Else went into the bedroom to pack her valise.

Knut came in with a couple of books. "These will be enough at first," he said.

"Thanks, you can always bring more when you come to visit me – though for such a short time ..."

"Eight or ten days at the most," Knut sighed. "Are you ready?"

In a short while Else had put on her coat. She went out to the kitchen to say good-bye to the maids and ask them to be kind to Tage. Then she came back, lifted the child onto her lap and, fighting back tears, promised she would come back soon to tell stories and play with him.

"You must come now, Else."

Else kissed the child again and again. Then she set him down and whispered good-bye.

The carriage drove through the hospital gateway, across the large courtyards, and stopped outside the long building at the back. They rang the front door bell, but learned from the woman who unlocked the door that they had made a wrong turn. This was the men's ward; they had to go around the corner to the next entryway and go upstairs.

There was no impediment this time. The front door was unlocked, the wide staircase illuminated by gas jets. There was only one door at the top, where they rang the bell. Immediately they heard the sound of footsteps and the clank of keys. Knut squeezed Else's hand. He was very pale and did not say a word.

The lock turned and the door swung open. A tall woman with a delicate, pale face stood there, dressed in a tidy nurse's uniform, with a large bunch of keys hanging on the front of a grey-white rubber apron.

"Mrs. Kant? Come in. Let me take that," she said, reaching for the valise.

"Yes, well good-bye, Else," Knut said in a trembling voice and kissed her.

"I don't want to go in. The doors are locked – it's like a prison." Else took an unwilling step backwards.

"Don't worry about that, Else. The outer door has to be locked, of course."

"Will you come tomorrow?" Else inched reluctantly toward the door.

"Yes, Else."

"Are you sure?"

"Yes. Good-bye."

"Good-bye." She gave her husband one last look and turned to the woman standing on the threshold with the valise in her hand.

Chapter 5

Else walked quickly past the woman into a long corridor illuminated by gas jets mounted high on the walls. Then the door shut with a click, the bunch of keys jangled and the lock turned twice.

A shiver ran down Else's back.

"It's just like any other outside door," the woman explained, giving Else a searching look.

Else walked hesitantly down the mat-covered corridor. On one side there were high windows, under which stood long yellow tables, yellow wooden chairs, and, here and there, potted plants on rustic stands. Women in shapeless blue cotton gowns were sitting on some of the chairs. One sat with her arms crossed, staring listlessly in front of her. Another gave Else an inquisitive, sullen look, and a third sat hunched over her knitting. On the other side of the corridor were doorways at widely-spaced intervals.

Else walked on until she reached the wide double doors at the end of the corridor.

Then she turned to the woman, who had stopped a little further back, and asked, "Where will I be?"

"The professor thought in here," the woman said, opening one of the doors on the long wall.

Else turned and entered a spacious, half-darkened room with a wide window that faced the door.

"Why are there two beds? Is someone else in here with me?"

"A lady, a quiet old lady. She's so quiet we never know if she's here or not."

"But don't private patients have rooms to themselves?" Else burst out. "I can't sleep with anyone else in the room," she said, walking quickly back and forth across the room. A painful uneasiness came over her. Those creatures out in the corridor whose clothes looked like prison uniforms, the high shuttered windows that reminded her of ones she'd seen in Turkish harems, the gas jets that were too high to reach except with a long ladder, the jangling keys on the tall woman's cold rubber apron – everything alarmed and irritated her.

"No," she continued vehemently, "I can't sleep with anyone else in the room. I must have a room to myself." She paced back and forth on the rush mat that extended from the door to the window, and repeated the same thing, more and more excitedly: "I must have a room to myself."

Suddenly she noticed, squeezed into a corner of the chaise longue behind the table, the huddled figure of a thin, very tiny woman, who was following her with dull eyes.

"Is that her over there?" Else burst out, stopping in front of the tall woman, who was observing her attentively. "I want to get out of here, now! Now, this instant, do you hear?"

A young nurse came in. She glanced at Else for a moment, and exchanged a few words with the tall woman, whom she called Nurse Stenberg.

"You can have a room to yourself if that's what you want," Nurse Stenberg said calmly. She left the room and, followed by Else, walked to the wide double doors where Else had stopped before. She inserted the key and turned it in the lock, pushed half of the door in to the wall, stepped forward to another double door, one side of which she also pushed ajar, and said to Else, "Come along now."

Else hurried through both doors, which Nurse Stenberg carefully closed and locked, and they found themselves once again in a corridor of the same length and width as the previous one. The same high windows, the same yellow tables and chairs, the same figures in shapeless blue cotton gowns. Only there were more doors on the long wall, and all of them were open. The gas jets high on the wall were enclosed in wire mesh cages, set into rectangular alcoves, one above each door. There were no

potted plants, or mats on the floor, and to Else, it seemed even more naked and more like a prison than the previous corridor.

On one of the yellow chairs sat a tidy little old woman wearing a white
night cap, her eyes light blue in her pale, gentle face. Her shriveled hands
were clasped around a white folded cloth, and she chattered good-
naturedly to herself. A rather young girl with a sallow, exhausted face
came walking by, swaying slowly back and forth. She wore white wool
socks on her feet. Her brown cropped hair stuck out in all directions and
her hands were thrust into the sleeves of her sweater. Her large head
drooped, sometimes forward, sometimes to the side, as if it were too
heavy to support, and she cast frightened, sidelong glances at Else without interrupting her walk. When she met Else's glance, she made a sour
grimace and hid her face behind a lifted arm. In one of the open doors
another young girl was standing on tiptoes, her arm raised in a semicircle
around her head. "The nightingale," she whispered as Else walked past.
Suddenly she sang a few high clear trills, then started sobbing hysterically.

"Here," said Nurse Stenberg, stepping through one of the open doors.

Else followed her, then stopped and stared. In the middle of the oblong
room stood an iron bed, and at the head of the bed, a little yellow night
table. Nothing else. The window was high on the wall.

"You can be by yourself here," the nurse continued.

"But this is like a prison cell," Else blurted, when at last she found her
voice again. "No furniture or anything. Not even a chair to sit on."

"You won't need it," answered Nurse Stenberg. "You'll be in bed."

"In bed!" Else almost laughed. "Do people have to stay in bed when
there's nothing wrong with them?"

"Why have you come here then?" Nurse Stenberg asked severely.

"Bed!" Else said with a genuine laugh. "How long, may I ask? A whole
day, perhaps?"

"That depends. If you are very quiet, you might get by with a week."

Else turned her back indignantly. Nurse Stenberg had to be making
fun of her. "Isn't there a better room?" she asked, walking out into the
hall and looking into the remaining rooms with open doors. They were all
exactly the same – a bed in the center of the room and a little night table.

In one of the beds lay an old, wasted creature with the face of a mummy, skin the color of yellow parchment, and sunken eyes. She lifted her arms slowly when Else appeared on the threshold and stammered out something that sounded like a cry for mercy. In another bed sat a younger woman with wild frightened eyes, clasping her arms around her drawn-up knees. She was rocking her upper body back and forth, uttering muffled sounds.

Cells – the thought sprung suddenly to Else's mind. She was on a ward with isolation cells. But that didn't make any sense.

"You see, everything is the same in here," said Nurse Stenberg's voice from behind her. "You have the only empty room."

"But you can't possibly put me here," Else said. "These are cells, and I'm not insane."

"We shall see."

"Can't I speak to the professor?"

"Yes, tomorrow morning. The resident physician comes this evening.[2] Go into your room now – you can't stand around out here." Nurse Stenberg took Else by the arm and conducted her into the cell.

"Take off your things."

"You mean just my coat and hat, of course."

"No, you're going to bed."

"Now, at six o'clock? But why?"

"That's the rule."

"I never go to bed until after midnight. Oh, do let me stay up."

"That's impossible, you have to be in bed when the resident physician makes his rounds." Nurse Stenberg walked over to Else and took off her hat. Just at that moment they heard a commotion and a terrible scream rang out; a figure in a chemise and night-jacket flew past the open door, her bare feet slapping.

Nurse Stenberg ran into the corridor and took firm hold of the figure, who kicked and yelled and put up a fight. A young nurse came to help. She was a stocky woman, with thick strong limbs, round rosy cheeks, and a kind face.

"I can manage her by myself," she told Nurse Stenberg with a cheerful laugh. "Now, Madam Hoff, calm down, let's go to bed – there now, no tricks." She clamped her arms firmly yet carefully around the madwoman and dragged her down the corridor.

"Nurse Stenberg!" called a frightened voice nearby, and Nurse Stenberg hurried away.

Else went into her cell and began to pace the floor. What kind of a place had she come to? She pressed her hands against her feverish temples, and angry tears filled her eyes. She was going to be here all night with lunatics. With lunatics! Knut wouldn't come until morning and she would have to bear up until then. Because it didn't look as if they were going to let her out. But perhaps when the resident physician came? Naturally he would say right away that there had been some mistake and take her to another room. If only the professor himself would come. Oh, how she longed to talk to him. A whole night in this place! How would she get through it? Thank God she had brought her cough medicine along, so she would be able to get a little sleep. She fumbled feverishly in her dress pocket, grabbed the little bottle, pulled out the cork and lifted it to her mouth.

Just then the stocky nurse, who Nurse Stenberg had called Thorgren, came rushing in. She grabbed Else's arms from behind and forcibly tried to open her hands. Else struggled. Then Nurse Stenberg was there, too. She clamped her arm firmly around Else's shoulder and said authoritatively, "You must get undressed immediately, in my presence. Immediately!"

Thorgren unbuttoned Else's coat and feverishly stripped it off. She whispered something to Nurse Stenberg, whose inquisitive fingers were probing every part of Else's clothing. Else, who had unobtrusively slipped the bottle back into her pocket, stared in terror from one woman to the other, while she made jerky motions to protect herself. "Why are you treating me like this?" she asked indignantly.

"What did you have in your hand?" Thorgren asked, her voice quivering with anger as she hurriedly unhooked the front of Else's dress, her fingers searching for something in her bosom. "What have you done with it?"

"Can't I please undress myself?" Else said, bursting into tears. "I'm not used to people tearing my clothes off."

"Then you mustn't play tricks," Nurse Stenberg replied. "What was the bottle you uncorked?"

"Just my cough medicine," Else sobbed, "I have to take it to sleep."

"Yes, we've heard that before. Hand it over, right now." Nurse Stenberg again pressed her hands around Else's body.

"Won't you let me keep it, Nurse Stenberg? I cough so much at night. My doctor gave it to me."

"You will get all the medicine you need here. Give me the bottle immediately."

Else produced the bottle.

"So there," Thorgren nodded, finally releasing Else.

"Take off the rest of your clothes," Nurse Stenberg said.

"But can't you leave the room? I'd rather be alone."

"Go on, Thorgren, I'll see to this myself."

Again there was the sound of shouting and commotion in the corridor, and Thorgren ran out of the room.

Nurse Stenberg stood with her back to the wall. One hand firmly gripped Else's little bottle. "I have to stay here until you're in bed, Mrs. Kant," she spoke in a milder tone. "When you behave like this, well . . . It's very wrong of you to come here with secret opium drops."

"Why are they staring at me?" Else turned toward the open door, where several of the blue-gowned figures had gathered in curiosity.

"They're just patients."

"Can't you close the door, Nurse Stenberg?"

"That's against the rules."

Else undressed and laid the clothes on the end of her bed. Then she asked for her valise.

Nurse Stenberg put the articles of clothing over her arm and went out with them, leaving Else hunched on the edge of the bed, shivering and coughing in her underclothes.

She propped her elbows on her knees, buried her face in her hands and wept miserably. Then she heard a soft rustling and a mild chattering voice. She lifted her head. There stood the tidy old woman and the young girl with the white wool socks and the heavy head, watching her from a step away. When Else looked up, the girl made the same grimace as before and hid her face behind her arm; her upper body swayed and she turned her back as if offended. But the tidy old woman walked right up to Else and, leaning over her, whispered softly, "He was so fond of cabbage, my son-in-law, and then, you see, I was supposed to look after the little ones – I'm called Granny – yes indeed, the cabbage was simmering on the stove, but I could never eat more than three or four spoonfuls. No, never more. But I have some money in a savings account, my son-in-law took some of it out – how many days until the eleventh?"

"It's just passed," Else said.

"No, is that so? He was so fond of cabbage, my son-in-law, but it's clean and nice here. It's a lovely place to be, but we don't get any coffee."

Nurse Stenberg came back and handed a nightgown to Else. "What are you doing here, Granny?" she said, taking the old woman by the arm and the young girl by the hand, and conducting them out of the room, whereupon she immediately returned and watched as Else put on the nightgown and climbed into bed in her stocking feet.

"Can't I have my valise?" Else asked.

"No, that stays in my safekeeping."

"But there are so many things I'll need. My watch key. Have you taken my watch, too?"

"It's against the rules to have anything like that here."

"Will my door be open at night, too?"

"Day and night. Those are the rules," answered Nurse Stenberg, and went out.

Else propped her hands under her neck and looked out into the corridor where the young girl with the heavy head was still walking slowly, rocking forward and back. There was a continuous noise of slamming doors and banging windows, mixed with the sound of feet tramping back and forth. The gas jet flickering behind the wire cage hurt Else's eyes, and her fits of coughing came and went.

Suddenly a piercing scream rang out, and after that a furious thumping accompanied by a shrill torrent of speech. Else sat up in bed, her heart pounding in terror, and called for Nurse Stenberg. She heard rapid footsteps coming along the corridor, a door being closed and locked as the furious thumping continued, accompanied by a continuous stream of curses.

In a little while Thorgren came in. "Who is making all that noise?" Else asked.

"It's nothing for you to worry about. Just lie down quietly, now. But I must have that." Thorgren took hold of the ribbon in Else's hair and started to untie it.

"But why ever..." Else tried to push aside Thorgren's hand. "My hair will fall over my ears and make my head hot." But Thorgren insisted she wanted the ribbon. Else struggled and begged.

"Just wait until Nurse Stenberg comes," Thorgren said at last.

"Is she the one in charge?" Else asked.

"Yes, she's the head nurse."

"Mrs. Kant won't take off her hair ribbon," Thorgren told Nurse Stenberg, who had just walked in.

"Really, I can't see any reason why I can't keep it!" Else burst out.

"It's against the rules. But you can ask the resident physician when he comes."

Else lay back on the pillow again and tried to puzzle it out. What was going on? Both Nurse Stenberg and Thorgren were acting as if they were doing her a favor by letting her keep a measly hair ribbon. And when Nurse Stenberg left, Thorgren kept her hand on the pillow next to the hair ribbon. Either they enjoyed teasing her or they were absolute idiots.

Gradually the blue-clad figures disappeared from the corridor, and somebody went around restoring things to order.

The resident physician came in, a self-assured man of around thirty, with a warm, tawny complexion; a dark, full beard; and clear, phlegmatic eyes. He was wearing a long white linen coat, and was accompanied by a similarly-dressed young man. The resident physician wished her a friendly good evening and sat down on a chair that Nurse Stenberg had pushed forward for him, while the young man stood there looking solemn.

Else lodged her protests, angrily describing how they had torn off her clothes.

The resident physician exchanged a look with Nurse Stenberg, and then said, "Calm down, Mrs. Kant."

"But this arbitrary treatment! Why should I be in here with lunatics?"

The resident physician gave her a patronizing smile. "We can't start to individualize right away."

"They've taken all my things," Else complained. "And now they say I can't even keep my hair ribbon!"

The resident physician hesitated, then looked at Nurse Stenberg again. "How long is it?" he asked.

Else untied the ribbon and handed it to him.

"We'll cut it in half. You can make do with half of it, can't you?"

"Yes, if that will satisfy you!" Else answered disdainfully. She thought the resident physician wasn't any saner than the rest of them.

The hair ribbon was cut in two and Else given the shorter piece, which she wound around her braided hair; the resident physician ordered a sleeping potion, after which he departed, followed by the solemn young man.

Else lay there furious, filled with a painful astonishment that the resident physician had not said she was going to be moved, nor shown the slightest indignation at the way she had been treated. But Knut and the professor would come tomorrow. Oh God, God, if only the night were over.

"My name is Nurse Hansen, and I'm going to take your temperature," came a soft voice.

Else, who had closed her eyes because of the gas jet flickering above the door of the opposite cell, now opened them wide and saw leaning over her a pair of large beautiful blue eyes in the gentle face of a Madonna, framed by a mass of golden hair.

"Oh leave me alone," she begged. "I'm so tired."

"No, my dear Mrs. Kant, I have to do it. It will just take a second and it won't hurt."

Else felt like throwing her arms around Nurse Hansen's neck and begging her to stay there all night. Her gentle face and considerate manners comforted her. But Nurse Hansen gave a friendly nod and went out.

Then Nurse Stenberg came and held out her hand to say good night. "I'll do everything I can for you, Mrs. Kant," she said, stroking her hair. "As long as you are quiet and good."

"Thank you," Else mumbled, staring stiffly ahead.

It was fairly quiet now. The gas jets were turned down, and a delicately-built young nurse, with blond hair gathered into a thick knot at the back of her neck, gave her a sleeping potion.

"There are so many nurses here," Else said in astonishment. "Are you the one I'll be dealing with most of the time?"

"Yes, at night, as long as I'm on duty. During the day it will be Thorgren – you met her earlier."

"Is it quiet here at night?"

The nurse smiled. "No, Mrs. Kant. It's never quiet in this ward. You can hear for yourself."

There was a loud crash of something being thrown violently on the floor, and the nurse ran out of the room.

Else felt the violent noise like a bodily pain. She sat up in bed, wringing her hands, listening to the wails of misery that followed the banging. The cries came in an old, cracked, piping voice, interspersed with the calm, soothing voice of the young nurse.

"You should lie down, Mrs. Kant," the nurse said, somewhat crossly, when she returned a little later. "Here you have to accept whatever comes."

"But my God, what am I doing here!" Else raised her clenched fists above her head.

"Well, why did you come here?" the nurse asked indifferently.

Else eagerly began to tell her how it had happened, but she noticed that the nurse wasn't listening and broke off with, "What's your name?"

"Nurse Suenson."

"Who was making all that racket out there?"

"Do you call that racket?" Nurse Suenson gave a little laugh. "She's just throwing the bed-rails on the floor – a worn-out old soul who's so miserable she can't stand bedclothes. She's actually very sweet and pleasant, always raving about little Alma. I suppose that must be her daughter."

"Oh God! Oh God!" Else suddenly cried out in terror, nearly falling out of bed as she lunged toward Nurse Suenson, who was standing with her back to the door.

A tall white figure wrapped in a wool blanket, with dark unkempt hair hanging outside her nightcap, was standing there making faces.

"Now, now," Nurse Suenson said crossly, hurrying toward the figure and leading her away.

Else lay back in the bed and wept quietly.

A short while later, a stocky, dark-haired assistant in a white linen coat came and sat down in Else's room. He began to question and examine her.

"Isn't there anyone who wants to harm you?" he asked.

"No," Else replied, biting her lips to keep back her tears. She didn't know what he meant, but she went on, "Nobody wants to harm me. Do you mean in here, perhaps?"

"Persecuting or plotting against you? No one?" the assistant continued in an understanding tone.

He must think I'm insane, Else thought, turning her head away.

The assistant went on tapping at her chest, listening with a stethoscope, asking question after question. Finally he was finished.

"Are you out there, Nurse Suenson!" Else called out softly, when the sound of the assistant's steps had died away in the corridor.

"Yes, I'm sitting out here reading." Nurse Suenson's small, fair head appeared for a second in the open doorway. "Now you've got to sleep, Mrs. Kant."

Sleep, Else thought. How could she possibly do that, when under the most favorable circumstances it was such a problem, and when always in the back of her throat she felt this tickling constriction that made her cough.

If Knut knew...

An irresistible longing for her husband and child came over her. It pierced her to the heart and lay like an agonizing weight on her chest. She could scarcely breathe.

Suddenly there was the sound of thunderous blows, wild screams and furious squabbling. It seemed to be coming from directly under Else's bed. She leaped up in terror.

"Nurse Suenson, Nurse Suenson," she called.

"Hush, it's just the ones down below," Nurse Suenson said, coming in with a yawn. "The sound carries in here. Lie down calmly now, they can't hurt you."

"Are there lunatics down there, too?"

"Yes, it's the men's ward. My, they certainly are stirred up tonight."

The screams and banging grew louder and steadily more furious. Someone with a penetrating voice was holding forth, pouring out a stream of oaths and curses.

Else clung to Nurse Suenson and hid her face on her shoulder.

"Isn't there anyone who can speak kindly to them, like you do in here?"

"It wouldn't do any good. They are maniacs and their delirium has to run its course. Now, dear Mrs. Kant, don't be afraid. You understand, of course, that none of them can get up here."

"Yes, I know that – I know that." Filled with anxiety, Else lay back on the pillow and tossed her head from side to side. "They're locked up, just like we are, of course. But I can't help it. I'm so afraid. Oh God, God!" She threw her arms around Nurse Suenson again.

"If only you would sleep, Mrs. Kant. Listen, it's a little quieter now."

"He's still shouting just as terribly."

"He'll stop eventually. Lie down, now. Don't you feel at all drowsy after the sleeping potion?"

"Not a bit."

Nurse Suenson straightened the blankets over Else. "You've got your stockings on," she said in surprise. "How could that have happened?" She started to take them off.

"I prefer to keep them on – my feet are like ice."

"It's not allowed, Mrs. Kant. I can't understand ... And garters, long, black garters." Nurse Suenson looked upset.

Else sat up in bed and drew her feet toward her. "Yes, garters," she said. "What's wrong with garters?"

Nurse Suenson looked at Else, and her young face reflected uncertainty. "No," she said, finally. "I don't dare do anything else. It's my duty to be suspicious." She made a hasty grab at the garters.

"Suspicious?" Else looked bewildered. "Hush, who's coming?"

"It's the resident physician on his night rounds." Nurse Suenson covered Else up. "Don't say anything about the garters," she whispered. "Thorgren will be in trouble if this gets out." She went out into the corridor, from which Else could hear the sound of quiet conversation.

Then the resident physician slipped into the room and expressed his regret that Else hadn't slept, though it was after eleven o'clock.

"No later than that!"

"Now get some rest. I'll give you something more to make you sleep."

When the resident physician had left, Nurse Suenson gave her another dose of the rusty, vile-tasting mixture; then it was the garters again, which she feverishly insisted Else surrender.

"But why – why?"

Her answer was evasive. Finally it dawned on Else. They were afraid she was going to kill herself.

"You were going to drink that bottle of opium," Nurse Suenson said, "and we've been instructed to watch you."

Else lay there speechless. That was why Nurse Stenberg and that stocky little Thorgren had swarmed over her as if she were a criminal. That explained the scene with the hair ribbon and the look the resident physician had given Nurse Stenberg. So Knut had told Hieronimus. Yes, of course. She wished to God he hadn't done it. She felt indignant and humiliated, as if she'd received an undeserved rebuke in public.

"Some strange things have happened here over the years, believe me," Nurse Suenson went on. "And when something goes wrong, it's the nurses who are blamed. Thorgren was as white as a ghost when she thought about what might have happened."

"Yes, now I understand everything," Else mumbled. "But it doesn't make any difference – I won't be here after tomorrow."

"Do you think so?" Nurse Suenson asked, with a doubtful look.

A wild, piercing cry reached them.

"She's having convulsions again," Nurse Suenson exclaimed, dashing into the corridor; Else could hear her struggling with someone as the cries grew louder and took on a rattling sound.

Else couldn't bear to lie still any longer. Struggling against her own impulse to scream, she got out of bed and went into the corridor, where she saw Nurse Suenson carrying off a howling woman, whose rigid body in a ripped chemise dragged along the floor. They disappeared into one of the cells.

Else sat down on the edge of a chair and pressed her hands to her heart, which was beating as if it would leap out of her chest. After a long time the screaming stopped and Nurse Suenson reappeared. She jumped slightly when she caught sight of Else and said brusquely, "My God, what are you doing, Mrs. Kant? You must never get out of bed – never. If you do, I'll have to report you and we'll have to take stricter measures."

"Don't be angry," Else begged, holding out her hand. "I didn't know it was forbidden, and I was so frightened I couldn't help it."

"Do you think it will be quiet here now?" Else asked, when she was back in bed again.

"I told you, it's never quiet on this ward."

She had scarcely spoken when another furious racket began down below, even louder and wilder than before.

Else was nearly in despair.

"Oh stay here, dear Nurse Suenson! Do stay here."

"No, I'm going out to have my dinner now. We sleep in the daytime when we're on night duty, so we have to eat at night."

"What are you having tonight?"

"Soup and meat."

"Oh give me a little."

"I don't dare."

"But I'm so terribly hungry. I couldn't eat the bread and butter they gave me. Just a little bit. Nobody will know."

But it was in vain. Nurse Suenson assured her sadly that she wasn't permitted to do it.

Nor was she permitted to spend so much time in Else's room, she added.

Chapter 6

SLOWLY THE NIGHT CREPT ALONG. At half-hour intervals Nurse Suenson looked in on Else, always finding her wide awake.

"It's been quiet for almost an hour and a half now," Nurse Suenson said, coming in once again. "And you still haven't slept."

"What time is it?"

"A little past five."

People were busy in the corridor. Doors and windows were banged and rattled open, chairs and tables were shoved aside, and there was the washing and slapping of wet scrub rags. Else felt every sound like a spasm in her heart, and the gas jet over the door, flickering in the draft worse than ever, irritated and stung her sleepless eyes.

Nurse Suenson brought Else a hand towel and a very small basin of water.

"Let me have my clothes so I can get up," Else begged. "I'm so tired of lying in bed."

"Then I'd catch it from the professor, all right," Nurse Suenson objected.

"But my soap and comb and toothbrush?"

"Nurse Stenberg has them. You'll have to manage without today." Nurse Suenson opened the cell window with a long pole and hurriedly started to wash the window sill, wall panels, and door. Else had to get up on her knees to reach her wash basin from the bed, and the draft was so cold her teeth chattered.

She got up while Nurse Suenson was making the bed, then she was brought tea and a couple of pieces of bread and butter, after which a woman came in with a water bucket and scrubbed the floor. The gas jets were turned off and grey daylight filled the cell. Finally Nurse Suenson swept the floor with a long-handled broom.

"Do you clean all the cells yourself?" Else asked.

"Yes," said Nurse Suenson breathlessly, as she continued her sweeping.

"The only thing we don't have to do is scrub floors. And then the patients get their tea, and most of them have to be washed, dressed, and helped with everything."

Nurse Stenberg was making her morning rounds of the cells. "I hope you slept well," she said to Else without waiting for a reply.

"Now I'll bid you good morning, Mrs. Kant." Nurse Suenson extended her hand.

"How tired you must be," Else said, looking closely at her delicate young face, and her ashen, hollow cheeks.

"Yes, I really am. I've been on duty for seven nights and I have seven more to go. The shift is fourteen days."

Else was overtaken by a paralyzing fatigue, and sank into a doze from which she was startled awake every few moments. The patients were calmer now, but there was the continuous noise of doors opening, windows rattling and banging, footsteps creaking and tramping, keys jangling, people talking, and every sound brutally penetrated the bare echoing room, sending rippling streams of fire and ice through Else's body.

After a few hours, Hieronimus finally arrived, stepping briskly and lightly in his long white linen coat. He was followed by five or six assistants and students, whose white clothes made them look like baker's apprentices. Hieronimus seated himself on a chair by the bed, while his white-clad retinue formed a semi-circle a few feet away; Nurse Stenberg and little Thorgren stood at the rear, their hands clasped before them, looking as solemn as if they'd been called as witnesses.

Hieronimus felt Else's pulse and asked some routine questions about her health, which she answered in pained monosyllables under the curious stares of the white-clad men.

"Why are all those people there?" she asked crossly.

"They're doctors," Hieronimus said. "Are you troubled by constipation?"

Instead of answering him, Else started to complain about her experiences during the night, insisting that she couldn't bear to stay there.

"Hasn't she slept?" Hieronimus asked, turning to Nurse Stenberg.

"Slept?" Else repeated indignantly.

"Well, then you can sleep now," Hieronimus said curtly, standing up.

"No, I can not! They've taken away my clothes, and they won't let me get out of bed."

Hieronimus walked to the door, his retinue respectfully giving way.

"I'm not permitted to speak to you?" Else cried out.

Hieronimus turned toward her slightly. "Not right now," he said with a wave of his hand. Then he left the cell, his steps as quick and light as when he entered, followed by his white-clad escort.

Else counted the minutes as she stubbornly waited, hour after hour, for Hieronimus. Thorgren brought her tea and plain buttered bread, exactly what she had received that morning, and leaned over her, rosy-cheeked and smiling as always, her hands tucked between her knees. "It won't be so bad, dear Mrs. Kant. As long as you're quiet. We'll be good friends, you'll see. Now you must eat something."

"I can't."

"Oh yes, just a little bit, all right?" She cocked her head to one side and smiled even more brightly.

Nurse Stenberg came, too, and in a kind voice urged her to eat. But Else shook her head and waited for the professor.

Out in the corridor by the yellow table opposite Else's door, one of the white-clad men was busy with some tall clear beakers, which he filled with various colored liquids. The young girl with the heavy head was wandering around in white wool socks as on the evening before, swaying back and forth; now and then the tidy old granny came into view, chattering and nodding.

Time passed but Hieronimus did not appear. Nor did Knut. Else listened feverishly to the footsteps in the corridor and wondered if she could recognize her husband's.

The patients had long ago started their racket again. Shrill howls, wild shrieks, kicking, stamping, ranting and raving beat in on her without respite. Else began to differentiate the individual expressions of misery. Dinner was brought in and Else discovered it was three o'clock. Despairing, she began to cry. So Knut wasn't coming today. Visiting hours were between eleven and twelve.

She was still crying when Nurse Hansen with the Madonna face came and asked how she was. Thorgren was off that afternoon and Nurse Hansen was taking her place. Else broke into loud complaints. Nurse Hansen took both her hands, squeezed them tenderly and whispered, "I feel so sorry for you, Mrs. Kant, and I wish you well, so I beg you to be calm. The more patient and quiet you are, the sooner you'll get better. Complaining does no good here. It just makes things worse."

"But they can't possibly want me to lie here another night," Else wept. "It will drive me mad."

Nurse Hansen gazed sadly at Else with the big beautiful eyes that recalled little Karin in the Swedish folk songs and said nothing.

"Don't you feel sure the professor will say I can be moved, when I've really had a chance to talk with him?"

Nurse Hansen shook her head. "You shouldn't expect your husband either, Mrs. Kant. There are no visitors on this ward. Shh..." Nurse Hansen put her finger to her lips and went out just as Nurse Stenberg was coming in.

Nurse Stenberg wanted Else to eat. It wouldn't do for her to lie there without taking any nourishment. Firmly she put her hands under Else's arms and sat her up in bed, then placed the tray on her lap.

There was porridge, with milk to pour over it but no sugar, and a tiny flounder in a puddle of melted butter.

Else swallowed a few spoonfuls of porridge, but the fish didn't smell fresh, and when she put a bite in her mouth, she had to spit it out again. It had a vile taste and had been boiled without salt.

The afternoon dragged on. Else was lying in dull despair, when she was again overwhelmed by longing for her husband and child. Never had she known that longing could cause such a violent physical pain. It was as if

Knut and Tage both were lying invisibly on her chest, crushing her to bits. Little Tage! How was he, she wondered. Oh, if she could just have a glimpse of him, even from a distance ...

Windows were banged open out in the corridor and in the cells. Else crept down under the covers to protect herself from the draft.

After a half hour, the windows were closed again and someone came tramping down the hall, banging something against the wall every few minutes. At the same instant, the shutters were fastened over the windows and a yellow light flooded in. Immediately the tramping steps and loud banging were explained. It was a man with a ladder lighting the gas jets over the doors of the cells.

Then suddenly Professor Hieronimus bustled into the room. He was wearing his overcoat and carrying a walking stick, and Else was immediately put off by his appearance of haste. Nevertheless, a ray of hope flashed through her.

"Thank God you've come," she said.

"I hope you are feeling better now," Hieronimus began in his thin, colorless voice.

"No," Else said, "how could I possibly? It's so terrible here."

"Terrible! On the contrary, it's very pleasant here." Hieronimus's tone was didactic. "You just have to think it's pleasant and then it will be. You've been feeling poorly recently, isn't that so?"

"Yes," Else answered. "But I'll never get better here."

"Things haven't been going well between you and your husband, I suppose. Do you have any complaints, any reproaches against him?"

"No," Else whispered, overcome with tears.

"He's a good husband and a kind father? He hasn't given you any cause for jealousy?"

"No, he's an outstanding man in every respect," Else stammered out. "But he had promised to come today."

"He did come to ask about you," Hieronimus said, speaking even more rapidly than usual.

"Then why didn't he visit me?"

"I wouldn't let him. You're getting something to make you sleep, aren't

43

you?" Hieronimus walked toward the door.

"Wouldn't let him – but why? Is he coming tomorrow then?" She sat up in bed and called after Hieronimus.

"No, not tomorrow," came Hieronimus's quick, cold reply.

"But when?"

"We shall see." Hieronimus was gone.

Chapter 7

"WE SHALL SEE, we shall see" – the words still buzzed in Else's ears as she repeatedly laced her fingers together and released them. Oh this gnawing pain in her chest!

"This is a lovely place to be." Granny was standing by the bed; her clean, shrivelled hands were clasped around a folded white cloth, and she was shaking her night-capped head in grateful wonder. "So clean and nice, but we don't get any coffee – no we don't."

"We shall see, we shall see" – no, he must have been joking. Yes of course, of course. Else was lacing her fingers together so tightly that her knuckles cracked.

But joking in a place like this? This ward, as they called it. And Hieronimus... He hadn't looked as if he were joking. Besides, he knew it wouldn't do her any good to lie in bed, and ... No, it was not a joke.

But perhaps he wanted to test her – to try her patience.

Oh nonsense, she hadn't come to a reform school, after all.

But perhaps Hieronimus saw that as his mission. What if he went through life with a burning desire to help and reform, to produce results that would amaze people and be a spur to him, a confirmation that he deserved the reputation he had earned. His manner and appearance were so peculiarly didactic – even ministerial. Yet surely he was not so young that he based his actions on dreams and theories. Surely life must have taught him, too, that the only thing worth knowing is that one knows nothing.

"We shall see, we shall see." Now she had it! He was going to surprise her – tomorrow Knut would suddenly appear in the cell. Yes, that was it. That was it.

But good God, it was still inexcusable for him to treat her this way. If he had told her Knut was coming tomorrow, maybe she could have slept tonight, but now ... No, Hieronimus was not as wise as she had thought.

And now she had the night ahead of her – the night, the night. Another night in this place.

"Well, Mrs. Kant, how are you getting along?" The resident physician gave Else a genial clap on the arm. "Dissatisfied with life, are you?"

How brutal these people are, Else thought. But then, catching a gleam of sympathy in the resident physician's phlegmatic eyes, she made him a silent apology.

"We'll make sure that you sleep tonight," said the resident physician. "We'll give you a double dose."

"That's what I had last night!"

"All right, a triple dose then. Just don't get the idea that you can't sleep. What would stop you? You have a comfortable bed and everything you could want. I'll look in when I make evening rounds."

Nurse Hansen took away the supper tray of tea and plain buttered bread, which Else had not touched.

"It's a pity you won't eat anything," she said.

"I can't get it down," Else replied.

Then things were readied for the night, everything just the same as the evening before. The blue-clad figures disappeared from the corridor. The gas jets were turned down, Nurse Stenberg made her evening rounds of the cells, and Nurse Suenson appeared for night duty.

"How have you been today?" she asked.

"Terrible," Else said, gripping both her hands.

"You were so sure you weren't going to be here today," the nurse said with a sad smile. "You see? I actually thought you would have been moved, though."

"What will the night be like, Nurse Suenson?"

"The same as usual, of course. Here's your sleeping potion."

"Do I have to take it? I won't sleep anyhow."

The nurse held the mixture to Else's lips. "You must never say 'no' to anything here. It's for your own good."

Then the horrors of the previous night began again. The same howls and shrieks, the same banging and thumping, the same furious, inhuman din from the maniacs raging and cursing below. Every few minutes Else sat up in bed and struggled to contain her fear. Every time Nurse Suenson looked in, Else felt comforted and begged her not to leave.

At a little past eleven, the resident physician appeared.

"What, you're not asleep?"

"The professor said my husband won't come tomorrow either," Else said. "He was joking, don't you think?"

"Now calm down, Mrs. Kant. Why are you so discontented?"

"Discontented! Don't you understand I'm being tortured to death here?"

"You're supposed to sleep. Then you wouldn't feel tortured."

"Sleep! Listen to the way they're shouting and yelling. And if there's a moment's peace, I start to cough."

"You're imagining things. But let me examine you anyway." The resident physician took out a stethoscope like the one the stocky assistant had used the night before.

"You have excellent lungs. Absolutely nothing the matter. Now, no more of this nonsense about the cough."

"Send a note to my husband and ask him. Or ask Nurse Suenson. Do you think I'm lying to you?"

"There, there, no offense meant. I'll give you something more to make you sleep." The resident physician disappeared.

"No, I won't take it!" Else cried. "Just give me some peace and then I'll sleep. The potion just makes it worse!"

"She's completely beside herself," the resident physician muttered, hurrying away.

Else's chest felt constricted by the weight of her despair. She looked at the high window, the tiny panes that gave the impression of iron bars, and she thought about all the locked doors that enclosed this terrible prison. She couldn't weep, didn't have the energy to speak to Nurse Suenson, who came and poured the sleeping potion down her throat, then gently and tenderly covered her up. If only she had kept her faith and could pray to the God of her childhood and youth. That would bring her peace and hope. Her heart swelled when she remembered how many times before she had found comfort and strength in prayer. A flood of hot tears relieved her, and she folded her hands involuntarily. Why, why had Jesus abandoned her! Then she remembered what Jesus had suffered, how he went to his shameful death without complaint, and by his patient suffering made his life and death a glorious example for all mankind, whether they believed or not.

A soothing calm descended on her. She closed her eyes and was on the verge of dozing off, when a shrill scream frightened her awake. The noise stabbed through her body like a wide, ice-cold knife. She leaped to the floor and called Nurse Suenson, but remembering she was not allowed out of bed, hurriedly climbed back in again.

The commotion continued. When one voice stopped, another started, and down below they carried on as if possessed. Little by little Else felt as if she were being battered and smashed to pieces. In the end all the tumult, all the shrieks seemed to be inside her. They ripped through her body, whirled and bubbled in her head; sometimes after a particularly violent shriek, she felt as if she were sinking into the depths, then slowly being lifted again. But there was one benefit: while she was being tossed around on these waves of terror, she did not cough.

As on the previous night, the patients became calmer toward morning, but then Else started to cough.

She thought about the professor. She could not understand how a physician, a man she had turned to for advice and help, could allow her to lie here exposed to these heart-rending upheavals. He knew how she had suffered from insomnia, how much she needed a quiet place to sleep. She was being treated exactly as if she were a lunatic, and for someone like her who was not insane, that was worse than being in prison.

"My goodness, Mrs. Kant, I thought you'd be asleep by now." Nurse Suenson had slipped in and was standing in front of Else.

"If it ever gets quiet here for a moment, I start to cough," Else answered.

"I really hadn't noticed. There's so much racket in here."

"Is the professor coming tomorrow morning?"

"No, the resident physician. The professor won't come until evening."

Again despair overwhelmed Else. She would have to stay here for another whole day. Dead-tired, confused, with no chance of getting a wink of sleep, shut inside these walls through which no cry or message could reach the outside world. Stretched on this hard bed where she would never find rest for her weary limbs, staring through that open door at the cell corridor and the blue-clad figures. And Knut would not come all day. She had asked Nurse Suenson if the professor could possibly be joking or planning to surprise her, and the nurse's answer removed all doubt. Oh Knut, Knut! How could he let them treat her this way? But perhaps Hieronimus really believed she was insane. He had barely talked to her, so he certainly couldn't know that. How strange, moreover, that he hadn't taken more time to arrive at an understanding of her condition – whether it really warranted keeping her in a cell. For without some urgent necessity, surely a person would not be put here.

Or perhaps he believed she had planned to use the opium drops to kill herself? The others had believed that, but now they knew better. She had carefully explained the circumstances to the resident physician and to Nurse Stenberg, and of course they had told the professor. No, Else didn't know what to think.

But when Hieronimus came tomorrow evening she would have a heart-to-heart talk with him. A calm one. Try to eliminate the misunderstanding that must have occurred. Then at least she could be sure that this was her last night in a cell. She clung obsessively to this thought. She kept repeating over and over the words she would say, until she knew them by heart. She imagined what Hieronimus would reply and formed his words into careful sentences. Her eyes filled with tears of longing, with kindly feelings toward this man who was so wise and so humane, whose life and powers were dedicated to the most unfortunate of his fellow creatures, people he helped more ways than he could know. Yes, tomorrow evening, tomorrow evening, her deliverance would come. She would get a quiet room in another place where she couldn't see and hear all the noise and misery, where she could live peacefully as a convalescent with one of these kind nurses and have daily talks with Hieronimus. Patience, patience – this day would also pass. It was a matter of concentrating all her strength and all her energy so she could bear up until Hieronimus came.

Chapter 8

Now it was morning at last. Doors slammed, windows were flung open, and a draft swept through the cell. The woman with the water bucket and scrub rag was clattering around in the corridor. Nurse Suenson was dashing back and forth in an endless rush, bringing washwater and tea, helping patients, and cleaning the cells. Nurse Stenberg made her rounds of the patients, and everything was the same as the morning before.

Else lay motionless on her pillow, her eyes closed, hands folded on her chest. Her body felt paralyzed with fatigue and ice coursed through her veins. Oh, if she could only sleep for a half hour. But that was impossible. Either the patients were screaming or there were footsteps in the corridor and jangling keys and the sound of doors being unlocked and slammed shut. But tonight, tonight when Hieronimus came ... Surely it was at least eight o'clock – from eight to twelve was four, from twelve to half-past six was eleven and a half. Eleven and a half hours! Dear God, that wasn't so terrible.

"How are you feeling, Mrs. Kant?" Nurse Hanson with the Madonna face was speaking to her.

"Don't ask me questions, don't talk to me." Else said darkly. "You're all paid to torture me."

"Dear sweet Mrs. Kant, we all want to make you as comfortable as we possibly can. Believe me, it's true ..." She bent down to Else and looked at her tenderly.

"Oh but I'm suffering so terribly," Else said, her eyes filling with tears.

"To lie here and know how dreadfully wrong all this is. To be powerless."

"Yes, I can well understand how you feel. But you mustn't show it. Everything here is interpreted as insanity. Just be calm, calm and good."

"But I am calm. I lie here as quietly as a mouse."

"If only you could win over the professor. He's so good to the ones he likes."

"The ones he likes!" Else said in astonishment. "But the people here are ill and insane."

"Yes, yes, I know. I'm giving you this advice because I like you. Do you want to read *Berlingeren*?[3] There's no harm in letting you have a newspaper, I suppose."

"No thanks. I'd rather have you. Sit down and talk to me."

"I don't dare. I'm on the quiet corridor and I just came to look in on you for a moment. I have to go now."

A large lazy fly buzzed incessantly above the doorway, trying in vain to penetrate the wire cage around the extinguished gas jet, where a small strip of sunlight played in rainbow colors. Else followed the fly's movements with tired eyes and thought how stupid it was not to settle quietly someplace and wait for the window to be opened. Then it could just fly out to freedom. Freedom – she had never before realized what a world of happiness that word encompassed. The day before yesterday she had been walking around as free as air, without feeling any gratitude about it. It was an eternal truth that blessings were only appreciated when they were lost. Suddenly the fly wheeled around and flew straight towards her bed, and the next moment she saw it swooping toward her face. Terrified, she struck out at the fly, which fell to the floor and crept away.

During rounds Else once again asked permission to get up.

"Why do you want to get up?" the resident physician asked. "You're better off in bed."

"But it's outrageous when there's nothing wrong with me. How am I supposed to pass the time! I've been lying here for forty hours and I haven't slept a wink."

The resident physician looked inquiringly at Nurse Stenberg, who was accompanying him on rounds as usual.

"No, Mrs. Kant won't sleep," Nurse Stenberg said jokingly. "She also has a cough, I hear."

"Well, sleep will come. Just be patient. Good day, Mrs. Kant." Then the resident physician went out into the corridor, where he busied himself with the tall beakers on the yellow table.

"I heard you coughing just now," he said suddenly, coming back into Else's room. "I'll give you some cough syrup." So she got cough syrup and breakfast – plain buttered bread and tea – which she scarcely touched.

"Now it ought to be quiet in here for a while," Nurse Stenberg said as she was taking away the breakfast tray. "See if you can take a nap."

Else turned toward the wall and almost immediately dozed off. But a moment later she was startled awake by a soft rustling sound from out in the corridor. The sound came again and again at short intervals, and in the unusual stillness, it seemed sharp and penetrating. Finally Else lifted herself on her elbows and peeked out into the corridor. Nurse Stenberg was sitting there reading a newspaper.

"My, but you're a difficult person," Nurse Stenberg said after questioning Else and finding that she hadn't slept.

After several hours had dragged by, Else was brought her dinner. Porridge and boiled fish, exactly the same as the previous day. She could only swallow a few mouthfuls.

Later in the day she heard sobbing and whimpering from the adjacent cell.

"Who is that crying in there," she asked Nurse Stenberg the next time she came in.

"A woman who's going to St. Jørgen's."

"Doesn't she want to?"

"Want to? They never want to."

"Poor, miserable creature! Imagine being sent to St. Jørgen's," Else shuddered.

"Oh it's not so bad. They're cared for very well at St. Jørgen's."

"Will her cell be empty then?"

"No, we're expecting a new patient. That's why this one is being moved. She won't go to St. Jørgen's until tomorrow morning."

A half hour later, the new patient arrived. It sounded to Else as if a battle were raging outside. A shrill female voice was screaming in desperation, scolding and threatening in the midst of a scuffle as somebody was being dragged down the corridor.

"Who dares lay a hand on me? I'll rip anybody who comes near me to pieces! Where is my husband – Carl, Carl! Help, help, save me, do you hear me, Carl! Oh God, oh God! Mother, Mother! You have no right to take my clothes off! Let me alone, let me alone!" The cries went on for a long time. Finally she was still. Then Else heard the shrill voice cry, "You out there, lady!" and ask for the professor. When Nurse Stenberg answered, the voice screamed, "Believe me, the professor will hear about this. He's a gentleman – he knows how a lady deserves to be treated!"

Else shivered with horror and compassion. Ah yes, the professor. If only he would come.

Finally he arrived, followed by Nurse Stenberg. As on the first morning, he asked Else a few routine questions, and then as he was about to leave, Else asked if she might speak to him alone.

"In a moment." He bustled out so quickly that his white coat fluttered around his legs. A few minutes later he came back and sat down by Else's bed.

"I would like to explain to you about the opium drops the other night," Else began, and after relating all the circumstances, ended by saying, "If you ask my husband, you'll find it's true that I've taken opium drops for my cough at times. Nothing else helps."

"Perhaps so, but you're not getting any opium drops in here," Hieronimus said curtly, in his dry, thin voice that sounded like it came from a diseased chest.

"No, of course not," Else said in a humble, bewildered voice.

"Above all, you must learn to subordinate yourself," Hieronimus continued in a reproachful tone. "The beginning was not promising. You brought things with you – books, drawing materials, and a number of other things you aren't permitted to have. That was strictly against my orders. I said explicitly, a few underclothes and the necessary toilet articles – nothing more."

54

"I didn't understand that," Else stammered. "I mean, I didn't have time to ask about it. And my husband didn't understand either. He gave me the books and promised to bring some more when he came."

"Hmph," Hieronimus said derisively, a sneer curling his thin, clean-shaven upper lip.

He thinks I'm lying, Else thought with astonishment.

"You can ask my husband, Professor," she said in a voice that shook with repressed outrage. "In any case, I absolutely can't bear it here any longer – it's impossible to sleep, for one thing."

"Oh really, and why is that?"

"Imagine, coming from one's own peaceful bedroom . . ."

The professor interrupted sharply: "The *peace* you achieved in your peaceful bedroom, for yourself and your husband, the less said about that the better, don't you think?"

"But then I would sleep a little in the morning, at least."

"As I recall, your husband said you kept making scenes until seven or eight in the morning."

Else was taken aback at Hieronimus's way of putting her in the witness box and cross-examining her.

"Then it was after eight," she said with trembling lips. "But here it's never quiet day or night."

"You're wrong," Hieronimus said curtly. "The patients often fall asleep for hours at a time."

"Hours! No, not hours," Else answered, "and then of course there are other kinds of noise here." And she told him about the slamming doors, the banging windows, the gas man tramping through, the footsteps in the corridor – everything.

Hieronimus bolted from his chair and was at the door in a second.

"Nurse Stenberg!" he called.

Nurse Stenberg came immediately.

"You know how often I've said that care must be taken to maintain quiet, even on this ward," Hieronimus said sternly. "The patients often complain about the slamming doors and banging windows."

"It's the maids, Professor."

"You are the only one I'm concerned with. You must make the maids obey. That is *your* concern."

"That's beyond me, Professor."

"You *must*. And what about the windows – are some of the hooks missing?"

"Yes, there are some hooks missing in a few places."

"That's disgraceful. What negligence! Why haven't you reported it?"

"But I have, Professor."

"It's not enough to report it, you must also make sure you get results. Do you understand?"

"Yes, Professor."

"What about the gas man? Does he wear boots?"

"Yes, I believe he wears boots, Professor."

"He should wear slippers. See that he wears slippers and walks quietly."

"I will certainly tell him, Professor."

"You have to see to all of this. It's your responsibility. Now what about Mrs. Kant? I understand she made quite a commotion when she arrived?"

"Oh, it really wasn't so bad, Professor."

"Not so bad?" Hieronimus cut her short. "Of course it was bad. I also heard about it from the resident physician."

"But I've just explained that to you," Else began, sitting up in bed and looking at the professor with astonished eyes.

"No, it really wasn't so bad." Nurse Stenberg came to her rescue.

"Then why did you put her in the disturbed corridor?" Hieronimus said in a sharp, dismissive tone.

"She was so opposed to sharing a room ..."

Professor Hieronimus did not let her finish. "You don't have to excuse yourself. You did the right thing. Well, there have been no incidents since," he said, turning to go.

"Do I have to stay here another night?" Else cried anxiously. "Oh no, Professor, you mustn't make me stay here another night!"

"I think you had better let me decide how long you should stay here,"

Hieronimus answered with lacerating coldness.

"Can't I see my husband tomorrow? I beg you, Professor."

Hieronimus, who was already at the door, turned and said in a milder tone, "As soon as you can tolerate it. Believe me, I have no desire to torture anyone longer than necessary. Besides, it's better for him not to see you while you're confined to bed."

As soon as she could tolerate it! Was there anything she hadn't tolerated in this place, night and day? Crushed, Else sank back on her pillow and burst into violent, heartbroken sobs. Nurse Stenberg, who had left with a sullen expression, came back and sat by her.

"There, there, dear Mrs. Kant. Don't cry so horribly – there, there, if only I could do something for you."

Else got up on her knees. She threw her arms around Nurse Stenberg's neck, and when she could get some control of her voice, said through her sobs, "Forgive me, Nurse Stenberg, forgive me for complaining about the noise ..." Her words came haltingly. "I didn't know that you would get the blame and I didn't know he was that kind of man either. I'll never do it again."

Nurse Stenberg patted her hair, kissed her cheek, and assured her that she shouldn't fret about it. She should just lie down nicely and be calm and patient.

Chapter 9

How SWEET AND KIND Nurse Stenberg was! Else had thought that she walked through this place of suffering without any feeling for the victims' misery, yet just now when Else had made trouble for her, she had been kind and sympathetic. Else would never forget that!

And the others, too, for that matter. Plump Thorgren with her smiling rosy cheeks. She had been in and out all day, speaking cheerfully and kindly, demonstrating her good will in every way. Not to mention Madonna-Hansen, whose large eyes glowed with goodness and heart-felt compassion. And of course Nurse Suenson, the night nurse, whose mere appearance soothed Else's agony. Thank God for the nurses! What if they had behaved like Hieronimus? She had the impression, though, that they instinctively did not want to reveal the good relationship that existed between them. Whenever Hieronimus came in their faces became rigid and severe. It was as if the atmosphere instantly turned to ice when he appeared.

"You really must try to win over the professor," they all told her. "Even if we do everything we can to help you, it means nothing if he's against you."

"Win over the professor," Else brooded. Wasn't she a suffering human being who had freely entrusted herself to his care? What if she had been utterly raving mad – desperate, uncontrollable – could he be "against" her on those grounds?

No, she didn't understand it.

And how should she go about winning over the professor? She hadn't shown any rebelliousness, only cried and bewailed her fate. And her complaints had been only a ripple on the sea next to the suffering she had already experienced. Should she pretend to be humble and repentant – prostrate herself before this man who seemed so tyrannical? Conduct herself like some wretched underling, beseeching his majesty for an unmerited favor?

No, a thousand times no! Not if they burned her at the stake!

But suppose she did try to "win" him over, as they put it. Appeal to his kindness and sympathy. Surely he must possess both. Otherwise he would certainly not feel he was the right man for this place, where his duty, above all, was to show humanity and discretion, to try to understand as much as possible, and through understanding, exercise a helpful, calming influence on his patients.

His behavior was probably just a mask that he found expedient to assume for some reason or other. Tomorrow morning, when he made his rounds, she would try again.

Tomorrow morning! A whole night of terror lay between tonight and tomorrow morning. Yet another night in this place. This would be the third.

Now Tage was being put to bed at home. Oh God, Tage, Knut, home – how her heart ached. She wrung her hands and pushed her face deeper into the pillow. Little Tage – was he asking about her? And Knut. What was Knut thinking? Didn't he think it was dreadful that he couldn't see her? He had promised so faithfully to come ... A pent-up groan escaped her.

"Here is your sleeping potion, Mrs. Kant."

Else lifted herself up on the pillow and took the mixture Nurse Suenson gave her.

"You seem very calm tonight. Are you feeling better?"

Else shook her head.

"Haven't you slept today?"

"No, I've given up sleeping. I've given up everything." She hid her face in Nurse Suenson's breast and shook with sobs.

"I was so sure you were going to be moved by tonight," Nurse Suenson said. "This corridor isn't the right place for you. What does the professor say?"

"The professor is a beast," Else wept.

"You mustn't say things like that! The professor is a fine man. But you must really try to win him over."

"Yes that's right," said Thorgren, who had come into the room and was now standing beside Nurse Suenson with her hand on Else's shoulder. She gave it a gentle shake and said, "The day you win over the professor, we'll see shooting stars in the sky."

In the cell next door, the new patient went on screaming and scolding and desperately calling for Carl. Now she was utterly beside herself, pounding furiously on the door, uttering profane demands that it be opened.

"Is she locked in?" Else asked.

"Yes, she's uncontrollable. She kept running out into the corridor, demanding to go home."

"She's going to be a handful," Thorgren said with a laugh.

"Uh," Else said, shuddering. "She'll beat her hands until they're raw."

Then the banging stopped and they heard the sound of a body crashing heavily to the floor, followed by wails and convulsive sobbing.

"Aren't you going in to her?" Else asked.

"It's better for her to wear herself out. She's had so much chloral it won't take long."

"Good night, dear Mrs. Kant," Thorgren said, extending her hand and patting Else on the cheek. "Good night, Suenson."

"The sleeping potion doesn't help at all," Else said when Thorgren left. "Look at me, it's as if I've been drinking water."

"Yes, you're quite remarkable, Mrs. Kant."

"Does it usually work?"

"Yes, except with the maniacs. But we don't give it to them."

"Don't the maniacs ever sleep?"

"Yes, after the first three – four – five nights."

The hours passed. The patients had rumbled and shouted as usual, and the maniacs had carried on more wildly, if possible, than the nights before. For the last few hours Else had heard nothing from the patient in the cell next door.

Suddenly somebody let out a prolonged howl that seemed to go on forever. It sounded muffled and hollow, as if it were coming from someone buried alive.

"Nurse Suenson, Nurse Suenson!"

Nurse Suenson came in with her mouth full of dinner.

"Who is that?" Else asked, her face terror-stricken.

"It's a young girl."

"Why is she howling like that?"

"God knows!"

"She must be suffering terribly!"

"No, she doesn't know what she's doing. When the resident physician comes, I expect he'll give her a morphine injection."

"Will the resident physician come soon?"

"Yes, it's almost half-past eleven. He should be here now." Nurse Suenson went out to finish her dinner.

Else sat up in bed and listened for the resident physician's footsteps.

She was seized by a rush of anxiety that rose to a state of terror as the unbroken, muffled howling continued. How could a person keep howling like that! How did she have the strength, the breath for it? Oh God, God, what an abyss of misery it was to be here.

Then she heard the resident physician come walking quietly along the corridor and exchange a few whispered words with Nurse Suenson.

"Good evening! Just as wide awake as ever?"

"How do you think I could possibly sleep?" Else said irritably. "Please don't give me that nonsense about how I will sleep and ought to sleep. You can't really believe that!"

"What can one say to you?" The resident physician shrugged his shoulders.

"Listen to that howling, listen to the maniacs down there; in a minute the woman in the next cell will start, and then all the others! Oh God, God, I'll go mad!"

"Don't be such a spitfire." The resident physician's half reproachful, half teasing tone irritated Else, but his calm, compassionate face soothed her.

"I have to exert all my force," Else went on in anguished haste, "to keep myself from howling and wailing along with the others."

"You are quite hysterical, you know."

"How could a person in here be anything else?" Else continued, twisting in agony. "It is inexcusable, inexcusable. When I think that I left my home for some peace and rest!"

"But this is the place for that kind of patient," said the resident physician, trying to make his voice friendly and soothing. "It can't be any worse for you than the others."

"That kind of patient!" Else exclaimed. "Well, God help that kind of patient! But why can't my husband visit me? What do you think he would say if he were here now?"

"He's the one who brought you here. He must have thought it was necessary."

"Nobody brought me here. I came on my own accord because I chose to, myself. But if I had known then what I know now ... And the same is true for my husband. I'm positive he had no idea how I would be treated. Why shouldn't he have a chance to see and hear for himself? To lie here – in a place like this! And under the care of a man like Hieronimus. God have mercy on me!"

"He's the best in the field," said the resident physician.

"But why doesn't he let my husband visit me?" Every muscle in Else's face quivered with agitation. "Can you understand that? Do you defend it?"

"The professor is afraid of exposing you to excitement. That's easy enough to understand."

Else laughed. "Excitement! To see my husband would be a pleasant kind of excitement, not the kind I'm exposed to here ..." She broke off and hid her face in her hands.

"Calm yourself, Mrs. Kant," the resident physician said, putting his hand on Else's shoulder. "You'll see, it won't be as bad you think." His gentle voice and earnest tone aroused Else's hopes.

"Will you speak to the professor for me?" she asked, looking at him in desperation.

The resident physician nodded.

"And tell him you think he should let my husband visit?"

"I will, in a few days. Good night, Mrs. Kant. Just settle down."

Just settle down ... What kind of people were they anyhow? Physicians they called themselves – executioners was more like it. What was going to happen to her? How long would her strength hold out? Else lay back on the pillow and again wept the bitter tears that she had shed so freely during the last few days. She felt as if she were at the bottom of a deep well over which someone could clamp a lid at any moment. Oh no, that mustn't happen – it must not. She would work her way up – all the way up, so she could at least get her head over the edge.

When the professor came in the morning she would talk to him. He would be touched and understand what she suffered, and speak kindly and say she could have another room right away. Yes, of course, because there was no sense in this. Surely he didn't intend to drive her mad. If she actually were what they called insane, or her mind were less clear, perhaps she might have believed he was trying to drive her mad. But thank God, she wasn't as bad off as that.

Chapter 10

SHE BEGAN TO THINK about all the different tortures and agonies that the world's multitudes had suffered during the course of time – the people who had languished in underground prisons; the innocent young girls who had been abused and burned, suspected of being witches or the minions of witches; the many Russian men and women who had been condemned to death and executed for their political opinions; the victims of religious persecution, thousands of them; the people who had been mistaken for dead and buried alive – and an infinite compassion for all the wretched of the earth filled her breast. What did her suffering signify compared with theirs?

Her mind grew calm and still. "A little while and ye shall see me," Jesus had once said to his disciples. For a little while she would be here, but then in a little while Knut would come and set her free. Certainly. Anything else was unthinkable. Hieronimus was just pretending to be harsh. Why should he wish her harm? She had never met him before and never done anything to him. And even if she seemed unpleasant and repellent to him, that wasn't a sufficient reason for a man like Hieronimus. Quite the contrary, he would be doubly careful then.

The resident physician was right. She should stay calm. Now the muffled howling had grown fainter. Later that night the maniacs would perhaps also grow calmer and then in the morning the professor would come. Thank God, she had gotten her head over the edge of the well.

"You're not asleep." Nurse Suenson had tiptoed into the room.

"Did she get the morphine injection?"

"Yes; she'll fall asleep right away. The resident physician is pleasant to talk to, don't you think?"

"Yes, he seems very nice."

"But you mustn't let him notice that you're upset or excited, Mrs Kant. I gather he thought you were worse this evening."

"Worse," Else asked brusquely. "How do you mean, worse?"

"Up here," said Nurse Suenson, touching her index finger to her forehead.

Else wanted to sink to the bottom of the well again, but she pulled herself together and drove the thoughts away. Nurse Suenson had misunderstood, of course. It was impossible that the resident physician could interpret her justifiable complaints as a sign of mental disturbance.

"Tell me a little about yourself," Else said, lying on her side, her cheek propped on her hand so she could have a better view of Nurse Suenson's bright, delicate face. "Do you like being a nurse?"

"Yes, I like it very much – very much. I've been a nurse for five years and I've never regretted it for a single hour. The only thing that makes me sad is the thought of my sweet old father. 'You have a hard life, my girl,' he always says; then he heaves a deep sigh and strokes my hair."

"Still, I think it must be terrible to wrestle with these mad people. Aren't you frightened? Or weren't you at first?"

"Well yes, there were times when I was a little frightened at first. But you get used to it. And you get some pleasure now and then – take Granny, for instance. She's so sweet and grateful. And the old lady in there who throws the bedrails on the floor – a couple of times when I've been leaning down to do something for her, she's put her arms around my neck and whispered, 'Thank you, Alma. You're so sweet.' She always takes me for Alma, the one she raves about. From such a sick, worn-out creature that's a great deal," smiled Nurse Suenson, touched and happy.

"What is the old lady's name."

"Mrs. Fog."

"Do you think the professor is a kind man?" Else asked.

"Kind?"

"A good person, I mean."

"Oh heavens, yes. Of course I do. You should see the way he behaves towards someone he likes."

"What about you, Nurse Suenson, do you like him?"

"Like him?" Nurse Suenson repeated the question timidly, as if the idea it suggested were altogether blasphemous. "Like him? I have such immense respect for him – reverence, even."

"You don't think he could be mean toward people he doesn't like?"

"Mean toward people he doesn't like?" She turned the words over and over. "No, but he's very strict, oh very, very strict. I tremble with fear when he comes into the corridor, yes, I tremble an hour before, because I'm so afraid that everything won't be exactly as it should be. One time during his rounds, I spied a hair twisted around the soap in the corner of the washstand. I was trembling from head to foot. I didn't dare go over and take the hair away, didn't dare move from the spot, and I'm sure he saw it. He sees everything. If I had a hole in the toe of my stocking I'm sure he could see it right through the shoe."

"You're not that afraid of the resident physician, are you?"

"No, not the resident physician." Nurse Suenson, whose expression had been strained while she talked about the professor, now smiled easily. "He's so good-natured, you know."

"If only morning would come," Else sighed.

"Yes, it will be four o'clock soon."

"Thank God."

Just then they heard the sound of bare feet hitting the floor in the next cell, and a moment later, thundering blows on the door and a fearful scream.

"Oh God, she's starting again!" Else cried, hastily sitting up in bed. "You mustn't unlock the door or she might come in here."

"Now just be calm."

"Who is she?" Else asked.

"A young woman named Mrs. Syverts – very beautiful."

A moment later a figure in a chemise and a short jacket, with knees so bent she was almost sitting, came darting past the open door with unnaturally long steps and her arms flailing wildly.

The nurse dashed out at once.

Mrs. Syverts in the cell next door kept on shrieking and hammering at the door, begging and pleading for them to unlock it, desperately calling for Carl and threatening to tell the professor. Else held her hands tightly against her temples. Something was pressing behind her forehead and she felt as if her head were going to burst.

Chapter 11

THE SCRUBWOMAN ARRIVED and the windows clattered open. Nurse Suenson brought the usual ration of water in a tiny dish of cream-colored faience.

Else was kneeling on the bed washing herself while Nurse Suenson cleaned the cell, when a figure with bare white legs under a short chemise glided swiftly through the door and stopped to stare at Else. Her face was extremely pale, her eyes dark and lustrous. A mass of black hair framed her beautifully shaped wide forehead and fell in a long braid over one shoulder.

Else was moved by the beauty of the white face. She studied her eagerly.

"She's so pretty, that woman over there," the figure said, in an expressive yet strangely veiled voice, pointing to Else.

"She's so pretty," she repeated dreamily, "and she looks so unhappy."

"Go back to where you belong, Mrs. Syverts," said Nurse Suenson, who was washing the cell paneling with her usual breathless haste.

"Where I belong – yes, let me go home where I belong." There was bitter sorrow in her voice. Suddenly she stamped her foot and screamed furiously, "I'm a respectable woman, I tell you! I want to be a respectable woman, so I'm not staying here – not an hour, not a minute longer! Do you think I want to be with this pack of criminals?" She kept on stamping her bare foot and uttering a stream of ugly curses. "There's not one decent person in here!"

Nurse Suenson let the washrag fall into the soapy water, walked quickly over to Mrs. Syverts and took her by the arm.

"Don't lock me in!" Mrs Syverts shouted, terrified and imploring. "Don't lock me in!"

"Then you mustn't make a fuss," the nurse said, hauling her away.

"Carl, Carl, Carl! Help me, save me!" came the grief-stricken cry, and then stillness.

"Have you locked her in again?" Else asked when the nurse returned.

"No, I got her into bed and left the door open a crack."

A little later, when Else had finished washing and was lying alone in her cell, Mrs. Syverts came darting in again. In a couple of strides she was at Else's bedside, lifting the blankets as if to climb in.

"You're a man," she whispered through clenched white teeth. "Let me get in there with you. Do you think I don't know you're a man?"

Terrified, Else scrambled up and tried to push her away.

"I'll take you by force," hissed the madwoman. She seized Else firmly by the arms and forced her back on the pillow as easily as if she had been a baby. Without loosening her iron grip on Else's arms, she put one leg on the bed.

Else let out a cry for help. Nurse Suenson came in immediately, and hastily yanked Mrs. Syverts away.

"She was frightened, the fool, she was frightened!" Mrs. Syverts shouted and laughed as the nurse took her away.

Else burst into convulsive sobs. She put her head under the covers and bit the sheet so no one could hear her.

Violent twinges spread in waves from her neck to the back of her head; her temples pounded and something kept pressing, pressing, behind her forehead. The pain ripped and tore in her chest, moving inexorably, like a coiled snake, up into her throat.

After a long time, Nurse Suenson came in and gave her some water.

"Get hold of yourself, they're making rounds in a few minutes. It won't do any good to be so emotional."

But Else continued to cry. "I want to get out, out, out! – home to Knut and Tage!" a voice kept crying inside her, and the thought of these dear ones gradually calmed and quieted her tears.

"Now tell me why you are crying." Nurse Stenberg sat down on the edge of the bed and took Else's hand.

"I'm so terribly homesick."

"You have to get over that. Rest assured that the best thing for you is to stay here."

"No," Else answered violently. "It was a terrible mistake for me to come here. My husband would be frantic if he knew the truth."

Then Else heard once again that it was her husband who had brought her here, that there must have been something wrong with her or she wouldn't have come.

"Yes," said Else. Something had indeed been wrong, but she had not been insane. "Have you noticed any signs of insanity in me?"

No. But of course one could never tell. There were so many kinds of insanity and mental disorder. The ones who seemed the sanest were often the most severely afflicted – and since she was here, well . . .

Else gave Nurse Stenberg a desolate look. "It's hopeless," she muttered, turning her head away.

She was lying in a semi-conscious state with towering green-stained walls close around her. At the top the walls slanted inward, leaving only a tiny open square, covered by a wire cage with a gas jet burning inside it. A pale twilight flooded down the green-stained walls and she could hear a muffled roar, like the sea rolling monotonously in the distance. Nobody could see her, and the wire cage over the opening would never be taken away, and she would never be pulled up from these depths to life and time, the sounds of which she could dimly perceive. She would lie here forever, lie here with frozen arms and outstretched legs.

"Is she asleep now?"

Else opened her eyes. The resident physician and one of the assistants were standing there; Nurse Suenson was at the foot of the bed. She looked around in bewilderment, brushed her hand across her forehead, and remembered everything.

"Her eyes are swollen," said the resident physician.

"Yes, she's been crying quite a bit. She's homesick, she says."

"The professor was supposed to come today," said Else.

"He's been detained. You'll have to make do with my humble self," the resident physician said with his kindly smile.

"Didn't the professor say I was going to be moved?"

The resident physician looked at Nurse Stenberg, who shook her head.

"I can't take any more, I just can't take any more," Else wailed. "Will you see the professor today?"

"Won't you tell him that?" Else continued, when the resident physician had nodded that he would. "Please do it, Doctor! Isn't that right, Nurse Suenson? I can't bear it any longer, can I?"

"There isn't an empty room," Nurse Suenson looked at the resident physician uncertainly. "That's what's so unfortunate about the situation."

"How is her appetite?"

"She hardly eats a thing."

"You must do that," the doctor waggled his index finger threateningly. "You won't be moved as long as you don't eat."

"How could I possibly eat in this place! Besides, what kind of food do I get? Nothing but porridge and boiled fish every day."

"That's a fever diet."

"But I don't have a fever!"

"Mrs. Kant hasn't had a fever?" the doctor asked, with a quick glance at Nurse Stenberg.

"No, she hasn't had a fever."

"Well, it doesn't really matter. We can put you on another diet now. I'll write a note about the food. Good day."

"Be sure to tell the professor that I've got to be moved!" Else called after him.

All morning Else waited in agonizing suspense for someone to bring a message from the professor that Mrs. Kant should be moved to another room. The idea of staying there another night she could not, dared not consider. Every time Thorgren or Nurse Stenberg appeared she raised her head from the pillow and looked at them with breathless inquiry. Once she heard a man's voice in the hall and thought it was Knut. A cry of jubilation rose within her. With a lighting quick movement, she sat up in bed and held out her arms. The voice grew more distinct, the male footsteps came closer. It was Knut. She could hear that clearly. Oh God, God, she was saved, saved, saved! The blessed professor had wanted to surprise her after all ... Her whole face quivered with a smile of delight, her eyes filled with happy tears, and her heart pounded with excitement. Then one of the assistants walked past the door. "You're not allowed to sit up in bed," he told Else, as he hurried by and disappeared.

Chapter 12

ELSE SAT, BLANK AND UNMOVING. So he was the one she had heard and not Knut.

She felt as if all the blood in her body had sunk to her legs and a clammy chill was seeping from her head downwards. In a short while the blood flowed back to her heart, and rushed, red hot, to her head. Everything was dancing around her; she felt the bed swaying as if at sea. Gripping the night table for support, she slowly sank back on the pillow.

How could she have imagined anything as ridiculous as Knut being allowed to come today, she wondered later. That would be too delirious a joy. Besides Hieronimus had told her, "There's no point in letting him see you as long as you're here."

What did he really mean by *that?* Why shouldn't Knut see her as long as she was here? Should Knut be kept in the dark about the way she was being treated? It was almost as if Hieronimus was conceding that he couldn't defend the way he was treating her. No, Hieronimus surely believed he was treating her properly, but he thought Knut wouldn't understand and would meddle and insist she go home.

There wasn't an empty room, Nurse Stenberg had said.

But it was really too outrageous that she had to lie here for that reason, running the risk of going under. She had come here voluntarily. Shouldn't it also be a voluntary matter if she and Knut were to say: "We made our decision to come here under false assumptions, and now we want to reverse it."

No, again Else didn't know what to think.

73

She pondered and finally said to herself, "If I can just move today and avoid the horrors of another night, I'll be content." Perhaps the assistant she thought was Knut had brought orders to Nurse Suenson. Yes, of course. Why else would he have come at this time of day. They were putting the room in order now. A cheerful Thorgren was going to come in, a wide smile on her sweet, plump face and say, "You're going to get up, Mrs. Kant, and follow me to a lovely, quiet room." She wouldn't ask any questions, she would just wait patiently. They were looking forward to surprising her with the good news. Mustn't interfere with their pleasure.

When dinner was brought in – fruit soup and two pale meat patties that looked like buckwheat cakes – she immediately sat up in bed and ate as much as she was able to swallow. Fruit soup was the thing she hated most in the world, and she had always detested meat patties. But that didn't matter. Surely her dislike of the food could be overcome.

When Else had finished her dinner, she heard the door slam hard in the corridor and, at the same instant, a frightful howl. A moment later two attendants came past her door carrying a stretcher on which a thin, pallid woman was sitting bolt upright, waving her arms. She was wailing continuously. Shortly afterwards the attendants came back with the empty stretcher; the wails grew wilder and wilder, and Mrs. Syverts, who had been quiet for a long time, began to rage and shriek in the cell next door.

This is Hell, Else thought. Whoever invented the doctrine of torments of Hell had undoubtedly been a mistaken visitor on a Ward Six somewhere, presided over by a Hieronimus.

"What do you make of this farce?" Mrs. Syverts, dressed in a chemise, her long white legs a bit too thick at the ankles, had come into Else's cell, where she paced rapidly back and forth with her hands on her hips. "I'll go mad here. By God I'll go mad! My husband has a little place on the coast. I was supposed to go there but then the doctor came and said I had to talk to Professor Hieronimus first. He's all the rage these days, isn't he?" She stopped in the middle of the cell, and looked at Else sharply. "Everybody thinks they are going to talk to Hieronimus," she went on, "but we don't get to talk to him, you know. Bla bla bla bla – he says, then he's off."

"You should go get into bed, Mrs. Syverts," Else admonished.

"But it's so horrible to lie there staring at the walls all day. I'm not used to it."

"Of course it's horrible. This is the fourth night I've been here. You just came yesterday."

"And they fill me so full of chloral I get all mixed up. You wouldn't believe the way my head is ringing. Oh, Carl, Carl..." She covered her eyes with her hand and burst into tears.

"Is Carl your husband?"

"Yes, my husband, my kind, decent husband. We've only been married for eight months."

"Now go in and lie down, Mrs. Syverts. If the nurse finds you here, she will just say you're terribly sick and restless and then you'll have to stay in bed much longer."

"Be patient and good," Else continued, when Mrs. Syverts kept on weeping silently and didn't answer. "That's what they all tell me. So I pass it on. There's no point in rebelling here. Go now, before someone sees you."

"Yes, I will," Mrs. Syverts said, nodding vigorously. "I'll do it because you ask me." She walked quickly out of the cell.

A couple of minutes later a woman flew past the open door, wrapped from the waist down in a sheet that was soaked with blood in front. In a hollow sepulchral voice she screamed with all her might, "Knu'ssen! Knu'ssen!" Almost instantly she was dragged, almost lifted, back to her cell by Thorgren, as the cries for Knu'ssen continued.

"It's a puerperal maniac,"[4] Thorgren told Else, when she came in to see her later. "She gave birth two days ago."

"Is she the one who is still screaming?"

"Yes, but it's nothing for you to worry about. Courage, Antonius," she laughed, patting Else's cheek. "Think what a good situation the patients have here – nursed and cared for in every way, clean sheets on the beds twice a week. I think it would be fun to be a patient here for a little while ... With a man like our professor! I'm quite serious, Mrs. Kant."

How could these good, kind people have such blunted perceptions of other people's sufferings? It was the same old story again. The confidence in authority that in every century led men to believe in and submit to one person, one person with enough audacity and contempt for mankind to pose as someone who led the way and knew the truth. "With a man like our professor!"

Nurse Stenberg entered. Else thought she could see in her face that she had good news to report. But she wouldn't let on that she knew. Nurse Stenberg could tell her herself. But when Nurse Stenberg said nothing more than her usual kind words, Else could no longer contain herself and asked if she wasn't going to be moved.

No, Nurse Stenberg hadn't heard anything about that.

"But don't you think a message might still come?"

"That's impossible. It's five o'clock. Besides, as I've told you before, we have no empty rooms."

"No empty rooms," Else repeated, shivering at the thought of the coming night. "But tell me one thing: Is it impossible to find a room other than the cell I'm in now?"

"Impossible? No, it's not impossible. Changes can be made here and there. There's also the ward for nervous diseases and a corridor over in the pavilion that we sometimes use."

"Dear sweet Nurse Stenberg," Else gripped her hand and looked into her eyes with a gaze that cried for help. "Do whatever you can for me. Say that I'll die if I stay here. Oh be kind, be kind, and I'll remember it all my life."

"Yes, dear Mrs. Kant. We all want the best for you." She patted Else's hand and went out.

So that's finished, Else thought, I'm going to be here again tonight. Her mood grew hard and embittered. The patients careened about, screaming and wailing; their noise seemed a fitting accompaniment to the words in her head.

Soon it would be time for evening rounds – the resident physician would come, not the professor. Oh well, it didn't make any difference.

Almost immediately the resident physician appeared in his white coat, followed by one of his assistants and Nurse Stenberg. He repeated his everlasting question: Was she still dissatisfied with life?

Else sat up in bed and gave vent to her indignation.

The resident physician made no reply. He just looked at her, sadly and kindly. But as he went out he turned to Nurse Stenberg and said, "She's getting worse and worse."

A moment later she heard rapid squeaking steps in the corridor, then Hieronimus, in an overcoat, his hat in his hand, stood in her cell.

"Your husband sends you his regards," he said.

Else wanted to thank him, but her throat was so constricted she could not utter a sound.

"He asked me to tell you he found a cook he thought would be satisfactory, starting the first of the month. So you don't have to worry about that."

"Am I going to spend the night here again?" Else asked in a voice that seemed hoarse and unfamiliar to her.

"Y-ess," he said unctuously, as if prolonging the word gave him physical pleasure.

"But I can't bear it. I'm suffering so terribly."

"Oh, really," Hieronimus answered with such sneering contempt that Else felt as if she had been slapped in the face. "And how did you feel at home?"

Else sat bolt upright in bed, quite beside herself. With a contorted face, her eyes ablaze, she looked directly into Hieronimus's cold pale eyes and said, "You know as well as I do that there's absolutely no justification for keeping me in a cell! You say you don't have a room for me, but then you have an obligation to tell my husband. 'Oh, really,' you say," and she mimicked Hieronimus's sneering, contemptuous tone, returning the slap in the face as best she could. "Wouldn't you like to stay here one night, one single night, and let me have your bedroom?"

"Nooo," he said, his voice like the neighing of a distant horse.

"You expose me to inhuman torture, day and night!" Else cried. "What right have you to do that?"

"Inhuman torture!" Hieronimus's pale face had become as white as chalk. He lifted himself on his toes, then rocked back on his heels. "You have a great need to learn self control! Your illness is your inability to control yourself. I had thought about moving you..." Smacking his short, plebeian fingers against his other palm, he almost screamed, "But now you can stay here!" and he was out of the cell in a flash.

A delightful man, Else thought contemptuously and laughed to herself.

"My God, Mrs. Kant," Nurse Stenberg spoke from beside Else's bed. Her delicate pale face looked paler than usual and her expression was frightened and reproachful. "How could you dare speak to the professor like that. I heard the whole thing."

"How dare he treat me the way he does! I'm only sorry I didn't say more."

"The professor can't bear criticism. Not from anybody, least of all a patient."

"Well that's a pity for the professor," Else said contemptuously.

Later on Thorgren came in, terror-stricken, and made a sign of the cross. "You really must apologize to the professor," she begged.

"I wouldn't do that if he killed me," Else answered.

Madonna-Hansen also appeared and talked in horrified tones about the matter. Everyone on her corridor was quite upset. Nothing like this had ever happened before. Hadn't she always implored Else to be quiet and good because she was fond of her and had her interests at heart? "Now you must humble yourself before the professor. Promise you'll do it," she ended.

"Never!" Else cried vehemently. And Madonna-Hansen went out, shaking her head sadly.

The night shift began and Nurse Suenson brought Else her chloral.

"You look as if you're angry with me," Else said.

"No. Just sad. You'll never be moved this way."

Chapter 13

THE HOURS PASSED, and the furious racket, the clamorous shrieking, continued above and below. The puerperal maniac suddenly dashed down the corridor, uttering her prolonged sepulchral cry, "Knu'ssen, Knu'ssen!" Finally she was locked in, and the cries for Knu'ssen sounded more hollow and muffled than before.

Gripped by fear and anguish, tortured by longing and a consuming physical restlessness, Else tossed back and forth on the hard bed. Tomorrow was Sunday. Knut would be taking Tage for a walk before breakfast. Oh, if only she could go with them! Why hadn't she just stayed home? She could have stayed there if she had wanted. But she had felt ill and was looking for peace and quiet and rest to cure her. What were her miseries there compared to those she had to suffer now?

The procession of brown horses – what had become of it? She hadn't seen it once since she had been here. And she hadn't thought about her work for a second. If only she could have had quiet, pleasant surroundings, where she could have seen Knut and shown him every day that she was improving.

Night rounds began. Contrary to custom, it was one of the assistants. Else heard him ask from the doorway if Mrs. Kant was sleeping.

"No," said Nurse Suenson. "How could she possibly sleep here?"

"It's quiet enough."

"Right this moment," Nurse Suenson said indignantly. "Just wait a few minutes and you'll hear. If one of us had to put up with what Mrs. Kant has to endure ..."

"It wouldn't bother me," the assistant said loftily and walked on.

"Can't Mrs. Kant get up for a while today?" Nurse Stenberg asked the resident physician when he came the next morning. "She's so tired of staying in bed."

"She's been pretty quiet since the first night," the resident physician answered thoughtfully. "Yes, you may get up for an hour, Mrs. Kant. After breakfast. Good morning."

A few minutes later, one of the young assistants – a tall, slim fellow with a thin moustache and a smooth handsome face – came in and wished her "Good morning."

"What shall I tell your husband when I see him, Mrs. Kant?" he asked with an encouraging smile.

Else gave the assistant a searching look, unsure if she should answer him. But then the thought crossed her mind that perhaps he felt sorry for her, and she said urgently, "Tell him he must exert all his energy to get in to see me. Tell him I'm in a terrible state and I'll go mad if he doesn't come soon."

"Do you think that will be productive?" the assistant asked, still smiling.

"Of course it will be productive. He'll take me away the instant he sees what it's like here. He hasn't the slightest inkling – that's what's so dreadful."

"You don't like being here at all?" The assistant twirled his moustache and continued to smile.

"Tell him he must come, he absolutely must come, and make him understand that you think so, too," Else entreated. "I'll be so grateful to you. Promise me you'll say that."

"Your husband can't do anything. He goes by what the professor says entirely. He's also well informed about your situation here."

"No," Else said in a faltering voice. "He does *not* know."

"Well, in any event, I won't be seeing your husband at all." The assistant's smile spread over his whole face.

Else said nothing more. She lay clutching the sheets, her eyelids blinking rapidly.

The assistant stood for a while, stroking his mustache. Then with a soft snicker he left the room.

Else neither wept nor stirred. She was rigid with despair.

After Else had finished breakfast, Nurse Stenberg brought in her under-clothes and dressing gown. Else asked for various trifles – her garters, some hairpins, and the small toilet mirror. The professor had ordered all of that sent home, she was told. Instead of garters, Nurse Stenberg gave her two pieces of twine.

When Else had dressed she went out into the corridor.

"Today is Sunday," Granny chattered, sitting huddled up against the metal grate of the heater. "Clean clothes, from head to toe. Just look," she said holding out the folded white cloth to Else.

"Yes, Granny is always satisfied," remarked Thorgren, who was sitting, scrubbed and freshly ironed, at the yellow table reading a worn, cloth-bound book.

The young girl with the heavy head and the white wool socks was tak-ing short tacks, swaying back and forth, across the end of the corridor.

"I haven't seen her recently," Else said, pointing to the young girl.

"No, she refuses to walk past your door. 'That's not a woman, it's a ter-rible, wild bird,' she says, and she shivers with fear."

"Does she mean me?" Else asked.

"Of course," Thorgren laughed.

Else peeked into the cells. Mrs. Syverts was sleeping with her mouth half open, her white teeth visible between her young, full lips.

She was lying with her head at an angle, her hand under her cheek, a tear clinging to her long, black eyelashes.

Else slipped out quietly and went in to see the old woman with the yel-low mummy face – Mrs. Fog – the woman she had seen the first evening, who habitually threw the bedrails on the floor at night. She lay there, her half-open eyes as grey and cloudy as dirty bits of glass. From the sleeves of her hospital gown, which had slipped up above her elbows, two yellowish arms stuck out, as thin as canes of bamboo. The skin of her hands had the cracked and scaly look of dried haddock. As Else approached her, she lift-ed her arms imploringly, as on the first evening, and said something that died away on her sunken, bloodless lips.

"Poor thing," Else said, softly stroking her forehead, which was covered with little beads of sweat.

"Sweet Alma," came the faint whisper, as her hand moved slowly up and feebly clutched the front of Else's dressing gown.

When Else went back into the corridor, she came upon the young girl with the heavy head. The girl recoiled in fright, lifted her hand to hide her face, and cried as she lurched away, "Oh no, no – the wild bird wants to peck out my eyes!"

In the furthermost cell, the puerperal maniac was sitting up in bed groaning softly. When Else came in, she gave her a wavering, helpless glance and suddenly pulled the sheets over her head.

Else's felt dizzy and her knees were trembling. Better to go back to her cell and crawl into bed again. As her eyes drifted down the long, bare corridor, with its open cell doors and the securely-locked double doors at both ends, she thought with horror of that first evening when she had come here more or less confidently, never dreaming she was entering a prison for an unknown period, a place where she would be treated like a criminal, where none of her dear ones – not even her own husband – could gain entry.

Slowly she undressed and got into bed.

"Are you crying again?" Thorgren came in with her dinner. "Even when you've had the diversion of being up a bit and it's so nice and quiet here? You can almost tell it's Sunday."

Yes, Else could feel that too, and it just made the situation twice as dismal.

What kind of food was she getting today? She sat up and took the tray. Some yellow broth with small cream-colored dumplings. A slice of dry, roasted meat and boiled potatoes floating in thick, pale brown gravy. No salad, no cucumbers or pickles, none of the little side dishes she was used to and prized. But she must eat just the same. She had felt so feeble, so bone weary when she was up – and small wonder.

Eagerly she plunged in, but found it impossible to eat very much; the food tasted bland and disgusting.

As usual after an interval of quiet, the patients started banging and screaming again. Mrs. Fog threw her bedrails on the floor and uttered a muffled wail. The puerperal maniac dashed by, shrieking as if she were being stabbed with knives, and Mrs. Syverts carried on so violently that she had to be locked in. She started pounding on the walls of Else's cell, crying desperately for Else and the professor.

"I'm going to bed now, Mrs. Kant!" she called finally, after Else had admonished her. "I'll go to bed now and be good. Do you hear, Mrs. Kant?"

"Yes, I hear," Else called back. "That's fine, be quiet and go to bed now."

At a little past six, a few minutes after the gas had been lit, Hieronimus appeared. His greeting was unusually cordial.

"Well, how are you doing now?"

Else shifted on the pillow and did not reply.

"How is your appetite?" he continued, his cordiality undiminished.

"I'm hungry enough, but I don't like the food here," Else said sulkily.

"Perhaps you are used to other dishes?"

"To other cooking, at least. But that doesn't matter. The food doesn't make any difference."

Else shifted on the pillow again.

"Then what about sleep? You're still not sleeping?"

Else paused for a moment, then spoke in a voice that trembled with anger, "How can anybody sleep here who is more or less normal and not completely insane?"

"Well, let's hope for a good night." He spoke so quietly and kindly that Else was astonished. She had expected him to flare up as uncontrollably as the night before.

"Hope," she said contemptuously, thinking to herself: Throw a naked baby in front of a hungry tiger and then hope the beast won't eat it.

"Well, Mrs. Kant, if we mortals didn't hope . . ." Hieronimus suddenly was speaking deliberately, with a priestly unctuousness, his eyes filled with the expression she had seen in the waiting room, a look that reminded her of the young theology student.

Else had raised her eyebrows and something resembling a smile flickered in the corners of her mouth. A moment after Hieronimus uttered

83

"hope" he sprang from his chair and zipped out of the room like a conjurer.

The night was terrible. The maniacs below carried on uninterrupted. Spasms of pain gripped Else's chest. She writhed like a snake and moaned continuously.

When the resident physician made his evening rounds, he gave her some drops that helped for a while, but then the pain started again and continued all night.

"Nurse Suenson," Else said, during one of the intervals between her chest pains. "You do see how I'm suffering, don't you, how miserable I am in every way?"

"Yes, poor thing. You're not well at all."

"Then won't you take my husband a few words from me?"

"Not for love or money!" Nurse Suenson said, aghast, her voice more determined than Else could have believed possible.

"Don't say no, dear Nurse Suenson. I'm so afraid that I'll lose my mind in the end. Give me a piece of paper and a pencil, so I can write in bed."

"Not for anything in the world!" Nurse Suenson vowed in the same resolute voice. "Do you think I could dare go against the professor?"

"I beg and implore you! The professor would never know. I'd be grateful to you all my life, feel always in your debt. And so would my husband."

"No, no, no – don't even think about it, Mrs. Kant." She threw up her hand and smiled suddenly. "If I did that, my ghost would surely haunt this place after my death."

"Besides," she continued seriously, seeing Else's mute despair. "It wouldn't do the slightest bit of good. Once you get onto this corridor, nobody pays any attention to what you say. Your husband wouldn't do anything."

Chapter 14

"YOUR FACE IS AS YELLOW as wax today," Nurse Suenson said when she came in to see Else the next morning. "There's bound to be some change soon. The resident physician saw how ill you were last night."

The day passed. Else lay quietly in bed. When asked if she wanted to get up for a while, she shook her head. She gave in. Let herself slip down the green-stained walls to the bottom of the well. It was useless to struggle. The forces against her were too great.

Then suddenly Hieronimus was standing in the cell. Else viewed him through a haze, but noticed a gentle expression on his face.

"They're preparing another room for you now."

"Oh, just let me stay here," Else answered coldly, furrowing her quivering eyebrows. "The longer the better."

"The longer, the better?" The words came in a gasp through Hieronimus's narrow, grey-white teeth, and as on the evening before, he lifted himself on his toes and rocked hard back on his heels.

"Very well. That's my opinion, too – staying here will be good for you." A moment later he had disappeared.

Chapter 15

FOR THE THIRD TIME since Else entered the hospital, Knut was sitting, tense and uneasy, in the professor's waiting room.

So far, the information he had extracted from the tight-lipped professor had provided little comfort or illumination: "Your wife made a scene when she was admitted" ... "Visiting is out of the question" ... "In the beginning it's just a matter of winning the patient's trust" ... "No use making inquiries for a few days" ... "For now, I simply want to comment that your wife appears to be a very difficult patient."

Knut had done most of the talking during his visits. The professor had listened – not as interested as he should have been, in Knut's opinion. Why was this man so guarded – so cold, really? Was his mind made up, or had he still not come to any conclusion? Why hadn't the doctor been the one to lead the conversation? After all, it focused exclusively on the patient.

The clerk nodded from the doorway at Knut. It was his turn.

"Your wife is clearly insane."

Knut started. The word touched, with a violence that was almost physical, the painful web of anxieties that for a long time, bit by bit, had been spreading through his thoughts and feelings.

"Insane?" he asked.

"Yes."

"Disturbed?"

"Her madness takes the form of an almost total inability to control her emotions. At times she's an absolute fury."

Knut could not speak for a moment. So now it was settled, the certainty in his tone had left no room for doubt.

"Professor, have you taken into consideration her unique, impulsive force – the force so evident in her work?"

With no more than a half-second pause, Hieronimus answered, "Yes."

"Are you familiar with my wife's paintings?"

"Unfortunately, I've been too busy in recent years to follow developments in art here at home."

"May I send you some reproductions of her paintings?"

"Thank you. Naturally the choice of subjects could help guide my judgment of your wife's condition."

"And the treatment of subjects? The high level of artistry achieved?"

"That too."

The professor moved a few steps away from his desk toward the tile stove.

"My advice is to commit your wife to St. Jørgen's Mental Hospital for a period of time – not too brief."

Again Knut jerked as if he'd been stabbed.

"For how long?" he asked.

"A year."

"What would that accomplish?"

"Health," Hieronimus answered quickly, with a slight hint of displeasure at the question. When Knut did not respond, he added, "You don't have to make your decision now. Talk to Dr. Tvede. Your wife will stay here in the meantime. There's no rush."

"Still, it seems to me that if we're considering committing her to an insane asylum ..."

"Your wife must first of all learn discipline. She is unhappy about her stay with us. It wouldn't be good to move her just now. Besides it takes at least ten days to make the arrangements. Give me your answer some time this week."

"And it's your opinion that this will really produce a cure?"

"Without reservation. We have had many instances of it. The first six months will pass under protest from your wife. Then she will quiet down, and eventually leave the hospital with gratitude in her heart, quite cured."

"Through these purely mechanical methods – by separation and confinement?"

"Through these purely mechanical methods – yes," said Hieronimus, looking as if he had been struck by the phrase.

Knut felt as if he were faltering under a burden too heavy to drag. He could not move, and he purposely avoided noticing that his audience with the always busy professor was over.

"Then you will have peace in your home, as well," Hieronimus said from his chair, something resembling sarcasm in his voice.

Again Knut felt a twinge of pain. Were all his carefully chosen words being viewed as complaints about his own problems?

The man in the chair was hardly the learned doctor of the psyche he was reputed to be.

&

"THERE IS ONLY one thing to do: follow Hieronimus's advice," Dr. Tvede told Knut that evening. The next day, two physicians of Knut's acquaintance told him the same thing: Hieronimus was a man whose judgment in such cases could be relied on absolutely.

And so you must concentrate your efforts on that, Knut thought. He willed himself to accept the decision, though it ached like a painful abscess in his breast. Hieronimus's advice must be followed.

Chapter 16

ELSE HAD BEEN MOVED. The large double doors at the far end of the cell corridor had opened before her, and just beyond them lay her new room. In addition to the bed it held a chaise longue, a table and a chair. Here, too, the door was open night and day onto a corridor furnished with a yellow table and two chairs, enclosed like the cell corridor by firmly locked double doors. One side of the room abutted the cells, from which it was separated by an ordinary wall; on the other side lay a room with six beds, which at the moment were empty. Although the window above was hung with a piece of rust-colored wool curtain, its position high on the wall and its tiny panes of glass, created the same impression as the iron bars of the cell windows, and Else's sense of being in a prison remained the same as before.

After the move Else had a new day nurse, Nurse Ræder, who had come up from the men's ward downstairs – a powerfully built blond woman of about thirty. She wore a pince-nez and had a cheerful, well-bred manner. Humming softly, she went about her work, hips swaying slightly, addressing casual remarks to Else to help her forget her suffering. Else was glad of her company. In general, the nurses affected her like pale rays of sunlight on a dark and freezing winter day.

"Well," said the resident physician when he saw Else for the first time in the new place. "Are you contented now?"

Else, sitting on the edge of the chaise longue, stared mournfully in front of her. Except that the place was not a cell and the patients could not dash past her door or come into her room, there was no difference between then and now. She heard the whooping and shrieking just as clearly. The commotion, the banging of windows and doors, all the sounds of the day were just the same. Between half-past five and six o'clock, an icy draft announced the morning cleaning; at night the double doors to the cell corridor were opened so Thorgren, who had relieved Nurse Suenson, could look after both Else and the patients in the cells. And the night before she had suffered from a violent toothache.

"I can't sleep here either," she said wearily.

"Oh nonsense!"

"And it's so dreadful that I can never bathe."

"You can't bathe?" The doctor looked at her wide-eyed.

"Do you call that bathing? A cup of water in a dish, just enough to dip one's nose in. At home I took a cold bath every morning."

"You can take a bath here, too. See that everything is in order," he said, turning to Nurse Stenberg.

"The pipes leak and something's wrong with the heater," Nurse Stenberg said.

"Then they must be repaired. You shall get your bath, Mrs. Kant."

"Do you think it will be long before I can see my husband?"

"Put it out of your mind. Yes, it's likely to be a while," the resident physician added, responding to Else's look of despair.

"Didn't you speak to the professor for me?"

The resident physician nodded.

"Oh God, this is terrible," Else burst out. "What in the world am I going to do? I want so desperately to hear something from home."

"The professor is the best judge of what is beneficial for you."

"Beneficial for me," Else cried, standing up. "Oh yes, I know that old story by now." She took a few steps and sat down again. "How is it beneficial for me to be here under lock and key, suffering and worrying myself to death? What will become of me if I can never sleep? You know it's true that I never sleep. Even if you don't believe me, you've got the nurses' word to rely on. I will never be able to sleep here. I've said so from the first night and I keep on saying it. Do you think that's beneficial for me?"

"My, but you have a hot temper," the resident physician said in his usual amiable, low-pitched voice. "It's downright interesting to observe."

"What kind of man is this Hieronimus?" Else continued. "To say he's a petty pope – as arrogant and smug as a country preacher – still doesn't explain his behavior toward me. For my own good! Does he think I'll go berserk if I see my husband – not that he would cry about that – or is he afraid the hospital will fall to pieces when Knut comes?"

The resident physician tried as usual to pass it off with a joke, and Else listened without irritation. In spite of everything she was grateful to him – right from the first evening he had been sympathetic and friendly to her. And there was a gleam of compassion that sometimes appeared in his clear, phlegmatic eyes, especially at night when she was most upset and despairing, that consoled and soothed her temporarily.

"You are quite sure that I'm not mad, Nurse Ræder?" Else asked one evening after the gas was lit and they were waiting for night rounds. She had been up a few hours, but had gone back to bed again, worn out by the toothache that was torturing her for the third straight day.

Nurse Ræder, who was sitting across from her on the chaise longue with a large piece of woollen crochet-work, quickly removed her pince-nez and answered vigorously, "Well I, for one, haven't noticed the slight-est sign of it."

"Then won't you send a letter to my husband for me? You would be doing a good deed."

"It's out of the question, Mrs. Kant! Please don't ask that."

Else fell silent. She could tell from her tone that begging would be just as fruitless with Nurse Ræder as it had been with Nurse Suenson.

"Surely you understand that we nurses can't do that. It would be like a man violating his oath of office."

Else understood only too well. No rescue. No hope. She was buried alive.

"Your husband wouldn't do anything anyhow."

"How can you know that!" Else burst out. "You don't know my hus-band."

"When someone is under the professor's control, things happen just the way he wants. I'd advise you to start being friendly, or better yet, submissive toward the professor. That's what he expects. But you – if you knew how you look when he speaks to you," Nurse Ræder laughed. "You're not being very wise."

"The man makes my skin crawl," Else said with disgust.

Shortly afterwards rounds began. It was Hieronimus.

"Well here you are, sitting pretty," he said, bustling toward her.

Else did not reply. Every time she heard the professor's step her heart pounded and she shivered with repugnance. And when he spoke to her kindly, the way he did just now, Else found the jocular self-satisfaction in his voice more disagreeable than when he was sarcastic and irascible.

"And here you have the quiet you need to sleep, isn't that right?"

"Ask the nurses how quiet it is and how much I sleep," Else forced out. "You should have been in here last night and heard it."

"Well, sleep will come." He turned to go, then quickly spun on his heels and said, "You've had a toothache?"

"Yes."

"Is it over now?"

"No."

"Do you want the tooth pulled?"

"No, I'd rather see a dentist."

"Is that so!" He was gone in a flash.

During the night her toothache became completely unbearable. Her cough, which in the last few days had seemed to be improving, was worse again. No wonder, considering the draft every morning and evening when they aired the rooms. Hour after hour Else sat up in bed, groaning loudly in competition with the raving maniacs below. Thorgren brought her warm poultices. All night long she dashed back and forth. After a few minutes with Else, the screams and the uproar from the cell corridor summoned her back again. Whenever Else got a new poultice the pain eased a little, but then the coughing began. She wept, tears streaming down her face, repeating again and again, "I can't bear it."

"Why won't you have the tooth pulled?" asked the resident physician.

"It's not necessary," Else answered. "The tooth was just filled, it should last for years. Just let me go to a dentist. Surely he can let me go in a locked carriage with a couple of guards."

"We could put you in chains," proposed the resident physician.

"I'm going to go down right now and ask the professor for permission to drive to a dentist," Nurse Stenberg said, a couple of hours later. "I'd be the one to go with you."

"Thank you," said Else, who had been groaning all the while. Before long, Nurse Stenberg returned. She looked disappointed.

"Well?" Else asked.

"He didn't say anything, just indicated I should leave."

"What a beast!"

"I have some brown drops that helped me once," Nurse Stenberg said. "We'll try rubbing your gums with that."

That afternoon when Else went into the cell corridor, where she was allowed to stroll back and forth every day, she discovered a new patient in the furthermost cell, a woman who left a vivid impression of dignity and refinement, despite the hospital gown, the white wool blankets on the bed and the coarse pillowcase. She was lying quite still, her stony gaze directed straight ahead, tears streaming slowly down her impassive, swollen face. The young woman with the heavy head was in the cell, swaying and looking inquisitively at the new patient, while Granny leaned over her, chattering away. But the weeping woman took no notice. Only when the puerperal maniac dashed in and uttered her usual hollow cry for Knu'ssen, did she start up in terror and look around for help.

"Who is that?" Else asked the nurse who came in to fetch the puerperal maniac.

"A countess."

"Is she very disturbed?"

"Indeed she is. She was caught walking around a hotel with a loaded revolver, and now she thinks she's fallen into the hands of anarchists."

"Who would believe that's a lunatic in there – she does look desperate, but rational," Else thought, peering in unembarrassed each time her walk took her past the door of the countess's cell. "The poor thing... She doesn't have a revolver in there, I hope?" she asked anxiously, stopping in front of Thorgren.

"She has two!" Thorgren answered with a laugh, then added, "There, I got you to smile, Mrs. Kant. I won't be satisfied until I make you laugh."

No, Else said to herself later. I won't go stare at that unfortunate countess any more. She always gives me such a hurt, reproachful look. One should also be sensitive toward lunatics.

Else went in to see Mrs. Syverts, who was still confined to bed; she looked pretty and neat with her well-brushed, braided hair and her snow-white embroidered nightgown.

"How nice of you to come see me, Mrs. Kant." Mrs. Syverts grasped Else's hand in both of hers. The corners of her mouth trembled and the brown, velvety eyes filled with tears. "I'm still in bed, can you believe that? Every day I beg and plead to get up, but they don't even answer me."

"That's because you're not being quiet enough."

"It doesn't do any good, even if I'm quiet," Mrs. Syverts bit her under-lip and large crystalline tears trickled down her white cheeks. "I've tried that, too."

"What about the nights – you scream and carry on at night."

"That's because I'm so frightened. I feel like I'm in an underground prison, and when the others start in, I can't help joining them. And the way those doctors come into our rooms at night is also strange. They can't be decent, can they?" Mrs. Syverts smiled suddenly and gave Else a roguish wink.

"You were going to jump out the window, too," Else said.

"I did it to tease them," she giggled softly, the tears still rolling down her cheeks. "I like to tease those jailor scoundrels. That time I frightened you, I was just teasing then too. I didn't want to hurt you at all. Anyway, it's no wonder a person gets all mixed up lying here. All that chloral takes my wits away. Tell me, do you know why my husband is angry with me?"

"I'm sure he isn't."

"Oh yes – he promised to come and see me every day. Oh Carl, Carl, how can you bear to treat me like this?" She suddenly burst into loud sobs.

Else tried to soothe her.

"Come back soon, Mrs. Kant!" Mrs. Syverts called as Else was leaving.

Chapter 17

ELSE HAD GOTTEN THE IDEA that something must be wrong at home, because Knut never came. He had promised so faithfully to visit her; he knew that she never would have left home on any other terms. Every morning she had nursed the secret, anxious hope that in spite of everything he would suddenly appear that day in her room, and during morning visiting hours she had been nearly breathless with suspense. But he had never come. How could he stand being constantly turned away? If she were in his place!

Once fear about the situation at home had seized her, it held her fast, transforming itself into terrible images. Perhaps Tage was lying at death's door, or was dead already, and Knut didn't dare come, afraid his look of sorrow would reveal the truth right away. Or Knut had come down with diphtheria like the year before – no, Tage had diphtheria, and Knut couldn't come to the hospital for fear of contagion. Or there had been a fire, and Knut had rescued Tage from the burning nursery and had since died of his burns. Gradually, brooding over these images, she worked herself into a frenzy of dread that tortured her night and day and displaced all the other fears she suffered.

She had often wanted to discuss it with the resident physician, but whenever she was about to speak, fear of his response made her hold her tongue. When she finally managed to get it out, the resident physician assured her that it was all sheer fantasy.

Did he really know that or did he just believe it?

No, but surely she realized that if something like that had happened, a report would have reached the hospital. Besides, her husband was constantly coming to ask about her. He had seen him as recently as yesterday. But now the resident physician would make inquiries about the child, and he swore on his word of honor he would tell her the truth.

Nurse Stenberg and Nurse Ræder also tried to convince Else that she needn't worry.

Else felt relieved for a moment, but her doubt and fear soon returned. It seemed, as it always had, utterly incomprehensible that Knut would let her stay there without visiting her a single time. She had been there for twelve days now.

"What do you want your husband to do," Nurse Stenberg asked, "when the professor refuses to admit him?"

"But can't he get me out again if he wants to?"

"If your husband insists, you can be out in ten minutes."

Like a live ember, a hope flared up in Else's soul. Hope that Knut finally would lose patience and demand her release. She was consumed with impatience on her husband's behalf. If only he didn't wait too long – every minute of the day, every second of the night was a gnawing, lacerating torture to her.

"Why won't you ask the professor for permission to see your husband?" Nurse Ræder asked reproachfully one evening.

"The resident physician is asking for me."

"But perhaps the professor wants you to ask him yourself."

"I have asked. When I was lying in the cell, I asked constantly. Now I can no longer ask that man for anything."

Yes, of course, if it would do any good she would be happy to ask him. But since Hieronimus was so set on keeping Knut away, he must be making the assumption, incomprehensible to her, that it was the right thing to do. That was what the resident physician said, too. This nonsense that the professor would regulate his treatment according to how much humility she showed must surely be wrong. He was a physician, after all.

"Your child and your husband are both doing fine," the resident physician had said that morning. "On my honor." He had looked Else straight in the eye and she had believed him.

But the doubt had returned nevertheless. What if he had been ordered to calm her down by lying. "God, God, take away this cup from me," she moaned involuntarily.

"Well this is a sorry sight," Hieronimus said when he came that evening. Else, sitting by the window with her face wrapped in wet poultices for the aching tooth, rose as was her custom during evening rounds.

"You still won't have the tooth pulled?"

"No."

Hieronimus seated himself on the chaise longue and Else resumed her place.

"Your husband sends greetings," Hieronimus said cheerfully. "He asked me to tell you that the child is doing splendidly – eats, sleeps, and is fine in every way."

Else was speechless. She couldn't find the words of thanks that she knew she ought to express. Tears constricted her throat, and then Nurse Ræder, who was standing behind Hieronimus, signaled to her.

Hieronimus sat for a while watching Else, a smile of pity creasing his bloodless lips. Then he stood up and, with a cold "Good evening," walked out of the room.

"Why didn't you ask the professor just now!" Nurse Ræder exclaimed. "He was so gentle and kind tonight. He actually sat and waited for you to say something."

"I couldn't," Else said.

"You two will always be at loggerheads," Nurse Ræder laughed. "But you're not being very smart, Mrs. Kant. The professor had a very different look on his face when he left."

&

IT WAS NIGHT. The gas was turned down, and Thorgren came with warm poultices for Else's cheek. "If you could only get a little sleep, Mrs. Kant. It's quiet tonight."

Yes, if only she could get a little sleep. If she didn't sleep she would lose her mind in the end. There was no doubt about that. If she could just conquer this nagging disquiet inside her, get her heart beating calmly, instead of with these irregular, rebellious thumps; if she could crush herself into perfect compliance and suffer in silence, silent as the faithful who look upon the face of God and bow in devotion to his will. Suffering purified. Suffering was better than emptiness and vanity. Sorrow could have an uplifting effect, could give meaning and inspire respect.

Yes, she would suffer patiently, suffer devoutly, in spirit and in truth. A transport of something resembling joy made her tremble. Not everybody had the capacity to suffer like this, so that suffering became rapture. She had that.

Little Tage, your Mama is just fine tonight. And you are too. You're eating and sleeping and getting along marvelously. You don't have diphtheria, and you haven't been burned in a fire, and you aren't dead. Neither is Papa.

"No, neither is Papa. He's *not*," she suddenly heard Tage say distinctly, in his sweet clear voice. Else lifted her head involuntarily, and looked around. Where had it come from? Usually when her memory called up Tage's voice, she heard it within. But this time the sound was outside, close to her ear. Wasn't that an omen that perhaps he was dead?

No, no, mustn't let go of hope and faith. The resident physician had not been lying. His gaze had been firm and truthful.

Night rounds were in progress. "Does your tooth hurt?" the resident physician asked as he shook her hand.

"No," Else said, "not at the moment."

"Actually you really shouldn't be sorry you've got a toothache. It takes your mind off whatever you're brooding about all the time."

Else smiled weakly.

"I'm quite serious," the resident physician nodded.

"How long do you think I'll be here?"

"*Chi lo sa!*" [5]

"How long do patients stay here, usually? At the most, I mean."

"It varies – four, five, six months."

"Oh no, you don't mean it," Else said with an anxious smile.

"I really don't know, my dear Mrs. Kant. Good night." He shook her hand and went out. "Be good now and get some sleep."

"Four, five, six months," Else repeated. She took the poultice off her cheek and placed it on the nightstand. What difference did it make if she had a toothache? "You shouldn't be sorry you have a toothache." No, certainly not! The worse the better.

What had become of the well? The well with the green-stained walls and the distant whooshing sound, the pale dimness covered by a wire mesh cage that separated her from the ranks of the living for all time. Why wasn't she lying at the bottom of the well? Who had pulled her up? And who was jabbing this stinging, red-hot drill through her tooth up into her brain?

A child's bed hung unsupported in midair before her. A child's bed with a flowered coverlet and a lace-trimmed sheet. That coverlet – and the pillow. She had crocheted the lace on the coverlet herself on warm summer days in the arbor. Yes, it was Tage's bed, but where was her boy?

"Tage," she cried, sitting up.

"Did you call?" Thorgren asked, slipping quietly into the room.

"Please, dear Thorgren," Else said, "if I should die here, would you tell my husband I died of grief from being here, and from not being able to see him and not hearing any news about the child. Will you promise me that?"

"Yes, dear Mrs. Kant." Thorgren gave Else a firm handclasp. "But you're not going to die."

Else lay down again.

Now she was at the bottom of the well. She saw the green-stained walls, felt the damp subterranean air, noticed the distant whispering hiss.

Suddenly she heard a roar that had no trace of anything human about it, followed by what seemed to be the sound of heavy pieces of iron or lead being thrown violently on the floor. After that came the roaring of many different voices, accompanied by thunderous blows, piercing shrieks, and ear-splitting pandemonium. It sounded like the baying of mad dogs, the bellowing of bulls, the crowing of cocks, the hooting of owls; and all the while the booming strokes continued, as if the walls were being smashed by the blows of an axe.

Else wanted to get up but she didn't have the strength. Heavy chains bound her hand and foot, and a massive stone lay on her breast. The thunderous din sent icy bolts of pain zigzagging through her head and body.

She was in a deep, damp courtyard, facing an enormous iron gate that was slightly ajar. Through the keyhole and hinges she could see licking, dancing flames. In front of the gate on an iron chopping block sat a black woman with a shrivelled face and eyes that glowed in the dark like phosphorus. She wore a dingy rubber apron with a large bunch of keys at her waist.

"It's the entryway to Hell and she's going to open it for me," Else mumbled. "But I'll wait until she takes me by force."

Suddenly Tage was there in his nightshirt, his golden curls gleaming in the dim light, sitting on the black woman's lap. He waved his hand and cried joyfully, "Mama!"

Else struggled to free herself from the chains and the stone, and bounded onto the floor.

She felt herself enclosed in powerful arms, and Thorgren's genial voice said, "Come now, dear Mrs. Kant, you're not to get out of bed. You know that very well."

Else clung to Thorgren. "I'm going to die of fright," she said. "Listen!"

"Yes it's terrible," Thorgren answered. "There are ten maniacs down there and they're all on the rampage tonight. Even so, you were lying so still when I peeked in on you earlier. I truly thought you were asleep, as unlikely as that seemed."

"Listen, listen, now they're under my bed," Else whispered hoarsely. She huddled on the floor in front of Thorgren, wrapped her arms around the nurse's knees and hid her face in her dress.

"Dear little thing, do be sensible now. Remember that those people raging down there can't possibly get up here."

"Oh stay here with me! I don't dare get into bed. Don't leave me!" Standing up without releasing her grip on Thorgren, Else pulled her down on the chaise longue, where she buried her face in the nurse's lap and wrapped her arms around her waist.

The roaring and bellowing from below continued.

Suddenly they heard a shriek and the sound of something being overturned in the cell corridor. Thorgren hastily freed herself and stood up.

"Let me come with you – oh let me, let me," Else begged, nearly beside herself.

"That's impossible, Mrs. Kant. It's against the rules – I don't dare! I'll come back as soon as I can."

Thorgren ran out and Else hopped onto the chaise longue where she huddled on her knees with her face pressed firmly against the upholstery.

"It's not Hell-hounds, not roaring lions, not tigers who want to eat me," she said faintly. "It's just the maniacs downstairs. It's just the maniacs downstairs."

Oh God no, now they had all gotten into her head. How was that possible? All ten of them!

"Don't be so wild, don't hammer and crack my skull. I'll be quiet and good. Never cheat on my arithmetic at school, never again."

Tage came racing in and wanted to get into her head too. But now there wasn't room for him. Oh God, there wasn't any room. "My sweet, adorable Tage, don't go racing off again – don't go racing off."

"Where is Papa? Is he lying in that yellow coffin with the pane of glass in the lid? Have they roared and eaten him up? Knut, Knut, come save me! If you're not dead. Are you dead, Knut? Oh show yourself to me then!"

"Well, I've got them quiet in there for the moment." Thorgren put her arm around Else, who was still lying in the same position on the chaise longue. "Let's get back into bed, shall we?"

Else lifted her head, threw her arms around Thorgren and pulled her down beside her. "No, no, sit here with me! I don't dare go to bed."

"All right. For a little while."

They sat as before, Else with her arms around Thorgren's waist, her head in her lap. Thorgren gently stroked Else's back. The noise from below went on unabated.

Gradually Thorgren strokes grew more and more feeble and then stopped. Shortly afterwards the weight of her hand slipped off Else's back.

Else glanced cautiously up at her. Thorgren was asleep with her head tilted back against the side of the chaise longue.

Good, kind Thorgren. How unruffled and calm she was. Yes, of course. She wouldn't be fit to be here otherwise. Else lowered her face again and pressed closer to Thorgren.

"Knu'ssen!" The hoarse, hollow shout came from close by. Else jumped up with a cry. In the doorway stood the puerperal maniac, a folded sheet around her belly like a dressing.

Thorgren instantly shook herself awake and ran to the patient.

Else crept back into bed.

There they were again, inside her head, those lions and tigers and Hell-hounds. No, it was the maniacs. Ten of them. Imagine all of them having room in there. If only they didn't split her head open. They would fly in all directions and it would be so hard to find them when her head was put back together again.

A funeral procession went by. Dark figures in long coats were carrying an empty black coffin. "Let me lie down in it! Carry me away – far, far away!" Else sat up with a jerk and stretched out her arms toward the coffin ... But there was no coffin after all. And no figures in long coats ... No, of course, she was here in the hospital – or maybe she was up in the mountains? No, she was in the hospital.

"You are going mad," Else said to herself, carefully lying back on the pillow. "As soon as Thorgren leaves you are mad."

But then it really was better for her to put an end to it. Should Knut and Tage have to bear that disgrace? Never.

Her position was hopeless. Four, five, six months. She would be mad long before that. And her agony was a thousand times worse than death.

She could tear her handkerchief into strips, tie them together and hang herself.

Ai, there was a cock crowing inside her head. No, nonsense, it was only the maniacs.

If she could die now ... remove herself from the dominion of Hieronimus. The thought was soothing.

But even if she died, the institution would go on. Many human beings in a condition like hers might come here and have to deal with Hieronimus. If she could escape alive, she could tell her story – warn, and perhaps save, even one fellow being from the things she had experienced.

No, she *had* to live.

But wait, here they came again – the baying Hell-hounds, the roaring lions, the growling tigers, the howling wolves – trying to get into her head.

"There's nothing else to do. You *must* die." With feverish energy she tore her handkerchief into strips, tied the ends together and put it around her throat.

Then Thorgren was there. "It will be morning soon," she said, patting Else's hair.

Morning. There was an old echo of hope in the word. And in Thorgren's kind, reassuring touch.

Else was saved.

Chapter 18

THE RESIDENT PHYSICIAN came in the morning. Else lay motionless. Her head burned but otherwise her whole body felt dead, except when sudden, spasmodic twinges in her chest made her jump with pain.

"I can see you're not well this morning, Mrs. Kant," the resident physician said quietly.

Else immediately opened her eyes and stared at the resident physician in terror. "Oh no, no! I don't know you! What are you doing here?" she cried, and hurriedly put her hands over her eyes.

"Of course you know me. I'm the resident physician – you always like talking to me."

"Yes, but I'm so frightened. I'm frightened out of my senses." She uttered a muffled cry and again hid her eyes with her hands.

"What happened?" the resident physician asked. "She's never been like this before."

"They've had a bad night downstairs," replied Nurse Stenberg, to whom the question had been addressed. "And of course she never sleeps."

"Mrs. Kant is in a sad state today." Else opened her eyes slightly and saw the young assistant with the smooth face talking to Nurse Ræder in the doorway. He was twirling his thin moustache, and the smug smile she remembered from before extended all the way to his eyes. "I'm going to talk to her now," he said.

Else turned her body toward the wall so violently that the iron bed creaked, and the assistant left with his mission uncompleted.

Now I've reached my limit, Else said to herself. It's got to end today.

Neither angry gods, nor worried human beings, nor offended angels, nor wicked devils could demand more. Now even Mr. Hieronimus must think it's enough.

Lord God, what is my offense? What have they told Knut to keep him from forcing his way in here, armed if need be!

But today would be the end. Surely in our day a man wouldn't intentionally destroy another human being – at least not in this brutal way, under a mask of kindness and benevolence. Besides, Hieronimus was not really an enemy. He just enjoyed watching the death throes of the mouse being bitten and squeezed by the cat.

Else took courage and hope. The thought that she had safely weathered last night's crisis gave her new strength.

"You can't be a hero on an empty stomach," Nurse Ræder said as she brought in the lunch tray. "We're going to live, things are going to be nice and cheerful – here's a warm cutlet and some lovely bread and cheese."

"Let's eat now," Nurse Stenberg said. "I'm going to do what I did that time in the cell," she said with a smile, taking Else under the arms and sitting her up.

"All right, I will," Else said taking the tray. "Nurse Stenberg, please listen, you've meant more to me than you'll ever know – won't you go to the professor right now and tell him I'm not going to stay here any longer. I insist, I demand that he send me home, or at least let me speak to my husband. Last night I had to fight off madness. Oh, you don't know what I've been through."

"No," said Nurse Stenberg. "You probably should never have come here. But these are matters I know nothing about," she added nervously.

"Maybe not, but go now and tell him. Say I insist, I demand that he send me home."

"Yes," said Nurse Stenberg. "I'll go now."

Else waited confidently, almost cheerfully. Her knowledge and her own judgment of the situation reassured her.

As on the previous occasion when Nurse Stenberg went to ask permission to visit the dentist – she returned looking glum and crestfallen.

The professor had not said a word.

"Don't think about it, Mrs. Kant. It's no use."

Else's blood boiled with rage. Who was this man, this wretched Hieronimus? What did he think and mean and want? But there must be other ways. The resident physician. He was a human being, at least.

"Would you ask the resident physician to come see me?" Else asked Nurse Ræder a few hours later.

Yes. He was in the quiet ward at the moment. She would tell him.

Soon afterward the resident physician stood before Else's bed, calm and mild and reassuring as usual.

"I was confused this morning when you were here," Else said. "I couldn't remember anything, and I didn't recognize you – not even you. But now I beg you as a human being in the direst straits, to find my husband, the only person I dare trust, and tell him what's happening to me. Will you do that?"

The resident physician nodded.

"Tell him," Else said, sitting up in bed and grasping the doctor's hand, "tell him I've been in a cell among lunatics, and I'm living in a Hell that would drive the sanest person mad. Will you do that?"

"Yes, I'll tell him the next time I see him."

"No, you must go see him at home! Do you hear – you must! It could be ages before you meet him by chance."

"All right. I'll do what I can for you." He squeezed Else's hand and left.

Thank God. Thank God. The resident physician would do what he could. Surely! He understood the whole situation. And even though officially he did not have permission to meddle in Hieronimus's affairs, he nonetheless said to himself that necessity knows no laws. Oh thank God. Thank God.

Now she would get up and go out in the corridor and visit the patients. The darkest hour was always closest to dawn. Today the resident physician was going to see Knut, and Knut would instantly come and free her.

"My dear Mrs. Kant, you look so chipper today." Madonna-Hansen came hurrying into the room while Else was sitting on the edge of the bed putting on her stockings. "I miss you during the day, you know. You seem to be so far away from me. But what's this?" Her tone was filled with pity.

"You're using string instead of garters?"

"Yes, they've sent everything home. Everything. Even my large fur piece. I freeze walking around the corridor in my robe. Good heavens, I couldn't possibly have hanged myself with my fur piece."

"Now, now!" Madonna-Hansen shook a warning finger though her large eyes smiled. Then she quickly took off her crocheted woolen vest. "Borrow this," she said, "it's nice and warm."

"Thanks. But then you'll be cold yourself."

"No I won't. I have other things to wear. But now I must go. Good-bye, dear Mrs. Kant." She hurried out with a nod at Else, who gave her a grateful look.

Chapter 19

Eʟsᴇ ᴘᴀᴄᴇᴅ ʙᴀᴄᴋ ᴀɴᴅ ꜰᴏʀᴛʜ in her room. Through the open door she could see the countess, tall and stately in her fine black woollen dress trimmed with black lace, standing with crossed arms by the double doors to the cell corridor. Else had talked to her several times and had felt comforted by her gentle, quiet demeanor. But today she was trembling with excitement and preferred to be alone. The resident physician had promised to talk to Knut.

The poor countess! Else found it inconceivable that anything could be wrong with her mind. At first she had thought so. The countess's story had sounded so incredible. Through trickery and force she had been lured to the hospital by Hieronimus and a relative, and then, without warning, had been told she was being held as a lunatic and would be confined to bed. She knew of no grounds for this except that her family was angry because she was a practicing Christian and had adopted a fisherman's two small children as her own, making them heirs to part of her fortune in her will. And then there was the pistol Thorgren had mentioned. The countess had owned the pistol unchallenged for twenty-two years. And the box of white powder, suspected of being poison, was nothing but ordinary face powder. Similarly, she had slept for a period of her life with a candle burning, and was accused of being terrified of anarchists.

Yes, the story sounded peculiar. And Else had assumed it was partly a figment of her imagination. But when she talked to the nurses, she had not been able to discover any reasons beyond the ones the countess had

mentioned for the presumption of madness on which she had been confined.

"Won't you come in and sit with me for a bit?"

Else, who was walking toward the window, quickly turned around. In
the doorway stood the countess, with her suffering face and her gentle,
dark-blue eyes. Her brown hair curled in little waves around her white
forehead and covered her temples to her ears.

They walked together into the spacious room next to Else's. It had
been fitted out for the countess with two beds, and between the high windows whose small panes gave the impression of iron grating, a sofa with a
worn, black damask cover. There was also a table and an old armchair.

"What do you really think of the professor?" the countess asked when
they had seated themselves.

"Nothing," Else said sadly. "I don't understand him."

"But he must be open to persuasion. Don't you think so? He must be
able to see that this business about my insanity is sheer nonsense."

"One would think so. But God knows."

"He must let himself be persuaded. The power of God's words will persuade him!"

"Can you really talk to him? I'm not capable of it."

"Oh yes," cried the countess. "I believe in the man. He isn't a fervent
Christian, but he is an honorable person. I believe that. I must believe it."
The countess wrung her hands and turned her eyes upward. "Oh, if only
I had my Bible."

"Can't you ask for a Bible?"

"That was the first thing I asked for, of course, but I haven't been given
one. Wouldn't you also like to have a Bible?"

"Oh I don't know," Else answered, an oppressed sigh escaping her.

"You do believe in God!"

Else nodded.

"And in Jesus Christ?"

Else nodded again. She didn't think this was the time or place to explain her lack of faith. And she had no desire to wound this good-hearted
human being.

"Shall we pray together? For where two or three are gathered together in my name, there am I in the midst of them. Now let us pray that your toothache will be relieved. Let us both pray at the same time. Oh, I heard you groaning last night. And the maniacs! Imagine, I slept in spite of it – not the whole night of course, but some."

"You're lucky you can sleep," Else said.

"That is God's power and grace. Every night I lie down in Jesus's arms, and I am delivered from all evil. You should do that, too."

"Yes," Else sighed.

"Haven't you gotten word that you can see your husband yet?"

"No, but the resident physician promised to talk to him today. As soon as my husband gets a full report, he'll come at once." Else felt hope coursing warmly within her.

"Yes, it is strange that you should be here," the countess mused. "This is a place for lunatics and criminals. It's really quite beyond me how you can walk around in the cell corridor. Today I stood in the doorway a little, and it pained me so terribly to look at them."

"It's a kind of diversion," Else answered. "Now they all know me, and some of them smile when they see me."

"I just don't understand it!" the countess suddenly exclaimed, clasping her hands. "I've never in my life had the slightest trouble with my nerves! And my doctor . . . I've asked to have a visit from my doctor, but they refused. Can you understand that? Yes, if I didn't have God I'd go mad brooding about it. But God is my strength."

જી

THAT AFTERNOON Else was in the cell corridor. Granny was crouched in her usual spot by the door of the tile stove and the heavy-headed young woman was standing behind a door peeking timidly out at Else, who was pacing slowly back and forth with her hands behind her back. The other patients were in their beds.

It was now half-past four, Nurse Suenson had said. But Knut could still come and get her. The night she arrived it was six o'clock. If a person could come in at six o'clock, surely it must also be possible to leave at the same hour.

Suddenly Else heard rapid male footsteps coming up behind her. Quickly she turned around. A chill of anticipation shot through her.

The resident physician was coming toward her.

"Your husband sends you his regards," he said, his voice not as low-pitched and unhurried as usual, but speeded up somehow.

Else could not speak. She felt her eyes burning with questions.

"I had the good fortune to run into him just now down in the court-yard."

"What did he say?" she asked breathlessly.

"Well, they're doing very well, both he and the child."

"He won't take me away?"

"No," said the resident physician, with a look of surprised displeasure.

"Didn't you tell him how I've been?"

"I said you've been rather ill."

"And he didn't want to see me? Didn't want to do something?"

Again the resident physician said "no," with the same look of surprised displeasure.

"Then you haven't delivered the message!" Else cried, and her voice, filled with despair, was angry and accusing.

"I have no idea what you mean," the resident physician said in an irritated, reproachful tone. "What do you expect your husband to do? He can't possibly have you at home. My God, a man's at his wits end when he puts his wife in Ward Six. Now that he's entrusted the case to the professor's skilled hands, all he can do is stay out of it."

Else stood looking blankly in front of her. She felt as if she were sinking, sinking, and as she sank her insides turned to stone, her body turned to stone.

"I can't imagine why you're so discontented," the resident physician continued heatedly. "Look at the others..." He glanced at the ever-cheerful, chattering Granny. "You're perfectly comfortable. What more can you ask? All this time I've been expecting you to calm down here – we all wish you well, you know – but it doesn't look like that's going to happen." He turned on his heel and quickly left the cell corridor. Then for the first time, Else fully realized her plight.

Chapter 20

SHE SANK DOWN ON THE CHAIR by the yellow table. Her hands lay limply in her lap, and she felt cold sweat beading up on her nose and forehead. It seemed as if she were surrounded by an endless wasteland, a wasteland whose terrible emptiness surged into her brain, down through her body, surging, surging, trying to make her part of the emptiness, part of the dreadful wasteland's barren nothingness.

"So you have to die after all," said a still voice inside her. And tonight. The ripped up handkerchief she had stuffed into her pillowcase. Thank God she hadn't thrown it down the toilet as she had planned.

"You should put something over your head, Mrs. Kant," Nurse Stenberg said as she walked by, "Now while we're airing things out. Remember your toothache."

Else returned to her room. She sat down in the large chair by the window, quietly staring into space, until Nurse Ræder brought her supper at seven o'clock.

Tomorrow at this time her room would be empty. The corpse had to be taken away six hours after death at the latest. Where would they take her, she wondered – home? No, there had to be a morgue here at the hospital where they put the dead. She saw herself lying on a long, wooden bier, side by side with the other corpses. She wondered if they put men and women in the same morgue. Oh, what difference did it make . . . In death everyone was the same.

And then Knut would come with a coffin to get her.

So it was going to cost her life to get out of here. Well, that was not too high a price. No price was too high for deliverance from this place.

She would never see Knut again. So that was the final time, when he said good-bye and kissed her on the stairway. Oh Knut, Knut – you have been good to me!

Tage, little Tage. She felt a stabbing pain and her heart contracted in her chest. Never again. Never again see your blond, curly head.

But thank God he was too young to know grief. He would talk about her a little from time to time, and then forget her forever.

To be able to believe in an everlasting life where one would be reunited with loved ones after death ... She would have waited patiently for eternities if she were certain of being able to hold her child in her arms again.

Yes, it would have been a solace at such a time to have the countess's faith. Then surely she would have been able to weep. Oh, it would have done her so much good to weep.

But shouldn't it be possible to simply imagine she was a believer, to cling to Christ's beautiful words: "In my Father's house are many mansions. I go to prepare a place for you."

She folded her hands and tried to pray, but it was no use.

Suddenly she rose and went in to see the countess, who was just finishing her evening meal.

"Did you get good news from the resident physician?" the countess asked, coming to greet Else.

"News ... resident physician ..." Else was taken aback.

"He had promised to speak to your husband."

Now Else remembered. "No," she said quietly, shaking her head.

"Don't lose heart." The countess placed her hands on Else's shoulders and looked lovingly into her eyes. "Remember that Jesus loves you and is near you."

"You mustn't despair," the countess went on when Else made no reply. "I'll pray for you. A Christian never despairs. Promise me that you won't despair, all right?" She kissed Else on both cheeks.

There was a commotion in the cell corridor – hard, jolting footsteps of people carrying a heavy burden, accompanied by other lighter, quicker steps.

"Perhaps it's a new patient?" said the countess.

Else nodded listlessly.

Shortly afterward the powerful stench of carbolic acid penetrated the room.

"How intolerable not to be able to close one's door," the countess exclaimed, pressing her handkerchief to her nose.

When Else left the countess, she saw through the open double doors a nurse and one of the assistants running down the cell corridor. Mechanically Else followed them.

In the end cell, the same one where the countess had been, a woman was lying propped on a high headrest, drawing hollow rattling breaths, her chest heaving. The contour of her rigid, outstretched body was visible beneath a blanket that came to her chin and hung down loosely along the sides of the bed. Her wide, square face had a leaden cast, with dark streaks under her eyes; dark cropped hair lay in damp clumps around her forehead and ears. A nurse and an assistant were bending over the rattling body.

The assistant pulled up her eyelid and touched the pupil with his index figure. "She's done for," he said, taking out a small syringe. The nurse threw the blanket off the woman's shoulder and the assistant gave her an injection.

"Put a bit of ice in her mouth every half hour," he said, and went out.

"What's wrong with her?" Else asked in horror.

"She swallowed carbolic acid," the nurse replied. "She's the wife of a workman. Imagine, she's left six little children. They've had such a miserable life, and her husband has mistreated her. Today she got dinner ready and when the husband came home and made a row as usual, she said, 'You've seen the last of me,' and went out to the kitchen."

"The poor woman," Else said with a shudder.

"Her husband just laughed and told her she always said that. But right afterwards he heard her fall and then terrible shrieks. The poor children! They threw themselves screaming on their mother, and wouldn't let go when she was being carried away."

"Do you think she will die?"

The nurse shrugged her shoulders and looked noncommittal.

Else went into the cell and looked at the woman who had tried to kill herself. She lay as before, her breath still rattling, a blue-white froth trickling out of the corners of her wide mouth. Her chest rose and fell, racked now and then by a violent spasm.

Else was shaking with horror, sickened by the stench of carbolic acid, but she couldn't tear herself away from the riveting sight. She forgot all of her own sufferings and knew only one thing, that she was standing before the most irrevocable part of life: death. Death by one's own hand. And not if the world came to an end, not if a thousand people gave their lives to buy her back, could this human being be restored to the ranks of the living. Irrevocable – gone forever. Death, death by one's own hand. This was what it looked like.

Suddenly she realized with surprise that she felt not only sympathy, but disgust. Mostly disgust. This woman had fled like a coward from her sufferings and her responsibilities. Left her children cruelly and faithlessly in the lurch. The poor babies, who had clung to their mother, unwilling to let her go.

The image cut Else to the quick, and suddenly tears came in a flood. Oh, what a relief. The stone in her heart melted and flowed away with her tears. And here facing this woman who took her own life – her rattling breaths, leaden face, the blue-white froth on her lips – Else vowed that she would not commit suicide. Not if she were locked up here for the rest of her life.

"Don't stay here any longer. It isn't good for you." Nurse Stenberg took Else by the shoulder and led her out.

Chapter 21

"I'VE COME TO SAY GOOD-BYE," Thorgren said later, when Else had gone to bed. "We've been ordered to keep the door to the cell corridor locked at night. You and the countess are going to have your own night nurse as well. Here she is! This is Nurse Bøhn."

"Good evening, Mrs. Kant." A tall thin woman, with a dark complexion and the expression of a kind but resolute schoolteacher, extended her hand.

"What nice easy work you will have." Thorgren sat down on the chaise longue and leaned forward with her arms crossed in her lap. "Now see that you're kind to Mrs. Kant," she nodded and laughed. "I won't hear of anything else. She's my special charge, you know."

"We'll get along just fine," Nurse Bøhn said with a gracious smile, giving Else's hand a cordial squeeze. "I'll bring your chloral now."

"That awful chloral. If only I didn't have to take it!"

"We're good children here," Thorgren said and laughed again.

"How is she doing in there?" Else asked pointing at the wall next to her bed, which adjoined the suicide's cell.

"It will be over soon," Thorgren said, still smiling at Else.

"Will she be there all night?"

"Yes, until tomorrow. She has to be washed and laid out, of course. That's Suenson's and my job."

"Don't you dread that?" Else asked with a shudder.

"No, we're used to it. Of course when a corpse is very dirty, it can be a little unpleasant. Sometimes the feet and legs are filthy. Now good night, dear Mrs. Kant. Be a good, sweet girl."

"I can hear her rattling in there," Else said to Nurse Bøhn when she brought the chloral.

Nurse Bøhn listened for a moment. "No," she said, shaking her head.

"Yes, when I'm in here alone."

"You must be mistaken, Mrs. Kant."

"It's darker than usual tonight," Else remarked.

"Yes, I've purposely turned the gas a little lower. I thought you might find it easier to sleep. Would you like me to turn it up again?"

"No, thanks. Let me try now. Good night."

Oh that smell of carbolic acid – Else couldn't get it out of her nostrils. The smell of carbolic acid and suicide – suicide and the smell of carbolic acid. They melted into one in Else's imagination.

What strange things happened in the world.

She was lying here on the other side of a wall from an unknown suicide. Who would have imagined it, two weeks ago? But if any other patient had come into that cell tonight, Else would have been the suicide, and the one in there would have lain alongside her, perhaps feeling the same fear and disgust that she did now. These coincidences governed and determined the whole of life. A suicidal woman had saved her from suicide. Trembling with a terrible sense of gratitude, she put her hand into her pillowcase to make sure that the torn up handkerchief was still there. It was. Thank God Nurse Ræder hadn't found it this morning when she made the bed. She would have to get rid of it tomorrow, because the day after tomorrow they would change the sheets.

How far had the death struggle advanced? She lifted her head, put her ear to the wall and listened. No, she could hear nothing.

Just as she was about to lay her head back, she heard a sound like the wheezing of a corroded pump. Did it come from in there? It seemed to Else that the sound came from behind her, right at the back of her head. She wanted to call Nurse Bøhn, but she couldn't utter a sound. Fear drove her blood in rapid pinpricks against her eardrums. She kept her head in the same position, raised up off the pillow as if propped by a brace.

Then she heard a prolonged gurgling. Forcibly she wrenched her head free of the brace and peeked out into the corridor. The chair was empty. Else carefully lowered her head back on the pillow.

How quiet it was here tonight. No sound from the cell corridor and nothing audible from the maniacs below. It was as if everybody knew that death was paying a call.

She closed her eyes and folded her hands on her chest. Her mind was filled with an oppressive solemnity and she breathed without a sound.

Then suddenly the woman who killed herself was lying beside her on top of the blanket. She heard the grating, rattling breath, sensed the nearness of the leaden face with the blue-white froth on its lips; and the smell of carbolic acid filled her nostrils.

Swiftly she sat bolt upright and stared in bewilderment at the blanket by her side. Nothing was there. She pressed her hands to her eyes and tried to collect herself. In a muffled voice she called to Nurse Bøhn, who immediately came quietly into the room.

"How is she doing in there?" Else whispered.

"She's dead."

"When did she die?"

"Fifteen minutes ago."

"How do you know that?"

"I went to look in on her."

"Listen, somebody's talking in there!" Else seized Nurse Bøhn's hand with such a sudden movement that she jumped.

"It's Suenson and Thorgren preparing the body." Nurse Bøhn put her free arm around Else's neck and pressed her head to her breast. "You're not afraid, Mrs. Kant?"

"Yes," Else whispered, squeezing her hand convulsively.

"But whatever for?"

"I don't know. Stay here with me. Pull the chair over by the bed and sit here."

"It's against the rules, Mrs. Kant. I have to sit out in the corridor. Remember I have to look after the countess too."

"She's asleep."

"No, she isn't. I just went in there and she was sitting up in bed."

"You mustn't go! Don't go!" Else threw her arms around her waist and clung to her.

"I wish I didn't have to. I'd gladly stay, because I see how frightened you are. But calm yourself, now. The others say you're such a sensible woman."

"All right," Else said with a convulsive sigh. She released Nurse Bøhn and lay back in bed.

"Call me whenever you want, I'll come right away. I'll hear you instantly." Nurse Bøhn smoothed Else's blanket over her. "I'd better turn the gas a little higher."

Else began listening to Thorgren's and Suenson's voices inside the cell. A couple of times she thought she heard Thorgren's muffled laugh. Then she heard water splashing and what she thought was the sound of their scrub brushes.

When the resident physician made night rounds, he joked with Else and spoke more kindly than usual. But she made only the most necessary replies. She had believed the resident physician's kindness was based on understanding, on compassion that flowed from understanding. Since this afternoon she knew better. She was left entirely on her own. She would have to rely exclusively on her own powers in the struggle to keep herself from perishing here.

"I'm pleased to find you so calm," the resident physician said finally. He stood there a moment, giving her an appraising look that was also tinged with surprise.

Then he said good night and went out.

Now it was perfectly quiet in the cell. They were finished then. They would have removed the wool blanket and covered her with a sheet. Would have turned off the gas so she was lying in pitch blackness. Closed the cell door. No, locked it. Otherwise one of the patients could suddenly tear open the door and run in there. Did they really turn off the gas? Wasn't it customary to leave a light burning in the death chamber?

The poor sobbing children who hadn't wanted to let their mother go. Now they no longer had a mother. But they didn't know that. Now she was lying here dead in a cell for lunatics, criminals and suicides. Else had lain there too. And now she was lying nearby.

But she was not dead, and she wasn't going to die either. Little Tage's mother was still alive. Little Tage ... Suddenly a tearless sob escaped her. Yes, she would live for Tage's sake.

Her eyes closed, but sleep was far away.

Then the woman who committed suicide was beside her again. But now her breath wasn't rattling. Unmoving and quite naked under a sheet, she lay on Else's blanket. Else distinctly felt the cold emanating from her dead body, and the stench of carbolic acid blended with the smell of the corpse.

Else wanted to scream and open her eyes, but it was no use. The corpse had glided onto her chest and was suffocating her. She struggled violently for air, for the power to move. But she couldn't lift a finger. Now she was dying – she was dying. Oh God, she was dying after all, suffocated to death by this unknown suicide. She was dead already. There was just a tiny little place inside her head, at the very top, that was still alive. The last remnant of bodily life had retreated to that place, where the fear of death bored like a red-hot spike.

Then she distinctly heard something snap in her head.

Else made a final violent effort, and with a sound in her throat of a cork being pulled from a bottle, drew a breath, and opened her eyes.

The corpse was gone. She wanted to sit up and call Nurse Bøhn, but she didn't have the strength to do either. Her body felt paralyzed. She tried raising her arm a bit. Yes, it worked.

What good would it do even if Nurse Bøhn came in? She wouldn't dare report this hallucination about the dead woman. Everything here was interpreted as insanity, Madonna-Hansen had said one of the first evenings. And that had made her cautious.

Again her eyes drooped with fatigue, but she quickly opened them. She dared not keep them closed for fear the hallucination would return. Finally she couldn't manage any longer. Her lids were so terribly heavy. In spite of her efforts, her eyes closed again.

And instantly the woman who committed suicide was beside her once more, ice cold, heavy, reeking of carbolic acid and decay.

"I'm going mad," Else said to herself. She cautiously sat up and called Nurse Bøhn.

"Please, give me a glass of water," she said.

The nurse did as she was asked, and Else drank a little. She began to ask Nurse Bøhn about one thing and another, so she would stay with her a while. Nurse Bøhn made cordial but brief replies. "You know you ought to sleep," she said as she turned and carefully smoothed Else's pillowcase. "It's quiet here tonight."

Else dipped the corner of her handkerchief into the glass of water the nurse had left on the bedside table and bathed her eyes. Perhaps that would help her keep them open.

She didn't dare lie down again. The hallucination was more likely to come back if she did. She leaned her shoulder and head against the wall and tried with all her might to keep her eyes open.

Nevertheless they soon closed again, and a few seconds later the woman who killed herself was lying beside her.

Else hastily sat up, clenched her fists, and writhed in fear and anguish.

"Are you really going mad? Is your strength all gone? Has your brain cracked somewhere, is it starting to go soft?"

If only she were allowed to get up and walk a bit, or Nurse Bøhn were willing to sit with her.

Should she call her in and take her into her confidence? For a moment the temptation was great, but she resisted it. Nurse Bøhn would consider it her duty to tell the professor. They were so dutiful, these nurses.

No, no, no! She would fight, fight to the bitter end. She was still perfectly sane. It was only when her eyes closed and this soft whispering and humming started in the back of her head, only then that she lost control of her imagination.

Yes she would fight, get on her knees in the bed, fold her hands and cry from the depths of her soul for help. Gather all her fear and horror and suffering into a burning cry – to herself, to her reason, to her will, to her physical strength, which had always been great. And to her loved ones who were dead. Perhaps they could hear her. Who could tell? The spiritualists said they were in the air around us and could be made to speak. But there had to be a medium for that – and she didn't have one. The dead would have to make an exception and temper justice with mercy. She knelt in the middle of the bed, with clasped upraised hands, and now her eyes were wide open, her heavy lids and fatigue were gone.

Then she heard a roar that sounded like wild animals and the booming of a storm breaking loose at sea.

Else stiffened in terror for a moment, but then she realized it was the maniacs below, and something like relief swept over her. Quietly she lay back on the pillow. Thank God for the maniacs! As long as they kept on, her eyes would not close and the woman who committed suicide would not come.

"Yes," said Nurse Bøhn, who was standing by the bed looking anxiously at Else. "We're used to it, of course, but it must be terrible for you."

"I'm beginning to get used to it, too," Else said with a strange smile, grasping Nurse Bøhn's hand and holding it tightly in hers.

"I'm coming right in to sit with you for a while," Nurse Bøhn said, loosening her hand. "I know how frightened you must be. But first I have to see to the countess – she's awake, too."

~

"GOOD MORNING, and congratulations!" It was Nurse Bøhn's voice.

"Congratulations?" Else repeated, looking at her in amazement.

"Yes, you've been asleep. Slept quietly for an hour and three quarters. The maniacs quieted down at four o'clock, and fifteen minutes later you were asleep. It's six now. It's the first time since you came here. I seem to have brought good luck with me."

"Congratulations," said Nurse Stenberg when she made her morning rounds, patting Else on the cheek.

"Congratulations." Thorgren came in, smiles creasing the pink cheeks that no night duty seemed to fade, and cordially gave Else both hands. "It had to happen eventually."

"Congratulations." Suenson greeted her with a beaming smile and quietly shook her hand.

Nurse Ræder was there, too, as well as Madonna-Hansen, and everybody was glad Else had slept.

Congratulations, Else thought. But none of them knew what the word meant to her. Does everyone in this earthly life speak and act out of ignorance?

Yes, ignorance.

But Else felt her inner self undergoing a change. A lethargic calm took over her mind, a melancholy resignation to her fate. If she had not gone insane these past two nights, she would surely be able to save herself in the future. The thought of suicide was a thousand miles away. Now she could bear anything, no matter what happened. She felt battered and shaken, but at the same time, strengthened.

She got up as usual to wash and tidy herself, after which she normally went back to bed for a couple of hours. She felt so exhausted that she could scarcely totter to the little washstand in the corner. Head swimming, blackness clouding her eyes, she groped her way along the wall, and even though she had slept, her head felt as heavy as lead.

Before going back to bed, she slipped down the cell corridor and looked through the peephole of the locked door at the woman who committed suicide. She was lying on a bare sackcloth mattress, wrapped in a sheet, her body encased so tightly that it looked like an elongated, formless bundle. Her belly was so swollen that Else could see only the top of her head outlined beneath the covering sheet.

There was nothing else in the cell. A pale sunbeam fell in through the window and gleamed grey-gold on the swollen belly.

Chapter 22

THE DAYS PASSED and the nights passed. Else maintained her apathetic calm, but a weight that hampered her breathing lay upon her chest. And she had a headache that never went away. The pain settled in her temples and hammered so violently that it seemed to Else as if her temples would eventually come loose and fall off. Never before in her life had she known such a headache as this.

One day, when Hieronimus asked her if she felt any other pain than the toothache, which still persisted and for which they now gave her morphine injections twice a day, she had complained about the headache and added that it was something she had never experienced before.

"Hmm," Hieronimus had responded with a thin, suspicious smile, and Else had sent him a glance that glittered with contempt. This wasn't the first time his scornful "hmm" had branded her a liar.

What a man, Hieronimus!

Luckily, he didn't make rounds as regularly as the resident physician. On Wednesday evenings he was absent because of his lectures, and on one occasion he had been away on a trip. Else was thankful when she was spared the sight of him.

The resident physician was as friendly and good-humored as usual, but Else no longer engaged him in conversation as in former days. She felt it was a waste of energy, and she had none to spare.

"What stoic calm," he occasionally remarked to Nurse Stenberg during rounds.

On occasion, however, the resident physician again caught a glimpse of

Else's "fiery temper." Once he mentioned that he had promised to show the countess, who had never seen Else's paintings, a reproduction of one of them.

"Oh no, don't do that!" Else blurted in a disapproving tone. She knew very well that someone with the countess's background would not be interested in her work. "Oh come now, you needn't be ashamed of your paintings," the resident physician had said consolingly. "Oh, is that so!" Else had replied in a such a scornful tone that the snarl was perceptible even to her own ears.

But mostly she answered only "yes" or "no" to both the resident physician and Hieronimus. Her only consolation was the nurses' constant, indeed increasing, kindness and care.

Through Nurse Stenberg Else had received permission to make a list of the things she originally had brought with her, now that there was no reason not to let her have them back. Nurse Stenberg had taken the list to the professor, who promised to send it immediately to Else's home. Since then Else had been waiting impatiently, with a secret hope that Knut would smuggle a note to her in the package. It had now been three days.

In the afternoon Else went to bed around five o'clock.

Her head hurt, her tooth hurt, and she was so exhausted that she couldn't sit up. Since the hour-and-three-quarters nap that had so overjoyed the nurses the other day, Else had been sleepless again. The morphine soothed her head and tooth, and held the pain at bay. But it did not bring sleep. Even though they continued to give her the choral.

Else was lying on her side in bed, a hand under her cheek, listening to Nurse Ræder who was seated on the chaise longue, crocheting and talking about her childhood in Jutland. Her words, uttered in a smooth, rather monotonous yet soft and agreeable voice, reached Else's ears as if from a distance, and the images they evoked were shrouded in mist and shadow. Then Nurse Stenberg sat down on the chaise longue beside Nurse Ræder. They talked back and forth, but Else didn't keep up with them.

Suddenly Nurse Ræder said, "You mean the Karen who ran away?"

"Where did she run away from?" Else asked.

"Here, from the hospital. Right in front of our noses."

"I didn't think it was possible for anybody to get out of here."

"Oh yes. It does happen," Nurse Stenberg laughed. "That Karen was so crafty. She was smart enough to ingratiate herself, so I had given her permission to help with the morning cleaning. That gave her access to the kitchen. She only needed a moment alone to steal the key to the kitchen stairs – it was hanging on a nail out there – and off she went."

"But when she came down from the kitchen, what then?" Else asked, interested.

"She only had to walk across the courtyard and through the little gate out to the street."

"The gate was open?"

"Yes, it's always open."

"And the key was hanging in the kitchen?"

"Yes. But not any longer. Just so you know, Mrs. Kant, in case you're thinking about running away." She laughed and wagged her finger at Else.

That was exactly what Else had been thinking. Like a cold chill of fear and hope, the thought had flashed through her mind.

"They're starting their rounds now." Nurse Stenberg rose abruptly and walked over to the head of the bed. Nurse Ræder put away her crocheting and did likewise.

Hieronimus walked in and seated himself on a chair by the bed.

"You did send my list home, Professor?" Else asked, when the usual few questions were over.

"Yes – several days ago."

"I can't understand it – Nurse Stenberg says nothing has come."

"No," Nurse Stenberg confirmed, "I haven't received anything."

"It's quite incomprehensible," Else went on. "The note can't have reached my husband, otherwise he would have sent the things I asked for right away."

"But I said there was no rush." The words came with slow relish from Hieronimus.

"Oh, did you!" Else burst out angrily. "No, there's no rush – I just would be freezing every day for lack of clothes if one of the nurses hadn't loaned me a woollen shawl."

"Well, you aren't freezing then, are you?" Hieronimus said with the same relish in his tone.

"But why should I borrow when I have clothes of my own? Why should I be deprived of the clothes I need?" Her voice trembled with indignation.

"There's no harm in learning to do without," Hieronimus said piously.

Else raised her eyebrows and said nothing more.

A contemptible man, this Hieronimus.

Hieronimus sat a while longer, tilted back in his chair. He seemed lost in thought.

If only he would leave!

Suddenly he rose and hurried off with a curt "Good night."

Chapter 23

THE NEXT MORNING Nurse Stenberg came in carrying Else's things in her apron. She had opened the package and carefully investigated the contents before delivering it into Else's hands.

No note from Knut. No, of course not.

But thank God, now she had her garters and could get rid of that string that was so painfully tight below her knees. Her watch and the watch key were there, too. And nail scissors and the little mirror and the porcelain box with lip pomade and a bottle of perfume. Also her crochet work and her large fur piece. What riches.

"Oh, here is our sweet lady," Granny said when Else appeared in the cell corridor. She was sitting in her usual place, clean and smiling, chattering about how much her son-in-law loved cabbage soup.

"Oh thank you," she cried eagerly when Else held out her half-filled coffee cup. She wrapped both her cold hands around the warm cup. Then she looked around carefully and leaned toward Else, as if to hide behind her as she quickly slurped the coffee.

"Thank you," she said again, as she handed back the cup and then kissed Else's hand. "It's so soothing, you know."

"You can have my coffee every day, Granny."

"Shh – they all ask how old I am, and my son-in-law ..." Granny's face had taken on an almost crafty expression, as if she didn't want the nurse who just walked by to hear them talking about coffee. Apparently she thought coffee was the world's most forbidden fruit.

"We were so happy together, my husband and I, in the beginning." Else was perched on the edge of the bed by Mrs. Syverts, whose white fingers were busily pleating a handkerchief which she held up to her face; she was speaking in the sad, expressive voice that Else had noticed the first morning. "But a woman can't help it if she's pretty and men like her. The few times we went out the men flocked around me. And my husband thought ... well, I guess he didn't like it. I just had too many things to worry about, but it certainly wasn't me who couldn't leave the men alone – they were the ones who ... Listen ..." Her face lit up suddenly with an eerie smile and her voice became low and lascivious. "I knew a Norwegian once and that man really *was* my lover! Yes indeed!" She nodded and laughed softly, a strange, rough, but still engaging laugh.

"Ah well, that's all over now," came the same sad voice as before, and she sighed deeply. "To think that I'm in here now." Suddenly she burst into tears and pressed her handkerchief to her mouth, while her shoulders and chest heaved with sobs.

"Ask Nurse Stenberg if she'll let me get up, Mrs. Kant. I've been lying quietly for days."

Else nodded.

"They've taken away my wedding ring, too," Mrs. Syverts continued, drying her eyes. "I don't know any more if I'm married or not. If only I could have my wedding ring! I could at least keep myself amused with that."

After Else left she asked Nurse Stenberg if Mrs. Syverts couldn't have her ring.

Nurse Stenberg hesitated.

"But why? She misses it so much."

"There are people who swallow their rings to put an end to themselves, Mrs. Kant."

Else shuddered. She remembered her torn up handkerchief.

"Can't she get up, at least?" Else asked.

"In fact, I've asked the resident physician, but he felt it was too soon."

When Else turned away from Nurse Stenberg, she saw the young woman with the heavy head run behind the door in fright.

"You mustn't be afraid of me," Else said, following her.

"No, she's especially fond of Mrs. Kant," the nurse remarked. "Isn't that right, Mariane?"

Mariane hid her worn face behind her lifted arm and gave a grudging, sulky smile. "Everything is evil and disgusting," she fretted, "and it's never going to get better."

"Oh yes," Else said, "Pretty soon you'll be well."

"I'll never get well. I've just been in Hell again for two days."

"Mariane has been locked in her cell because she was a bad girl and tried to hurt herself," the nurse explained. "She got hold of a pair of scissors and slashed her wrist right next to the artery. Let Mrs. Kant see the cut, Mariane."

Mariane, who still kept her face covered by her arm as she twisted and turned her upper body, quickly stuck the other hand behind her back.

"It's completely healed," said the nurse, pulling her firmly forward and showing Else the wrist, where a dark ridge of scar tissue was visible.

"Don't do that, don't do that," Mariane whined.

"Mariane is going to be a good girl, now." The nurse patted her thick, bristly hair. "In a couple of days, though, she's going to St. Jørgen's."

"Of course nothing will come of that," Mariane said with a grimace of displeasure.

"Does she want to go?" Else asked.

"Yes, poor thing. I suppose she's looking forward to the change. She's been here such a long time."

"Now I have to feed Mrs. Fog." The nurse took a dish from a large, steaming food tray that a maid brought in, and entered Mrs. Fog's cell. Else followed and held the dish while the nurse raised the head of the bed under the mummified old woman whose dim, glazed eyes looked from one to the other in helpless inquiry.

"Let's eat nicely, now," the nurse said, tipping a spoonful of bouillon and egg into her patient's mouth. "That's the way."

"Oh, oh, oh," Mrs. Fog groaned, making a face of weary repugnance as she swallowed down the soup with a hollow, choking sound.

"You know you really must eat," Else said, patting her pale forehead.

"Yes, but I don't like it," the woman whispered through toothless gums, watching Else with a gaze that seemed transfixed with misery.

"There now, dear Mrs. Fog. That's good," the nurse murmured, as she continued to carefully feed the patient, who was having more and more difficulty swallowing. Finally she spit it up again and the bouillon dribbled down her sunken chin.

"All right, she's had enough," the nurse said, drying Mrs. Fog's mouth and making her tidy. The patient lifted a gnarled, scaly hand and gripped Else's fingers. Her eyes closed wearily.

"She will die soon, don't you think?" Else asked the nurse after they had left the cell.

"You would think so, but people like that are amazingly tough."

Else went in to see the puerperal maniac, who was sitting up in bed with her arms locked behind her neck, uttering lingering groans.

"Do you have pain anywhere?" Else asked.

The puerperal maniac grew quiet and watched Else with a suspicious, questioning look that seemed, at the same time, to beg for help. She released her arms from behind her neck, grabbed Else's wrist tightly, and laid her head on her shoulder.

"What are you frightened of?"

"Oh, frightened," said the puerperal maniac. She moved her head away from Else's shoulder and looked at her with the same inquisitive gaze as before. "I'll tell you." She stopped and seemed to grope and struggle to find words, while she convulsively squeezed and stroked Else's arm. "It's the baby – do you know where the baby is?"

"Yes, the baby is doing fine," answered Else, who had found out from the nurses. "It's in another hospital."

"The baby isn't dead?"

"No, it's not dead."

The puerperal maniac stared into Else's face. Her gaze was now only helpless. Then a tear slipped out of one eye, a long, slow tear that she wiped away with her forefinger.

IN THE CORRIDOR outside her room, Else met the countess, weeping and wringing her hands.

"I'm nearly in despair," she said in her usual quiet way. "Imagine, my children, my poor unfortunate children have been put in the care of some horrible people who hate me and my boys."

"How do you know that?" Else asked.

"Through the professor. Oh my children, what can you think of your mother! One of them rode in the carriage with me when we came here, and they tore him away from me at the door. That was the heaviest blow. Oh my poor, poor boys..." She wept violently but without a sound.

"It must be terrible for you," Else said.

"And I'm not allowed to write a letter. Not allowed to send a message. And no one can visit me. What will become of me?"

"You mustn't be so distraught, dear Countess. You're always such a calm person. This can't go on very long. The professor *must* realize soon that you're not insane."

"Yes, that's what I thought, too." The countess forced back her tears. "But my hope grows weaker every day. He assumes that I'm mad. All his questions are designed to lure me into a trap."

"You have to be patient, Countess," said Nurse Ræder, who had just come in. "Resign yourself to being here for three weeks or so. By then a decision will have to be made."

"Three weeks," the countess burst out, her face swollen with tears. "Good God! Must you suddenly resign yourself to being locked up in a place like this, when there's nothing wrong with you, when you've committed no crime?" She was again overcome with tears. Then she walked quietly into her room, knelt down in front of the easy chair, and lost herself in prayer.

Chapter 24

As on the previous day, Else was in bed when the doctors made rounds.

"I've brought you something to read," the resident physician said, laying two small yellow booklets on the night stand.

"Thanks, that's kind of you." Else picked up the booklets. It was a subscription edition of Bertha von Suttner's writings, entitled *Memoirs* and *A Mother to her Daughter,*[6] or something of that sort.

"Now don't say we aren't nice to you," the resident physician smiled as he was leaving.

Shortly afterwards Hieronimus arrived in his overcoat, hat in hand. He sat down by the bed, and it seemed to Else that there was something almost self-conscious about him this evening. He leaned over toward the nightstand and his eyes came to rest on the yellow booklets.

"Now you've gotten all the things you wanted," he began after a moment's silence, without looking at Else.

"Yes, thank you."

Another brief silence. His hand approached the table and touched first the box of lip pomade and then the perfume bottle.

"What is this?" he asked in a friendly tone, still without looking at Else.

Else told him what it was in her usual abrupt way.

"Ah – and this?" He picked up one of the yellow booklets.

"The resident physician loaned it to me."

"So you have entertainment then."

He set the booklet aside and sat there for a while, looking undecided about something.

Suddenly he straightened up and grabbed something from the pocket of his topcoat. "By the way, I have a surprise for you tonight," he said hurriedly, putting a letter on the nightstand as he stood up.

"Thank you," Else said, instantly recognizing Knut's handwriting and flushing with pleasure and excitement. She seized the letter, then threw it down the next moment, exclaiming, "It's been opened!"

Hieronimus was already gone.

"You have a letter, I hear," Nurse Ræder said, coming in with Nurse Stenberg.

"Yes, but I won't accept it!" Else exclaimed, flicking the letter across the table with her fingers. "Do you think I would read my husband's letter after the professor opened it? That man! Tore it open with his skinny little midwife's fingers. Look at the way he's ripped it open."

"Now you're not being good," Nurse Stenberg said placing her entwined fingers behind Else's neck. "The professor opens all the patients' letters."

"Don't be angry with me, Nurse Stenberg! You mustn't," Else sobbed violently and put her head on the nurse's breast.

Nurse Stenberg let her cry. "Now read the letter," she said gently. "You know you've been longing so terribly for news from home."

"No, I can't, I won't! What could he possibly say if he knew the professor was going to read it. Take it away, Nurse Ræder. Oh take it away, I can't bear the sight of it."

Nurse Ræder hesitantly took the letter.

"You are being pigheaded," Nurse Stenberg scolded.

"No, I'm not. Just look at you – you can make me do anything you want. Except read a letter that *he's* opened," she added hurriedly.

Nurse Stenberg lowered Else's head onto the pillow. Then she kissed her cheek and said good night.

"You really ought to read the letter," Nurse Ræder entreated, when Nurse Stenberg had left. "I think you're torturing yourself by not reading it." Her normally cheerful voice sounded serious this evening.

"Just imagine that man!" Else burst out, sitting up again in bed. "Of course he got my husband's word of honor not to write anything that would upset me – upset me! Hurray! Upset me, here in this idyllic place! And even so! Does he think that all human beings lie and cheat? He might have opened it carefully and glued it back together. But he ripped it open, just to infuriate me."

"Hmm," Thorgren murmured coming into the room. "I keep waiting for the shooting stars, but the prospect seems pretty remote." Shaking her head, she gave Else a farewell handclasp and went out.

Nurse Ræder continued trying to persuade her. Finally Else agreed that Nurse Ræder could read the letter and tell her what was in it.

"Well it really doesn't say very much," Nurse Ræder said, after she finished reading.

"No, of course not, it couldn't possibly."

"Your husband writes that the little one is doing fine, and the more patient you are, the sooner you will see each other again."

"Patient," Else said with a bitter smile.

"Don't you want your letter?"

"I wouldn't lay a finger on it! Do whatever you want with it, as long as it's out of my sight."

"May I come in?"

"I'm feeling calmer now," the countess said, standing by Else's bed. "The professor came and told me that it wasn't true about the children. They aren't being cared for by those wicked people."

"Why did he say the opposite before?" Else asked.

"It must have been to test me. Do you see how God answers my prayers? He's a faithful Father to his children. Now I'm going to pray very hard that you'll be able to see your husband soon. Tonight I can do it, with my faith so strong."

"Thank you," Else said. "You are kind."

"Just think, they gave me my Bible, too. I'm almost happy tonight. I'm going to read a chapter now and then go to bed. The professor was so pleasant to talk to this evening. Good night."

The professor – pleasant to talk to. Why did she waste her words on that man?

136

A little later one of the assistants came in and gave Else an injection of morphine for her toothache.

Then Nurse Bøhn appeared with the chloral.

Chapter 25

THE NIGHT HAD BEEN pandemonium, and again Else had a hard struggle to endure her fear and despair. Now it was morning and they were waiting for rounds.

Else lay quietly in her bed. Her head burned with fatigue and her body felt as if it had been torn apart limb by limb.

Thunderous crashes that seemed to shake the bed made her jump in agony. It sounded as if they were firing cannons.

"Where's that awful banging coming from?" she asked Nurse Stenberg faintly.

"It's the front door down below."

"No, I know that sound. This one – do you hear?" The banging came again.

"Yes, it is the front door. It's stormy today."

When the resident physician arrived, Else pretended to be asleep. She didn't have the strength to open her mouth.

"She's had a bad night," Else heard Nurse Stenberg say. "It's deplorable the way the sound carries in here."

"Is it really that bad?" the resident physician responded.

"Is it bad? Once I even heard the professor complaining about it when he was showing someone around. There's some structural defect, he said."

In spite of the continuous banging Else fell into a doze, and after lunch in bed at eleven o'clock, she felt somewhat better. She picked up one of the yellow booklets and tried to read.

The sound of light squeaking footsteps made her look up just as Hieronimus came in, spanking-new from to head to toe in an elegant overcoat, shining boots, and lustrous brown leather gloves. He placed his hat on the table, pulled up a chair and sat down.

"Well, now you have your garters," he began in a soft, conciliatory tone. "They're contraband in here you know."

"Do you want them back?" Else asked sharply.

"No-oo," Hieronimus replied with a dismissive wave of his hand, then after a short pause, "But you must give me a firm promise that you won't misuse them."

A little late for him to be thinking about that, Else thought, remembering her torn-up handkerchief; then with a derisive smile she said, "The string they gave me for garters could also have been misused, if that had been my intention."

Hieronimus, who was sitting slightly inclined toward the bed, glanced down. His gloved hands were resting on his knees, and he spread his fingers slightly.

"Something has got to be done about that door!" he suddenly exclaimed, starting nervously and turning his head toward the corridor. The door had banged shut twice since he had come.

Nurse Stenberg appeared on the threshold and was about to say something, but Hieronimus waved her away. Then resuming his former position and adopting the same soft, conciliatory tone, he spoke, his body making slight movements in his urgency to put his words as carefully as possible: "You remember what happened that first night."

"Are you bringing that up again?" Else burst out angrily. "Do you think I was lying when I explained what happened?"

"Well, you've quieted down since then," Hieronimus went on. "That night you spoke of inhuman treatment."

"Inhuman torture," Else corrected him. "And I stand by that! I was supposed to learn to subordinate myself. That was why you put me here, isn't that right?" She spoke with icy derision.

Hieronimus started and looked as though he was going to flare up, but then he collected himself, and after a short pause continued with undisturbed placidity, "You have had those kinds of thoughts before. That can happen when one is mentally unbalanced and feels harassed and unhappy." Once again he shifted in the chair and paused for a moment. "But perhaps you weren't entirely serious about it. You will ..."

Else moved abruptly on the pillow. "I really don't want to talk about that now," she snapped, trembling with resentment. "I think this comedy has gone on long enough, or it would be comic if it weren't so tragic. My husband really cannot afford to pay four kroner a day to have me tortured here!"

"Comedy ... tragic ..." Hieronimus had straightened up, his voice was as quick and sharp as usual. "I think it's comic." Suddenly he sprang out of the chair and dashed to the door, calling out shrilly, "Is Mrs. Kant always such a difficult patient? Doesn't she eat her food? Doesn't she get proper care?"

"She is always friendly toward us," answered Nurse Stenberg, who was out of Else's sight. "She was a little excited last night because her letter was opened, but since then ..."

"Does she perhaps imagine that we keep her in here for our sake?" Hieronimus continued shrilly, half turning toward the bed. "We would just as soon be rid of her! We could close up shop and go for a stroll in the woods! But I'll tell you this," he took a quick step toward Else and slapped his fingers against the palm of his hand. "Your husband can take you away whenever he pleases – he's very welcome! But he may not come here to visit you!" He snatched his hat from the table and was gone in an instant.

"My God, Mrs. Kant." Nurse Stenberg came in clasping her hands.

And then Nurse Ræder: "Whatever could you have said to put him in such a fury?"

"I'm shocked, Mrs. Kant." Thorgren's cheeks were almost pale. "I could hear him all the way out on the cell corridor."

Then the countess appeared too. "Did you tell the professor the truth?" They all lined up in front of the bed, with horrified faces.

Perplexed, Else looked from one to the other. Then she started to laugh.

"God knows what will come of this," Nurse Stenberg said anxiously as she left the room.

"You aren't my favorite any longer," Thorgren shook her head gravely.

"You wanted to make me laugh, Thorgren! I'm laughing now!"

Chapter 26

"But what exactly is her condition?" Knut asked. He was sitting, as so often before, in the professor's office at the hospital.

"I've only been aware of fluctuations in my wife's health. Before, there would always be calm after a storm, unless, like this last time, there were constant tensions that overtaxed her nerves – and even then . . ."

He paused.

Why doesn't the man speak? Knut thought. Why doesn't he show me, once and for all, that he has an opinion about the patient that makes all this talking unnecessary?

"And here in the hospital," Knut continued, "here in this peaceful place where everything is arranged to spare the patient's nerves?"

"Your wife is stark, raving mad," Hieronimus replied, getting up from his chair.

The phrase drilled its way into Knut's consciousness like a dull blade. His mind was divided between two images: Hieronimus, stripped of his starchy dignity, making rounds in shirtsleeves with his assistants – and his wife, "raving mad."

Hieronimus took a few quick paces across the floor.

"She feels great bitterness toward you. The other day she threw your letter on the table. She wouldn't read it."

Knut stared at the professor in astonishment. Else's condition was becoming more and more of a painful mystery to him. True, he had given the professor his letter unsealed, so he hadn't felt able, nor had he wished, to write anything but the most commonplace things. Naturally the professor had sealed the letter before he gave it to Else. So it was better, really, that Else hadn't read it, because she would have assumed he had been able to send it uncensored. But this bitter mood toward him – what could have caused it?

"So you still believe it would be inadvisable for me to visit my wife?"

"Absolutely."

"And a visit from Dr. Tvede?"

"Not for the time being."

The audience was over.

He wondered if the people here at the hospital really understood the ailing temperament they had under their care. Everybody said Hieronimus was a careful and humane physician, the most knowledgeable of the specialists in mental diseases. Strange how mysterious these things seemed to the uninitiated.

Chapter 27

BEFORE DINNER Else went to take a bath, accompanied by Nurse Ræder. The bathroom, downstairs and adjacent to the men's ward, was a large dismal room with a stone floor and an uninviting zinc bathtub. The whole place had the look of a cellar. Afterwards Else had to go to bed so she wouldn't catch cold, they said, and she ate her dinner in bed.

Later in the afternoon when the gas was lit, Else sat and crocheted in the cell corridor with Granny and Mariane, who was wandering around with her usual swinging gait, uttering deep sighs and groans. She was even more nervous than usual because tomorrow she was leaving for St. Jørgen's.

Nurse Stenberg came in from the quiet ward. "We're expecting Bella Holm," she said to Thorgren, who had been in looking after Mrs. Fog.

"Ah, so she's in a bad way again!"

Else was about to ask who Bella Holm was, but just then the lock rattled, the double doors burst open, and two attendants came in carrying a stretcher on which a female figure was sitting hunched over, grabbing and plucking at her blanket.

"Here she is already," said Nurse Stenberg. "Merciful heavens, look at her! It must have been bad this time."

"I'm only asking where I am – I'm just asking." The figure on the stretcher lifted her head and seized one of the attendants by the arm. "I don't understand any of it, and that's what I told Mrs. Lund when they wanted to move my chest of drawers."

Else, who had approached the stretcher, retreated with a start. She had seen a face that was as round as a billiard ball and so swollen that the eyes were barely visible. One cheek was streaked black and blue, with a gaping, bleeding cut. To think that this face belonged to that soft, well-bred voice.

"Sit absolutely still and tend to your insects," said the attendant, who Bella Holm had grabbed by the arm. Setting the stretcher down outside the end cell, which had been empty since the suicide, the attendants picked up Bella Holm, blanket and all, and carried her in.

"Has she taken poison?" Else asked Nurse Stenberg.

"You could call it that, I suppose. She has delirium tremens."

"Do you think she'll die?"

"Oh my no. In three or four days she'll be all right again."

After the attendants had left, Else went to the door of the cell and looked in. Bella Holm was sitting erect, just as she had seen her on the stretcher earlier, eagerly examining the blanket and chattering away in her soft agreeable voice.

"You there, haven't you got a drop of beer?" she said suddenly and looked up.

"She's asking for beer, Nurse Thorgren!"

"Oh yes, I'll give her beer all right!"

Thorgren stood in front of Bella Holm's bed. "Lie down, there's nothing for her to find anyway." Thorgren took her by the shoulders and forced her down on the pillow.

"Not even small beer?"

"If you want milk, you can have that. Nothing else."

"What's she looking for?" Else asked.

"Flies, anything that crawls. All delirium patients do it."

"Yes, poor thing," Nurse Stenberg concluded, after answering Else's eager questions about Bella Holm. "She's from a good family. Her father was a schoolmaster, I believe. He was an incurable gambler, and when he had gambled away everything, even his bedclothes, he put a bullet in his head. And the mother had something wrong with her, too."

"But how can you treat her so coldly then?" Else asked tremulously. "You haven't shown her a bit of sympathy."

"A person like that deserves nothing but contempt. When she first came here, I stood up for her. But I don't any more."

Else went in to say good night to Granny, who always went to bed at six o'clock. Sweet old Granny, the only happy, peaceful soul in this hell.

As usual when Else came in after Granny had gone to bed, Granny pulled Else close, threw her arms around her neck, and confided the few ever-recurring fragments that occupied her mind.

"Yes," said Else, "but I really must go now. Good night, Granny."

"Good night." Granny kissed both of Else's hands as usual. "Tomorrow you'll give me some coffee again. It's so soothing."

"Mrs. Kant!" Mrs. Syverts cried out as Else walked by her door.

"See, I've got my ring now." Mrs. Syverts rubbed the ring with her handkerchief and extended her right hand. "Carl hadn't taken it back, Nurse Stenberg had it. They say that as soon as I get up I can write to my husband. But last night the doctors came in here again ... I don't know what you think ..." Whispering the last few words, Mrs. Syverts shook with husky and muffled laughter.

Chapter 28

During the night, Nurse Bøhn came to check Else often. Bella Holm was having convulsions in the next cell. She shrieked and howled, and periodically there was the sound of a heavy fall and something that resembled hiccoughing.

"Is she disturbing you?" Thorgren spoke from the doorway.

"Yes, she's really bad," answered Nurse Bøhn, who was standing by Else's bed.

"She keeps jumping into the water," Thorgren said, coming closer. "'Shh,' she says" – Thorgren placed the palms of her hands together, held them above her head and bent her body sharply forward – "and then she dives smack on the floor and gets the hiccoughs. Actually I've come to make up with Mrs. Kant and beg her one more time to be humble toward the professor."

"Yes, I've told her the same thing," said Nurse Bøhn. "Mrs. Kant has gotten off on the wrong foot with the professor."

"I've told you, it's impossible for me to talk to that man," Else moaned.

"Then write to him. Could you do that more easily?"

Else shook her head.

"It's all the same to us," Thorgren continued. "But for your own sake – the shooting stars, you know. Ah well, in any case we're good friends again, aren't we?"

Else held out her hand with a smile.

"When you write, you're the one who decides what to say," Nurse Bøhn continued after Thorgren had left. "And there would be no need for you to lose your temper. You should see how good-natured the professor can be."

Should she try it? Else lay musing on her pillow, listening to Bella Holm, who kept jumping into the sea. Try to make him understand how terribly she was suffering here and beg him to let her out. Since that time in the cell she had not poured out her troubles to him. Perhaps he believed she was now relatively content.

In the morning, Nurse Stenberg and Nurse Ræder both told her that she really ought to write to the professor.

After lunch Else asked for writing materials, and lying on her side in bed – she felt too exhausted to get up – she propped herself on her left elbow, her chest against the writing table, and wrote a letter that began, "Dear Professor: In the present state of pain and exhaustion in which I find myself, it is nearly impossible for me to find words for what is in my heart." Then she began to describe her condition, not as it really was, but as she hoped the professor could bear to hear it described without flying into a rage. She mentioned her persistent insomnia, the impossibility of getting any sleep in such a place, the noise of the patients, the many other sounds, etc. Finally she begged that her husband be informed of her urgent desire to leave as soon as possible.

When the letter was finished, Nurse Stenberg took it immediately to the professor.

Afterwards, Else got dressed and went out to the cell corridor where a pungent odor greeted her. The smell came from the end cell, where Nurse Suenson and Madonna-Hansen, amid jokes and laughter, were busy washing Bella Holm's head. They were scrubbing away at it, as if they were scouring the bottom of a kettle.

Else took a step closer. In a bucket on the floor lay a quantity of long hair.

"You cut off her hair?" Else asked.

"We had to – it was just swarming. But now those lice are getting their comeuppance. The smell of that stuff – " Nurse Suenson poured something from a bottle into a basin of water on the night table " – could fell an ox." Suenson sneezed.

Bella Holm, her neck and shoulders firmly gripped by Madonna-Hansen, squirmed restlessly and struck out with her arm, her cupped hand swooping through the air, fingers wiggling and ready to pounce.

"You've got to let me catch my canary, for God sake," she said in the tone used by girlfriends to reproach each other in jest. "Look! There it goes."

Else stood and watched. Bella Holm grabbed and snatched and chattered about birds and white chickens.

"There," Nurse Suenson said, taking away the basin and bucket. "I'm going to change my clothes from head to toe. It will just take a minute."

Madonna-Hansen stripped the blankets off the bed and pulled down Bella Holm's chemise. Else saw a pair of thin, dark legs with bony knees and flat, gnarled feet.

"Come, let's go," Madonna-Hansen said. But before she and Else had reached the doorway, Bella Holm had sprung out of bed and was moving along the wall, tracking the canary.

Madonna-Hansen closed and locked the door of the cell and Else went up the corridor.

In Mrs. Fog's cell a man was sitting on a chair beside the bed. He was holding his hat in his hand, watching the unmoving, yellow mummy face with a gaze filled with sadness and love.

"It's her son," Madonna-Hansen whispered.

"But you said nobody on this corridor could have visitors."

"No. But there are always exceptions in life. They sent for him."

"Is she going to die?"

"Yes, it can't be long now."

Else went in to see Mrs. Syverts and was surprised to find her standing by the window in a blue and white striped cotton dressing gown. Her long brown braid was hanging down her back.

"Oh, it's you, Mrs. Kant," she said happily when Else touched her arm. "I thought it was one of the others. I'm watching for my husband. I can't imagine why he doesn't come."

"So they've given you permission to get up. Are you happy about that?"

"Yes, but I'm freezing in this thin gown. Is it really true that you are married to Mr. Kant?"

"Yes."

"All the same, he looks like a man who would have quite a different kind of wife. Yes, because I know him." Mrs. Syverts nodded vigorously.

"What kind of wife?"

"A blond little clinging vine with velvet hair ribbons and a chignon. Someone who whispers sweet little nothings in his ear. I'm going to write to my husband now."

"Ask him to send you a warmer gown," Else said, going out to the corridor again and pacing back and forth. The man by Mrs. Fog's bed was still sitting in the same position and the mummy face looked lifeless.

After a while Else went in to see Granny, who had bronchitis and was confined to bed.

"You see, they've put me to bed," Granny said, smiling and nodding. "But that won't kill me. I was born February the 17th. How long ago was that?"

"Well, that depends on what year it was," Else said.

"Well, it doesn't really matter because last year there was such a good crop of cabbages. But mustn't one be happy and thankful to God for being in such a nice, clean place?"

On her way down the corridor, Else walked past the cell of the puerperal maniac, who was sitting up in the bed beckoning to her. Else went in.

"The baby," she said gripping Else's hand convulsively.

"The baby is fine. I told you that the other day."

"Yes, but it would be much better off dead."

"Now you're talking nonsense. Of course you want your sweet little baby to live."

The puerperal maniac watched Else intently, and something hard and angry came into her eyes. "We have so many already, and the minister says the Lord shall demand every child's soul from our hands."

"Don't think about that," Else said. "Just try to get well. Everything will be all right."

"But there was this kettle," the puerperal maniac whispered, "this big black kettle. There were so many little heads sticking out and Knu'ssen didn't have any money."

"There, there, lie down nicely now."

"Will you come back soon?"

"Yes, tonight."

When Else left the puerperal maniac, she peeked into Mrs. Fog's cell. The stranger was sitting in the same position as before. Suddenly he got up quietly, and placing his hat on the floor, fell on his knees with his hands over his eyes and buried his face in the white bedcovers.

Chapter 29

WHEN THE RESIDENT PHYSICIAN made evening rounds, Else asked for more of the yellow booklets.

"The professor says I can't."

"He's afraid they'll harm me?" Else laughed.

"The professor wants you to be a little more friendly first."

"Oh? Well, that suits me just fine. I'd do the same if I were in the professor's shoes. Exactly the same."

The next morning's rounds were later than usual. Else, who had been sitting with her crocheting by the window, put her work aside and went out to the cell corridor.

"I said I wouldn't interfere in Mrs. Lund's affairs," said Bella Holm, who had stopped prowling along the wall when Else peeked in at her. She was wearing a chemise and a short jacket and her face was even more bruised and swollen than before.

"No, a person shouldn't meddle in other people's business," she went on, turning to Else. "Why should anybody care how many schnapps I drink with my meals? I never drink schnapps except at mealtime, and that can't do any harm. I also think it's very peculiar that Mrs. Lund would help them move my chest of drawers."

"Did she move your chest of drawers?" Else asked.

"Yes, see for yourself. Is there a chest of drawers in here?" Bella Holm looked all around her. "I'm not blind, you know – oh look, there's the canary." She ran over to the window.

"Into bed with you," commanded the nurse, who had just come in.

"Yes, yes, yes, I'm going to bed now," answered Bella Holm in a voice that mildly reproached the nurse for her unreasonableness.

"You can hear right away that she's a well-bred person," said the nurse.

Else went in to see Mrs. Syverts, who was sitting up in bed combing her hair. Granny was bending close to her, chattering and whispering. Else fetched a chair from the corridor for Granny.

"You look so much like my Norwegian," Mrs. Syverts said to Else with a playful smile, as she removed the loose hair from the comb, twisted it together and tucked it carefully away in a scrap of newspaper. "I saw that immediately that first morning." She wiped the comb with newspaper, blew on it and placed it on the night table. "If only I had a little wash water," she said, looking at her fingers with displeasure.

"I looked for you in your room." Else turned around. There stood the countess in her black lace-trimmed dress.

"What's she doing here?" Mrs. Syverts burst out, pointing at the countess. "Look at her!"

"We are all sisters before God," said the countess in her soft, mild voice, placing her hand on Mrs. Syverts' shoulder. "I'll pray to Jesus for you. Do you know Jesus?"

"I was baptized and confirmed, I assure you. But you mustn't touch me – my fingers are greasy."

"Ah yes, Jesus, Jesus," prattled Granny, shaking her little night-capped head.

"Well, this is quite a siesta." Else and the countess turned with a start. Hieronimus was standing in the cell wearing his long white coat. The light from the bright February sun, peeking through the window, fell directly on his face, and Else was struck by the pure blue color of his eyes. She would have sworn his eyes were pale and icy. How mild and charming his manner could be. She was moved, nearly confounded, like someone strolling through the woods on an early spring day who suddenly feels spring in the air.

"I would like to talk to you, Mrs. Kant," he said with an almost imperceptible smile, and he walked quickly out of the cell. Else followed, thinking of Thorgren and her shooting stars.

153

"I have received your letter," he said when they were seated in her room, "and read it carefully. Not only that, I have faithfully presented it to your husband and your doctor. Now we shall see."

"Thank you," said Else, giving him a look that expressed even more gratitude than her words.

"So you will probably hear from your husband soon."

Else thanked him again.

"By the way, wouldn't you like to see your family doctor, too? There's no reason why he can't visit you."

Else hesitated before answering. Knut was the one she wanted to see, nobody else mattered.

"You do have confidence in him?" the professor asked.

"Yes. He's been my doctor for ten years. But I don't feel any urgent need to see him."

"Is that so? You take an interest in the patients, I notice."

"Yes, Granny is so sweet."

"Indeed. Well, good morning."

Else was full of hope and anticipation. Hieronimus had delivered the letter to Knut and Tvede. There could be no doubt about what would happen. This very day Knut would come and fetch her. So Hieronimus was the man he was supposed to be, after all. His previous behavior? Well, it didn't make sense to her and she would therefore erase it from her mind.

But both that day and the next passed and none of Else's expectations were fulfilled. Slowly she realized that she had been wrong again.

On the evening of the third day, when Hieronimus was sitting in her room during rounds, she said suddenly, "So my husband and Dr. Tvede have followed your advice and decided I must stay here?"

"Yes," he replied with evident satisfaction.

Else pondered for a moment. Then she said, "Then in your opinion, I am insane?"

"Yes."

His "yes," uttered with such ruthless pleasure, struck her like the blow of a whip, and she felt the ground giving way beneath her feet. What could she do? Nothing. She was in his power.

"Well," she said, getting up, "When Professor Hieronimus and my husband and Dr. Tvede say that I'm insane, then I must be insane." She paced back and forth across the room. "But then I've been insane all my life."

"Perhaps you have been."

"Perhaps you have been, too," Else mumbled to herself. Who could know?

"In most people one can probably find something or other that can be labelled insanity, if one has a mind to," she said aloud, looking at Hieronimus.

"I have recently become acquainted with your work," Hieronimus said. "Your paintings reflect an interest in the abnormal that is very unpleasant."

Interest in the abnormal, Else reflected. Wasn't it the professor's interest in the abnormal that had given him his authority and placed him in this position?

"Your paintings seem to me absolute proof that you are abnormal. I assume that you have tried in your work to represent your own inner life."

Else did not reply. She just stared at him.

"And the fact that you never sleep. That's also a sure sign of mental derangement."

"Hasn't my husband asked to see me?"

"No, he hasn't said anything of the kind."

His answer stabbed like a knife blade to her heart. She paced back and forth again, but her knees were so unsteady that she had to sit down.

"I don't understand," she said finally, wiping the sweat from her forehead. "He told me I would be here eight to ten days."

"Hmm."

Again this "hmm" that called her a liar. But she was oblivious to that now. Her thoughts revolved like scorching flames around one thought: Knut had not wanted to see her.

"I don't understand," she repeated. "Has something happened since I've been here, something I don't know about?"

"No. But now that your husband has you at a distance, he can see you more calmly and clearly."

"Is he irritated with me?"

"Irritated. Do you mean angry? One is not angry with those for whom one feels compassion." The words were spoken with calm and lofty dignity.

Else said nothing. This was the darkest hour of her life.

"Consider," Hieronimus said, standing up and walking to the corner of the room, where he positioned himself with his elbow propped against the wall, his hand under his chin. "You used to throw yourself naked on the floor, writhing and howling, isn't that correct?"

"Never!" said Else. "Naked? It would be impossible for me to do that."

"All right, perhaps you did it with your clothes on."

Knut didn't want to see her! Knut didn't want to see her! a voice inside Else shrieked. What was all the rest compared to this. "A man's at his wit's end when he puts his wife in Ward Six," the resident physician had said. Had Knut deceived and betrayed her?

"On the whole, the way you've behaved leaves me no doubt about your condition."

"I was in despair because I couldn't get on with my work."

"But you don't really know that," Hieronimus continued. "You couldn't remember afterwards."

"Yes I could remember, but sometimes I pretended not to because it was so painful to me."

"There! That's just what I told your husband," Hieronimus burst out triumphantly.

"Will I be here long?"

"Yes! Very long."

Again there was such rich enjoyment in Hieronimus's voice that Else thought he belonged to the category of the executioner who delights in his work.

"Can't I be moved to some other place?"

"Yes, to St. Jørgen's," he snarled.

"Fine. I'd rather be in St. Jørgen's. The sooner the better."

Hieronimus walked out.

"The professor was in here a long time tonight."

Else was sitting with her face in her hands; she lifted her head and nodded at the countess.

"Did you have a pleasant talk?"

Else repeated her conversation with the professor.

"My God!" the countess exclaimed in dismay.

"If he says you're insane, then of course he can say the same about me ... though it seems inconceivable!" She paced back and forth for a few minutes with her arms crossed, then stopped in front of Else. "Aren't you going to demand that he tell you the nature of your insanity?"

Else shook her head. "I have no desire to hear that man's opinions. Besides he's said more than enough already."

"It's outrageous," the countess declared. "I'm going to ask him about it in the morning."

"You shouldn't do that," Else said. "If you want my advice, you had better not ask about yourself either. It's a waste of words. As for me, he must have decided almost immediately that I was insane. And of course I was ill when I came here. If one had a mind to, one could justify calling that insanity, I suppose."

"You are unnaturally calm," the countess said.

"Oh this insanity business is nonsense. But to think that my husband doesn't want to see me ..."

"Come into my room and I'll read you a chapter from the Bible." The countess took Else by the hand.

Else rose listlessly and followed her.

Chapter 30

THE NIGHT THAT FOLLOWED seemed to Else the most terrible of all the terrible nights she had spent there. It wasn't the irrational fear that before had driven her to the edge of madness. The maniacs' raging and Bella Holm's puttering and chattering in the adjacent cell struck her now as nothing out of the ordinary. Nor was it that Hieronimus had pronounced her insane. What was that to her? She was not insane and never would be. If her mind had not snapped during her stay in this Hieronimic Hell – considering the wretched state she was in when she arrived – what could drive her mad? It was that Knut had not wanted to see her, that to get rid of her, he had coaxed and tricked her into leaving voluntarily. He certainly hadn't needed to do that.

She felt as if her soul were being broken on the wheel. She had thought before that she had reached the height of suffering. But only now had she reached it. And Tage, the child, the boy at home, what would become of him?

So she was being sent to St. Jørgen's, too. She remembered how she had shuddered that time in the cell when Nurse Stenberg mentioned the patient who was moving to St. Jørgen's. But St. Jørgen's? Dear God, if she had to be locked up, anything was better than this place with Hieronimus in command.

Hieronimus – what a strange man! His position must have gone to his head like an intoxicant. Not a single question about her state of mind. Never once asked about those sensations in the back of her head, what they felt like or how often they occurred. And the things that had affected

her here – the terror and despair, the ruinous consequences of sleepless-
ness which had almost finished her for good – of these he had not the
faintest inkling. He was just like an old-fashioned schoolmaster who disci-
plines and subdues his naughty, rebellious pupils with whippings and
rough treatment – this was the way he had treated her.

And he imagined he knew all the answers! Dared to say, quite curtly
and confidently, "You are insane, and you must be locked up in St. Jørgen's." And say it with the avid, joyful expression of someone swallowing
a delicious morsel.

She wondered if this wasn't a covert attempt to make her angry, to provoke an outburst that would provide the final proof of her madness. The
proofs he had must seem unsubstantial, even to him: her work showed an
interest in the abnormal; she was supposed to have thrown herself wailing
on the floor; and she wasn't able to sleep on Ward Six.

Ah well, it didn't make any difference. Hieronimus was an enigma to
her. He had his theories, presumably, and acted on them. Poor Hieronimus, one of these days he would be unmasked.

But Knut! Knut had not wanted to see her!

If only she could get out of here soon! She would actually miss the
nurses. Hour after hour they had helped her endure her misery. But
imagine being spared the sight of Hieronimus!

જી

"I WOULD LIKE YOU to see your family doctor." Hieronimus said to Else
the next day. "Then you'll discover I'm not the only one who thinks you
ought to be sent to St. Jørgen's, but so do Dr. Tvede and your husband.
For that reason I have given orders that Dr. Tvede can visit you whenever
he wishes.

"You should also go down and walk in the garden," Hieronimus continued, "Get used to fresh air. At St. Jørgen's, you'll go out every day."

"Now come along," the countess said to Else that afternoon. She was
dressed in her coat and hat, ready for a walk. "One owes it to one's body,
even in a place like this."

Else had been urged to go walking many times before, but this time she went along to humor the countess.

But when she returned twenty minutes later, she vowed to herself that this would be the first and last time. Walking back and forth inside the high fences that surrounded the bit of ground they called the garden, along two paths through the naked trees, followed and watched like a prisoner, under all the staring eyes of the neighboring windows – no – this was an extra drop in the cup of bitterness she had to swallow every day.

The next day when Else went out to the cell corridor, she saw an unfamiliar man between two of the white-uniformed assistants disappear into one of the cells. Else had only one thought, to conceal herself from this stranger. She hurried back to her room.

But what was happening? Were they coming in? Hearing the unfamiliar footsteps approaching, she fled, fearful and anxious, to the window and turned her back to the room.

"Here is an acquaintance who would like to say hello to you, Mrs. Kant," said one of the assistants from the door.

Else remained where she stood. Blood flooded to her heart and she had to grasp the window frame for support.

"Good day, Mrs. Kant," said a strange voice from close by.

Else turned around.

A stocky, dark-haired man stood there smiling profusely.

"I'm here to inspect the ward and I wanted to say good day to you while I was at it. You remember me, don't you?"

"No," Else stammered.

"Yes, of course you do – I'm Anton Ringe – we've met at the Hahns' a number of times."

Yes, of course, she remembered him now. "You've changed a great deal," she said out of sheer confusion.

"Of course. After ten or twelve years, it's not surprising," and Else read in his glance: "You should see how you have changed, yourself."

"I'm a physician, you may remember." The man went on smiling and smiling, presumably lacking any other way to express his good wishes. "So I go around to the hospitals."

"Ah yes," said Else, wishing the earth would swallow her.

"How are you doing, by the way?"

"Oh, all right." Else felt as if the ground beneath her feet was red hot.

"Well, things can always get better. Good-bye, Mrs. Kant." He extended his hand. "It was nice to see you."

Nice to see you ... Else threw herself into the easy chair and wept.

"So, you've had a visitor today," the resident physician said when he came that evening.

Else gave him an indignant look.

"Oh, we thought it would please you."

"Please me? Oh yes, of course! Everything you do here is dictated by what will please me! I mustn't see my husband, God knows I couldn't bear that, just this stranger, this man I've met at parties when my circumstances were the same as other people's!" Her face quivered with suppressed tears.

"Yes, it was a mistake, Mrs. Kant," the resident physician said gravely. "I told you it was done with the best intentions."

The best intentions! If only she had a cannon and gunpowder she would blast that loathsome phrase out of existence.

The next day, Else again went to take a bath. Nurse Bøhn, who had replaced Nurse Ræder on the day shift, accompanied her.

"Is this the only bathroom for Ward Six?" Else asked as she was dressing. "Does everybody take baths here no matter what kind of diseases they have? Even the criminals who are put here for observation?"

"Yes."

"That Konradi Schøller, the one who smothered her son, did she take baths in this same tub? Were you here with her?"

Nurse Bøhn nodded.

"Didn't you discover she was a man then?"

"No, because I didn't look at her. When I saw her in bed it occurred to me once or twice that she looked like a man around the shoulders. But who could have guessed ..."

This is the last time I'll take a bath here, Else said to herself.

Upstairs in the cell corridor Bella Holm was pacing in her hospital gown, bending down every few minutes to pick up something from the floor.

"I tell you, there was a krone on the floor," she told Else. "When you see a krone lying around, you pick it up, by God."

"She's no better than when she came," Else remarked to the nurse.

"Yes. She still hasn't slept. It's going to take a while this time."

That night Else lay silent and motionless hour after hour, brooding and grieving because Knut hadn't wanted to see her. Her heart felt like an open wound. And Tage – sweet, adorable little Tage – would his heart also turn away from her?

In the morning when she entered the cell corridor, she went in to see Mrs. Fog, who was lying with closed eyes, her arms stretched out stiffly on the blanket. "It's impossible that she could be alive," Else thought to herself, bending down to listen to her breathing.

Then Mrs. Fog opened her eyes and gave Else a look that was like a loud shriek. Else felt a cold chill go through her. Who could have imagined this mummy could look like that?

Mrs. Fog's lips moved slightly, and her eyes begged desperately as her hands rose and fumbled toward each other.

Else whispered in her ear, "Shall we pray together?"

The eyes spoke agreement.

Else took Mrs. Fog's hands and helped her fold them together. Then she folded her own and recited the Lord's Prayer. The mummy's beseeching eyes remained fixed on Else's throughout.

When the prayer was over, Mrs. Fog slowly lowered her eyes, a trace of a smile trembling on the sunken lips. Her breathing was almost inaudible. Else stood for a while and watched her.

Ten minutes later, as Else was walking back to her room, she again looked in on Mrs. Fog, who lay as before. A distinctly yellow tint had spread over her face, imparting a faint glow.

"Wouldn't you think she was dead?"

"She is dead," said Nurse Suenson.

Chapter 31

"IF YOU WANT TO SEE THE BODY you must come now, Mrs. Kant," whispered Nurse Suenson, beckoning to Else from the doorway. Else rose and followed her into Mrs. Fog's cell after which Nurse Suenson closed the door.

The corpse was lying on a bare sackcloth mattress, like the woman who committed suicide, tightly wrapped in a sheet through which the outline of the body was visible. It was so small, Else thought, it might have belonged to a half-grown child.

Nurse Suenson threw back the sheet and Else recoiled, shuddering. Mrs. Fog's body was a mere skeleton covered with translucent, sallow skin – the forehead and head a skull, the lower jaw sagging so that the mouth stood open and the chin rested on the chest. The joints of the shoulders and elbows seemed unnaturally large, and the belly was shrivelled and hollow. The protruding ribcage was crisscrossed with wide blue lines.

"What are those?" Else asked pointing to the lines.

"The doctors draw them on the bodies sometimes. I really don't know why."

What must this human being have suffered to have wasted away like that, Else thought, gazing at the fearful sight.

"There," Nurse Suenson said, putting the sheet back over her. "They're coming now to take her away. A new patient has already been assigned to the cell."

Else went back to her room and thought about Mrs. Fog. This human life had come to an end now. What had it been like, she wondered. Dying all alone in this place, among strangers, without a loving hand to close her eyes. And yet she had a son who had looked at her lovingly, sadly, and who had kneeled by her bed. Surely he must have wanted to be with her during her last moments. But life did not take one's wishes and desires into account.

Perhaps she too would one day be dying alone and abandoned in a strange place, and her son, possibly the only person she had left in the world, would not be able to be with her. Her son, sweet little Tage – she put her head on her knees and wept tears of longing for the child. If only she could hear some news of him. Eighteen days had passed since she had left him at home.

Perhaps his nursemaid might be allowed to visit her since Knut did not want to. Oh Knut, Knut . . . she wept again.

Yes, she would write to the professor one more time, humble herself to him, as the nurses put it, beg him to allow her to see the nursemaid.

In the afternoon she obtained pen and ink and wrote among other things: "But even if I really am insane, I can't understand why you, who are in authority over me, should make it your business to cause me as much pain and suffering as possible. Just being deprived of personal liberty is an unbearable misery, and now this – not being able to see or hear about my child . . ." She ended by earnestly begging that the child's nursemaid be allowed to visit.

Nurse Stenberg immediately took the letter away and returned with a message that the professor had received it, but he was going to be away tomorrow and would not be back until the following day.

Else's heart sank at the thought of this delay. But there was nothing to do about it. Now at least she had hope to live on in the meanwhile. She took her work and sat down by the window, but she could not bear to crochet because of the constant throbbing in her head. Her tooth also ached night and day, more or less violently, and she was still getting morphine injections. She put her crocheting aside and sat quietly with her hands in her lap.

Then she heard raised voices and loud sobbing coming from the cell corridor; when she got out there she saw Nurse Stenberg dragging away

Mrs. Syverts, who was screaming and struggling.

"How do you like this, Mrs. Kant! I'm being forced back to bed!" shouted Mrs. Syverts as they entered the cell. "I won't go! I won't go!" She tore herself loose and stamped her foot. "I'll go mad lying on that torture bench!"

Without so much as a word, Nurse Stenberg seized her firmly, forced her down on the edge of the bed and unfastened her dress.

Mrs. Syverts wept and scolded a little, then she grew quiet and, with a cold stare, helped undress herself.

"Why does she have to go to bed again?" Else asked.

"The professor's orders."

"How long do I have to stay here this time," Mrs. Syverts mumbled from her bed. Suddenly she clenched her fists and screamed, "Why don't you poison me right now? I know that's what you want." She burst into sobs and turned her face to the wall.

"She had written a letter to her husband that the professor didn't like. It was quite deranged."

"Poor thing," said Else. "She had been doing so well."

In Mrs. Fog's cell the new patient had already been installed. Else went in to see her.

She was a forty-year-old woman with a plump, ruddy face, thick chapped lips, and dark cropped hair that bristled out of her night cap. One temple had a large, white scar. She lay with her eyes closed, apparently asleep.

Suddenly, with a lightning quick movement, she sat straight up in bed, shook a sallow, clenched fist in Else's face, and burst into a torrent of coarse abuse. Else was so shocked that she flew backwards out of the cell.

A minute later, she curiously peeked at her again, this time only sticking her head inside the door. The woman was lying quietly on her pillow and seemed to be asleep. But just as suddenly as before, she sat up in bed and shook her fist at Else, calling her vile names.

"What a dreadful person," Else said to Nurse Stenberg, hurrying away from the door.

"Yes, and her name is Madam From,"[7] Nurse Stenberg laughed.

No, the puerperal maniac was altogether different. Not to mention Granny. Else went in to see them before she went back to her room.

Chapter 32

ELSE WAS PACING back and forth in her room, restless and expectant. Tonight Hieronimus would make his rounds and she would hear his reaction to her letter. It was four o'clock now. In two and a half hours he would be there.

Oh, this oppressive weakness! Feebly she let herself sink into a chair, leaned back with her hand over her eyes, and fell into a doze from which she was soon awakened by the sound of someone entering the room.

Hieronimus was standing before her in overcoat and gloves.

She rose quickly, her whole body trembling.

Hieronimus sat down on the chaise longue and Else resumed her former place.

"You have written to me again," Hieronimus began, with a tone of displeasure. "The language you use is much too strong."

Else didn't know if she had heard him correctly. She had taken such pains to express herself as mildly as possible.

"You talk about pain and suffering and being deprived of liberty," Hieronimus continued scornfully. "You have more liberty than is good for you."

Else was about to reply when she saw Dr. Tvede in the middle of the room.

"Ah yes, here is your doctor," Hieronimus exclaimed.

Tvede greeted Hieronimus first and then Else.

"Thank you," said Else. She couldn't manage anything more. Her lips quivered as if she were on the verge of weeping.

"How are you sleeping?"

Else shook her head. "I can't sleep here. This room is so terribly noisy."

"That's an exaggeration. This room is not noisy," Hieronimus said gruffly.

"And the patients make such a commotion," Else continued, looking intently at Tvede.

"Commotion," Hieronimus exclaimed. "I think it's quiet here." He directed a glance at Tvede, as if for confirmation.

"The one who makes the biggest commotion is Mrs. Kant," he snapped.

Else gasped audibly, stunned by Hieronimus's words. She felt as if she would collapse under the weight of this false accusation. But then it suddenly occurred to her – He wants to goad you into an outburst so that Dr. Tvede can observe your madness – and she answered calmly, though with a trembling voice: "Except for the first night, when I cried and pleaded because I was frantic and didn't know what was happening..." She had to stop, the words stuck to her tongue.

"Well, now you can have a talk with your doctor." Hieronimus rose and left the room, bustling away in his fussiest manner.

Tvede came over to Else and held out his hands. "I see how much you are suffering," he said.

"Is it really true that I'm going to St. Jørgen's?" Else asked, as soon as she could find her voice.

"Yes, you'll be well cared for there."

"So you and Knut agree with Hieronimus. Is your confidence in him so great? You just saw what he's like."

"I have confidence in him as a physician. I don't know what he's like as a human being."

"Why doesn't Knut want to see me?"

Tvede's small eyes widened. "Not want to see you! He can't get permission from the professor."

"Is that really true?" Else let out her breath with inexpressible relief. "You mustn't deceive me."

"I assure you, Mrs. Kant. Your husband has been in despair because he couldn't visit you."

"Oh thank God, thank God!" Else squeezed Tvede's hands and wept, her face against his shoulder. "You've lifted a stone from my heart."

Tvede continued to reassure her that Knut had been frantic because he couldn't get permission to visit her.

"Hieronimus has been lying then," Else said, drying her eyes. "Lying, on top of all the other revolting things he's done. What he said about my 'commotion' was a bare-faced lie, something he made up on the spot to suit his purposes."

Tvede did not reply.

"What did Knut say when he read my letter?"

"What letter?"

"The one I wrote to the professor, the one he showed to you and Knut."

"We haven't seen any letter – neither I nor your husband."

"Are you sure of that?"

"Yes, Mrs. Kant."

"So it's another lie! And you're still going to leave me in the hands of that man?"

"No, we want you in St. Jørgen's as soon as possible."

"Oh please, not St. Jørgen's," Else begged. "Why should I be locked up with lunatics? I've had enough of that here. I'm not so deranged that it's right or necessary to lock me up against my will."

Tvede shook his head. He looked as if the conversation were painful to him.

"Take me away from here right now and let me go home – just long enough to see my son and pack a suitcase," Else implored tearfully. "Then I'll go wherever you and Knut want. Just not to another madhouse."

"No, I don't dare trust you," Tvede said sadly. "Once you get home, well ... You won't keep your word. When the child was sick this winter, you promised not to get up at night and tend to him, but you did it just the same."

What does that have to do with this, Else thought miserably, continuing to plead. She also told him about the visit from the outside doctor.

"Well, I don't think that ought to happen here," Tvede said disapprovingly. "It must have been painful for you, Mrs. Kant."

"Painful!" Else raised her eyes to the ceiling. "What do you think it's been like for me, confined to bed in that cell, surrounded by raving lunatics, never sleeping day or night? Do you think it's any different now?"

Tvede gazed at her with a compassionate expression in which Else could also read doubt and a firm intention not to let himself be moved.

"Will you at least promise me that you'll tell Knut everything – how Hieronimus has been torturing me and telling lies and saying Knut didn't want to see me?" Else said at last.

"Yes, Mrs. Kant." Tvede took her hands again.

"Tell him I've been in a cell and I'm still living with lunatics, that I hardly ever sleep, and that they let strangers come and stare at me as if I'm some kind of freak. Will you do that?"

"Yes, yes. Everything."

"Couldn't you ask the professor to let Knut visit?"

"Better ask him yourself."

Else heard Hieronimus's footsteps in the cell corridor. "There he is," she whispered hurriedly. "You must help me – tell him it's not true that Knut doesn't want to see me, really give him a piece of your mind."

"Well," said Hieronimus, looking intently from one to the other.

Else gave Tvede an imploring look.

"Mrs. Kant would very much like to see her husband," Tvede said in a tone that humbly begged the professor's pardon.

"All right, if Mr. Kant wants to see her, he's welcome to do it as far as I'm concerned. Obviously. But I must say I've gotten quite the opposite impression."

"Oh yes, he really does want to," said Tvede. His tone was so hesitant, his expression so irresolute, that Else began to fear he had deceived her.

"Wouldn't you also like to see your child?" Hieronimus asked, his face and voice changing suddenly.

Else gasped again, this time with pleasure.

"Thank you so much," she said.

"Then we'll see about arranging it. In the meantime the nursemaid you were so eager to see can come."

"Thank you so much," Else repeated.

Tvede left with Hieronimus. As Else took Tvede's hand to say good-bye, she was smiling from ear to ear.

"Really, that man is unbelievable!" The countess came in with an almost indignant expression on her gentle face. "Imagine, having the nerve to say Mrs. Kant made the biggest commotion! I was standing right outside and I heard him."

"Yes," said Nurse Stenberg, who had also come in. "The professor must have a reason that we don't understand."

The professor is a boor and a liar, Else thought with disgust. But what did that matter? Now they were going to visit her, both Knut and Tage. Glowing with pleasure she recounted her news.

"The part about the child puzzles me," Nurse Stenberg said. "Children are never admitted to the hospital, but I guess that's up to the professor."

⁂

IN HER LETTER to Hieronimus Else had given her word that if the nurse-maid came to visit, she would not use her to carry secret messages or letters, which she knew to be forbidden. But now she inwardly retracted this promise. With a man like Hieronimus, who lied about her and rebuked her in front of Tvede, she felt no obligation to keep her word. Just to be safe she would have a letter ready when Inger arrived and ask her to deliver it to Knut. Possibly Hieronimus would postpone Knut's visit. He seemed to enjoy torturing her. And Tvede's behavior hadn't inspired her with hope. In front of Hieronimus he had seemed far too subservient.

Out on the yellow table in the corridor she found a piece of paper. The pen and ink had been in her room since the other day. She started to write, but every time she heard footsteps, she had to hide the paper quickly beneath her crochet work. As far as haste allowed she described her situation, intentionally avoiding strong words so that Knut would not think she was exaggerating. Even so, the letter became a cry for help from a soul in distress, an urgent appeal that he come at once. And if he maintained his resolve to send her to St. Jørgen's, against her vehement protests, he absolutely had to see her first. After many interruptions she had filled the paper. She folded it and slipped it into her bosom.

For the first time since she arrived, the crushing pain in her chest was gone. She went out and took a walk in the cell corridor. Every time she passed Madam From's door, the woman sat up in bed and cursed her bitterly.

"You affect her like a red flag in front of a mad bull," said Nurse Stenberg, pushing the cell door shut.

"She's nasty, that one," Granny said with a shudder, pointing at Madam From's door. Then with a broad smile she nodded and prattled: "Granny's going away now."

"She's leaving?"

"She's moving over to the quiet corridor," Nurse Suenson said. "Someone new will be in her cell."

Else bid Granny a tender farewell. She was not permitted to visit the quiet corridor.

"Who will give you coffee now, Granny?"

"Oh, coffee, yes," Granny laughed silently. "Our sweet lady will bring Granny coffee," she nodded confidently.

Mrs. Syverts was protesting loudly from her bed. "You're play acting, the whole lot of you," she said as Else entered her room. "If only it were amusing, this charade of yours! But I can't be bothered to watch it. It bores me, simply bores me."

"Just calm yourself now," said Else, taking her hand. "You'll soon be able to get up again."

"I'll never get out of bed!" Mrs. Syverts shouted, bursting into tears. "I'm so miserable, so miserable. They're driving me mad here!"

Else looked through the peephole in the cell door at Bella Holm. She was lying quietly in bed, asleep.

But the puerperal maniac was sitting up in bed, crying, the tears flooding down her face.

"Don't you have a handkerchief?" Else asked, when the puerperal maniac wiped her eyes with the sheet.

She looked at Else uncomprehendingly for a moment, then wept again.

Else handed the woman her handkerchief.

"What a rag," the puerperal maniac said, holding the handkerchief out in front of her. She crumpled it up in her hand and stuffed it under the pillow.

"Your husband is coming, I hear," the resident physician said during evening rounds. "So you're making your peace with the professor?"

"Yes, and my child," Else said joyfully.

"Did the professor say that?" the resident physician asked dubiously.

"Yes. But don't think for a minute that I'll believe it until I see it," Else added. She was so happy and full of hope tonight that she could afford to act as if she were skeptical. Even if the professor deceived her, she still had the letter for Inger to deliver hidden in her bosom.

Chapter 33

BEFORE BEDTIME Else took advantage of the opportunity to write still more to Knut, using scraps of paper she got from the countess under the pretext of making a list of some trifles she wanted sent from home. Again and again she implored him to come, adding, "If you are not here by Friday evening at the latest, I will sink into bottomless despair."

That night Else slept for six hours – after her usual dose, to be sure.

The next morning she continued writing. Eventually she had accumulated quite a lot. Full of confidence she wrapped it in a piece of newspaper and hid it in her bosom again. Shortly after eleven o'clock, Inger actually appeared. Else burst into tears at the sight of her and begged for news about Tage.

Inger talked about all sorts of things, and Else sat and listened and asked questions.

"It must be terrible for you to be here, Madam," Inger said at last.

"Yes, it's terrible. Be sure to tell the master that. And here is something I've written to the master," Else hurriedly took out the little package and slipped it into Inger's bosom. "No one must know," she whispered. "If you're asked when you leave if I've given you anything, be sure to say no. Otherwise I'll be in trouble."

Inger nodded knowingly: "You can depend on me, Madam."

At that moment, Hieronimus came in. "Well, is this the nursemaid you wanted?" he asked agreeably.

"Yes, thank you," said Else.

He stood there for a few moments and then went away.

As Inger was leaving, Else walked up the cell corridor with her. "Here you can see the company I keep," Else said, stopping by one of the open cell doors.

"Oh no," said Inger, holding her arm over her face. "It's horrible to see them."

During the afternoon Else heard a strangely muffled, breathless moaning coming from the cell corridor, followed by the crash of something falling and breaking. As Else came into the cell corridor, a young woman flew past her in wool socks and a sackcloth gown with the sleeves sewn together at the wrists; she was dashing back and forth at furious speed, shrieking and chattering continuously. Over in the corner lay an overturned washstand, its water pitcher broken on the floor.

"Oh God," she moaned. "Oh Rasmussen, oh Jakobsen, oh Jesus Christ, Mother, Mother, Aunt, Rasmussen." Her face was crimson and the whites of her wild eyes gleamed with fear.

"There is God the Father!" she shrieked suddenly, throwing herself on her knees before Else. "Oh God, oh Rasmussen!" She banged her face on the floor and grabbed the hem of Else's dress.

Else jumped away in terror.

"Come along," Nurse Stenberg said, bending over and lifting the howling woman. She sat down in a chair and took her on her lap.

"Who is she?" Else asked.

"A Miss Foss. She's twenty-four."

Miss Foss howled and screamed for Jesus and Rasmussen, Jakobsen and God the Father, Mother and Aunt. The entire cell corridor echoed with her cries. Every few minutes she tried to tear herself free, but Nurse Stenberg held her with an iron grip.

She went on like that the whole day. Every time Nurse Stenberg was called away and let go of her, she would dash back and forth at furious speed. The morphine injections she received had no effect.

When Else went to bed that night she could hear the muffled uproar of her cries, even though Miss Foss had been put in the farthest cell. But Else fell asleep just the same. The thought that Knut had read her letter by now calmed her spirit.

The next day was Thursday. Outside the weather was dazzlingly clear and the morning sun lit up the sky. Else felt the sunlight penetrate all the way to her heart. The wailing tumult from Miss Foss went on unchanged, but it did not register on her consciousness. Today Knut would certainly come.

> *Do you know the land where the blue Dnieper flows*
> *And rich, golden wheat fields toss in the wind?*
> *Where the fragrance of daisies and new-mown hay*
> *Wafts in the breeze from the distant steppes?*
> *Ah, that's the place where my heart yearns to fly,*
> *To be young again and free from care*
> *Hear Gritskov's songs of olden days*
> *Braid wildflowers in Marusja's hair.*

She had read these verses on a piece of torn-out newspaper that she had found this morning on a table in the corridor, and the lovely lines still reverberated in her mind; her heart swelled with joy at the thought of spring, which now must be in the air outside, and with longing for sunshine and freedom.

Imperceptibly, on wavering currents of feeling and memory, an image rose before her of youthful summer days, where lofty, snow-capped mountains stood proudly in the glittering sunlight, while below in the valleys streams bounded through the water-sprites' tiny mills, down the mossy slopes of the hills. Where the sun winked, warm and bewitching, through the tender, leafy branches of the silver birches. She felt the summer wind rustle around her and smelled the scent of new-mown hay.

> *Ah, that's the place where my heart yearns to fly,*
> *To be young again and free from care*

Her eyes filled with tears as she stood at the window and watched for Knut. In the corner of the high wooden fence was a small door, which she could just make out. Through it visitors came and went.

"Today you will probably see your husband," the resident physician had said during rounds. And since then Else had not left her post by the window.

Now it was half-past ten: visiting time.

At eleven o'clock Else was still desperately waiting and watching. Her hope was beginning to fade.

At eleven thirty she was still there, restless and feverish. She couldn't stop fidgeting.

"You mustn't wait for your husband any longer," Nurse Stenberg's voice said from behind her. "It's twelve o'clock."

Else sat down in a chair and wept bitter tears of disappointment. But then her hope revived. Tomorrow was another day. She would wait patiently until tomorrow.

"Even so, I won't be sent to St. Jørgen's," Else said to Nurse Ræder.

"You don't think so?"

Nurse Ræder's friendly, skeptical face made Else uncomfortable. But she shook it off and said, "Just wait and see."

"I've never known the professor to want anything he didn't get," Nurse Ræder replied.

If only I dared tell her about my letter to Knut, Else thought. Then she wouldn't disagree with me any more.

ა

"How CAN SHE keep it up?" Else said to Nurse Stenberg that afternoon, sitting in the cell corridor and looking at Miss Foss, whose condition was unchanged. Her lips were bloody and raw and there was an ulcerated sore on the end of her tongue. "Why doesn't she collapse?"

"She's had six morphine injections," answered Nurse Stenberg. "Now we're going to pack her in wet sheets."

Nurse Suenson came in with a bucket of water and some sheets over her arm. Nurse Stenberg hauled Miss Foss into the cell where Nurse Suenson had set down the water bucket. Else followed them and watched while the two nurses removed the clothes of the struggling patient.

Miss Foss was laid on a mattress on the floor. Nurse Stenberg kneeled and held her firmly while Nurse Suenson dipped wide bandages of folded sheets into the water and wrung them out; then the patient, whose mouth never stopped for an instant, was wrapped in sheets from head to foot in spite of all resistance. She was then rolled up in wool blankets, which they fastened with large safety pins. Sweat dripped down the nurses' faces and poured off Miss Foss. They left her and locked the cell door.

Else stayed in the cell corridor, looking in through the peephole in the door. Miss Foss was chattering and howling the same as before, sometimes jerking her whole body six inches off the mattress. Finally she managed to work her way off the mattress and lay jerking on the bare floor.

"Hasn't your husband been here today?" the resident physician asked during evening rounds.

"You know very well that he hasn't," Else answered.

"You can be sure he'll come, since the professor has promised," nodded the resident physician.

"He also promised that my child can come," Else said, "and I believe that's against the rules."

The next morning was another bright sunny day, and again Else stood by the window and watched, humming to herself, "*Do you know the land where the blue Dnieper flows.*"

"Today your husband will surely come," said the resident physician.

"Yes, surely," Else thought. Today was Friday and she had written that she would wait until Friday.

But this day passed like the day before. She stood there until twelve o'clock. Then she turned away from the window and sat down in the chair, sick and humiliated.

"You haven't been out in the cell corridor, today," Nurse Stenberg said, pulling Else out of the chair by both hands. "Come on, we miss you out there."

Well, Knut might still come. By Friday evening at the latest she had written. Oh Knut, Knut – if she could only talk to him, make him understand that she simply must not be sent to a madhouse. He had never, never failed her when it counted. She went with Nurse Stenberg down the cell corridor and looked through the peephole at Miss Foss.

Miss Foss was pacing back and forth, stark naked, howling and moaning and calling for Rasmussen and God the Father and all the others. On the mattress lay a few scraps of torn cloth.

During the night she had torn her way out of the wet pack. They had given her some clothes, which she had ripped to pieces and tossed away, Else heard later.

During the afternoon Else could not sit still for a second. A nagging disquiet make her skin prickle, and suspense painfully constricted her chest. The day passed and Knut did not come. Finally, at six o'clock Else gave up hope.

Chapter 34

AND THEN ALL THE TENSION and restlessness were gone. In their place came an icy indifference that gave her peace. It really was true, after all, that Knut hadn't wanted to see her. The fact that he hadn't come, after the letter she sent . . . She couldn't understand it in the least – but it didn't matter.

When Hieronimus came during evening rounds, Else asked if her husband had been told he could visit her now.

"No," said Hieronimus in a cheerful tone, "there's no hurry."

"It doesn't matter anyway," Else answered. "I no longer want to see my husband."

"You'll no doubt change your mind." Hieronimus bustled out.

During rounds the next morning the resident physician again brought up the subject of Mr. Kant visiting. The professor never went back on his word.

"I don't want to see my husband any more," Else said vehemently. "Never again in my life!"

"Shame on you," said the resident physician.

"He's let me stay here without visiting me one single time. It's no credit to him that I haven't lost my mind."

"Be reasonable, Mrs. Kant." The resident physician took Else's hand and looked at her intently. "You don't know the pressure your husband has been under."

"But where did he get this sudden respect for authority? And for a man as misguided as Hieronimus?"

"But one must have faith in physicians, don't you agree, Mrs. Kant? That's what well-bred people are taught."

"And so one exposes one's closest relations to ruin for the sake of good breeding!" Else cried bitterly.

That afternoon around five o'clock, Dr. Tvede suddenly appeared in Else's room. She was sitting by the window, crocheting.

Else received him with icy calm. He brought her warm greetings from her husband.

"So I am going to St. Jørgen's?" Else asked simply.

"Yes, Mrs. Kant."

"Then we have nothing more to say to each other. You did a splendid job of delivering the message I gave you for my husband."

Dr. Tvede stammered and appeared pensive and distressed. He only stayed a short time. As he was leaving he extended his hand.

"Good-bye," Else said, standing up. "This is probably the last time I talk to you, because when I get out of St. Jørgen's I won't come to you again."

Tvede left the room.

An hour later Hieronimus came in. Again Else asked if her husband had been told he could visit her.

Again she heard the same cheerful "no" and the same "there's no hurry."

"By the way, I have something for you." Hieronimus put a letter on the table in front of Else. It was from Knut, and Else saw immediately that the envelope had been ripped open like the previous letter.

"I refuse to read a letter from my husband that you have opened," Else said, hurriedly rising.

"Then I feel sorry for your husband," Hieronimus replied.

Else moved away a few steps. She stood with her back half turned to him.

"What's more, this indignation is just a sham," Hieronimus said scornfully. "You've been in an asylum before – you know that a mental patient's letters are always opened."

"The people who wrote me letters then didn't matter," Else answered.

"It's different now. Besides, my letters were not opened."

"Hmm. Your memory is obviously incorrect."

Else measured him with an icy look.

"You still need to work on controlling your temper," Hieronimus continued sarcastically. "Of course there will be ample opportunity for that at St. Jørgen's, where you'll be for quite some time."

Else did not utter a syllable.

Hieronimus took his time about leaving.

After he left, Else picked up the letter between her thumb and index finger and tossed it onto the table in the corridor.

"You've been in an asylum before." And this "specialist in mental diseases" scornfully threw that in her face as well.

That time. What peace and quiet she had found in that institution, supervised by a humane and kindly old physician who was now long in his grave. That time, too, constant insomnia produced by emotional disturbances had made her ill. And that time she had been far more sick than now. She had not recognized her family, and there was a fat little grey man hopping up and down on the table who kept getting the lamp caught between his legs. But as soon as she entered the institution she had been able to sleep. The fat grey man went away and a soothing peace came over her. After a period of barely two months, when she was about to be released from the institution, she had begged to be allowed to stay longer. But the kindly old superintendent had smiled, shaking his grey head, and said he could not justify keeping her there any longer because she was occupying the place of someone who was genuinely ill. It was precisely the memory of her peaceful, beneficial stay with the endearing old superintendent that had made her so willing to go to Hieronimus for help.

To Hieronimus! This man who had written a few articles that had created a stir and who gave lectures that interested the young medical students! Nothing else was known about him. Oh yes, he was also known to have poor digestion and a rather irritable disposition.

The next morning the professor made rounds, accompanied by a white-clad assistant.

When he arrived Else was walking back and forth in the little corridor outside her room. She heard his footsteps but didn't turn until she reached the end of the corridor.

"Good morning," said Hieronimus.

"Good morning," murmured Else.

"How are you feeling?"

"The same as usual." Else swished past him into the room and went over to the window, where she stood with her back to him.

"I understand Dr. Tvede was here yesterday," she heard the professor say out in the corridor.

"Yes," Nurse Stenberg answered.

"Did she make a scene?"

"No, there was no scene. I was sitting out here in the hall and it was very quiet. But Dr. Tvede was only there for a moment and when he left he said Mrs. Kant had been angry."

"Note that Mrs. Kant displayed anger toward Dr. Tvede," Professor Hieronimus cackled. Probably addressing the assistant, Else thought.

"You might have spared me that, Nurse Stenberg," Else said when rounds were over.

"Dr. Tvede asked me to say that. So I was obliged to do it."

"Is that really true? He asked you to do that?"

"You know I wouldn't have done it otherwise, dear Mrs. Kant." Nurse Stenberg's tone was mildly reproachful. "Do you think I would cause you any unpleasantness if I could help it?"

Else was speechless. Tvede, the man she had regarded so highly and who had been her friend. What did this mean? "Once you get on this ward, nobody pays any attention to what you say." Oh yes indeed, she was being watched and peered at like a strange animal.

Chapter 35

ELSE'S LETTER had struck Knut like a bombshell, scattering his thoughts in every direction. He'd had no idea that the situation was anything like that. He trembled with sympathy, and in his heart was the nagging fear that the whole business of putting her in the hospital had been a mistake. But in a case like this, he dared not act on his own. He went immediately with the letter to Dr. Tvede.

"What shall we do?" Knut asked, with the secret hope of seeing Tvede as uncertain and ready to give up the thing as he was himself.

"You have to bear up," Tvede replied gravely. "To interrupt the cure now can only do harm."

"But this continuous mental and physical suffering..."

"Yes, I don't understand why Hieronimus is keeping her on that ward. It's clearly not the right place."

"Or he's not the right man. I'm starting to think that he and Else have been fighting a battle of some kind, and Hieronimus has been getting the worst of it. He's keeping her in there to break her."

Tvede shook his head doubtfully. "Let's both write to the superintendent of St. Jørgen's," said Tvede. "She will have to do better there."

"Will you talk to Else? I'm not allowed to visit, and it probably wouldn't do any good anyhow."

"Yes."

That same day Tvede fell ill. He sent a message to Knut that it would be impossible for him to see Else for at least a couple of days. Knut felt the full misery of the postponement. He wrote a letter to Else. The veiled phrases might console her and at least it would be an answer before Else's deadline. But in spite of Knut's urgent request, the letter remained for some time in Hieronimus's pocket.

Finally on Sunday morning Knut received Hieronimus's confirmation that the transfer to St. Jørgen's would take place. His wife's condition, however, had worsened. She was very ill, and the visit he had promised before she moved would be very inadvisable. It could only result in a painful scene that would be harmful to her.

For the first time there was something friendly and expansive in the professor's tone.

"You don't need to put your wife in the private section of St. Jørgen's," he said in passing. "It's just used by rich people. The ward there corresponds to the private section here."

Knut thanked him for the information. He did not know at the time that it was wrong.

Chapter 36

Oh, what a long, long dreary Sunday. Else lay on the chaise longue most of the day, quiet, disconsolate, paralyzed.

In the afternoon Nurse Stenberg came and sat next to her, and started patting her hair and stroking her arm.

Suddenly Else said, "Will I be leaving soon?"

"Yes, Mrs. Kant," Nurse Stenberg said in a mild, affectionate voice. "Early tomorrow morning."

Else threw her arms around the nurse and wept.

"A little while ago the order came to prepare your things. A package from your home has also been sent."

"Your home" – the words pierced Else to the heart. She didn't have a home any longer.

"You mustn't be unhappy, Mrs. Kant," Nurse Stenberg said consolingly. "You won't be at St. Jørgen's long. Believe me."

"No," Else said dully. "Well, I won't have to see Hieronimus."

Then the countess came and sat and wept with her. She was just as disconsolate as Else.

The hours passed and the resident physician appeared in the evening.

"You see, my husband didn't come after all," Else said.

"Yes, I don't understand it."

"A man of his word, our Professor Hieronimus."

"Now we'll make rounds together," said the resident physician, putting his arm through Else's and accompanying her into the cells. All the good will and gratitude she had felt for the resident physician in the beginning

186

flooded back at that moment.

Bella Holm had been moved, and in her cell lay an old farm woman whose hip had been crushed by a kick from a horse. In a shrill, cracking falsetto, she wailed and complained about the hellhole she had been locked up in, and demanded to be sent home. She had to cook her husband's dinner.

"Put in a good word with the professor. You, lady, there!" she shouted after Else.

"She's come to the right person," Else said, and almost laughed.

သ

THE LAST MORNING had arrived and Else had packed her things. She wrote a hurried letter to Hieronimus in which she vented her contempt and indignation, making her accusations point by point. Finally, she promised the professor that as soon as she was released from St. Jørgen's she would hold him accountable for the way he had treated her. She signed herself, "Your sincere enemy, Else Kant."

She was just finishing the letter when the resident physician came in.

"May I speak to you alone for a moment?" Else asked. "And will you answer me just as you would answer a person who wasn't in a madhouse? Will you do that?" Else asked after the resident physician had closed the door.

"Yes," said the resident physician. "I will."

"Will you tell me then if you have ever observed any trace of insanity about me while I've been here?"

"No," the resident physician replied gravely.

"And in spite of that, you think it's right to send me to St. Jørgen's?"

"That's none of my business."

"Does a man have a legal right to lock his wife in an insane asylum against her will, simply because he and a physician say she's insane?"

"Yes. And vice versa."

"A system like that can easily be abused."

"Yes, it happens quite often," was the resident physician's reply.

"And I don't have any rights? I'm not permitted to speak to a lawyer or friend?"

"No, not when you are here. And the superintendent of St. Jørgen's can keep you there for years if he feels like it." There was a smile of triumph in the resident physician's eyes, as if he enjoyed the power held by the physicians.

"But he won't do that," he added a few moments later. "He's such a good-natured man."

"And is that what determines how long a patient is kept locked up – whether the superintendent is good-natured or not?"

The resident physician shrugged his shoulders.

"Well, that's all I wanted to ask. But I am letting myself be taken to St. Jørgen's under the most strenuous protest. You are my witness. Because it is wrong that I'm being sent to St. Jørgen's."

"Good-bye," said the resident physician, extending his hand. "What fine weather you have for your trip."

"I'd rather have foul weather," Else said.

"Such a pessimist. Always discontented."

"Can you truly not understand that bad weather would be more in harmony with my mood?"

"Oh yes. Naturally. Well, good-bye then."

"Good-bye," Else said, heartily shaking the resident physician's hand. "Many thanks for your kindness to me."

"Don't mention it. Good luck to you."

Then Else put on her coat and hat. She said good-bye to the countess and the nurses, kissed them all and thanked them for their kindness. She also went in to see the patients. Mrs. Syverts extended a limp hand in farewell and said a few bad-tempered words about this disgusting charade.

When they came into the quiet ward, Else asked about Granny, but Granny was in bed and time was running out.

Then the big double doors at the end of the quiet ward were unlocked. Else recognized the rattling keys from the first night when she had come here with Knut. She looked back down the long corridor, where some of the patients were seated on yellow chairs, among them Bella Holm, who kept her head bent over a large piece of knitting and looked ashamed. Suddenly Else was seized by a sadness that brought tears to her eyes. She was known here now, almost at home. Here she had suffered, and fought, and won. What lay ahead of her in the new place?

Nurse Stenberg accompanied her all the way out to the doorstep. Again Else thought about the night she and Knut had come this way. Twenty-five days she had been there. Twenty-five days that weighed on her like twenty five years.

In front of the doorstep was a carriage and two horses, with two attendants seated on the driver's box. Beside the carriage stood a friendly old woman, who was going to keep watch over Else on the long drive to St. Jørgen's.

When Else came out onto the steps, she turned to Nurse Stenberg and embraced her with heartfelt thanks for all her kindness. Then she climbed into the carriage, followed by the old woman.

The sun was shining brightly in the hospital's tidy courtyard. Else looked through the carriage window and thought with something like envy of Mrs. Fog and the woman who committed suicide, who had also been taken away from this place.

And then she was finally on the way to her new prison.

ST. JØRGEN'S

Chapter 1

HOW STRANGE IT WAS to be driven away like someone under arrest . . . Else kept turning her head from right to left, peering out through the carriage windows.

People were walking along the muddy March roads, free as the breeze in the lovely spring sunshine, thinking about nothing in particular. Trolleys, carriages, work carts, vehicles of every variety were moving to and fro in whatever direction they wanted. Only she was being transported to someplace she didn't want to go.

How many times had she read in the newspapers that the police had apprehended someone, put them in a carriage and driven off to the station, and not given it another thought? Now she was in the same position.

The same position? No, it was not at all the same. For people taken into custody by the police, there was law and justice: interrogation, acquittal or conviction. But for her? She now belonged to a caste for which society made no provisions.

Through the carriage window she caught a glimpse of an elderly gentleman, neat and tidy though poorly clothed, whom she had met in this same street many times before. He always walked with his head stooped forward and his hands clasped behind his back. From time to time he would stop, straighten his neck and stare straight ahead with eyes that saw nothing. And then he would move his lips silently and wag his head a little. Else had often observed him from a few steps away and thought that he was an unfortunate soul whom life had tormented and broken, but not embittered. For his eyes were so mild and lifeless.

As long as Hieronimus didn't get his hands on him! Hieronimus would, of course, immediately put an eccentric like that in a cell. And then the man would be finished for good. Because the poor soul surely didn't have the strength to bear even the physical torments of the Hieronimic Hell. Much less the mental anguish of knowing he'd been deprived of his freedom and locked up in a madhouse.

An eccentric like that...

Wasn't Hieronimus himself an eccentric? Else continued turning her head from side to side so she could look through the carriage windows. How distant and foreign the traffic in the streets seemed to her! Like a world she contemplated from someplace in another life.

Good Lord – why were these people plodding along, struggling and toiling like this? And why did they spur their horses on and drive them to exhaustion?

One fine day death would sink its claws in all of them. Or – a thousand times worse – they would be taken by the scruff of the neck and hauled away by a Hieronimus.

She tried to think about Knut and Tage, but couldn't. A vast and endless wasteland separated them from her. It was as if they no longer had anything to do with her. She had no one in the world anymore. There was only herself. Herself and ... Hieronimus.

For she carried him with her. The man and his conduct obsessed her, were wholly inside her; he lay upon her like an evil spirit, above, within and without.

She and Hieronimus. No one and nothing in the world except him and her.

Yet, as she sat peering out the carriage windows, she kept feeling her heart suddenly start to pound whenever she spotted a figure she thought was Knut. It started as soon as she drove across the hospital courtyard. Knut had to be standing there, to see her and nod to her before she was transported to her new prison. Or at the last, big gate. Or out on the street right next to the hospital. But he had not been anywhere.

This did not grieve her. She simply couldn't understand it.

Chapter 2

"You needn't be afraid," Else said, smiling at the friendly old woman on the opposite seat; she had watchful eyes and her hand rested on the door handle. "I'm not planning an escape."

"No," the woman said and nodded gently, her hand still in place. "It's just a habit of mine."

"Have you ridden out to St. Jørgen's with many others perhaps?"

"Oh yes, ma'am," the woman smiled and her face broke into tiny wrinkles. "For twenty-six years. My husband is the porter at the hospital, and this has been my post."

"For twenty-six years," Else repeated. "Then I can't understand why you are worried. Surely you must be used to dealing with lunatics."

"Oh yes," the woman nodded. "But they all behave differently. The calm ones are the craftiest." Her tiny black twinkling eyes looked warmly at Else, and an inscrutable smile played around her wrinkled lips.

"Well, you know what they say – nobody in the world is as crafty as a lunatic," Else replied, barely able to keep herself from laughing.

The woman blinked her eyes and nodded with the same inscrutable smile, staring unabashedly at Else's face. Her expression said: You won't fool me.

"Where are we now?" Else asked.

"On Kongeveien. The big old park is over there." The woman pointed out the left carriage window.

The big old park. Else had taken walks there with Knut on clear, warm summer days, and they had sat up on the lookout point, gazing down at the city. She had been so happy strolling there, because she was walking with Knut, and because there were a couple of little places in the big old park that reminded her of her native country.[8]

"Did the people you rode with ever try to escape?" Else asked.

"Oh my yes. Many times."

"But never successfully, I suppose."

"No. Because it's impossible of course. I'm right here – I used to be so quick on my feet that even if the patients ran fast ... And then there's an able fellow up on the box, as well as the driver. And besides, everyone you meet joins in on the hunt as soon as they hear it's a lunatic."

Yes, Else thought. Once you've been labelled a lunatic, there's no pardon.

"They were all caught, then, the ones who tried to escape?" Else continued.

"Yes indeed. All except two. Two in twenty-six years. That isn't many."

"How did they manage to escape? Tell me!"

"I don't know, ma'am, I honestly don't. They seemed to just sink into the earth. One had hidden in a field of rye, we later heard, and the other had jumped clear across the fence and gone headfirst into a pond."

"Those poor people." Else clasped her hands tightly and let out a deep sigh.

"Oh, it was the foolishness of insanity that drove them, after all," the woman remarked. "So it's hard to know what to think."

Else continued looking out the carriage windows. There were wide, rolling fields on all sides. The sky was blue, the sunshine golden, and on the horizon lay a delicate, purple-white haze; every now and then fantastic outlines of the forest's edge broke into view.

"My, but it's warm," Else loosened her fur coat. "Do you mind if we open the window a little?"

"Not in the least." The woman stood up and pulled the cord, so the window slid halfway down.

"Thank you," Else said. "I'll take out my crocheting and keep myself occupied. The time will pass more quickly then."

"How long is the trip to St. Jørgen's?" Else asked after she had crocheted in silence for a while.

"About five hours. But we'll stop and rest along the way."

"Why?"

"For the horses. And for madam to have some refreshment as well. Coffee and rolls. At a tavern midway between town and St. Jørgen's. Coffee will taste good," the woman nodded. She still sat with her hand firmly gripping the door handle.

That's where Knut will be, Else thought and a tremor went through her body. Oh, if she could just have this one demonstration that he shared in her suffering. That even though he hadn't done a thing after her letter of despair, he was nonetheless with her in his thoughts and in his sorrow. How could someone hand over a loved one to the discretion of strangers without at least once coming to see and hear for himself?

No, he would be standing outside the tavern, he would walk over, open the carriage door, and then . . .

Just think how undemanding she had become! Imagine being so moved by the thought that Knut would be there on her path of suffering, if only to see her and say the words that took all pain away.

Undemanding? No, it was not undemanding. The most important thing in life was having someone who shared in your sorrow as well as your happiness. And that was just what Knut had always done.

She lost herself in remembrance and contemplation of the past, and while her fingers were busily crocheting on the wide curtain lace, she became more and more convinced that Knut would be standing outside the tavern, halfway between town and St. Jørgen's, where they were going to stop and rest . . . What was this quiet, clicking sound that seemed to rock her deeper into her reverie and awaken a faint feeling of homey cheerfulness? Else lifted her head, which had been bent over her crocheting. The woman sat nestled into the corner of the carriage, her hands knitting away on something large and black. So she had settled back, and no longer feared that Else was contemplating escape. Else was so pleased at the experienced old woman's show of confidence that she could have kissed her.

"Perhaps you are cold," Else said. "Wouldn't you like my fur piece? I'm much too warm."

"Oh no, ma'am. I'm very snug sitting here. Thank you all the same."

"Please do," Else insisted. "I can see you are worried about the draft."
Else stood up and put the fur piece around the woman's shoulders. "Now
be good and keep it on," she entreated.

"Madam is much too kind," the woman smiled and shook her head.
"Well, all right, thank you very much."

"Do you have children?" Else asked a little later.

"Oh my yes," the woman answered, busily knitting. "We've had so
many, but the Lord has taken all of them but two."

"You poor thing. You have certainly been through a lot."

"Yes indeed," the woman said. "When the first one dies, you think you
can't bear it, but then when they're plucked from you one after another . . ." She laid her knitting on her lap and, taking a white cloth out of a
bag, she dried her eyes and blew her nose.

"And such wonderful, bright children . . ." The woman had once again
started to knit. "Anton had just turned seven – he said to his father the
evening he died: 'Father,' he said, 'I believe it is true that we get wings
when we die, because I can feel them growing on my shoulders.'"

"Did you know he was going to die when he said that?"

"Yes. Because we had watched the others of course. It was consumption. He died as quietly as a candle going out. I was sitting in the chair by
the bed and had nodded off – I'd been sitting up with him so many nights,
and I'm only human after all. Then I hear my husband snoring over on
the bed and I wake up, and when I look at the boy, he's cold and dead."
The woman once again put her knitting down and blew her nose.

"Didn't you wake your husband then?"

"No, heavens no. He was so tired from the day's toil and trouble, you
see, and Anton was the seventh one to die."

The seventh one to die, Else thought. One does get used to it then.
Even seeing one's children torn away by death. Well, she herself had
grown so used to the Hieronimic Hell that she had actually felt sad about
leaving it.

"I really can't imagine how you could ever get over seeing your children die," she said. "That must truly be the worst thing in the world."

"Well, I really don't know what I would say is the worst," the woman replied, shaking her head as she knitted intently. "Suppose your husband is seeing other women?" She bit her lips and bent her face deeper over her knitting. "We women are worn down by drudgery and childbirth, and the men ... they always want something to keep themselves amused. Then they come home to a tired, sulky, cross old woman." Again she took out her cloth and blew her nose.

"But still, there are many men who love their wives even if they are old and tired," Else said. "Aren't there?"

"Do you really believe that, ma'am?" The woman let her knitting fall into her lap and gave Else a searching look.

"Yes, I do. Because they have such good memories from the past. From the days when the wife was young and pretty and happy. And that binds a man and makes him see his wife with the eyes of youth."

"It sounds so beautiful, the way madam puts it." Small tears rolled down along the woman's nose and her thin lips quivered. "But when there aren't any good memories. When the wife has always been tired and miserable and cross and suspicious ... Oh my, I'm running on like this, because I can see madam is a person who understands."

A few minutes passed during which Else crocheted and the woman knitted. Then Else said, "So you've come to the conclusion that life is an evil?"

"A what?"

"Well, that life is so hateful and disgusting that it would be better never to have been born?"

The woman stopped knitting and considered for a minute. "No," she said, slowly shaking her head. "I simply can't imagine never having been born. In spite of everything, I've had so many distractions and, to tell the truth, adventures and joys in this life. And then there's my post. Who would have ridden with the lunatics, if I hadn't?"

"They would surely have have found someone else," Else said.

"Found someone else? Yes, but then it wouldn't have been me. All these years I've been riding back and forth. Dear me."

"Hasn't that been terribly difficult for you – I mean, haven't you felt awfully sorry for them?"

"For whom? For the lunatics... No, good Lord, they're people you don't really care about. And then they're so frightfully vulgar. I simply can't tell madam the kinds of words that come out of their mouths and the kinds of gestures they make."

Else felt more and more at ease in the friendly old woman's company. She would not have spoken this way if she had considered Else to be mad. But naturally she wasn't conscious of this. It happened completely instinctively.

"Yes, it must be awful to see and hear them," Else said. "But I would feel terribly sorry for them nonetheless."

"Oh, I don't know, ma'am. Creatures of that sort are more like a kind of animal."

Else took up her crocheting again and the woman knitted away. After a while Else said, "But the two children you still have, have things gone well for them?"

"I thank God for the ones he has taken," the woman answered darkly.

"So they're spared the sorrows of this earthly life, you mean."

"Yes indeed," the woman said and hastily looked up. "Take my son, now – he married a bad woman who has dragged him down so deep, so deep into unhappiness and depravity and brought sorrow and shame on us all."

"But perhaps he is happy with her nonetheless."

"Happy! Oh no, God help us," the woman took up her knitting again, "there's nothing but fighting and scenes between them all the time. She runs around with her old lovers, and there he sits."

"But surely he doesn't know about that."

"He most certainly does! But what difference does it make once a woman has charmed a man? Everytime we mention it he flies into a terrible rage. But every so often he comes crying to me, and when I put in a good word for her – trying to get on his good side, to tell the truth – he calls her the worst names and asks how I can be so simple as to defend a person like her."

"People are strange," Else said.

"Yes indeed," the woman exclaimed, giving Else a look of surprised assent. "Yes, aren't they strange," she went on thoughtfully. "Our only consolation is that the grave will soon take us all." The last words were uttered in a quivering voice.

"Yes, there is something consoling in the thought of death," Else remarked.

"Yes indeed! And to think how afraid of it we are at first. But after we've lived for a while, we feel more kindly toward it. And then of course, it's not just us and the ones we live with who are going to die, but all those who come after as well."

"Do you believe in an afterlife?" Else asked.

"Dear God, yes, I should say I do! We learn that at our mother's knee. But it's beyond my understanding."

"Would you like to live on after you're dead?"

"Oh no, indeed I wouldn't. As far as I'm concerned one life is enough. But you're not a respectable person, you know, if you don't believe in those passages. And good Lord – it certainly can't do any harm ..."

Else looked out at the fields where patches of snow were lying here and there. The sun was hidden behind the haze that had risen higher on the horizon, and the landscape had taken on raw and wintry tones.

"It seems a little chilly now," Else said.

"Yes indeed! Dear God, how sensible madam is. I was just thinking the same thing. We'll shut the window then. At any rate, we'll be there soon."

Chapter 3

ELSE ROLLED UP HER CROCHETING and put it in her sewing bag. Then she leaned back in the seat and closed her eyes. They were stopping at the tavern now, the carriage door was opening up, and suddenly Knut was standing in front of her . . .

Would Knut recognize right away that she wasn't insane? Understand from a single glance that it was an outrageous injustice to lock her up in a another madhouse?

No, he most certainly would not. He had blindly and resolutely believed in Hieronimus. So the mere sight of her and a few minute's conversation would probably not overturn his unshakable belief. After all, wasn't there something called the lunatic's lucid moment?

But then it would be better if he weren't there. Oh yes, yes, a thousand times better!

Besides, she was so hardened and embittered by his conduct toward her since the day he left her at the entrance to Ward Six, that she couldn't bring herself to make any attempt whatsoever to change his decision. In all likelihood, she would tell him exactly what she had told Hieronimus that time in the cell: Just let me stay here. The longer the better.

Oh God, no. If only he weren't there! The carriage stopped. The woman stood up and put her hand on Else's shoulder. "Here we are."

Else sat up straight.

At that moment the carriage door opened. Else gave a start. Thank God, the attendant was standing outside, not Knut.

The woman stepped out first, then held her hand out to Else who, a moment later, was standing on the road, shyly looking around. No Knut. Nothing to see except the wide, undulating fields and a glimpse of the forest's edge through the haze which was now grey and wet. Farms and buildings here and there, and close by to the right, a long, low structure; above its entrance, in large, white letters, the word "Inn." Directly across, a shed with the inscription "Travellers' Stable."

Else breathed a sigh of relief that Knut wasn't there, and in the next instant felt the disappointment like a nagging ache in her chest.

But he'd be sitting inside the inn. He would greet her warmly, take her by the hand and ask if he could speak with her. Once again she felt the same trembling sensation creeping through her body, and the fear of seeing him again came over her.

As the driver and the attendant began to unhitch the horses, the woman took Else by the arm and led her up the inn's low, stone steps into a damp and chilly room; against the wall running the length of the room was a counter with bottles on it and, on the opposite side, small tables and chairs. There were also tables and chairs in front of the two small windows. Pasted on the walls were notices and advertisements with large block letters and colored pictures of Tuborg bottles. A listless woman in a black, knitted vest stood behind the counter, her arms folded across her protruding stomach. The room smelled of gas, alcohol and coal, and the floor was strewn with sand.

No Knut here either.

The woman seated Else at one of the tables. Then she ordered two cups of coffee and pastry.

"Can't I have bread and butter instead?" Else asked. "I don't like pastry."

"Well, I don't know, ma'am. The regulations say pastry. But it probably doesn't make any difference."

Their order was brought right away by the listless woman.

Else watched the old woman greedily gulp down the scorching hot coffee from the thick, blue-rimmed cup. She herself had to blow on the coffee for a long time before she could start to drink it.

The door from the hallway opened quietly and a strange couple came in: a woman with a gaunt, greenish face, who was holding the arm of an ashen man in ragged clothes, with unruly tufts of hair sticking out around his sparsely stubbled face. The woman was wearing a pair of dilapidated men's boots, a short blue-checked cotton skirt, a black homespun jacket and a woolen scarf that completely covered her hair. One of the man's legs was wrapped in a dirty bandage from ankle to knee, and he had a pronounced limp; supported by his stick and the woman, he thumped over to one of the tables, where the woman helped him to sit down.

Else peeked at them. The two of them sat there, stiffly and silently, staring straight ahead.

The listless woman behind the counter went over to them carrying a lager and a schnapps glass in one hand, and in the other a bottle of liquor from which she filled the glass.

The man thrust stiff fingers into his tattered pocket and took out some copper coins which he handed to the innkeeper. He drank the schnapps and then lifted the beer to his mouth and emptied it in one swallow.

At that point he took a small pipe and a box of matches from his pants pocket. He poked his index finger in the pipe, looked at it for a minute and lit it. A hideous stench of burnt wood immediately filled the room.

Then he grabbed the stick that he had placed between his knees; whereupon the woman, who had been sitting the entire time as straight as a board, staring emptily into space, immediately rose, took him by the arm and helped him up from the chair. And without uttering a word they thumped out of the inn.

Else stood up and watched them through the window.

There they were, walking toward the road, the woman with the gaunt, greenish face dragging along the tattered, limping man.

"Who are those people?" Else asked the woman, who had come over right away and was standing beside her.

"Wayfarers, on their way to town. Most likely to look for work."

"But why didn't the woman get anything? Why did he drink everything himself?"

"Oh well, ma'am. The man is the most important, you know."

"But the poor woman! She was about to collapse from exhaustion and hunger."

"Yes indeed! But that's the way the world is, after all."

"How did you know that he wanted schnapps and lager?" Else turned to the innkeeper who had resumed her place behind the counter.

"What else would he want?" was the woman's sullen reply.

Just then a howl rang out. A narrow door in the wall behind the counter flew open, and a four-year-old boy came running in: "Mother, he's hitting my chickens!"

The listless woman picked the boy up in her arm, and with her knee sent him flying toward the door. The boy was seized by a fit of violent coughing accompanied by hollow hiccoughing noises. He doubled over and fell flat on his face, coughing and gasping for breath.

"He's having a convulsion," Else cried in terror to the woman who was standing there, calm and unperturbed.

"Oh, it's just this idiotic whooping cough." Grudgingly the woman lifted the boy up from the floor and carried him out.

"Wouldn't it be possible for me to go inside somewhere and freshen up a bit?" Else asked, wiping her fingers on a paper napkin.

"Yes, this way please." The old woman opened a door into a little room that contained a couple of beds and a washstand hung with a curtain of white shirting. A door, slightly ajar, gave onto a littered courtyard, and in a far corner a gate opened out onto wide, brown fields.

Muttering about the open door, the woman minced along right on Else's heels, never leaving her side. She held her nervously trembling hands slightly raised, as if she needed to be ready to pounce on something.

"Now you're worrying again," Else said as she dipped her fingers in the washbasin.

"Oh no, ma'am. But one can never know. And now my legs are so old and stiff. Years back my feet were as nimble as you please. A person had to be an early bird to run away from me," she smiled and gently shook her head.

"You needn't be suspicious of me," Else said. "It's quite unnecessary."

"Yes indeed ma'am. But I do have my post, you know. And it isn't very nice if something happens."

Chapter 4

ONCE AGAIN they were sitting in the carriage as it rolled away, the woman knitting and Else crocheting.

Well then, Knut would be at St. Jørgen's. That would be better, too. There in the tavern in those unpleasant surroundings ... Although at St. Jørgen's he probably wouldn't be allowed to see her. The tavern would at least have been a kind of neutral territory.

"Why exactly is madam going to St. Jørgen's?" the woman asked suddenly looking up from her knitting.

"I wish someone could tell me," Else answered with a feeble smile.

"But isn't madam's husband alive?"

"Yes. But Hieronimus is also alive."

"Yes indeed," the woman laughed quietly. "And he is a hard taskmaster."

"Well, he hasn't been easy to deal with. Can you imagine, he doesn't know the slightest thing about me and he just decided, without the least bit of concern ..." Else stopped suddenly and asked herself, What is the use of telling her this? Then she added with a sigh, "He's a strange man."

"Yes indeed. They're all different, ma'am. The one we had before Hieronimus was such a mild man. He let them go, just let them go when they weren't stark raving mad. And I haven't heard that things are any the worse for that. Indeed I haven't."

"Madam mustn't be so downcast," the woman continued by and by. "Everything will be fine, wait and see."

Everything will be fine, Else thought. Well, she'd escaped from Hieronimus with her life, of course. But that was a miracle and miracles didn't happen every day. Suppose the superintendent at St. Jørgen's was like Hieronimus – a shudder went through her and she felt her face stiffen. True enough, the resident physician in Ward Six had said the superintendent was so "good-natured." But hadn't rumors also circulated about Hieronimus's friendly disposition and insight?

"Naturally I'll be put in a cell again," she said with a trembling voice, involuntarily reaching toward the woman.

"Dear me no, madam won't be put in a cell." The woman squeezed Else's hands warmly. "Rest assured. Rest assured."

"But how can you know that?" Else bowed her head and cried over the woman's hands.

"How can I know that? What would be the good of putting a person like madam in a cell? Calm yourself now."

"Yes, but in Hieronimus's ward – I went down there with no idea that I'd be in a cell or surrounded by lunatics."

"Yes, Hieronimus's ward – that's in a category of its own."

"Isn't the superintendent at St. Jørgen's the same?"

"Dear me no, no, ma'am! He's so even-tempered and friendly, so good and kind. He's not one to scold, or make himself mysterious, or put on airs. He would never put madam in a cell!" The woman freed her hands and stroked Else's arms affectionately.

Else dried her eyes and took up her crocheting again.

Ah well. As long as she wasn't put in a cell, it might be bearable. Not that it mattered – she no longer feared losing her reason, even if she were put in a cell. She was used to it, after all, and should be capable of holding her own. But she so dreaded all the horror and suffering she would see and be a part of there. And even if she kept her reason, her soul would be damaged beyond repair. She felt such consuming anger at the way she was being treated. What would become of her in the end? Her inner self would be ravaged, turned to rubble and ashes as if by a fire storm.

"There's the old cathedral," the woman said, pointing out the right-hand window.

"So we'll probably be there soon," Else said dully; she cautiously shifted her position on the seat, and did not look at the old cathedral.

"Yes. In ten minutes."

They drove through a hilly, winding street with small, oddly shaped houses on either side. Then they came out on a country road. Through the carriage window Else saw, off in the distance, an extensive complex of light-colored buildings, the most distant of which lay higher up as if on terraces. "Is that St. Jørgen's?" she asked.

"Yes. That is St. Jørgen's."

A flood of emotion welled up in Else's breast and threatened to spill from her lips in a mindless shriek. She clenched her teeth and covered her face with her hands.

Would it be possible to jump out of the carriage? Flee from this brutal violation? Could she actually be as crafty as a lunatic?

She peeked through her fingers at the woman, who was calmly winding yarn around her rolled-up knitting. What if she quickly threw open the door, jumped out, ran like a madwoman and threw herself on her face in a ditch. She felt a quivering, tingling sensation throughout her body, but she didn't move.

Oh, the agonies she would have to go through again, with new doctors, new nurses and new lunatics. She would be in there with them, a person who had been committed and abandoned, someone who had no one, no one but herself and Hieronimus.

No, no, no, she couldn't bear it! Death was preferable to this. She took her hands from her face and sat up with a jerk.

"Well, my dear, we'll soon be there." As if to quiet her, the woman laid her hand on Else's arm.

Else looked at her with an expression full of pain and wonder. How calmly and matter-of-factly she accepted the idea that a fellow human being who had committed no crime should be put in prison against her will, held under lock and key at a place inhabited only by lunatics.

Else continued to look at the woman, and while she looked everything inside her grew calm. This was how life and people were. Life ran its course, never heeding how many trampled and bleeding souls it left in its wake. And people watched indifferently. They had all they could manage with their own affairs.

Yield to the inevitable. Yield and be thankful that it wasn't any worse. If she leapt out of the carriage now, there would be no rye field for her to hide in, no pond to jump into, and so the friendly old woman would catch her and think she had new evidence of how well lunatics could dissemble.

No, there was nothing to do. Yield. Meekly bow her head.

But to be brought down by a man like Hieronimus! That was miserable beyond words!

Now they were on a long, steady incline. There were young, naked trees separated by big spaces on either side and on top of the hill a long, low, gleaming white brick fence with a tall, open entrance gate in the middle. Behind that an impressive two-story building with a tower and wings, and behind that, higher up and to the sides, many large buildings of various shapes and sizes, surrounded by gardens and open spaces. And all around an expanse of forest and hills. It was like a whole little world of its own.

Suddenly Else jerked herself back in the carriage.

"Was that someone madam knew?" the woman asked, having seen a gentleman on the road curiously peeking through the carriage window.

"Yes, one of my husband's relatives – he works in the office at St. Jørgen's."

"Madam shouldn't pay any mind to that. All kinds of people will end up here one fine day. Today me, tomorrow you."

Else just shook her head. She felt as if there were a plug in her throat.

"Madam will soon be free and unfettered again. Believe me."

Chapter 5

THEY DROVE into a large archway, and it was as if darkness fell outside the windows. At that moment the carriage stopped.

"So," the woman said. "We're here now."

The carriage door opened and Else and the woman stepped out and climbed some steps. A moment later they were standing in an oblong waiting room with only one window; no one was there.

"Why am I here?" Else asked.

"The superintendent will be here right away."

Else walked slowly back and forth across the room. Knut was most certainly here, but for the time being he was keeping out of sight. If only the superintendent would come! But he was probably making arrangements with Knut right now.

"Madam should sit down." The woman had seated herself at the table in front of the window. "It makes a better impression."

"I can't," Else answered. Suddenly stopping, she smiled at the woman and said, "I have to try, after all, to act a little bit like a lunatic. What do you think, should I start making faces? Or should I answer 'bla, bla, bla' to everything he says?"

Shaking her head, the woman laughed soundlessly; her shoulders shook and her eyes disappeared completely. Then the door behind her opened quickly. Else spun around and saw coming toward her a tall, broad-shouldered and powerfully built gentleman in his forties; he held himself erect, his shoulders slightly back. Extending his hand to Else, he said, with a smile that brushed across her like a breath of calm and trust,

"I know that you have come here under protest."

"Are you the superintendent?" Else asked, examining his large, tan face with its dark moustache and alert eyes whose curious, keenly observant gaze seemed to take her captive and hold her fast.

"Yes, I'm afraid so. But let's not start by being too angry."

"Not at you," Else answered.

The superintendent nodded and laughed, a short sympathetic laugh, and the smile that lit up his dark eyes made his appearance extremely captivating.

"And presumably you don't find that strange," Else continued, "since you know that I have come here against my will and, in my opinion, without reasonable grounds. Is there anything wrong with my mental state?" She turned to the woman, who was looking very interested as she sat smiling and nodding.

"Not in the least! But the superintendent will figure it out, like I told madam earlier."

"Here's Nurse Schrader, the nursing supervisor at the sanatorium." The superintendent turned toward her as she entered, a tall, slender woman with shiny brown hair that was parted in the middle and combed smoothly down along her temples. Her eyes were dark and intelligent and she gave the impression of being very neat and orderly.

Nurse Schrader greeted Else without smiling and appraised her with clear and penetrating eyes.

"Come with me and I'll show you around." The superintendent went toward the door.

"Good-bye then," Else said and held out her hand to the friendly old woman who had stood up and curtsied. "Thanks for your good company during the trip."

"Oh, not at all."

"Please say hello to Nurse Stenberg and all the nurses, and tell them that I've been calm and well-behaved during the trip."

"Yes indeed. And good and sweet and friendly," the woman added with her sunniest smile as she curtsied once again.

Else followed the superintendent, who quickly left the room and

descended the short flight of steps in front of which the carriage had earlier come to a stop. Then they walked across the archway and through a
door, opened by a porter, and came in on a landing leading up a wide
and well-lit staircase; decorating the landing was a marble bust on a dark,
inscribed pedestal. They walked up the stairs to a spacious vestibule; the
doctor opened a door and they found themselves in a wide and very long
corridor with many high windows, a couple of small tables and chairs, a
huge baseburner, many doors, and a carpet runner on the floor. Else was
constantly on the lookout for Knut.

"It's light and spacious here," the superintendent said, stopping in front
of one of the windows. "Down there is the garden and farther away the
park. The view is pretty and cheerful. A person can be happy here. Don't
you think?"

"If one comes here voluntarily." Else stood next to the superintendent
and stared at a row of windows in the side wing. From one of these windows Knut would see her, if he were in there. And he had to be there.

"Very seldom does anyone come here voluntarily," the superintendent
said. "You shouldn't even think about that."

"But then a person should be crazy, or at least mentally disturbed. And
I am neither."

"So much the better."

"Because this is a madhouse, of course," Else continued.

"An asylum, if you please."

"A madhouse," Else said energetically.

"An asylum," the superintendent repeated.

"A madhouse!"

"Oh come, come. Let's not start squabbling right away." The superintendent laughed again – the same short, charming laugh. "We'll be nice
to you. Your husband has written a long letter to me."

"Don't speak about my husband," Else said vehemently.

"You have no reason to be angry at your husband. I can assure you of
that."

"Oh yes, I suppose you know all about that," Else said, smiling bitterly.

"Yes, indeed I do."

"I suppose I have no reason to be angry with Mr. Hieronimus either?"

"Don't you like him?"

"Like him?" Else laughed. "I love him from the bottom of my heart. I love him so much that I carry him with me incessantly, constantly, wherever I go. Might I ask, if you know the gentleman?"

"I do indeed. He's an excellent man. More capable and outstanding in his research than anyone else in the country."

"Yes, I know that. That's why I went to him," Else said with a sound resembling laughter.

"Now I'll show you to your room." The superintendent turned away from the window and, with Else behind him, walked down the long corridor, through an open double door into a short hallway that formed a right angle with the long corridor. There was a high window and on the wall opposite the window, three doors spaced close together. There were tables and chairs, a couple of closets, and on the far wall a double door.

"You were supposed to have been on the ward," the superintendent remarked, "but it seemed to me ... So I got this for you." He opened the middle of the three doors and they stepped into an oblong room with a carpet on the floor and a double set of curtains. Along the wall and close to the window was a small sofa with an oval table, and the room was so narrow that the chair on the other side of the table had to stand sideways up against the wall in order to fit. There was a bed and a washstand against the same wall as the sofa, and along the other wall, a chest of drawers, a rocking chair, and a tiny little round table with simple crossed legs. A gas lamp hung from the ceiling.

"This isn't very luxurious," the superintendent continued, "but habitable nonetheless. Don't you think?"

Else nodded, thinking that the friendly old woman had been right after all. Thank God. This wasn't a cell.

"Making these arrangements was a bit difficult, because we're overcrowded. But then we got the lady in here to share a room with another lady, and that's how we were able to do it. Because the ward is, well ..." The superintendent squeezed one eye shut and wrinkled his nose.

"Thank you," Else said. "That was kind of you."

"Come along and I'll show you the rest of the place right away." The superintendent left the room and Else followed in her long, buttoned-up fur coat, the boa over her shoulders, her hat still on.

"You'll see, you'll soon start to feel at home here," the superintendent chatted away as they quickly walked back through the long corridor and down a wide and comfortable, slightly creaking stairway that descended from the corridor.

It looked exactly the same as upstairs. A long, wide corridor with a carpet runner, chairs and tables, many windows on the one wall, and many doors on the other.

"Here is the living room." They were standing in a spacious room furnished with lots of large plants on the floor over by a wide, curtained window; there were arm chairs, a piano, a round table with newspapers and illustrated magazines, framed pictures on the walls, and a gas chandelier hanging from the ceiling.

"And here is the dining room." It was a room with a long table and many chairs along the walls.

"It is nice here," Else said. "But I don't want to be down here with the others. I would like to have my food brought up to my room."

"All right, to begin with. Later on you'll join the others, I expect."

"Later on? Am I going to stay here for a long time?"

"Well, if you're not well-behaved and good, you'll be here for a long time," the superintendent said, smiling. In the midst of her unending anguish, Else felt secure in this man's hands. The resident physician had been right. The superintendent was a kind human being. And an honorable one. Else could see that by looking at him. His figure reminded her of a knight from the Middle Ages and his firm and handsome hand seemed created to grip the hilt of a sword. And what was best and most reassuring: He was the diametric opposite of Hieronimus.

"Thank God, you're not the least bit like Hieronimus," the words suddenly slipped out of her mouth.

"Come now, are you going on about your Hieronimus again!"

"Yes, I simply can not think about anything else." They had gone back upstairs and were once again on the long corridor. "Superintendent, if you knew how he has treated me. It is so inconceivable that I never would have believed it if I hadn't experienced it myself."

"All mental patients are angry at their doctors," the superintendent commented.

"No," Else said. "Not all of them, by any means. I know that very well. Besides, I'm telling you that I was not and am not mentally ill."

"Your husband must have had a different opinion since he brought you to Hieronimus."

Else felt herself grow warm. Was she going to hear, once again, the story of how she had been brought there?

"You are mistaken," she said curtly and, walking beside the superintendent back to her room, she told him how it had all come about and what she had experienced on Ward Six.

"Yes, I know all about that, Mrs. Kant." The superintendent stood still in the middle of the floor, two fingers of his right hand stuck inside the front of his vest. "It cannot be otherwise on Ward Six. Hieronimus is not to blame for that."

"Who is to blame then? Didn't he admit me, decide that it was a suitable place for me to stay, keep me there by force in spite of all my pleas and suffering, and forbid my closest family to visit me?"

The superintendent shrugged his shoulders. "There, there, let's not talk about Hieronimus. What about your husband, why are you angry at him?"

Else explained why she was angry at him.

"Your husband has acted out of love and concern for you," the superintendent said earnestly. "You must take that as a given."

"Such splendid concern! Do me the favor, would you, of not mentioning my husband."

"Get yourself settled in now." The superintendent nodded good-bye.

Chapter 6

When else had taken off her coat, a pale and cheerful girl in a blue cotton dress and white apron came in. She said a friendly hello, placed a tray with dinner on the table and then left again.

Else started to eat. It was fruit soup and veal roast. She must have been very hungry because even the fruit soup was tolerable, and she finished everything.

A little while later Nurse Schrader brought coffee. She sat down to talk for a couple of minutes. There was something stiff and guarded about her, and her intelligent, penetrating eyes regarded Else searchingly, somewhat coldly.

Later, when the pale, cheerful girl, whose name was Maren, had removed the trays, Else sat down with her crocheting in the rocking chair by the little round table.

So Knut had not been here.

Thank goodness, this really was a quiet place. She hadn't seen or heard any sign of the patients. And the superintendent was so sympathetic and agreeable. That was, at least, one stroke of luck in all this misfortune.

But nonetheless, she was locked up for an indefinite length of time, among people with varying degrees of madness. And ahead, a hopeless, enervating struggle to assert herself and exonerate herself from blame. Among strangers, utterly new and unfamiliar people. Oh, if only she had Nurse Stenberg and the other nurses!

⁊

SUDDENLY there was an inarticulate scream from one of the adjoining rooms, and then a weird and vociferous gabbling, interrupted by piercing shrieks and intermittent gasping for air. It sounded like the shrieks and utterances of a person with a cleft palate.

Else gave a start. The crocheting dropped to her lap and she sat and listened, trying in vain to find some meaning in the words streaming out of there. They went on and on.

Then a voice started speaking from the room on the other side, loudly and angrily, accompanied by sounds like hands clapping and thunderous blows on tables and walls. Else leaned her head forward to listen and discovered that the person in there was raving in English.[9]

"God damn these pigs, these beasts! I shall bruise you all together! I wish to see you hanged, burned! I wish to see your brains braised, and I shall walk upon your bloody faces, walk with my heels, and I shall tear you into pieces, and throw your torn limbs through the windows, into the water, no! into the burning flaming hell itself, you damned pigs and beasts and robbers and rascals!" The voice grew wilder and wilder, more and more strident; it ended in a roar and some crashing blows, and then, after a few minutes pause, started up again.

Else bent forward and cried. This was just like Ward Six. And the demented souls on either side went on and on.

Oh, it was torture to be surrounded by lunatics! These agonizing conditions assailed her soul like lashes of a whip. How could people condemn their fellow human beings to this? Once again, as when she was on Ward Six, she wrung her hands and asked herself what crime she had committed to justify being tormented so terribly. No calm, no rest. Only fear, anxiety and resentment. And sleep – the sleep that her brain and whole body so desperately needed! No, she wouldn't be able to sleep here either.

"Es ist bestimmt im Gottes Rath,
Dass ich zu Grunde gehe" [10]

She sat up, dried her face and leaned back in the chair. *"Es ist bestimmt im Gottes Rath"* – what was it she was recalling, where did those words come from? She didn't remember and didn't feel like pursuing it. Nor was she capable of gathering her thoughts amid continuous roars and screams from the rooms on either side of her.

"Some vessels are made unto honor, others unto dishonor." Ah well, in the name of God – she was one of those vessels made unto dishonor. She had been caught and put in chains. Chains that she could not break. So she was destined to perish. For never, never! would she calmly and voluntarily submit herself to this! This nagging and defiant resentment would spread itself over the entirety of her inner life, ever more stifling, darkening her reason and making her thoughts circle continually and forever around one and the same thing. So she would fall apart in the end and Hieronimus, bearing the palm, would say, "There you see, I was right! She is mad and will never be otherwise."

The door slowly opened, and an old, haggard face with grey hair neatly combed and done up, and a funny black cap perched on top, peeked warily in, looking around in all directions. Then through the crack in the doorway slipped a shrunken little woman in felt slippers, wrapped in a dark shawl with fringe that reached down to the edge of her short petticoat. She moved over toward Else, slowly and stealthily, and said in a squeaky, tearful voice, "Well, so you're the new patient."

"Who are you?" Else asked.

"Oh God, oh my God," squeaked the weepy voice. "My son was here the other day and I pleaded with him that I had to leave this place. But it's no use. No, it's no use."

Else looked at her. Her face aroused absolutely no sympathy. It was as if every trace of goodness and kindness in these features had been wiped out and was gone. The thin blond eyebrows were arched at sharp angles, and the sole expression in the small cloudy grey eyes, in which the pupils seemed to be permanently turned toward the center, was one of peevish despondency. The mouth was completely without lips, and the long protruding chin was like an impertinent question mark.

"What is your name?" Else repeated.

"It doesn't matter what your name is in here," came the whimpering response. "But anyway, my name is Mrs. Seneke, and I'm seventy-six years old."

"Who are those people!" Else exclaimed anxiously sitting up in her chair. Her neighbors were still at it, and now one of them had started stomping on the floor in a violent rage.

"Oh dear God, that's Miss Hall," whined Mrs. Seneke. "But why should she be locked up? She was so sweet and good today when I looked in on her. God knows she was."

"Is she English?"

"No, but she'd rather speak English than Danish. Well, of course I don't understand any of it."

"I'm so afraid of her," Else whispered.

"There's no need for you to be. She is so kind, God knows she is. But in a place like this – you should see how the maids treat us."

"There was one who brought me dinner – Maren – she looked so sweet."

"Sweet – sweet, you say?" Mrs. Seneke's mouth twisted to a grimace and she gave a little snort. "Just wait and you'll see how sweet she is. Maren? She is the devil incarnate, and the others are too. But they just follow the ones on top. Go along with everything. So you can't really expect anything else. Dear God, dear God! To think of ending up here in your old age. But there's no consolation. Not the slightest bit. No one understands you..." Mrs. Seneke pulled the dark shawl more tightly around herself and slunk back toward the door. Then she turned around and came back. "Don't say that I've been in your room," she sqeaked imploringly. "For God's sake, don't tell."

"No," Else said. "But why should it matter?"

"Oh, you've no idea," Mrs. Seneke had moved very close to Else and she clutched her hand: "Promise me you won't say anything."

Else promised.

"You don't know," Mrs. Seneke angrily waved her skinny yellow hand. "They're utter devils, every one of them. Utter devils," she kept on muttering as she silently slipped out of the room.

Else sat bolt upright in the rocking chair, listening in anguish to her neighbors' racket which now seemed to be abating. Tears rolled slowly down her cheeks.

"Well now, Mrs. Kant, why so despondent?" The superintendent came in and sat down on the sofa across from Else.

"One of them is stone deaf," the superintendent continued in response to Else's complaint. "Mrs. Henderson, poor thing. A good and decent person. Just talks to herself."

"But these shrieks, listen!"

"She's calling Frants. That's her husband. And the other one is angry."

"At whom?"

"At me, mostly," the superintendent answered with the short laugh that was so becoming to him. "That is her illness."

"Just as long as they don't come in here." Highly agitated, Else rocked back and forth in her chair.

"Of course not. Though they may very well disturb you somewhat. But there wasn't any other room." His last words sounded apologetic.

"Why didn't you write to say you didn't have room for me then?"

"Then you would have had to stay with Hieronimus even longer." The superintendent looked at Else with his quick, keen gaze in which she now perceived a roguish glint.

His remark gave Else the chance to bring up Hieronimus again. The superintendent was evasive and tried to steer the conversation to other topics, but Else kept coming back to the same thing.

"Let's not talk any more about Hieronimus," the superintendent finally exclaimed. "It bores me!" His tone was firm, but there was a smile in the corner of his eye.

"Yes, of course. I can certainly understand that." Else stood up and paced the narrow floor. "But why won't you listen to me and say something – acknowledge that what I'm saying is true. If you did that, I could probably be finished with this someday."

"Your only thought should be that you are not with Hieronimus, but here with us, people who want to be kind and good to you. Don't you believe we want that?"

"Yes of course," Else answered sitting down again. "But what good does that do? I'm still a person who's been locked up, and that's what I'll remain."

"You mustn't feel that you're locked up here. If you don't like having the door locked, we'll unlock it. The same with the shutters on the windows, and the door on the tile stove. Everything will be the way you want it. If you'd like to have the gas burning at night, we'll let it burn! We want to do everything we can to make you happy."

"Thank you very much," Else said. "I would appreciate all of that."

"And my newspaper – you can have it the instant it comes; I don't have time to read it until later in the day anyway."

Else thanked him again.

"So, you'll be good and behave yourself, all right? And give me a message for your husband when I go into town on Friday?"

"No," Else said severely.

"Well, well, there's plenty of time before Friday. Perhaps you'll change your mind."

"You don't know me," Else mumbled. "Nor do you know what has happened."

"I know that your husband deserves a greeting."

Else stared straight ahead. It had suddenly occurred to her that Knut was here after all, and that the superintendent's talk was leading up to his appearance. In the letter she sent from Ward Six she had begged to speak to him just once before he committed her to the new prison. How could he deny her that? Even if she were no more to him than the most insignificant of his fellow creatures? No, he must be here. Why didn't the superintendent say anything? She couldn't ask.

"What are you thinking about so intently, Mrs. Kant?"

Else regained her composure and drew a breath. Then she said, "What I'm going to write about Hieronimus when I finally get out of here!"

"Write – you're going to write about him?"

"I most certainly am!"

"You shouldn't do that, Mrs. Kant. The only one to suffer will be yourself." There was a hint of both superiority and compassion in the superintendent's tone of voice.

"Only death can keep me from doing it," Else replied.

"What do tales like that accomplish?" the superintendent went on with his friendly admonishment. "The author becomes the butt of ridicule or, in the best case, the object of pity."

"I can bear that pity."

"There have been so many other cases, which you know about, I'm sure. An authority like Hieronimus is not brought down by that kind of assault. For Hieronimus and all the rest of us it will just be entertaining reading, but for you the consequences will be deadly serious."

"You may just as well ask the rain to stop falling or the river to change course and run up the mountain," Else said calmly.

"Ah yes, you and your countrymen . . ." the superintendent laughed, "obstinate and hot-headed, isn't that right, Mrs. Kant?"

"Yes, and thank God for that. I'm certainly obstinate and hot-headed enough."

"Well, I'll say good night, Mrs. Kant. How have you been sleeping? Do they usually give you chloral?"

"On Ward Six they gave me huge amounts. But I would rather not take it – I don't sleep anyway."

Chapter 7

So that's how things stood after all. Knut had not been there.

"Here you are." Maren brought Else her supper.

"Can't you ask them to be quiet?" Else asked, pointing in both directions.

"It doesn't do any good," smiled the pale, good-natured Maren. "And they don't do any harm either. You needn't be afraid."

"Are they quite mad?"

"Oh my no, they're not mad," Maren answered hesitantly as she moved toward the door.

"Yes, but they surely don't have all their faculties?"

"Not quite all of them," Maren said with the same hesitant intonation, and with an expression that was half embarrassed, half reluctant. "But nobody does in here, you know." She glanced at Else with a strange smile, and quickly slipped out.

"Nobody does in here." No, of course. And that was the reason proper little Maren didn't want to get involved with her. How could she go on talking and asking questions like any other person, forgetting that she was supposed to be insane? As Else ate her supper, tears dripped into her tea and fell on the buttered bread, slices so thick it seemed they were intended for hungry schoolboys.

She was soon finished eating. She shoved the tray away, and took up her crocheting again. The tormenting thoughts seemed to have less effect when she had something in her hands.

There was a knock on the door and a tall young man stepped in.

"Good evening," he greeted her. "My name is Vibe and I'm the resident physician here."

Else stood up and extended her hand. The man had a pale, beardless face, sandy hair and good, gentle eyes. Else was agreeably impressed by the air of refinement that pervaded his entire being.

Dr. Vibe spoke of the long, boring trip in the carriage and expressed his pleasure that the weather had been nice; finally, he hoped that she would be relatively content at St. Jørgen's.

"My stay in Ward Six was good preparation, at any rate," Else answered, starting in on Hieronimus.

Like the superintendent, Dr. Vibe tried to get her to talk about other things, but he met with only momentary success. Dr. Vibe listened politely, but made no reply.

"Now I'm going to stop," Else said at last, with a dismissive gesture. "It certainly can't be pleasant hearing about this."

"Oh," Dr. Vibe smiled sympathetically, and his expression said: You should forget about all that.

"But I can't," she exclaimed, standing up. "I have to think about him, and I have to talk about him." She sat down again.

"In time you'll put it behind you, you'll see," Dr. Vibe consoled.

"Yes, God willing," Else said. "Not while I'm in here, though. It's *his* doing that I'm here, you know. How can a person do such a thing and go unpunished! And on top of that, the way he's treated me – mocking me, taking me for a liar, a criminal – Oh dear, now I'm off again." She put her hand over her mouth and shook her head.

"If you'd like to read my newspaper, I'll send it up to you every day as soon as it comes. There are papers delivered to the sanatorium as well, but there are already so many who want to read those."

Else expressed her thanks and told him the superintendent had also promised to send along his newspaper. "This certainly is a very different place than where I've come from," she added, smiling.

"As far as talking about Hieronimus is concerned, I'll do better, I will," Else continued as she shook Dr. Vibe's hand and said good night.

But when Nurse Schrader looked in on her evening rounds, Else had already forgotten her promise and once again started talking about Hieronimus.

Later Maren came and announced that it was time for bed. Else immediately put her crocheting away and undressed. After she was in bed, Maren brought her chloral and turned down the gas a little, remarking that the superintendent had told them not to turn off the gas in Else's room without her permission.

"Do you turn off the gas in other people's rooms?" Else asked.

"Yes. All the others sleep in the dark."

"Aren't they afraid?"

"They don't have the sense to be."

"What about these two, Mrs. Henderson and Miss Hall, or whatever they're called – do you think they'll be quiet tonight?"

"Yes, for a while anyway. Good night, Mrs. Kant."

Good night, Else thought. Good night? How long would it be, she wondered, until she had a good night? Would she ever again have one? Or, in a larger sense, would she ever again be entirely human after all this? Oh, these anguished thoughts and this weight upon her chest, these heavy sighs forcing their way up from inside her every minute. And then the commotion all around her. From Mrs. Henderson's room came a sound like a dog snapping at flies, interspersed with inarticulate sounds that resembled talk, and a periodic howl that the superintendent had said was a call for Frants. It had actually quieted down somewhat, the sound was fainter at times, as if it were dying away. Miss Hall was also less violent, thank goodness. Oh no, Miss Hall was starting to sing, but her voice wasn't as shrill and piercing as when she had been raving before.

Still, why let it cause her so much pain and anguish? She was used to things a thousand times worse. She shuddered, remembering what she had experienced on Ward Six; involuntarily folding her hands she mumbled, "Thank God that's over, at least."

Now Miss Hall was humming an English lullaby and Else's thoughts immediately flew to Tage, whom she had thought about only vaguely and half-consciously throughout the day.

Now he lay sleeping in his little bed at home, unaware of the way his mother was being treated. Not knowing the tears of grief she had cried for him and herself. Would she ever get to see him again? And if so, under what sort of circumstances. Else cried and cried, but the tears brought no relief.

"I thank God for the little ones he has taken," the friendly old woman in the carriage had said, when the talk had turned to her children. Oh yes, Else understood at that moment how a mother could have such thoughts. If Tage were dead now, she wouldn't be worrying and longing for him; she wouldn't feel such a crushing burden on her chest. Yes, there was a kind of solace in knowing with certainty that one's child would not have to experience any of the evil that life on earth could bring.

What if now, here in St. Jørgen's, she heard that Tage was dead – would it seem like a relief? She saw him lying in his little casket in a white nightgown, a bouquet of wild chamomile between his little fingers, which, even in death, were round and chubby; and suddenly it was as if something snapped inside her. She sat bolt upright in bed and sobbed, clenching her handkerchief between her teeth.

No, no, no! Tage must not die! She couldn't bear the sight of his sweet eyes, closed for eternity, with dark circles and swollen yellow lids; his plump, smiling child's mouth ajar, small dark blotches on his upper lip; his perky little nose, pointed and bluish-white, the nostrils sunken; his curly hair plastered against his wide forehead, damp and lifeless. That was how her little brother had looked when he died of croup and was lying in a casket strewn with flowers. How vividly she remembered, had always remembered that sight! When they covered him with an embroidered sheet and led her out of the living room and she could hear from the side room the hollow blows of the hammer on the coffin lid, she had cried – a girl of fourteen – cried as if she believed, even hoped, that she could cry herself to death, and she had been certain that she would never again have a happy moment. And her sorrow consumed her for a long, long time, an entire year. She had gone to the cemetery every day with flowers for the grave, and many years later the memory of her little brother's face, which through death had undergone such a ghastly transformation, could suddenly give rise to such pain, that she had to rush away from whomever she was with, hide away somewhere, and cry. Yes, to this day it could pierce her heart when some coincidence or other made her think about it.

No, no, Tage must not die! Anything but that. She'd pay any ransom, gladly consent to be imprisoned for the rest of her life to keep him from being nailed into that cold, black coffin. Yes, she'd even stay in a cell with lunatics, become the maddest of them all. "A vessel made unto dishonor."

Her handkerchief was completely soaked with tears. She quietly crept out of bed and found a new one in her valise.

When she again lay back on her pillow, she felt a sense of calm within her. And then she noticed there was no more noise coming from her neighbors. They had been quiet a long time, she now realized.

She turned toward the wall with a yearning desire to fall asleep. Perhaps sleep would come after all. If only for an hour or two. She was so tired, so desperately tired.

Chapter 8

BUT ELSE'S HOPE FOR SLEEP was not fulfilled. After a few minutes, she felt a twinge in her sore tooth and then a piercing, throbbing pain set in.

She pulled the wool blanket up over her cheek, breathed into it to make it warm and lay very still.

But the pain only got worse. Finally she sat up, and holding her head in her hands, moaned softly.

She could thank that ogre Hieronimus for this too. If he had let her see a dentist, she would have at least been spared this pain.

Wasn't there something called abuse of authority, and weren't there laws against that sort of thing? If they existed, Hieronimus should be punished.

"You really shouldn't be sorry you've got a toothache." That had been the truly comforting consolation the resident physician on Ward Six had offered her. She was reminded of the anecdote about the Yankee who was acquitted by the jury after he had been accused of killing a man who had told him, while he was groaning from the terrible pain of a toothache, "You should just stop thinking about it."

She might possibly have had a couple hours of sleep, but now that she was in such terrible, senseless pain... Rocking her head back and forth, she continued to moan.

Then the door opened silently, and in glided an enormously tall, thin female figure; her head was wrapped in a black kerchief, and an angular, wax-yellow face jutted out from beneath the scarf. A bunch of keys hung at her side, and a lamp dangling on a cord glowed at the edge of her long apron. As the stiff, narrow figure approached the bed, Else thought she looked like one of the Norns. [11]

"What's the matter?" she whispered.

"Toothache."

"Hmm. That's not good. Shall I get a warm compress?"

"Yes, thank you. But who are you?"

"The night nurse."

The Norn disappeared as silently as she had come, and she was soon back with a steaming bowl of water, cotton batting and a piece of rubber sheet hanging over her arm.

"There," she said, when she had quietly and carefully wrapped Else's head and secured the bandage with a safety pin. "Perhaps that will relieve you somewhat. I'll look in on you again in an hour."

When the Norn returned after an hour, Else was again sitting up in bed moaning.

"Didn't it help?" the Norn whispered.

"Yes, for a while. But now it's started again."

Once more the Norn disappeared and returned with the steaming bowl of water.

"Thank you very much," Else said when the new compress was in place. "You're very kind. But I'm sorry to cause you so much trouble during the night."

"No," the Norn whispered. "It's no trouble. I'm on duty anyway. I just hope this helps."

"Are you on duty every night?" Else whispered like the Norn.

"Yes. I'll look in on you again in a while. And give you another compress."

Else had scarcely settled herself before the lady next door, Miss Hall, whose bed must have been right next to the wall by Else's, sat up, bed creaking, and started to rail and swear in English. The ugliest profanities came screaming into the room and then she clapped her hands and pounded on the wall.

Else jumped in fright, but then she suddenly noticed that the pain in her tooth was gone and tried to comfort herself with the thought that the fear had succeeded in driving away the toothache.

A moment later Mrs. Henderson started up, worse than before. It was as if sleep had given her new strength.

Else lay staring hopelessly at the large pink paper rosette, shaped to look like a sunflower, that was hanging from the globe of the gas lamp to protect her eyes.

Then the Norn came back. "Well," she whispered, "how are you feeling?"

"My tooth feels fine, thank you. But listen to that!"

The Norn gave Else a perplexed look. "Oh, them," she said. "Why do they bother you?"

"It's impossible to go to sleep," Else groaned.

"Don't listen to them," the Norn soothed. Once again Else was reminded of the story about the Yankee.

"How can I not listen to them," she said, half crying. "Besides, I'm so terribly afraid of them."

An expression of compassionate wonder spread across the Norn's quiet face like a faint glow.

"There is absolutely no need to be. They're locked in their rooms, you know, and besides, they wouldn't harm a flea."

"But can't you go in and ask them to be quiet?"

"That would only make them worse. I'd better turn off the gas now."

Chapter 9

"Good morning, Mrs. Kant, how are you?" a busy voice called.

Else opened her eyes halfway and drowsily looked at Nurse Schrader.

"You've had a toothache and not slept, Sibylle tells me."

"Sibylle?"

"Yes, the night nurse. The one who gave you the compress."

"But I was sleeping just now. Why in heaven's name did you wake me up?"

"It's nearly seven o'clock. Maren will be here soon to light the fire, then you'll have tea and after that you'll have to get up. Unless you'd rather stay in bed," Nurse Schrader nodded and left.

No, Else wouldn't rather stay in bed. She'd had enough of that in Ward Six. But now she was so heavy with sleep. Nearly seven! Then she had only dozed for half an hour, for long after the Norn had turned off the gas she'd been kept awake by her neighbors. She turned over toward the wall and nodded off, but was immediately startled when someone came in and started poking and rattling in the stove. She lay absolutely still hoping that when this was over she would fall back asleep, and she did finally. But then Maren brought in the tea and loudly announced, "Here you are, Mrs. Kant."

Else turned over with a sigh and told Maren that she would a thousand times rather have gone without tea.

That was impossible, Maren explained. Rounds were at half past ten, the rooms had to be cleaned, the patients had to be finished with breakfast, etc.

When Else was dressed, she went out to the long corridor and paced up and down the carpet runner. She walked slowly, a little unsteadily, for her body felt terribly heavy and her knees weak. Most of the doors to the rooms were open, and Maren and another maid were busy with long-handled brooms and dust cloths. Some rooms were empty; in others patients were in their beds.

A young girl with a clean and meticulous appearance – fair, smooth hair done up in a neat bun at the nape of her neck and a light tartan shawl over her shoulders – appeared in the hallway and started trotting up and down. Her grey dress of soft woollen material was so short at the bottom that her long, slender feet and thin ankles were visible. The girl's small, fair head was perched on her delicate neck as if at the end of a stem, and her child-eyes, frightened and questioning, darted curiously at Else every time she approached her on her route. Finally she fell into pace with Else, though staying a step behind her. Else, sensing that the young girl wanted to say something to her, stubbornly turned her head away and did what she could to get rid of her – slackening her pace, walking faster, sometimes standing still. But the young girl faithfully did the same thing and continued to follow her.

"I don't like having her on my heels," Else whispered to Maren, who was standing by a table down at the end of the corridor, busy with a huge stack of buttered bread on a large tray.

"I'll speak to her about it," Maren answered as she quickly portioned out the buttered bread onto plates.

"Oh no, don't! She looks so nice, poor thing."

"You should go down to breakfast now, Miss Thomsen," Maren said, momentarily turning her head toward the young girl who was standing a couple steps away.

Miss Thomsen wrapped the shawl more tightly around her arms, tossed her head and made a face which said, "Mind your own business."

Just then a bell rang.

"There's the bell!" Maren shouted to the young girl, who turned after a while and slowly moved down the corridor.

"Is she deaf?" Else asked.

232

"Yes, she doesn't hear much."

"Poor thing. She's a mere child."

"She is twenty-seven years old," Maren answered with her usual, good-natured smile.

"Is that possible? She looks so childlike, so good and proper."

"Oh, she's really not so good."

"Is she mean?"

"Sometimes. I'll set your breakfast in your room now, Mrs. Kant."

Oh, these thick pieces of bread! Else was sitting in her room by the breakfast tray, and after she had picked the bread up, had no desire to eat it. Suddenly she had an idea. She went out to Maren and asked to borrow a knife. Maren looked a little doubtful, but nonetheless handed her what she'd asked for. Else sliced the bread crossways with the knife so it was less than half as thick, and then it tasted just fine.

"It would be very sweet of you to give me a knife both morning and evening," she said to Maren when she came for the tray, and Maren saw no reason why that couldn't be arranged.

Just then the superintendent appeared and Else told him about her night.

"Yes, I know what you mean. A toothache is a terrible affliction. But now we'll see what we can do about it."

"My two neighbors are almost worse," Else said.

"I see. Try to be patient. As the days get longer Miss Hall usually gets better. We've had her here for fourteen years. During the summer she's sent home for a couple of months, but in the autumn she invariably returns."

As the days get longer, Else thought. While the grass is growing, the cow is dying.

"And Mrs. Henderson will also calm down later on, you'll see. Just keep a stiff upper lip, Mrs. Kant."

"I can't," Else mumbled. "It's so dreadful for me to be here."

"Nonsense," the superintendent said cheerfully; he had seated himself on the little sofa while Else sat on the chair by the window, squeezed in between the wall and the table. "You know we're being good to you. If you want to write a letter, go right ahead! If letters come for you here, you'll get them right away – I won't open and read them beforehand. If you want your husband to visit, I'll write to him immediately."

"You know that I don't want that."

"All right, then I won't do it. But a message – no, no, I won't ask you for a message," the superintendent interrupted himself when he saw Else fidgeting on the chair.

"You do see how everything is arranged just as you want it," the superintendent continued in an amiable tone. "Food brought to your room and everything – though you really ought to go downstairs. The patients who take their meals downstairs are calm and nice."

"No thank you," Else said. "I'd like to be excused."

"If there's anything you'd like – an egg at breakfast, a glass of milk now and then, small beer with dinner – just let us know."

"Thank you," Else said. "I feel so miserable and weak."

"We'll give you an iron compound. It will help you regain your strength. And then you'll have to go outdoors and walk."

"I can walk in the corridor out there. It's nice and airy, you know."

"All right, to begin with. And reading material – if you want anything to read, just say so. We have an entire library."

Else didn't answer. She sat and thought about the immense difference between the superintendent and Hieronimus. Mechanically she put her hands to her face and shook her head slightly.

"Is it your tooth again?"

"No, it's Hieronimus. He didn't even let me see a dentist! I guess that's not part of the treatment for people presumed to be insane – no help for physical ailments?"

"Are you starting that again?" the superintendent smiled admonishingly at Else. "Why don't we make an agreement that you will never again mention that man's name in my presence?"

"I wouldn't be able to keep it," Else said.

"If you really set your mind to it?" The superintendent knit his eyebrows and made himself gruff.

"You should have been there to see for yourself!" Else cried. "For one thing, he always believed I was lying! I had gone there in order to tell him as much truth as I could. How can a sick person be helped without telling her doctor the truth?"

"Well, I'm leaving now," smiling, the superintendent stood up. "Let me find you in a better mood when I come by this evening."

In a better mood ... Hmm, how could she be in a better mood as long as she was here? But thank God for the superintendent. She was beginning to like him.

Chapter 10

An hour later there were rounds again. It was the second resident physician, a short and stocky man with thick hair and large, somewhat misty eyes. His name was Sejer and he was accompanied by Nurse Schrader. Else returned his greeting and responded curtly to his questions.

"You find everything perfectly satisfactory here?" This remark came after Dr. Sejer had stood for a while observing Else in silence.

"Yes," Else responded in an irritated tone. "I've never in my life enjoyed myself as much as I do here."

Dr. Sejer looked offended. "Most of our patients are contented here," he said testily. "And there is, of course, every reason for that."

Else pressed her lips together determined not to respond, but the words slipped out in spite of herself: "Don't you know that I've come here against my will?"

"That's your problem, you know," Dr. Sejer said sympathetically.

Else, who had turned her head away, sent him an impatient sidelong look, and as she did, caught a glimpse of Nurse Schrader's face, whose expression seemed to say, "How can you torment her with such talk?"

She turned her head toward Nurse Schrader and got a look that radiated such warmth and understanding, that she completely forgot her irritation over Dr. Sejer. Dr. Sejer continued to talk about how it was her duty to be happy and thankful, etc. When Else didn't answer, he finally left, followed by Nurse Schrader who turned in the doorway and nodded at Else.

In the afternoon as Else lay curled up on the short sofa trying to take a

nap after dinner, Mrs. Seneke came creeping in. She was in the same out-
fit as the evening before, and her face looked, if possible, even more twisted and haggard.

"I just wanted to hear how you're doing," she squeaked. "No, don't get
up," she persisted as Else sat up.

"I'm fine, thank you," Else said.

"Well, what do you think of the superintendent and Nurse Schrader?"

"Wonderful."

"I see." Mrs. Seneke's face turned as sour as vinegar. "So you're one of
those. Well, I certainly won't bother you any more by coming in here."
She turned and walked on her soundless felt shoes toward the door.
There she turned her head and added "You don't so much as offer an old
lady a chair." And with that she was gone.

Else lay down again and curled up on the sofa. What cheerful company
she had. And Knut had thought she wouldn't be able to stand being
among hysterical women at a private clinic!

No, it was impossible to lie here any longer – the sofa was too short.
Else got up and went out to walk in the corridor, and immediately the
young girl with the meticulous appearance and the short dress fell in behind her. Else pretended not to see her, but when the young girl stayed at
her heels, she went over to one of the windows and stood with her back to
the corridor.

A minute later she was aware of the young girl standing behind her.

"What do you want?" Else suddenly asked, turning around.

"My name is Miss Thomsen," the young girl said; her face contorted,
she pressed the words out, and her snuffling voice was low and colorless.
"What is your name?"

As Else was saying her name, Miss Thomsen stared intently at her
mouth.

"Wouldn't you like to go for a walk in the garden?" Miss Thomsen
asked after repeating Else's name. "I'll go with you."

Else shook her head.

"No? You ought to, though. Fresh air is good for you. I go down every
day. You ought to go down and eat at the table too. You can help yourself

to the best pieces, drink milk and get a juicy piece of meat. Do you like the food here?"

"I've been here such a short time."

"It's revolting, isn't it? But down at the table you can at least take what you want. I always hurry and grab the best pieces. Why do you have to be here?"

"Oh, I don't know."

"Were you tricked into coming here? No? I was. They said we were going to take a drive, and then, all of a sudden we were here."

"Have you been sick then?"

"Not the slightest bit. But I'm a phenomenon. Shh," she suddenly put her index finger to her lips. "Don't tell anybody I've talked to you. Do you hear, you mustn't."

"No," Else said.

"They're such awful riffraff."

"Who?"

"The superintendent, Nurse Schrader, all of them, pah!" Miss Thomsen stuck out a long, thin tongue.

"Come in and see where I live. Please?" Miss Thomsen cocked her head a little and there was a touching expression in the frightened, questioning child-eyes. "Oh please, do," she went on, taking Else by the arm. "I like you. You look so nice."

Reluctantly Else went with her.

When they came from the large corridor into the short hallway, the door next to Else's room was standing open. Else peeked in and saw the back of a female figure in a long nightgown up on the bed, pawing through bedding that had been thrown helter-skelter. A large, white comforter formed a pointed mound in the middle of the bed and suddenly the figure began punching at it with all her might. Else stood stock-still, staring into the room. "It's just Mrs. Henderson," Miss Thomsen said, pulling Else by the sleeve.

"So she's the one who screams and says those horrible things. Wait, I want to look at her," Else said as Miss Thomsen again tugged at her sleeve. "She won't harm us, will she?"

"No. She's a decent sort. But why do you want to look at her?"

In her struggle with the bedding Mrs. Henderson had reached the foot of the bed which abutted the wall with the window. She suddenly turned around, furiously kicking at the comforter. Just then she caught sight of Else and stood petrified, her large, terror-stricken eyes flashing darkly in the grey-white, emaciated face. She had a large, thin mouth, a long, flat nose with wide nostrils, and protruding ears. Lank brown hair hung down to her shoulders.

"Come over here, come over here!" she exclaimed suddenly. Her face contorted terribly as she eagerly waved her hands.

"I don't dare," Else whispered.

"Yes, of course you dare," Miss Thomsen said. "She's just curious because you're a new patient."

"Come over here, come over here," Mrs. Henderson repeated.

Else moved hesitantly toward the bed.

Suddenly Mrs. Henderson threw herself on her knees, leaned over the edge of the bed, and seized Else with skinny, grasping fingers. Else wanted to run, but Mrs. Henderson had already locked her arm around her neck and pulled Else's face down to hers. Her staring eyes seemed to devour Else, and a foul smell poured out of her open mouth. Her face hideously contorted as before, she asked, "What is your name?" then placed her protruding ear by Else's mouth. All of this happened in an instant.

Terrified, Else tore herself loose and ran over and clung to Miss Thomsen, who had remained in the doorway.

Mrs. Henderson stared at her in astonishment. Then she called to Miss Thomsen who immediately went over to her and shouted in her ear that the stranger was a new patient whose name was Mrs. Kant.

"Oh." Mrs. Henderson was again standing up on the bed. She looked sulkily at Else, started making faces and waved her away with her long skinny hand: "Go, go, you mustn't stand there." She shook her head helplessly and looked as if she were about to burst out crying. "Go, go," she repeated, hiding her face behind her upraised arm. "I'm going to tell Frants."

Miss Thomsen put her arm through Else's, ushering her past Else's and

Miss Hall's doors into a square little hallway with a high window.

"That's where Maren sleeps, the beast," Miss Thomsen said pointing at a bed that just fit in the far end of the hallway. "That's to keep an eye on me, of course. What riffraff!" They entered a spacious corner room with two windows, one on each wall, from which there was a lovely, expansive view. There was a light Brussels carpet on the floor, armchairs upholstered in velvet, a writing table and pictures on the walls.

"My, but this is nice!" Else exclaimed.

"Yes, it's nice here," said Miss Thomsen, who the whole time had been standing right up against Else, staring at her mouth whenever she spoke. "It's called the princess apartment. Here is my bedroom." She opened a door to a smaller room with a wide bed, a washstand and dressing table.

"Well, if you have to be here, you do have a comfortable place."

"He makes you pay blood money," Miss Thomsen remarked. "I pay twice as much as the others, and he still goes around in a threadbare coat. He's a miser, the scoundrel!"

"Who?" Else asked.

"The superintendent, of course."

"How can you think he's the one who gets the money!" Else cried.

"Oh I know, all right. They want to trick us! But of course he gets the money, or else he steals it. Surely you can see that. Why else would he keep us here? I've been here for nine months now, and all my begging and pleading to leave hasn't helped the slightest. Please sit down, Mrs. Kant. Oh yes, do! It's so nice having someone to talk to. Look here, I have something for you." From a little cabinet she took two porcelain dishes with candy and chocolates, and some small dessert plates.

"I got this from home," Miss Thomsen continued after she had taken her place next to Else and they had both helped themselves. "I have to keep it under lock and key, and even so, it doesn't do any good. They steal like ravens."

"Who?" Else asked in surprise.

"The maids and Nurse Schrader and everyone. Just wait, you'll see, if you ever have anything special."

Else tried to convince her that she was mistaken, but soon realized it was to no avail, and gave up.

"If you knew how they have treated me," Miss Thomsen chattered on. "I've been locked up for seven weeks, and then they've taken me by force and poured chloral down my throat. That Nurse Schrader is Beelzebub himself, yes, that's what I say – Beelzebub himself – and Maren is even worse."

"No," Else said shaking her head. "You are wrong about that."

There was an exasperated look on Miss Thomsen's pale, childlike face. "Maren has grabbed me and held me by the wrists so I turned black and blue," she said angrily. "One time I was so furious I broke my umbrella on her back."

"For shame, that was a horrid thing to do."

"No," Miss Thomsen said. "It served her right, they use her as a spy. You mustn't think I was bad, Mrs. Kant." She took Else's hand and laid her head lightly against her shoulder, peeking up at her with an imploring look.

Else patted her cheek and said nothing.

"Don't you think they'll have to let me go soon?" Miss Thomsen asked, straightening up. "Because I'm really not insane. Am I?"

"I suppose your relatives have to ask for you to come home," Else answered.

"Yes, but the superintendent tricks them into believing I'm insane and have to stay here. So what can I do?"

"Don't they come and visit you?"

"Yes, from time to time. But the superintendent always takes them aside and whispers and gossips – pah! Have you noticed how he stinks, his male smell?"

"No," Else said. "I think very highly of the superintendent, and I'm sure the man doesn't keep anyone here any longer than necessary."

"Then you must think I'm insane," Miss Thomsen exclaimed.

"No. I don't think anything. I don't know anything about you, I don't know you at all."

"Well, just wait. Just wait. Why has he locked you up, if I may ask?"

Else didn't answer. For a moment she sat staring straight ahead, and then she rose.

"You're not mad at me, are you, Mrs. Kant?" Miss Thomsen quickly clasped both of Else's hands.

"No, of course not. Why should I be? But your ideas are utterly absurd."

"Why are you leaving then?"

"Because I'm very tired. I didn't sleep at all last night. And soon there will be rounds. I think it's best for us to be in our own rooms."

"Yes, you're right about that. Shh," Miss Thomsen was touching her index finger to her lips. "Don't tell anyone I've spoken with you. Promise me."

"Yes."

"Come see me during the day. You think it's nice in here. And you have such a miserable room, the narrowest and most miserable of them all. Bring your work and sit in here. You are so industrious."

"How do you know that?" Else asked.

"Because I've peeked through the keyhole!"

Chapter 11

INSANE, ELSE THOUGHT, when she was back in her room and once again sat with her work. Yes, Miss Thomsen was indeed an eccentric with absurd ideas, but insane – insane in a way that required keeping her locked up?

What did it really mean to be insane? It was easy enough to call each other's quirks and more or less irritating peculiarities insanity, just like that. Who could prevent it? One person had an aversion to cats; another couldn't be persuaded to do anything on a Monday; a third didn't go to bed without first placing his shoes backwards outside the bedroom door; a fourth believed in dreams and governed his life by them; a fifth had spoken to spirits of the dead and knew he would enter ninth heaven when he died; a sixth, in a revelation from the apostle Peter, had received the power to heal by laying his hands on the sick; a seventh became insomniac out of desperation that he couldn't make progress in his work; an eighth felt so unsuited for life on earth that he willingly chose to make his exit; a ninth had stomach troubles that made him impossible company; a tenth drank, and in his drunkenness did the strangest, most disgusting things; an eleventh loathed the opposite sex; a twelfth couldn't bear the sight of children; a thirteenth went into convulsions around rats and mice; a fourteenth was a megalomaniac and imagined he knew exactly what should be classified as insanity and what should not, and so on and so forth, *ad infinitum*.

How many people would be walking around at liberty, she wondered, if a Hieronimus were installed on every street corner, invested with the authority to lock people up whenever Hieronimic judgment declared them insane? What if the state appointed an Overhieronimus, commissioned to monitor all the little Hieronimuses? Would all of these minor popes be put into carriages, one after the other, with one guard and two attendants, and transported to the madhouse one of these days? Imagine how many insane asylums would have to be built. Many more than there were Hieronimuses to manage them. A multitude of enclaves populated by insane people, stretching all across the land, which of course was also populated by insane people of one sort or another, who had to run loose because the institutions were all full. And what about the real lunatics, the ones who were a danger to public safety, to their neighbors' life and limb? Quick, chop off their heads and bury them, or burn them up straightaway.

The superintendent came in and sat down. As before Else was pleasantly touched by his amiable manner and appearance. But as usual it didn't take long before she started in on Hieronimus.

"I really can't understand your anger toward that man," the superintendent said suddenly. "Your stay there actually made you better."

"Better. How am I better? I still can't sleep, you know."

"If you had been the way you are now, I don't suppose you would have gone there."

"Oh, Hieronimus has no idea how I was when I arrived or how I felt while I was there!" Else exclaimed indignantly. "If he had examined me and understood my condition, he would have immediately told my husband Ward Six was not the right place for me. It's no credit to him that I'm not insane today, or that I'm still alive, for that matter. Better, you say? Hieronimus couldn't have thought I was better since he made my husband send me here."

"There you go, blowing off steam again," the superintendent laughed.

"If only I had come here to begin with," Else said. "It would have been much, much better."

"Yes, I think so too. But you probably wouldn't have agreed to that."

"No, if only I had," Else sighed. "If only I had known, I would have."

"Miss Thomsen," Else said, when the superintendent made a move to leave. "Why is she here?"

"Oh her. It's a form of idiocy – she'll never change."

"Yes, but why does she have to be locked up?"

"What can be done with a person like that? Her family can't possibly put up with her. They have really been more than patient. Imagine having responsibility for someone like that. Anything might happen to her when she's out on the street by herself. Naturally, she always wants to walk alone. The first rogue to come along could lure her away and . . . Well, she can be happy she has such a nice place to stay. Good night now, Mrs. Kant. See that you get some sleep tonight. How is your tooth?"

"It will start up, of course, as soon as I get in bed."

"You should let Dr. Sejer look at it. He's quite the dentist."

"No," Else said. "Not Dr. Sejer."

"Now, what's the matter with Dr. Sejer?"

"Nothing," Else answered.

ᨀ

"WELL, MRS. KANT, you look utterly content." Nurse Schrader was making her evening rounds.

Else put her work away to make room for Nurse Schrader.

"No, I am not content and I won't be as long as I'm here."

"You're not being very nice, Mrs. Kant. We treat you very well, you know."

"You do, but just the same. Tell me honestly, do you really think it's necessary to keep me here against my will?"

"That's not for me to say."

"But have you noticed any kind of insanity or confusion in my behavior?"

"No, not yet. Come now, Mrs. Kant, let's talk about something else instead," Nurse Schrader added hastily when she saw Else's indignant expression. "You'll see, your time with us will pass quickly. When you get used to being here, you'll settle down and end up in good health and good spirits."

"Never," Else cried.

"Are you really so contrary? You don't look it." Nurse Schrader laid her delicate, slender hand with its long, shiny fingernails on Else's shoulder and smiled warmly. "Can you imagine, I dreamt about you shortly before I heard you were coming here."

"Really?"

"That day I had seen one of your paintings, and at night I dreamed you came and asked if you could share a room with me."

"Here at the madhouse?"

"Shame! Yes, here at the sanatorium."

"But how did you know me?"

"I have no idea."

"Did I look like I do in real life?"

"No, you looked frightfully arrogant and unpleasant."

Else laughed.

"I can't help taking note of what I dream," Nurse Schrader went on. "Because sometimes my dreams come true."

"Mine do too," Else replied.

Nurse Schrader sat for a while. They talked about mutual acquaintances, patients who had been there, and relatives of patients who had come to visit, and Else was astonished and pleased about how much they agreed in their opinions about people, as well as other things. Finally Nurse Schrader asked if Else would like to have coffee with breakfast.

Else thanked her and said she had been getting coffee.

But that wasn't part of the arrangement, Nurse Schrader explained. Else was supposed to have been a ward patient, of course, and they didn't get coffee there.

"What's it like on the ward?" Else asked.

"The food is exactly the same except they don't get coffee and dessert on Sunday. But there are eight to ten beds in each room, and for that reason the price is somewhat lower."

Else shuddered.

"I don't have my clothes," Else remarked. "The valise I brought is missing too."

"Yes, your things must be counted and labelled. We haven't had time to do that, but I'll see about it tomorrow. Good night, Mrs. Kant. Anne will soon be here with the chloral."

"Won't it be Maren?"

"No, not this evening. The two of them share the patients up here and Maren isn't working this shift." Nurse Schrader squeezed Else's hand and left with a friendly nod.

Eight to ten beds! How could Knut possibly have wanted to put her in a ward? He knew her fear of sharing a room with anyone, even if it was someone she knew very well. And here among strangers, insane people no less? What was behind all this? What had come over Knut? She pressed her hand to her heart and shook her head, bewildered. A stranger, the superintendent, had taken pity on her and out of the goodness of his heart, spared her the horror of being locked up with eight or ten insane people day and night.

Oh well, there was no use brooding or grieving over this. She had more than enough with everything else. And besides – Knut was no longer any concern of hers.

Anne came with the chloral and said that it would soon be nine o'clock. Mrs. Kant ought to be in bed. There was something chiding in her voice. Else glanced at her and saw she was older than Maren. But Anne was friendly and kind too.

Chapter 12

THE NIGHT PASSED much the same as the previous one. The Norn came in several times and gave Else a compress for her toothache, and Miss Hall and Mrs. Henderson screamed and carried on. In the morning after the Norn had turned off the gas, Else drifted off to sleep, but then Anne came and lit the fire and Nurse Schrader came in to say good morning; by the time Else got out of bed, she felt so worn out and aggravated that she wept as she was getting dressed.

In the afternoon Else got her suitcase and valise.

"The top closet in the corridor is yours," Nurse Schrader said; she was accompanied by a maid who carried the suitcase. "You can hang your dresses and coats there."

As Else was putting her undergarments in the dresser drawers, she looked to see how they had been labelled, and saw "6660" in red back-stitches on every single article. Not only on her undergarments, but on her dresses, capes, corsets, stockings, handkerchiefs, gloves, even on a tablecloth she had started to embroider at home that had been sent along so she would have some work to "amuse" herself with. These red numbers had a strangely annihilating effect on Else. She was no longer a person, simply this or that number, like prisoners and soldiers. Her initials were on all of her undergarments. Why these red numbers then, which obliterated her as a person?

But of course. No doubt they had to do it. Among all these hundreds of patients there could be many whose initials were E.K., and it would, of course, be difficult to keep track of everything when it went to the laundry. But oh, it was horrible just the same.

While she was out in the hallway hanging her clothes in the closet, Else heard a low snicker. Directly across from the closet a door was ajar, and Else knew that Miss Hall lived behind this door. She didn't dare turn around. She was afraid of Miss Hall.

But when she was finished and about to go back to her room, Miss Hall's door flew open and an oily, whispering voice said, "Good afternoon, Mrs. Kant."

Else stood still in front of the open door. At first she could only see darkness and an intense, rose-colored glow behind the darkness, but gradually, in the middle of the darkness, she made out a short, squat female figure in stocking feet, slip and white nightshirt; her head was bobbing up and down and her hands gesticulated excitedly.

"Let me look at you," the figure said suddenly, stepping onto the threshold so that the light from the window fell on her large, middle-aged face, with its pale, baggy cheeks and shiny, jet-black hair.

"Are you Miss Hall?" Else asked.

"Yes, that's what they say," she replied and took Else's hands as she stepped out in the hallway. "You've got a lucky room, I want you to know."

"Lucky?"

"Yes, because none of the people who live there stay very long. I've noticed that now, year after year. I always come back here, you see. It's because my mother is so egotistical."

"Why is it so dark in your room?" Else asked.

"Because that's the way I like it. I'm so hideous this time of year. And when these confounded doctor-brutes come, I don't want them to see me," Miss Hall spoke with twists and nods, that resembled the quick, supple movements of a sparrow's head. She smiled and snickered without interruption and her chubby, pale hands weren't quiet for a minute. " 'Bla, bla, idiot!' is all I say and I just turn my back," she stood pointing her fingers and laughing quietly. Then she suddenly stepped backwards into her room.

"But that glow in there." Else couldn't understand where the rose-colored light came from.

"That's the way I like it. You're not so hideous when you close the windows and cover them with red curtains."

Now Else understood. There were white shutters reaching halfway up the window and above them the glittering rays of the March sun shone through the red curtains, creating the rose-colored light.

Miss Thomsen came out of the little hallway leading to her room. She was wearing a hat, cape and large, shiny galoshes.

"Won't you come down and walk in the garden, huh?" she nudged Else's arm. "Oh, there you are, my child!" Miss Hall exclaimed, and came to the doorway, arms outstretched.

Miss Thomsen put both hands on Miss Hall's shoulders and, embracing each other, they kissed repeatedly.

"Come walk with me," Miss Thomsen repeated, nudging Else again. "You don't want to, is that it?" She shook her head a little and looked disappointed.

"Go on," Miss Hall said. "You can go down with her. She's my child, I'll have you know. She's such a sweetheart." Miss Hall wagged her index finger at Miss Thomsen and gazed at her with an infatuated smile.

"Yes, the two of us," Miss Thomsen burst out, jauntily tossing her shoulders back and kicking out with one foot. "We've really fooled that riffraff." An impish look on her face, she let out a low, cooing laugh. "They're riffraff, aren't they, Miss Hall?"

"Riffraff!" Miss Hall shouted, and her contorted face grew angry and threatening. "They're rabble and riffraff and scoundrels and criminals! I will see them hanged! God damn!" She hit her clenched fist against the palm of her other hand.

"Don't do that," Else said terrified, but Miss Thomsen laughed and seemed to be enjoying herself immensely. "We've fooled them, haven't we, Miss Hall?"

Miss Hall was suddenly beaming again. She nodded and snickered.

"That time we were locked up, do you remember, Miss Hall?"

"Yes, that was splendid," Miss Hall laughed. "It was her idea, the little scamp."

"But when you were locked up, what could you do?" Else asked.

"We weren't at the same time," Miss Thomsen explained. "Well yes, for a little while, but after they let me out, I slipped notes to Miss Hall down there between the floor and the door." She laughed again with the low, cooing sound. "Almonds and raisins too. Once I stuck in a piece of almond cake, but it crumbled."

"I ate it anyway," Miss Hall said in her oily, hurried voice, smacking her lips.

"And when I was locked up again later, Miss Hall slipped notes to me. Isn't that right, Miss Hall?"

"And newspapers and chocolate drops," Miss Hall added, all the while nodding and twisting her head and waving her busy hands.

"Yes, the two of us have had some fun from time to time. Isn't that right, Miss Hall? Do you remember how you pounded on the door – ha, ha, ha, look, Mrs. Kant." Laughing, Miss Thomsen pointed at a number of small indentations on the door.

"Did you really make those with your hands?" Else asked in astonishment. That explained the numerous marks of the exact same appearance she had seen on her own door. "You must have ruined your hands."

"Yes," Miss Hall replied with a snicker, "my skin was in shreds. But I think it's fun. Once I turned over the tile stove too," she exploded in a loud guffaw.

"But didn't you get a terrible scolding?"

"Oh, that pack of riffraff!" Miss Hall screamed, stamping her foot. "Do you think I care about them? The more I tease them, the better. Do you know what I told the superintendent the other day? 'You ought to be in jail, you old windbag,' I said." Miss Hall let out another guffaw and Miss Thomsen joined in.

"Shh, who's that now?" Miss Hall suddenly exclaimed, a storm cloud passing over her face as she poked her head forward and listened to steps coming down the long corridor.

"Is someone coming?" Miss Thomsen whispered, and instantaneously the expression on her face became suspicious and hostile. Touching her index finger to her lips, she hurried away.

At that moment Anne appeared with a tray and said, "You are to have an iron compound, Mrs. Kant."

"Iron compound," Miss Hall screwed up her face and stuck out her tongue. "Did the nuts you stole from me this winter agree with you? What d'you say, you thieving hussy?"

Else gave Anne an apologetic look on Miss Hall's behalf, but Anne just smiled and shook her head a little, while she good-naturedly gave Else her medicine.

Suddenly Miss Hall slammed the door with such a bang that Else jumped and grabbed Anne's arm. Then she started ranting and raving in her furious English.

"Don't let her bother you," Anne said unperturbed. "She is a good person at heart. She just can't stand the sight of us."

Else peeked in through Mrs. Henderson's door which was half open.

Mrs. Henderson was in her nightgown. Her arms hung stiffly at her sides, and on large flat feet she paced across the grey- and red-patterned carpet that covered the floor. Her thin, lank hair fluttered in time to her small, measured, slightly hopping steps. When she reached the window, she didn't turn around, but walked backwards to the door, hopping and staying in time. Then across the room again, always in step, and backwards to the door, again and again. The bedding was just like yesterday, thrown helter-skelter on the bed, and a few pillows were lying on the floor.

All of a sudden a spasm went through Mrs. Henderson; uttering a stifled shriek, she turned around, her anxious, searching eyes darting in every direction. When she spied Else, watching her intently through the half-opened door, she appeared to take fright. "Ugh," she said, covering her face with her arm.

"You're not allowed to stand there," she said after a minute in a slurred voice, as she peeked at Else from behind her arm. "Go away, go away." But when Else didn't respond, she moved backwards, her arm covering her face. At the window she turned her back to Else and stood hunched over, her hands clasped in between her knees.

After a moment she slowly turned her head and whimpered, "Go away." Then she started marching in place, up and down, her big flat feet slapping the floor with hollow thuds, while her thin brown hair fluttered around her neck.

Else moved one step, positioning herself by the crack between the door and the frame and continued to watch.

Before long Mrs. Henderson again turned her head, directing her watchful gaze in all directions. When she saw that Else was gone, she started up her previous, measured march, forwards and backwards, but now with her face toward the door.

Else was nailed to the spot. She could not tire of watching this figure who, in spite of everything repellent, had a touching, childlike look of sadness in her eyes, in her humble, hunched-over posture, in her helpless, hanging arms, in her thin, fluttering hair, yes even in this measured pacing back and forth, this stubborn determination to walk backwards instead of turning.

Suddenly, with a movement as if someone had whispered in her ear, Mrs. Henderson stood still and stared through the crack into Else's eyes. She let out a scream and jerked so violently that she shook from head to toe. And then she cried, her voice beseeching and on the verge of tears, "Go away!" Else ran into her room. Mrs. Henderson's terrified look and intense fright, so unexpected, went through her like a jolt of electricity. Her entire body trembling, she sank into the rocking chair and wept.

Chapter 13

IN THE EVENING when Else had finished eating and was about to take up her needlework, there was a knock on her door; a stout, dignified woman with a broad, coarse-featured face and sparse hair streaked with grey came rushing into the room.

"May I come in?" she asked and burst into muffled laughter.

"Yes," Else said, her surprise mixed with displeasure. She had noticed this woman a couple of times before, and she knew that her room was in the long corridor and that her name was Mrs. Winther. "Won't you sit down?"

"Where shall I sit?" The woman laughed again until she shook. "It's so narrow here, a person can't get past you. I'd have to sit on the bed."

"I can move the rocking chair up to the sofa," Else suggested, but she stood where she was, her hand resting on the back of the rocking chair.

"Everything is round," Mrs. Winther said, pointing at the globe of the gas lamp, "and everything goes 'round, 'round, 'round." Once again she laughed her muffled, husky laugh and her eyes filled with tears which rolled down her broad, red cheeks.

Else didn't know how to respond and she tried laughing along with her.

"And can you imagine," Mrs. Winther went on, "now Eriksen has decided that the earth is round too. I don't know what you think!" Mrs. Winther was now laughing so hard that she was gasping and holding her sides.

"Yes, but the earth is round," Else ventured when Mrs. Winther finally stopped laughing.

The words were scarcely out of her mouth before Mrs. Winther burst into laughter yet again. "Flat as a pancake, hmm? Are we agreed?" She dried her eyes and breathed heavily from the exertion of laughing so much.

Else wished she would go. She didn't know how to answer or what to do with this person.

"Do you like it when I come to see you, hmm? Does it cheer you up, hmm?" Mrs. Winther's question came after a few minutes of silence and then there was a new torrent of laughter.

"Will you visit me too?" she continued a little later. "My room is much better. Pah, that thing," she moved closer and, making a sour face, grabbed Else's crochet work. "They sent me pretty stuff like that too – it was supposed to distract me." She laughed again. "But I say thanks just the same. I'll have nothing to do with that kind of distraction."

I won't say a word now, Else thought. Then she'll have to leave.

Mrs. Winther stood there for a while, looking at Else, her face quivering from suppressed laughter. Else took the crocheting from the dresser, put it on the table, nervously moved the rocking chair, pulled her handkerchief out of her pocket, folded it neatly on her knee and put it back in her pocket.

"You're fun to talk to," Mrs. Winther said suddenly, exploding with laughter again. "My youngest son Peter, who's seven years old, is every bit as entertaining." Then she left.

"Thank God," Else let out a breath and sat down with her embroidery. But she soon let her work fall to her lap. Tears welled up in her eyes, blotting out the sight of her stitches and dripping down onto the needle. The words "my youngest son Peter" had brought thoughts of Tage to the surface. How was he doing, she wondered? And what did he think about his mama never being at home any more?

"Good evening." Nurse Schrader had come in.

Else moved over to the edge of the bed and invited Nurse Schrader to sit down in the rocking chair.

"Always working. You're an industrious person. What's this, have you been crying?"

Else dried her eyes, and then her sobs burst out in earnest. Nurse Schrader tried to calm her, entreating her not to despair, assuring her that she'd feel better after a while.

"Don't you think the superintendent will let me go in another week or so?"

Nurse Schrader gave a little start, but quickly composed herself and said, "No patient has ever been released after such a short time."

"Yes, but I'm not insane," Else sobbed.

"Just the same, being here might be good for you, Mrs. Kant." Nurse Schrader rocked slowly back and forth, pressing the toe of her small, high-arched foot against the carpet in time with the rocking chair.

"No," Else cried. "It's not good for me to be in a place where I'm suffering such agony. No, no! It's not that anybody here is trying to cause me pain and suffering," Else continued, noticing the look of displeasure on Nurse Schrader's face. "Please don't think that's what I mean. On the contrary. All of you are so extremely kind to me. But even so. It's just that I can't possibly regain my strength as long as I don't sleep. And in order to sleep, I must have inner peace. And in order to have peace, I must be in a place I've chosen freely."

"Nevertheless, we have had many sensible patients, who have been delighted to be here," Nurse Schrader said. Then she recounted what had happened to this one and that one in such a lively and descriptive manner that Else felt herself captivated.

"And I miss my child so terribly," Else remarked when Nurse Schrader had stopped talking.

"Your child can visit you. I'll tell the superintendent."

"No thank you! I don't want to see my child while I'm here."

"But why ever not?"

"Because it would be ten times more painful to have to say good-bye to him. And besides, I don't want him to remember when he grows up that he visited his mother in a madhouse."

"Now, now," Nurse Schrader admonished.

"But tomorrow I'll write to the nursemaid and ask her to send me a letter telling me all about him," Else said.

"Write to your husband instead, Mrs. Kant."

Impatiently, Else shrugged her shoulders and threw out her hand. Then she described Mrs. Winther's visit and expressed her fear that she'd come back.

"I hardly think so," Nurse Schrader said. "She usually gets bored with people right away and keeps to herself for the most part."

She must have been thoroughly bored with me, Else thought.

Chapter 14

ELSE HAD GONE TO BED. Maren came with the chloral, turned down the gas and left.

Feel better after a while. "After a while" – the words gnawed at Else. When Nurse Schrader said "after a while," it was clear that she believed, or knew, that Else would be there for a long time. She just didn't have the heart to say it outright.

Oh well, no matter what happened, she mustn't forget to be happy that she had escaped from Hieronimus.

Perhaps she would be able to sleep tonight. Her tooth didn't ache and both of her neighbors were quiet.

"God damn these rascals!" There it was, Miss Hall had started up. "I tell you, I will murder you all!" Yes, of course. It was much too optimistic to think she would keep still.

"Maren!" screamed Mrs. Henderson, pounding on her door. "Won't you do it since Frants says so? It's bad enough that you won't listen to me, but Frants!"

Else was amazed that she could now clearly understand Mrs. Henderson's slurred voice. But she was just getting used to it, of course.

When Miss Hall had been at it for half an hour, Else could tell that she was getting tired. Her scolding sounded weaker and at the end her voice was quite thick. A little later she heard her snoring. Mrs. Henderson had also gradually quieted down.

Oh, if only her tooth didn't start aching now.

But her tooth did start to ache. An absolutely dreadful, unbearable toothache.

When the Norn came with her dangling lamp, Else was, as on the previous nights, sitting up in bed moaning.

The Norn went to get a compress, and after she had wrapped it around Else's jaw, she stood by the bed for a few minutes.

"It does help," Else said.

"That's good to hear."

"Have you been a night nurse for a long time?"

"For seven years."

"And you've been able to stand it?"

"Barely," the Norn whispered.

"You're so pale."

"Yellow. Yellow as a lemon. And thin. I've really gone downhill these seven years. There's no doubt."

"But are you bound here for life?"

"No. But they're reluctant to let me go. A place like this requires a dependable person, you know, and someone who's strong enough."

"I suppose you sleep all day long?"

"No. I'm never through until almost two o'clock. I also help bathe the sick patients."

"Well, then I hope you make at least a hundred kroner a month."

A shadow of a smile appeared on the Norn's face. "Hmm," was all she said. "Is it still helping?"

Else nodded.

"Good night then, Mrs. Kant," the Norn whispered and disappeared.

&

HER HEAD FELT so tired and fuzzy, her body heavy and weak. As usual, Else had been yanked out of her morning sleep. The fire snapped and crackled in the tile stove, and a strong, blue light streamed in through the unshuttered window behind Else's bed.

Well, she might as well get up and wash.

Over by the washstand, she stood shaking her head in annoyance.

Every day since she had come she'd asked Maren to please remember to give her two pitchers of water and two towels. At Else's request, Nurse Schrader had immediately given her approval, and she gave Maren instructions in Else's presence. Should she do as she had on other mornings, manage as best she could with one little pitcher of water and one skimpy towel, and remind Maren again this evening?

No, then Maren would most certainly keep on forgetting.

She opened the door and called to Maren, but no one answered.

Why wasn't there a bell? It was such a nuisance to get hold of a maid!

She quickly threw on her robe and walked down her short hallway out into the long corridor.

Coming toward her was a strange figure, a skinny little woman in a dark cotton dress that was pulled together under her bosom with a bunch of different drawstrings. There was a cap on her head and her tangled, grey hair hung down below. The skin on her face was like shrivelled, dark-brown leather and it was spotted with large black warts. Her eyes, popping out of their sockets, looked as if they were about to roll down her cheeks. Her mouth was open and she moved her thick tongue back and forth incessantly, from one corner of her mouth to the other. She was groping along the wall with one hand; she held the other out in front of her, moving it up and down like the forepaw of a swimming dog.

Else came a little closer to get a better look at this repulsive sight, and as she did so the clammy brown hand slapped her across the face. She felt like she'd been touched by a toad.

She shrank back with a muffled scream while the figure moved along, undisturbed, and disappeared through a door at the far end of the corridor.

Just then Maren came into view over by the stairway carrying a tray with a huge stack of buttered bread.

"I've seen a dreadful person!" Else exclaimed and started to tell her.

"That's just Miss Hahn. She always walks that way with her hands because she's blind."

Else turned around to go back to her room, but remembered that she had gone out to find Maren, and in an irritated tone asked about the water and the towels. She would rather not complain to Nurse Schrader, she said, but at this rate she'd be forced to.

"No," Maren said and looked up at her with such a winning smile that Else's foul mood evaporated. "I'll go get it now and I won't forget again. I promise you."

Dr. Vibe made the rounds. Nurse Schrader was with him, but she was called out almost right away.

Else was glad to be alone with Dr. Vibe. Then she could talk about Hieronimus uninterrupted. The fact that Dr. Vibe never said anything in response didn't bother her. Whether he concurred or not, it was still a relief to vent her feelings.

"You have been getting the newspaper every day, haven't you?" Dr. Vibe asked when Else finally stopped. "Yes, thank you. At precisely half-past twelve there's a knock on my door and then I know the porter has come with the paper."

Later on the superintendent came and commiserated with her over her toothache. He had heard from Sibylle that she hadn't slept last night either. He would send Dr. Sejer in to see her this morning. There must be something they could do about that confounded tooth. Then there was Miss Hall. Else ought to go into her room and ask her to not yell and scream at night. Miss Hall was really very sweet and she had let it be known that she liked Else very much. It might help if Else asked her herself.

Else asked if she could have a cold bath in the morning, and he saw no objection to that. She would be getting a catalogue from which she could choose books she wanted to read. And she had her needlework as well – what a lovely embroidery she was working on. If she would only take walks during the day, and go down for meals, then it wouldn't be long before she would be very happy there.

There was that awful word again, Else thought. But she was so anxious that she couldn't bring herself to ask what the superintendent meant by "long." Instead she said "Do you really think it's necessary to keep me locked up here?"

"Locked up, locked up," the superintendent repeated in irritation.

"Actually no," he said in another tone. "In my opinion you could just as well be staying at another place, with your relatives abroad, for example."

Else's heart leapt with joy at these words. But there was something about the superintendent, as if the words had slipped out halfway against his will. So her reply was simply, "Yes, that's exactly what I said to Dr. Tvede."

"All right then, good morning," the superintendent shook Else's hand and left, with his usual appeal that she keep her spirits up.

Well, that wouldn't be any problem at all, now that she knew the superintendent thought as she did. It wouldn't be long now before he came and said she was free from prison and could go wherever she wanted. Overcome with joy and excitement, she was unable to sit still, but had to get up and pace the floor.

"Come down to the garden," a voice whispered sharply behind Else and she quickly turned around. The door had opened a crack and Miss Thomsen's hat-covered head was poking into the room.

Else said she didn't want to.

"Come down to the garden," Miss Thomsen repeated, making a face as she usually did when she spoke, "and we'll send those scoundrels packing."

"Don't want to, huh? Don't want to?" Miss Thomsen made a pitiful face. "Come down to the garden," she started up again, repeating her appeal three or four times before she finally shut the door and left.

A while later Dr. Sejer came in with some dental equipment in his hand. After asking Else if she hadn't changed her mind and decided she was glad to be there, he started to examine her tooth over by the window. He stuck both his hands in Else's mouth, not bothering to use a towel. He picked at the tooth and dug around with a sharp instrument; part of the filling had fallen out, he said. He then put in a grey lump and took great pains to make it adhere.

"I certainly hope your tooth will behave itself now," he said as he was leaving.

Else hoped so too, after she'd had to stomach having both his hands, with their metallic odor, in her mouth. She went over to the washstand

and rinsed her mouth clean.

Around six o'clock in the evening the superintendent came into Else's room again.

"Can't I take along a greeting to your husband?" he said after they'd been sitting and talking a while. "Tomorrow I'm going into town."

"If you want to see him, go right ahead," Else answered darkly. "But I don't have any message for him."

"You are a stubborn one," the superintendent said.

"Should you meet my beloved Hieronimus, however," Else continued after a pause, "you must give him my most heartfelt regards."

"Hieronimus – ah! Can't you keep still about that Hieronimus of yours? I'm getting jealous, downright jealous!" The superintendent spoke with such a comical whimper and his face looked so amusingly vexed, that Else had to laugh out loud.

When the superintendent had gone, Else walked out into the corridor and was amazed at the unusual activity out there. Darkly clad female figures, old and young, tall and short, some singly, others arm in arm, almost all with bowed heads and self-conscious expressions, continued to emerge from the little side hallway where Else's room was located, walking past her and disappearing through the double doors at the end of the long corridor.

"What kind of a migration is this?" Else inquired when Anne appeared in the corridor.

"They are from the wards. They come through the double doors at the end of your hall; they're going to a party in the big meeting room."

Yes, of course. There was going to be a party tonight. Both the superintendent and Nurse Schrader had told Else about it and asked if she wanted to join them.

What a densely populated place St. Jørgen's must be! These were just the quiet patients, whose number was infinitesimal compared to the violent ones. Still, so many were coming. And then there was the men's ward, as well.

Chapter 15

"MAY I COME IN for a little bit?" Else was looking through Miss Hall's half-open door into her room; the gas was lit and the glass globe was wrapped in red crepe paper. Miss Hall was sitting in her bed propped up against the high headboard, and she waved eagerly at Else. She and the bed and everything in the room were enveloped in rose-colored light and there was a faint odor of stale musk.

"I have so many little black children," Miss Hall said with her oily, sniggering voice when Else stepped up to the bed. She threw her arm around Else's neck, pulled her down close and whispered in her ear a number of things Else didn't understand.

"I see," Else said. "But listen, Miss Hall, won't you please be more quiet at night?"

"Do I bother you?" Miss Hall quickly asked, suddenly looking ashamed.

"Yes. It's impossible to sleep with you ranting like that. Remember, our beds are right next to each other with just this thin wall in between."

"Can I sing, then? You don't have anything against that, do you?"

"Yes, singing is just as bad. Can't you just lie there quietly?"

"No, I can't." Miss Hall stuck her finger in her mouth and hung her head.

"I don't understand," Else went on. "Surely it can't give you any pleasure to lie there scolding people who can't even hear it?"

"No, but I can't help it."

"Oh, but I'm asking you not to. Won't you please stop?"

"Yes," Miss Hall nodded eagerly. Then she grabbed Else's hands and pressed them against her eyes.

Else bent down and kissed her on the forehead.

"Now you'll see," Miss Hall exclaimed, throwing her head back energetically. "Tonight you won't hear a peep out of me." Her eyes glistened with tears.

"Thank you. Now you're being very sweet."

"Look who's here! Good evening, my child." Miss Hall waved a welcoming hand. "Pull up a chair and sit down."

Else turned around. Miss Thomsen was standing in the middle of the floor, a newspaper in the hand dangling by her side.

"Ah, so you're in here," Miss Thomsen said, looking at Else with sad eyes. "You still haven't come into my room on your own."

"Don't pay any attention to what she says," Miss Hall took hold of Else's arm. "She's very sweet, but she's not quite right in the head. And she's so jealous, the little goose."

"What is she saying?" Miss Thomsen asked, staring into Else's face. "I'm saying you should sit down and read the newspaper to me, like you usually do!" Miss Hall shouted.

"Ha-ha-ha," cooed Miss Thomsen.

Else seated herself on the sofa and Miss Thomsen sat down on a chair she had pulled up underneath the veiled lamp bowl. She unfolded the newspaper and started reading in her snuffling monotone.

"No, I don't care about that!" Miss Hall interrupted. "What business is it of mine whether or not there's room enough in the poorhouse?"

Miss Thomsen started reading something else.

"Pah, this stuff about politics bores me!" Miss Hall interrupted again. "Isn't there anything about murder and drunkards?"

Miss Thomsen searched through the newspaper. "Yes, here's something about an infanticide. 'A young girl, Swedish by birth, left her service the other day,'" Miss Thomsen read. "'Her master and mistress, who couldn't understand what reason she would have to run away, started searching through her things, and in her chest of drawers they found a baby's corpse…'"

"Stop, my child!" Miss Hall exclaimed indignantly, emphatically throwing out her hands. "How can I bear to hear about such things? Read something nice, my child. Life is so beautiful!"

"Well, you've just heard how beautiful it is," Else ventured.

"Life is beautiful," Miss Hall asserted and in a pathetic voice declaimed:

> *Like the eagle I spread my wings –*
> *Soar toward the sun and heaven so blue.*
> *While in my ears the music rings,*
> *Strive on, strive on, I must be true.*

"Miss Hall is just magnificent," Miss Thomsen exclaimed enthusiastically. "But," she turned around completely and whispered to Else, "she's not quite right in the head, all the same."

"Can't you find something nice in your newspaper, you dear little goose?" Miss Hall said.

Miss Thomsen turned the newspaper over and over. "Yes, here is a poem," and then she read:

> *I languish with longing as the days disappear,*
> *As the days turn into weeks and years.*
> *I languish and cry with a voice so clear:*
> *When will our love's spring end my tears?*

"See, that was beautiful!" Miss Hall shouted. "That's the way it should be. Languish and long for love's rosy dawn. I'm going to write a poem for you, Mrs. Kant."

"Thank you," Else said.

"But you mustn't show it to anyone. And you must tell me honestly if you think it shows any talent."

The door opened and Nurse Schrader stepped in.

"Well, so here you are, all three of you together," she said with a friendly smile, and sat down on the sofa where Else had made room for her.

"I came in to see Miss Hall and ask her to be quiet tonight," Else said. "And she will, won't she, Miss Hall?"

Miss Hall set her lips in a pout and didn't answer.

Nurse Schrader sat down for a visit and chatted quietly in her usual intelligent, friendly manner. But the conversation never really got going. Else was the only one who responded. After a couple of minutes Nurse Schrader got up, shook everyone's hand and said good night.

"Bah!" Miss Thomsen blurted, sticking out her long tongue, when Nurse Schrader had gone. "What a ninny!"

"To hell with that battle-ax!" Miss Hall said, bursting into violent laughter.

"Nurse Schrader is a fine person," Else remonstrated.

"Just wait," Miss Thomsen said.

"Yes, just wait," Miss Hall repeated.

"Just wait, just wait." Pointing their fingers at Else, both of them kept up this singsong until she finally put her hands over her ears.

"Be quiet," she cried, getting up. "If you are sweet and kind to Nurse Schrader, you'll find she'll treat you the same way."

"Treat us the same," Miss Thomsen hissed. "Yes, she treats us the same all right, the devil."

"Who exactly are you?" Miss Hall asked when Else came over to her bed to say good night.

"I am Mrs. Else Kant, it's as simple as that."

"But why have you come here?"

"I haven't figured that out myself."

"But they have given you a lucky room. Believe me. You won't stay here for long." Miss Hall threw her arms around Else's neck and kissed her.

"You will remember to be quiet tonight, won't you?"

"Yes, my sweet."

"If she's going to kiss you, I want to, too." Miss Thomsen touched her cold lips to Else's cheek. "Good night."

After Else had left Miss Hall's room, she stopped and peeked in at Mrs. Henderson. There she was in her nightgown, pacing back and forth in her bare feet, hopping in step, forwards and backwards, her back to the door.

Else stood nailed to the spot, looking at her.

Then Anne came along with a glass of medicine and went in to Mrs. Henderson, halting her in her march.

Mrs. Henderson swallowed the medicine, and amiably remarked to Else, "Chloral is excellent. Excellent, I tell you."

"It's just water," Anne laughed.

"Does she always get plain water?"

"No, but often. She has had so terribly much chloral, and if she just thinks it's chloral, she sometimes sleeps anyway."

Chapter 16

ELSE HAD BEEN GIVEN a larger dose of chloral than on the previous evenings. Dr. Vibe's orders, Maren had explained. She lay with her face toward the wall, trying to sleep.

What was that strange sound? A rustling, whispering murmur that rose and fell, sometimes turning into a threatening growl. She lifted her head from the pillow.

"You black, dirty pigs, you vampires, bloodsuckers, you robbers and rascals," a sharp, penetrating voice whispered.

Poor Miss Hall! Yes, she was telling the truth. She just couldn't help herself. She lay there whispering her abuses so she wouldn't disturb Else. It was really very touching.

Else had almost dozed off when a shrill scream accompanied by pounding and loud noise roused her. She quickly sat up in bed and listened. She heard shouting and a high-pitched, terrified voice gabbling, rapid steps, the rattling of keys, a door opening and closing, and then silence.

Sighing, she lay back on her pillow.

A little later the Norn came in. Else asked what the noise had been, and learned that a young girl on Corridor Two had taken castor oil.

"Corridor Two – is that the ward?" Else asked.

"Yes, it's right next door, only a wall between your corridor and theirs. You've probably seen the double doors out there. I understand you're going to have a bath tomorrow, Mrs. Kant. Do you want a tub bath or a shower?"

"A shower, thanks."

"I'll be ready for you at eight o'clock. You shouldn't come any later because I have the others afterwards – two or three groups are coming for a warm bath."

"I'll be there right on time. But tell me – won't I be allowed to be alone while I bathe?"

"Yes, of course you will. For someone like you, I can't see any reason why not. How is the tooth?"

"It doesn't hurt at all, thanks."

"Well then, good night, Mrs. Kant. I'll look in on you later."

And the Norn was faithful to her word. She peeked in on Else three more times and each time found her awake. The Norn shook her head sadly and Else was beside herself. She didn't have a toothache now, and Miss Hall and Mrs. Henderson had both been quiet for a long time. She had also been given chloral, more than before, and still she didn't sleep. No, it was these nagging thoughts which never left her in peace. The fact that she was here. The uncertainty about how long. Impatience for the doctor, who couldn't possibly think she was insane, to let her out of here. Her longing for Tage and anxiety about the future. She could not live without the child, but she would never again return to her home. Just one of these torments would be enough to keep her awake and now there were so many – so many.

That splendid Norn! She hadn't hesitated a minute when Else asked for permission to bathe alone. The Norn didn't think she was insane either. Otherwise she wouldn't have said yes. Bless the dear Norn!

"And the fact that you never sleep – that too is an unmistakable sign of insanity." Oh yes, Hieronimus was a man who knew all the answers!

Chapter 17

ELSE WAS WALKING up and down the long corridor when rounds were made. It was the superintendent.

"Well, have you been out for a walk today?" he asked, stopping in front of Else.

"No, I did that once and I won't do it again. It's intolerable, walking around with the patients like a flock of sheep, with a guard right on my heels."

"Still, it's a pity you don't get out in this lovely spring weather. You've been here for ten or twelve days now, and you've only been out once. The grounds are really very beautiful." The superintendent stepped over to one of the windows.

"Well, I wouldn't know a thing about that," Else replied. "I see nothing, feel nothing, as long as I am here. All I know is this one terrible thing, that I'm being kept locked up in a madhouse."

"No one is hurting you in any way," the superintendent said brusquely, though the expression on his face was gentle. "It's for your own sake that I want you to go outdoors."

"Yes, I know. But it's much too painful for me this way. If you would let me go out alone, I'd go every day."

The superintendent gave Else a keen, scrutinizing look.

"Go out alone – well, you could do that, of course. But wouldn't you try to escape?" Else endured his penetrating gaze and waited a minute before she answered.

No, she thought. I don't want to lie to him. Now if it were Hieronimus . . . but this doctor has been much too good to me. "Yes, I probably would try to escape, if I were allowed to go out alone," she finally said.

The superintendent laughed.

"Well, you can see for yourself. I don't dare let you go out alone. But other than that, we do everything we can to accommodate you. We bring your meals up to your room, and the other day when we had a party for everyone, we didn't make you go."

"You would have had to drag me by the hair to get me to that party," Else replied.

"And when the resident physician from Ward Six was visiting and wanted to see you, we didn't let him come to your room because you said you didn't want to see him."

"Yes," Else said. "I'm tremendously grateful for everything."

"I've brought chloroform and cotton batting for your tooth since it's bothering you again." The superintendent pulled a package out of his pocket and unwrapped a little bottle which he held up against the light to scrutinize. "It's not enough to kill you." Smiling, he handed the bottle and cotton batting to Else.

"I'm not thinking about that either."

"How about the shower in the morning – are you happy about that?"

"Yes, extremely happy. And the Norn, I mean Sibylle, is so wonderful."

"You see! You are actually very happy here with us."

The superintendent made his rounds on the long corridor, in and out of every door, while Else strolled up and down.

When he went into the hallway that led to Else's room, she followed him.

Mrs. Henderson, whose door was open as usual, was walking as she always did, forwards and backwards across the floor. She turned her back to the door.

"Why can't she put on some clothes so she can walk in the corridor?" Else asked. "She clearly needs to move around, poor thing."

"No, because then she would be tearing from one end of the ward to the other." The superintendent was standing in Mrs. Henderson's doorway. "She's skinny enough as it is. The exertion would do her in."

"But would that be such a catastrophe, if the exertion did her in, as you put it?"

"You can't reason that way. Her husband is alive, and he feels he has nothing else to live for but her."

"But when she's like this and will never be any different..."

"He visits her every Sunday, and every week he writes her a letter." The superintendent spoke with a strangely lingering inflection and Else thought he sounded moved. "It's Mrs. Henderson's comfort and joy, and her husband's as well, I believe."

Mrs. Henderson threw out both arms and turned around in the middle of the floor. As soon as she caught sight of the superintendent, she ran over to him, grabbed his arm and said with the usual facial contortions, "The day after tomorrow is Saturday."

"Yes," the superintendent shouted into her ear. "And you'll get a letter from your husband."

"Yes, from Frants!" Mrs. Henderson nodded so emphatically that her hair flew up and down, and her face was so contorted that she looked like a wild person.

"But Maren is horrid," Mrs. Henderson continued. "She won't take the shutters off the windows even though Frants said she should. Frants said so, he did." She cocked her head and looked up into the superintendent's face with the eager, pleading expression of a child.

"That's all right, just wait until your husband comes," the superintendent shouted.

"Last night I slept on the mat outside Mrs. Mørck's door so I could watch over her," Mrs. Henderson said then. "I assure you, superintendent, it was a good thing I was lying there. What would she have done otherwise?"

"But I don't like her," Mrs. Henderson rattled on, pointing at Else. "No, I don't like you at all." She turned her face toward Else and, stretching and twisting her neck in snake-like motions, pointed at Else with her head.

"She isn't hurting you," the superintendent shouted. "She's a very nice lady."

"But I don't know her. I don't know her at all." Mrs. Henderson swung around with a graceful sweep and once again started trotting, oblivious, back and forth on her wide flat feet.

"Now I'll go see Miss Hall and get my usual scolding," the superintendent said with his short, sympathetic laugh.

"Miss Hall is really very sweet," Else remarked and proceeded to tell about the whispering. "When I told her that her whispering bothered me too, she stopped everything. I haven't heard a peep from her since."

"And you still want me to believe you don't sleep," the superintendent teased.

"Want you to believe – why should I want you to believe anything?" Else asked, offended.

"Nervous women always believe they don't sleep," the superintendent said in the same teasing tone.

Else felt like she'd been rapped across her fingers. That had also happened a couple times before. Just when she thought the superintendent was so amiable and reassuring to talk to, he made some remark that pulled the rug out from under her feet.

"Superintendent, you can ask the Norn – Sibylle – if I have slept or not. You do believe what she says, don't you? I dare say she's not a nervous woman who imagines things."

"There, there, Mrs. Kant." The superintendent's tone was once again amiable. "Many times I believe I haven't slept too, but then my wife tells me I've been snoring." The superintendent laughed and Else had to laugh too in spite of herself.

"But I don't snore, you can be sure of that!" Else exclaimed. "And I'll not be able to sleep as long as I'm here. Not really, anyway."

"Do you know what pleases me?" Else had been walking along with the superintendent and they were now standing in front of Miss Hall's door.

"No."

"Can't you guess?"

"Impossible."

"For three days now you haven't talked about Hieronimus. I call that progress."

"No. I swore to myself that I wouldn't utter his name again as long as I'm here. But don't think that means I've forgotten him."

Chapter 18

THE NEXT MORNING the superintendent came with a large envelope full of letters. Else wasn't feeling well and had gone back to bed after her shower and breakfast.

"You see, all of them are unopened," the superintendent said. "Read them and cheer yourself up now."

Else took the envelope silently. She wanted to clasp the superintendent's hand and kiss it. The gratitude she felt toward him – because once again he had treated her like a fellow human being – was enormous.

But she did not kiss his hand. That would look like hysteria. She expressed her deep thanks and left it at that.

The envelope contained all the letters which had come for Else while she had been away from home. In addition there was a reply from Inger, to whom she had written inquiring about the child.

She read that one first, again and again, while her eyes filled with tears. Tage talked about Mama every day and told everyone that mama was in the hospital and would soon be home again. He was healthy and active, was eating and sleeping, and doing very well in every way.

She lay there with Inger's letter in her hands, her thoughts filled with Tage. Thank God he hadn't forgotten her, and still knew he had a mama he expected to see again.

Then she read the other letters. They were from friends and acquaintances and her relatives abroad, and the news was all good.

The last letter she opened was a narrow envelope made of transparent paper and with a disguised handwriting. The envelope gave Else an unpleasant feeling which was more than borne out when she opened it and read the contents. It was an anonymous letter filled with the most poisonous insinuations about her husband's relationship with her.

Else got out of bed, tore the letter and envelope into shreds and put them in the tile stove.

In the afternoon she got dressed and went out to walk in the corridor. Miss Thomsen appeared out of nowhere and slipped her arm through Else's.

"Well, are you quite sure you understand everything," she began, poking her face right into Else's. "There are three conditions: the Christian, the marital and the bloody."

"I see," Else nodded.

"And I am a phenomenon – you know that, don't you?"

"Yes."

"But imagine how those monsters have tormented me with the bloody condition." Miss Thomsen took a firmer grip on Else's arm. "They've gone poking around in my bed, they've opened my window in the middle of winter, and one time they made a cross on the desk in there. What do you think?"

Else didn't know what she should "think." The superintendent's pronouncement that Miss Thomsen was an idiot and would never be otherwise had offended her at the time, but now she knew it was the absolute truth. A few days ago Else had given in to Miss Thomsen's persistent and increasingly urgent requests to walk in the garden, and when Miss Thomsen had Else all to herself down there, it was as if all the dams that held her muddled ideas gave way. Didn't Else know what had happened to her? Hadn't Else read about her bloody condition in the newspapers? Didn't she know the story about the stranger who had put his arm around her waist and carried her across a creek full of dangerous stones? Hadn't she heard how she had been persecuted on account of the bloody condition wherever she had been, both abroad and at home but mostly in here? Else had started out by trying to talk sense to her – Miss Thomsen was otherwise so childishly sweet and reasonable – but she had seen soon enough that it was impossible. Then she took the tack of agreeing to everything she said and patiently listening. But Else had gradually grown so tired and dizzy from her everlastingly repetitive chatter, day in and day out, that she felt something close to fear every time Miss Thomsen came rushing toward her, which she always did as soon as Else appeared outside her room.

"What do you think?" Miss Thomsen repeated. "Wasn't it shameless of them to make a cross?"

"What kind of cross?"

"They had taken a vase of chamomile and placed it crosswise to a photograph. D'you understand?"

"What did they mean by that?" Else sighed.

"They wanted to mock me, of course. You do know what the cross means?"

"No."

"What a goose," Miss Thomsen laughed. "And here you are a grownup! A cross means love, and when they set it crosswise to the bloody condition, well, you can figure it out for yourself. Pah, the scoundrels!"

Anne came along with a glass of milk on a tray and went into one of the rooms, leaving the door open. Else stopped and looked in.

"Come on," Miss Thomsen said. "Maren is a devil, but Anne is worse than the worst."

"What sluts!" cried a young blond woman from her bed inside the room. "I know you, you hussies, you bet I do," she continued, sitting up in bed. "You're the ones who took two chairs and straddled them in the middle of the garden this summer."

"Here is your milk, Miss Nielsen," Anne held the glass out to the blond woman who accepted and drank it.

Else walked in and stood by Anne in front of the bed.

In a loud, angry voice, Miss Nielsen talked about a series of unrelated things, all the while looking straight ahead, her glass in her hand. Suddenly she threw the rest of the milk right in Else's face and crowed, "Take that, you scum!"

"For shame," Anne said, taking the glass from her. "Hell and damnation to all of you!" screamed Miss Nielsen, throwing herself back on the bed and kicking her blanket up in the air. "Go complain to the prison warden, and I'll spit in his eyes!"

"Come along, Mrs. Kant," Anne said.

"Anne put her up to it," Miss Thomsen whispered when Else came out into the corridor. "You understand that, don't you?"

Else shook her head.

"I'm going down to walk with the patients now." Miss Thomsen had followed Else to her door. "Won't you come along?"

"No."

"Oh yes, come. The two of us can go ahead by ourselves. Then we can talk without the others hearing us."

Thanks, Else thought. That was precisely what she wanted with all her heart to avoid.

While Else washed away the milk spots, Miss Thomsen stood in the doorway, coaxing and begging Else to go with her.

"Come along now, Miss Thomsen!" Maren called at last, appearing in the doorway wearing her hat and shawl and a large white apron.

"All right, I'd better go then. Good-bye, Mrs. Kant." Miss Thomsen nodded at Else, stuck her tongue out at Maren, and was off.

Else sat down by the window and started sewing on her table runner. Almost immediately the door opened slowly and Miss Hall, in her night-gown and petticoat, peeked in.

"Please come in," Else said.

Miss Hall stepped inside and shut the door behind her. In the bright sunlight from the window, Else really saw her for the first time. Her sallow, puffy face had small regular features; her glossy black hair, neatly combed and arranged, was streaked with silver; her hazel eyes had a good-natured, though restless, expression; and her delicate red mouth, which never stopped quivering, revealed shining white teeth. Else could see that she must have been very pretty in her youth.

"Why are you always in your stocking feet?" Else asked when Miss Hall was seated in the rocking chair.

"Because I like it," Miss Hall sniggered, sticking her hands into the wide sleeves of her nightgown.

"And in your petticoat and nightgown," Else continued. "You should put a dress on."

"Tell that to the battle-ax," Miss Hall said angrily. "She's taken everything away from me."

"Ask her if you can have your things back. You're doing so well now. Quiet at night and calm and good all day long."

"That's right, isn't it? I never bother you anymore." Miss Hall looked at Else with a proud and happy smile.

"No. Now you're always sweet. I told that to the superintendent and Nurse Schrader, too."

"Oh, those scoundrels!" Miss Hall exclaimed, stamping her foot.

"I like them both very much," Else said.

"Do you really?" Miss Hall's face broke open in a hesitant smile which soon turned into her usual snigger.

"Anyway, there's no use asking," Miss Hall continued seriously. "One day the battle-ax will wake up and decide to bring me my things. I know how this place works, believe me. You should never ask for anything here."

"But now you have to see what my child brought me today." Miss Hall jumped up from her chair, ran out and returned immediately with a saucer containing a few anemones in a bed of damp moss.

"Look," she said, holding the saucer up to Else, her face beaming rapturously. "Aren't they lovely? Oh, I love anemones, the first ones of spring." She bowed her face and gently kissed the flowers. "God bless, bless, bless my little darlings!" When she lifted her head, her eyes were filled with glistening tears.

"They are sweet," Else said.

"Yes, aren't they!" Miss Hall cried. "For me they are ten times more beautiful and precious than for anyone else, because when I see the first anemones I know my evil time is over and every day I'll be better."

"Now you shall hear a poem I have written for you, Mrs. Kant." Miss Hall pulled a folded piece of paper out from under the collar of her nightgown and unfolded it.

"No," she said. "I don't want to read it out loud. It's so embarrassing."

"Oh, please do," Else begged.

"No, no," Miss Hall covered her face with her hands. "I'm sure you will just make fun of it."

"How can you think that?" Else said.

"Read it yourself then," Miss Hall handed the paper to Else.

"I can't understand your handwriting," Else said after looking at it for a while.

"All right, give it to me then. But you have to promise not to make fun."

> *Locked up inside a prison*
> *With many dreary rooms,*

Miss Hall read lugubriously, while a faint blush spread across her cheeks. "Oh dear, you're making a face now."

"Indeed I'm not! The beginning is beautiful. Let me hear more."

> *Locked up inside a prison*
> *With many dreary rooms,*
> *Sits the daughter of a king,*
> *Her fate is filled with gloom.*
> *She longs to beat her wing*
> *Up toward the sky so blue.*
> *But alas, she has no wing,*
> *It has been rent in two.*

"For God's sake, you mustn't make fun, Mrs. Kant."

Miss Hall suddenly ducked her head and hid her face behind the paper, which shook between her hands.

"Believe me, I'm not making fun, Miss Hall."

Miss Hall brushed her hand across her eyes and continued:

> *One day a queen arrives,*
> *Queen from a far-off land.*
> *She smiles with jet-black eyes,*
> *Her name is Mrs. Kant,*

concluded Miss Hall, bursting into embarrassed laughter. "Do you want it?"

"Thank you," Else said. "I would love to have it."

"What do you think of it? Does it show talent?"

"Of course it does."

"In my youth," Miss Hall sighed, "I could write poetry. You should have seen me at the balls in white gauze, holding blazing yellow bouquets. But everything in the world is vanity, you know. I think those who are beautiful and blessed with the greatest gifts, are lifted up by God so that they will plunge, like a brilliant shooting star, into darkness. God must amuse himself with that kind of thing. Because what other form of amusement could he have, Mrs. Kant?"

"Oh," Else said. "One can imagine any number of things."

"Ha! If only one didn't have such an egotistical mother, then one wouldn't have to be here. My goodness! I can hear my birds, my sweet, little birds." Miss Hall bounded out of her chair. "They come every morning and every afternoon and get food from me."

"What kind of birds?"

"Sparrows and bullfinches and ravens, all the birds who live in the trees out there. I give them all the bread I don't eat myself. But Maren and Anne, the greedy beasts, steal it from me whenever they get a chance. That's why I keep it on me."

"Where?" Else asked. "You're not wearing a dress so you have no pockets."

"Inside my drawers, where else?" Miss Hall snatched the saucer with the anemones, waved a farewell hand and left.

A moment later Else heard Miss Hall open the window in her room, followed by the sound of affectionate chattering interspersed with scratching and pecking and something that sounded like lightly falling hail.

Chapter 19

Miss hall was amazing, Else thought. In spite of all the misery connected with being at an insane asylum, she welcomed the little things life offered with enthusiasm and joy. Her delight over the first blossom of spring, her exuberant happiness at feeding the birds, her intense emotions which found expression in lyrical creations, the satisfaction she derived from her "child's" company, and now her proud joy over having controlled herself at night for Else's sake. It was as if she were revived by all this, and every day that passed found her more and more contented and normal.

Maybe that was the secret in finding contentment in this world – accepting the good, little things, living for them and being thankful for them.

Else set her work aside and took a deep breath. She longed for air. Should she go down to the garden for a while? Miss Thomsen was out now, so she would be left in peace.

She got her hat and jacket from the closet out in the corridor, and as she was slowly pulling on her gloves, she peeked in at Mrs. Henderson, whose door was, as always, open.

Mrs. Henderson was once again walking forwards then backwards, up and down the room. Else stood and marvelled, as so often before, at this slow, tireless, measured march. Would she notice that someone was looking at her this time too? It was as if Mrs. Henderson had eyes in the back of her head.

Sure enough. She turned around with a start and came running toward the door.

"I told you not to look at me," Mrs. Henderson said in a threatening voice. Bobbing and twisting her head, she spoke right into Else's face. "Who are you? You shouldn't be here at all, and I'm going to tell that to Frants and the superintendent!"

"I don't want to harm you!" Else cried.

"Go away!" Mrs. Henderson said. "Go away! You don't even know Mrs. Mørck!"

"I'm going now," Else said.

When Else came downstairs into the large corridor which parallelled the one above exactly, she saw through an open door an immense, ruddy woman who stood in the middle of the room lifting up her skirts, while her dull, swollen eyes stared straight ahead. Else stood still and gazed at her.

"Go away, Mrs. Kant," Anne said as she walked by with a tray.

"Why shouldn't I look at her?"

"Because she hits. She might rush over to you and knock you flat. She's terribly strong."

Else retreated hastily, found a maid with a set of keys to open the door to the garden, and hurried out.

One of the maids was walking with a patient who was carrying a large grey cat in her arms. She moved along hopping and swaying, kissing the cat repeatedly and talking to it with loving gestures. Her ankles were constantly turning in and the maid had to keep reaching out to catch her to stop her from falling.

The garden was wide and spacious, surrounded by a high wooden fence, with several paths all of which went in circles. There was a large lawn in the middle, naked beds of earth, and clusters of different kinds of trees which were beginning to bud.

Oh dear, there was Mrs. Winther sitting on one of the benches, a large brown fur piece over her shoulders, her head bare and her umbrella opened.

Else wanted to turn around, but Mrs. Winther turned her head and nodded at her, so she didn't dare. ———

"Well, out getting some exercise," Mrs. Winther said with a derisive laugh. "We go around in circles here too, 'round, 'round, 'round. What a lovely world we live in." Mrs. Winther laughed until she shook.

"Yes, these circular paths are a bore," Else replied, thinking she ought to say something.

"You needn't feel embarrassed," Mrs. Winther said bubbling with laughter. "You can just leave."

What a supercilious woman, Else thought as she walked on, downcast and self-conscious. She would certainly take care to not walk close to the bench where Mrs. Winther was sitting. She took small turns, back and forth, in the upper part of the garden.

Suddenly she heard running steps from behind and knew that it was Miss Thomsen. Oh, if only she could leap over that wooden fence and get away from her. Now, once again, she'd be pestered to death by this interminable jumble of deep-seated, crackbrained ideas.

"I figured you were here," Miss Thomsen said, breathlessly putting her arm through Else's. "When you go up to your room, you'll get a surprise."

"What?" Else asked.

"I won't tell," Miss Thomsen replied, quivering with joy. "But just wait. Something that will make you happy."

What could make her happy? A letter? No, there was no mail at this time of day. And besides, as long as she remained here, letters brought her no pleasure.

"Look," Miss Thomsen whispered. "There's a maid over there who is going to spy on us."

Else looked all around and couldn't see any maid except the one who was walking next to the tottering patient with the cat in her arms.

"Her?" Else said. "The only reason she's over there is to help that patient."

"That's just an excuse. Don't you see that? I don't understand how you can be so dumb, Mrs. Kant."

Else was silent. What was the use trying to make Miss Thomsen understand that she was mistaken. She had struggled in vain far too many times. "Just look, look at the way she's peering at us! Pah, the bitch! I'd like to skin her alive."

Coming from the fair-haired Miss Thomsen whose appearance was so childlike and mournful, these words seemed so comical that Else burst out laughing.

Miss Thomsen laughed along with her.

"Yes, you can end up going crazy," she exclaimed, visibly proud of having said something funny. "But there are these three conditions: the Christian, the marital and the bloody. And finally, you mustn't forget this – I'm a phenomenon."

Here came the whole song and dance. Else felt her muscles tighten and she stared glumly into space. Every time Miss Thomsen poked her face into Else's and said, "Isn't that right?" or, "Do you understand?", Else said "yes" and nodded. Her thoughts floated from one thing to another while Miss Thomsen's snuffling chatter buzzed in her ears. It was as if she were walking through some lonesome place, her foot hampered by a chain, rattling as it dragged across the ground.

She could of course be spared Miss Thomsen's incessant pestering if she complained to the superintendent or Nurse Schrader. They would simply forbid Miss Thomsen to talk to her. But Else didn't have the heart to do that. Miss Thomsen clearly found comfort and relief in confiding in her and, in spite of everything, Else felt some affection for her too.

"But now I've written my ultimatum." Miss Thomsen came to a sudden stop.

"Yes," Else thought. "You've said that before."

"I'm telling you, the superintendent was flabbergasted. Have I told you what he said?"

"Yes," Else replied, in an attempt to avert the response.

"I have now set myself a deadline of June 9th," Miss Thomsen went on. "It will then be one year since I came here. If I'm not out of here by then, I'll escape."

"Yes," Else said. And for the tenth time got a description of how Miss Thomsen would go about "escaping." Sew her sheets together around two or three o'clock at night, tie them securely to the hook on the window, and lower herself down to the garden. Then she would just have to climb over the fence and run into town.

"Then I'll come to your place," Miss Thomsen concluded. "I have your address. Because you'll be out of here long before then, I'm sure of that. Don't you think so?"

"I hope so."

"Then we'll travel together," Miss Thomsen continued. "Stay at a pension down in Switzerland, or up in Norway. You always travel in the summertime, don't you?"

Else nodded. Miss Thomsen had been going on about the two of them travelling together for over a week now.

"You see, there's nothing wrong with me," Miss Thomsen insisted earnestly. "I can make plans and talk sensibly about all kinds of things. I can write my ultimatum to the superintendent. I can be crafty too and trick those rascals. And I have a mission."

"A mission?"

"Yes, a mission for all the unhappy phenomenons in the world. That is why I have to suffer so much. Christ had to, too."

"Ah yes, Christ," Else said.

"Can't you see that it's exactly the same with me? What did Christ want? To save unhappy souls. What do I want? To save the phenomenons."

"There's the bell for supper," Else said, breathing a sigh of relief. "We have to go up."

In her room Else found a dish with some anemones and violets poked into a bed of damp moss and, adorning the mirror above the dresser, some boughs of spruce. So that was what Miss Thomsen had meant when she had talked about a pleasant surprise.

Later, after Else had eaten supper, Miss Thomsen came in and let her eyes, questioning yet rapturous, wander from Else to the anemones to the spruce boughs above the dresser. "It was a surprise, wasn't it?"

Else thanked her warmly.

"You haven't forgotten our evening together, have you, Mrs. Kant?" Miss Hall stood in the doorway, waving and bobbing her head.

"No, I'm coming now. Go along, Miss Thomsen. I just want to take a peek at Mrs. Henderson."

"Why do you want to do that?" Miss Thomsen pouted.

"Because I can't help it." As soon as she'd said it, Else realized her reply echoed Miss Hall's that time she had asked her to keep still at night.

Mrs. Henderson wandered up and down, her back to the door, in perfect step and imperturbable, head bowed and hair flying. Else stood nailed to the spot.

"What's become of you?" There was Miss Hall, in stocking feet and knee-length slip, and those huge legs.

"Isn't it strange that she can bear to keep on plodding like that?" Else said. "Look at her feet, the skin is worn to shreds."

At that moment Mrs. Henderson turned around and ran to Miss Hall with outstretched arms.

"Frants is coming on Sunday!" she shouted, noisily gasping for breath and grabbing Miss Hall by the shoulders.

"Congratulations!" cried Miss Hall.

"I've written a letter to Frants," Mrs. Henderson continued. "But I'm keeping it next to my heart. I'm keeping it next to my heart, I tell you!" Mrs. Henderson uttered the words with such force and such violent facial contortions that her pale grey cheeks took on a faint blush, and the veins in her forehead bulged. "The shutters are always locked and they could just as well be open now, because I'm not thinking about escape anymore. I'm not thinking about escape any more!" she repeated in a wild screech.

"Has Mrs. Henderson tried to escape?" Else asked when she and Miss Thomsen were sitting in the red glow of Miss Hall's room.

"Yes, she tied her sheets together and lowered herself down from the window, just the way my child is planning to do it." Miss Hall chided Miss Thomsen and then told how Mrs. Henderson had sprained her ankle at the time but had still managed to drag herself twelve miles, halfway to town, before she was caught and driven back.

"You shouldn't run away," Miss Hall continued. "One must be released from this place. So now you know, my child," she said, admonishing Miss Thomsen once again. "You won't accomplish anything – you'll just be grabbed by the scruff of the neck and brought back, and then you'll be a lot worse off than you are now."

"You would almost think that's what she wants," Miss Thomsen said angrily. "She looks so happy when she says it."

"It smells like spring in here!" Miss Hall exclaimed, clapping her hands in enthusiasm; she walked around the room sniffing each of the many spruce boughs and each dish of anemones and wild violets.

"And I have her, my sweet child, to thank for this."

"Yes," Miss Thomsen said. She was sitting on the little sofa next to Else; she sighed deeply and her mournful child-eyes took on an unaccustomed luster. "If we didn't have God's blessed spring, then what?" She threw her arms around Else's waist and buried her face in her lap.

"I'm going to bed now," Miss Hall said. "Don't look at me. Good night, good night, good night," she went around and kissed the spruce boughs and flowers.

"And my sweet, little birds, I shall not forget them in the morning." From behind the curtain she took a plate of bread crusts and put the contents under her pillow.

"There!" she said after she had jumped into bed and pulled the covers up. "Now you may read to me, my child."

"Miss Hall wants you to read!" Else called to Miss Thomsen, whose face was still buried in her lap.

Miss Thomsen sat up. "If I just had a knife, I'd do this." She held out her left hand and made a slashing motion across her wrist with the other.

"Now, now!" Miss Hall cried from her bed. "We've all thought about that. But it wouldn't do any good. How could we know that we wouldn't end up someplace even worse?"

Chapter 20

"I WOULD LIKE TO SPEAK WITH YOU for a moment," Else said to the superintendent one morning during rounds; he was accompanied by a young assistant she hadn't seen before.

"All right; but why do you refuse to go outdoors? Your cheeks are getting so pale and thin. Surely you could take walks in the garden."

"Walk around that wretched garden like a chicken inside a chalk circle!"

"Is the garden wretched." The superintendent laughed.

"I took a walk with Nurse Schrader the other day. I'd be glad to go out with her."

"Well now," the superintendent said a few minutes later when he was back in Else's room without the assistant. "Have you read this?" He picked up a book from the table and leafed through it. "What do think of it?"

"How long do you intend to keep me here?" Else replied.

"I don't know."

"You don't know? Who is supposed to know, if not you?"

"Calm down, Mrs. Kant." He sounded slightly impatient. "You should be happy to be here. That's my opinion."

"I've been put here because I supposedly suffer from some form of insanity. Could you tell me what it is?" Else asked, looking squarely at the superintendent.

"Form of insanity ... form of insanity." The superintendent looked annoyed. "You are here for observation."

"For observation!" Else exclaimed. "Wasn't I subjected to enough observation in Ward Six?"

"That wasn't the conclusion of those in charge."

"Those in charge! Who is in charge? Hieronimus! If he measured himself with the same yardstick he uses on other people, wouldn't he be in here too?"

"Who swore she would never again mention Hieronimus's name?" Furrowing his brow, the superintendent leaned forward toward Else.

"I don't understand this," Else said, holding her head in her hands. "I've been here for fourteen days, and you must admit, if you are honest, that you haven't seen any sign of insanity in me whatsoever. Neither you nor Nurse Schrader, who has been so attentive and talks to me at least three times every day."

"One cannot determine if a person is insane just like that."

"But imagine yourself in the same situation as I am now. What would you do?"

"Myself, in the same situation?" The superintendent wrinkled his nose.

"I know, but just suppose," Else went on. "You have been sick and unable to sleep, careworn and depressed, with or without foundation in the opinion of those around you. Year after year you have suffered from a nervous cough which has consumed all your resistance. Then you go to a person who is well-known for his insight and competence in treating cases of this nature and he takes you by the collar, says you are crazy and throws you in the clink, where nobody can get in to see you."

"Really now, the clink," the superintendent laughed. "Well, I would calmly accept the fact that I was there until someone released me."

"That's easy to say," Else said. "But God knows if you would be able to take it with such nonchalance when it came right down to it. Here I sit arrested for lunacy," she continued indignantly, "and I'm not even allowed to know the nature of my lunacy?"

"Well, in the first place there's your anger toward your husband," the superintendent said.

Else clenched her fists and raised herself slightly in her chair. She sat back down again and said, "Is that what my lunacy consists of?"

"Among other things."

"With Hieronimus it was my inability to control myself, my predisposition to paint abnormal pictures, my insomnia. And here – well, the possibilities are endless, if you are so inclined."

"Calm down," the superintendent said again.

"No, I will not calm down!" Else cried. "Why should I, when I feel I'm being treated disgracefully? Yes, disgracefully! I am not insane and I don't belong here. What do I say and do that isn't normal, if I may ask? I don't have hallucinations, no *idées fixes*, no obsessions. And even if I did, there's still the question of whether you are justified in keeping me locked up against my will!"

"But what would you do if I let you go?" the superintendent asked, irritated. "You don't want to go home to your husband."

"What business is it of yours what I do or don't do, as a citizen or as an individual? I thought you were the superintendent at St. Jørgen's, not Mrs. Kant's guardian."

"Write to your husband and ask him to visit you. Then perhaps the three of us can come to an agreement."

"Never!" Else cried. "Not if I have to stay here forever. I do not understand how you can confuse these two things. The question for you must be: Is Mrs. Kant insane, and is she insane in such a way that requires her to be kept under lock and key? The fact that a woman is angry at her husband is no reason to lock her up. If you were to take responsibility for all the angry wives, where would you find the space?"

"Well, we'll have to wait and see," the doctor said, as if he were reconsidering.

"Don't wait too long," Else pleaded.

"You must understand that when an authority like Hieronimus sends you to me, I have to keep you for the entire observation period."

"How long does the observation period last?"

"It varies." The superintendent rose and shook Else's hand. "Just stay calm, Mrs. Kant. I'm not going to hurt you."

Chapter 21

"I HAVE A COUPLE OF BOOKS for you," Nurse Schrader said when she came in the evening. "*René Mauperin*, it's one of my favorite books. And there's also one by Mrs. Edgren." [12]

They talked about books they both had read and Else was again struck by how similar their tastes and opinions were.

"We play ombre now and then in my room," Nurse Schrader remarked. "Dr. Vibe and myself and a couple of others. Wouldn't you like to join us sometime, Mrs. Kant?"

Else thanked her and said she would love to.

"I have to laugh when I think about the time I was learning to play ombre," Nurse Schrader said. "All night long I lay dreaming about ombre, and I actually learned the game in my dreams."

"That's exactly what happened with me!" Else exclaimed animatedly. "I learned it at night in my dreams. Literally!"

Nurse Schrader handed Else a package of silk threads she had purchased for her table runner and said she hoped it was what she wanted. "I've been looking at your apron," she remarked. "What lovely embroidery."

"It was actually a lamp doily that someone gave me for Christmas," Else said. "But I don't like lamp doilies, so I made it into an apron."

Nurse Schrader leaned back in the rocking chair and chuckled. Else gave her a puzzled look. "Isn't that funny?" Nurse Schrader said. "I got a lamp doily for Christmas, too, and I made it into an apron."

"Mrs. Kant, what's become of you?" Miss Thomsen poked her head in, but when she caught sight of Nurse Schrader she retreated, dumb-founded, and slammed the door shut.

Nurse Schrader stood up.

"Oh no, don't go," Else pleaded. "Talking with you is much nicer than sitting in Miss Hall's room."

"Oh my goodness, you really must go in and see them. Otherwise they'll think it's my fault. They've gotten used to having you there in the evening, and frankly, you've been a good influence on them both. And I think you enjoy it too – isn't that so?"

Else sighed. "Oh I suppose. If they were to suddenly vanish, I'd proba-bly miss them. People in prison can't be choosy."

"We'll go for a walk again soon," Nurse Schrader said. "And you must come and see my room some day. I actually have two rooms in the sum-mer, but not during the winter because one of them doesn't have a tile stove. Good night."

As soon as Nurse Schrader had gone, Miss Thomsen reappeared and motioned to her. Else rose and followed her into Miss Hall's room.

Chapter 22

"WHAT A CHARMING PLACE you have," Else said. She was standing in Nurse Schrader's room, which was abundantly furnished with a carpet, draperies and a portiere, a well-stocked bookshelf, pictures on the walls, and lots of bric-a-brac and embroidery.

"If you'd like to come in here occasionally during the day, you are most welcome," Nurse Schrader said and hurried out.

Else remained in the room and looked around. A number of photographs were displayed on the desk in the corner, and a couple of the latest books, their pages still uncut, were lying on the table in the middle of the room.

When Else stepped out into the corridor, the door next to Nurse Schrader's room was wide open, and Anne was inside sweeping the carpet. A fair-complexioned woman with a gentle face was lying in the bed by the window and when Else paused in the threshold, she gave a friendly nod.

Else went in and said hello to the fair-skinned, gentle woman, but a second later ran back into the corridor with her hand over her nose, terrified and sickened by the unbearable stench in the room.

"Oh Anne, Anne!" she cried from out there. "How can you stand it?"

"The smell you mean? You stand what you have to."

"But what stinks like that?"

"Her breath, poor thing."

"Good God," Else exclaimed. "Never in my life have I smelled anything so foul."

"It is pretty bad," said Anne, coming out with the broom and dustpan, her face a sickly yellow. "I often feel like I'm going to choke, but it's worse for her."

The fair-skinned woman in the bed smiled and nodded continuously. Finally she lifted her hand and beckoned.

"No," Else said to herself. "I can't possibly go back in there."

Back in Else's own hallway, Maren was standing by the table in front of the window, stacking cups and plates from breakfast.

"I've eaten now!" Mrs. Henderson came screaming into the hallway, dressed in her nightgown.

"That's good!" Maren shouted. "I'll be sure and tell Nurse Schrader."

"And then I'll get my letter. Won't I?" Mrs. Henderson seized Maren by the shoulders and looked at her with anxious, imploring eyes.

"Of course you will, Mrs. Henderson! You know that perfectly well!" Maren shouted.

Mrs. Henderson went back to her room where she marched up and down, keeping time, forwards and backwards, her back to the door while she repeated over and over again, "I've eaten!"

"She hadn't touched her food for three or four days," Maren explained with her sweet, shy smile. "So Nurse Schrader said that she wouldn't get her letter as long as she didn't eat. And that helped. Today she ate her breakfast all up."

Else heard the scuffing sound of Miss Thomsen's big feet behind her, and she shuddered.

"Come into my room," Miss Thomsen said, grabbing hold of Else. "Bring your work. All right?"

"You don't have to put up with Miss Thomsen's pestering," Maren said sympathetically. "It must exhaust you. Just tell the superintendent."

"What? Huh, the superintendent," muttered Miss Thomsen.

Else gave Maren a nod. Then she fetched her needlework, went into Miss Thomsen's room and sat down by the window. And all the while Miss Thomsen's eternal chatter was humming and buzzing in her ears.

Oh, how tired and beleaguered she felt. How could the superintendent have the heart to keep her there any longer? How could such a humane man consent to her being declared incompetent and treated like a criminal or dangerous person?

The door opened and in came a stout, heavyset woman in a pretty black wool dress with a lace collar; she wore a diamond brooch and a gold watch chain around her neck, and her fleshy, sallow face was beaming.

"Hurrah!" cried Miss Thomsen, jumping up from her chair.

"Well, the battle-ax has handed over all my possessions," the woman said contentedly. At that point Else recognized her. Who would have thought that Miss Hall with her stocking feet, knee-length slip, and white nightgown with the shapeless sleeves could look so neat and ladylike?

"Would you like one?" Miss Thomsen asked, tossing an orange into Miss Hall's lap, when she had seated herself on the sofa.

"Now, now, my child. We serve oranges with plates and silver knives."

"It won't be long now before I escape," Miss Thomsen exclaimed with an exuberant kick. "Look at her," she said, pointing at Miss Hall. "Isn't it a low-down mockery and disgrace that she should be here?"

"There, there, my child. I'll stay here until summer. Then they'll send me home. No one is keeping me here any longer than necessary." The nice clothes had brought a calm dignity and a quiet contentment to Miss Hall.

Then it was time for rounds. The superintendent came in. "Good day, ladies," he said with a friendly wave.

"Well, Miss Hall, you've blossomed into a butterfly, as you always do when spring makes its appearance."

Just then Miss Thomsen stormed over to the superintendent, her hands on her hips.

"What about me, why should I be here?" she shouted, and defiantly looked straight into his eyes. Her pale eyes were flashing green with indignation and her entire body trembled with hatred.

"We have talked about that often enough, you know," the superintendent said with a shrug of his shoulders.

"You ought to be ashamed of yourself!" Miss Thomsen stamped her foot and her face grew red. "You got my ultimatum a long time ago. But just wait til you're dead! The flames of Hell will be ten times hotter when the gates are finally opened up for you!"

The superintendent made no reply, just looked at her with a mixture of distaste and compassion.

Miss Thomsen stared intently at the superintendent for a few seconds. "Why should I be here!" she shouted again, threatening with her fist. "You won't answer that... you... you... Because you don't dare!" She turned around on her heel and walked over to the window where she stood with her back to the room.

"And you, Mrs. Kant," the superintendent said, turning to Else. "Industrious as always. If I grant you and Miss Hall permission to take walks alone, will you go outdoors then?"

"But my child has to come along!" cried Miss Hall.

"All right," the superintendent said to Miss Hall. "I know I can depend on you this time of the year. The three of you may take walks. But not yet – first you must get used to the fresh air down in the garden, Miss Hall."

Else let her work fall and she gave the superintendent a troubled, questioning look. He had no intention of releasing her. First Miss Hall was supposed to get used to fresh air, and then she would take walks with Else. That could take a long time.

"Was there something you wanted to say, Mrs. Kant?" The superintendent was standing with his hand on the door handle, ready to leave.

"Yes. I want to ask the same thing I did the other day: how long will I be here?"

The superintendent furrowed his brow and motioned impatiently.

"Since, after all, I am not insane," Else said.

The superintendent yanked the door open.

"No, answer me now!" Else cried earnestly. "Why won't you let me go?"

"Because you are not normal."

"You owe me proof of that!"

"There is proof enough," the superintendent replied brusquely. "Your anger toward Hieronimus, for example."

Else stood staring at the door through which the superintendent had disappeared. They were going to drive her insane after all. By hook or by crook. This stupid nonsense about her anger toward someone or other, presented as proof that she wasn't normal. How could she answer that? It was like fighting windmills. Despondency crept over her and she had to struggle to not give in to tears.

"Don't be sad," Miss Hall consoled. "You won't be here long."

"I've already been here much too long," Else answered darkly, sitting down and taking up her needlework again; eyes blinded by tears, she leaned over her work to see more clearly.

Miss Thomsen, who was still standing by the window with her back to the room, started muttering angrily under her breath. With a sudden, deep moan, she threw herself down on a chair, leaned her face and arm on the windowsill and burst into racking sobs.

Miss Hall went over to Miss Thomsen and tried to soothe her.

"Oh well," Miss Thomsen said at last, sitting up and drying her face. "It's all in vain. There's no hope. But they will be punished for their crimes, for there is a God in Heaven. In the name of our Redeemer, Jesus Christ, Amen." She leaned back in the chair with her arms dangling at her sides. Her head was bowed, her chin rested on her chest, and her twisted face was set in bitter sadness.

From her pocket Miss Hall took a small piece of needlework and a little case containing a gold thimble. She sat down on the sofa and started sewing, chattering away and laughing, completely unaware that neither Else nor Miss Thomsen were paying her any mind.

Then Nurse Schrader came with Miss Hall's hat and coat and wanted her to go down to the garden. Miss Hall was willing, but asked Else to come along. She had to have someone to lean on, and her "child" was not in a good mood.

Else got up immediately to fetch her wraps.

"You look so dispirited." Nurse Schrader had gone with Else to her room.

"Yes," Else said and she told her what the superintendent had said.

Nurse Schrader tried to cheer her up. What was the superintendent supposed to say when patients asked him over and over why they were there. It wasn't an easy matter, being the superintendent.

"But the other patients," Else remarked, "they're all abnormal one way or another, at least the ones I've seen."

"Do you believe any of them would agree?"

"No, but there is a difference, after all." Else was no longer able to hold back her tears.

"Just have faith and be calm, Mrs. Kant." Nurse Schrader put her arms around Else's shoulders and looked at her sympathetically. "You were being so sensible and cheerful just now. Take my word: the superintendent is treating you fairly. You and everyone else. He has the greatest interest in his patients. But he does have to keep you here a little while to get a clear idea of your condition. Right, Mrs. Kant?"

"I suppose," Else sighed. "There is nothing I can do."

A little later she was walking on the circular paths in the garden between Miss Hall and Miss Thomsen, one on each arm. They chattered and asked questions and demanded answers, both at the same time. Finally Else felt she was going to drop from exhaustion and she suggested they go up. But Miss Hall and Miss Thomsen were both full of energetic protests and they clung more tightly to Else's arms, insisting it was so invigorating to walk.

Chapter 23

ELSE HEARD ROUNDS being made in the corridor and hastily grabbed her dress. If she could just get it on in time to unlock the door. Otherwise she would have to explain why she had shut herself up in her room, and she didn't want to do that. She didn't dare confess that she often had to take off her clothes in the morning and search her undergarments for the fleas she picked up down in the bathroom. Fleas in the "sanatorium"! Could there be a better proof of Mrs. Kant's insanity?

She had just turned the key in the lock and sat down with her needlework when the door opened. It was the pleasant young assistant with the wide face and fair complexion. The superintendent was away that day, he explained, so he had come in his place.

Else kept busy with her sewing and said no more than was absolutely necessary in reply to his questions.

The assistant stood there, his round eyes directed at Else. His gaze was a mixture of curiosity and attentiveness.

"Well, you received a letter from your famous countryman and poet yesterday, didn't you?" the assistant finally said.[13]

"Yes."

"What did he write?"

"What did he write? He wrote as he usually does, of course, a friendly, gracious letter." Else shifted her position in the chair and didn't lift her eyes from her needlework.

"It's nice that you have made such good friends," the assistant ventured.

"Friends?"

"Yes. Miss Hall and Miss Thomsen. You are with them all the time."

Else made no reply.

"Miss Hall, by the way, will probably be leaving in a couple of months," the assistant went on. "But in the autumn you'll get her back."

Else gave a start and quickly looked up at the assistant. But without a word, she bent over her work again and went on sewing.

Eventually the assistant left.

"March, out you go!" Else heard Miss Hall shout a moment later from her room. "Who do you think you are, king for a day?"

Else had to laugh.

The next day was Sunday. Else was in bed when the superintendent and Nurse Schrader came in the morning. She had been down and showered but had gone back to bed again – rounds were so early on Sunday that she didn't have time to get dressed.

"Well," the superintendent said. "Here you are, lounging in bed while the rest of us are slaving away."

Else didn't answer. Since the other day in Miss Thomsen's room, a feeling of resentment toward the superintendent had been growing, and she made no attempt to hide it.

"Here are a couple of letters for you." The superintendent reached into his pocket and put the letters on the bedspread next to Else, who thanked him.

"You're sleeping at night now, aren't you?" the superintendent asked amiably.

"Yes, sometimes. For a couple of hours."

"Six, I'd say. That's not bad. Pretty soon we can start reducing the chloral."

"You know more about that than I do, I suppose," Else remarked. "Last night I didn't sleep more than an hour and a half. I keep my watch on the table, and the gas is lit, so it's easy enough to keep track."

"And we've sent the toothache packing," the superintendent went on.

"Yes. Thanks to the chloroform."

"There you see! We are doing something good for you."

"I've written a letter to my friend Mrs. Hein asking her to visit me. You did say she's welcome to come, didn't you, superintendent?"

"That would please me greatly. Are there other people you would like to see?"

"No thank you. No others."

"Still just as embittered toward your husband?"

"Yes."

"He comes so faithfully to ask about you whenever I'm in town, and he has such a disheartened look."

"Let him."

"Stubborn lady," the superintendent smiled. Then his expression changed, and he added with annoyance, "Well, I really don't know what to say. You can't be completely normal as long as you feel this bullheaded resentment toward your husband."

"No, of course not. So let me be abnormal then."

Nurse Schrader, who was standing at the foot of the bed shook her head disapprovingly at Else.

"Well then, good day Mrs. Kant."

One of the letters was from Inger and the contents were, as usual, about Tage. Else pressed the letter to her breast. She had a premonition that the constant aching to see her child and the gnawing anxiety inside her would turn to consumption in the end.

&

In the afternoon Else took a walk with Nurse Schrader, who led her down the loveliest paths, across fields and through woods, showing her the prettiest views. It was a glorious sunny day and spring was in the air. But Else was feeling so weak and unwell that she wasn't able to enjoy either the sunshine or the spring air. A couple of times she thought she might faint and every time they came to a bench, she wanted to sit down. Nurse Schrader talked about this and that, but Else only listened with half an ear. Her thoughts circled around the same thing that always occupied her. Finally she said:

"If you were to be absolutely truthful, Nurse Schrader, and tell me what you think – would you say that I am insane?"

"Not really insane," Nurse Schrader said hesitantly.

"What then?"

"Extremely nervous."

"Nervous – my God, nervous? I don't know what you mean by that word. That it's torture for me to have to stay in this place, that I can't resign myself – is that what you mean?"

"Yes, that's part of it."

"Suppose I were happy to be here, wouldn't that be viewed as evidence of insanity, too? Oh well – there's no use talking about it," Else interrupted herself. "Nervous – I've been so calm lately."

"Yes, you're calm enough," Nurse Schrader replied.

They had met a number of people on their walk – men strolling alone or in groups, accompanied by an attendant; a group of women with kerchiefs tied around their heads, ushered along by a maid. They had all greeted Nurse Schrader, who informed Else that they were patients from the hospital. Now, as they were walking up the hill toward the hospital gate, Dr. Vibe came toward them.

He called out a friendly greeting, turned and joined them on their walk.

Else nearly forgot that she was at a madhouse when she spoke with Dr. Vibe. He had such a sensitive and unassuming manner; nothing about him intimated that she was the patient, he the doctor. None of Dr. Sejer's admonitions, well-meaning though they were, about how she ought to feel grateful and glad to be there; not so much as a trace of the expression in the assistant's eyes when he looked at her, a look that put her in a class with objects on display.

They walked by one of the hospital buildings that was encircled by a garden with a tall picket fence. The garden was full of patients milling around. One of them called out, "Hey you, stranger lady, come over here!"

Else looked over. Waving at her through the picket fence was a slender woman in a tidy blue cotton dress. She was blond and had a pretty face.

"That's Madam Nilsen," Dr. Vibe said.

Else walked over to the fence and Nurse Schrader and Dr. Vibe followed.

"Can't you help me get out of here?" Madam Nilsen asked.

"I wish I could help myself," Else muttered, her eyes on a large square female figure who was sitting on her haunches on a little grassy mound inside the picket fence, making growling noises. Her arms lay crossed upon her belly, and her hands dangled restlessly; her face, round as a ball, was dark blue, with frightfully large open lips; and a yellow-checked kerchief was wound into a pointed turban around her head. The figure resembled a pagoda.

"Oh stranger lady, you must help me," Madam Nilsen entreated. "I have two daughters I could stay with down there on the mountain. Oh my, isn't that pretty," she said, pointing at Else's waistband of blue shot silk, visible under her fur piece. "Isn't that what they call a spencer?"

"I have to go home," Nurse Schrader said. "Come on."

"I'm counting on you to help me!" Madam Nilsen called out to Else.

"The desire for freedom is a strange thing," Dr. Vibe said. "It never dies in people. There are people who have been here for forty years and they have never stopped longing for freedom."

"Well, that just goes to show you," Else replied smiling. "I've only been here a few weeks – imagine how I must feel."

"Hmm," Dr. Vibe said, returning her smile. Then he bade her good evening and left.

Else had gone upstairs and was tiptoeing into her own hallway so Miss Hall and Miss Thomsen wouldn't hear her, when Mrs. Henderson came hurtling through her doorway. She grabbed the front of Else's fur piece and vehemently uttered some words which sounded more inarticulate than usual. A moment later she loosened her grip and pushed Else away.

"It's you!" she screamed and her pathetic, ashen face looked terror-stricken. "I thought you were Nurse Schrader. Go away, go!" She threw up her hands, turned and started to march.

"Good evening," Else said to Anne who was sitting in the hallway crocheting a wide piece of cream-colored lace. "How pretty," she said, pointing at the lace. "And how beautifully you crochet."

"Yes," Anne said with a happy smile. "I'm working on my trousseau."

"Are you getting married?"

"Yes, this summer. I'd like to show you what I've already finished." Anne got up and led Else into the tiny little hallway outside Miss Thomsen's bedroom, where she opened a large ottoman and showed Else layer upon layer of beautiful, handmade articles. There were curtains, ready to hang, with wide, lace-crocheted borders; candle doilies; embroidered napkins for bread baskets; a knitted bedspread and much more.

"Have you really done all this in your spare time?" Else asked and looked admiringly down into the ottoman.

"All of it. It is amazing what you can accomplish when you just keep at it, morning and night. That's what I'm doing now. And when it's for your trousseau, it's easier of course."

"Thank you for showing this to me, Anne."

"Oh, so that's where you've been keeping yourself," a voice whined when Else and Anne came out. Mrs. Seneke was standing in the middle of the hallway, wrapped in her grey shawl, her haggard face peeking out. Sticking out below were a pair of childishly thin legs and feet in felt slippers.

"Was there something you wanted, Mrs. Seneke?" Anne asked.

"Do you have to ask? Where's the glass of milk I'm supposed to get? I've been here for over an hour, waiting and calling you." Mrs. Seneke scowled and her scolding voice squeaked pitifully.

"I'll bring it now," Anne said pleasantly.

"I'll bring it now," Mrs. Seneke mimicked. "It doesn't matter anymore. I don't want a glass of milk. Spare me your glass of milk. You're the kind who enjoys pestering and tormenting a poor, sick person." The grey shawl turned and shuffled away, the long fringe swaying. Then it stopped, the head on top turned toward Else and the voice said: "And you, who are you, hanging around here, scheming with these wily hussies?"

Else and Anne glanced at each other and laughed to themselves.

"Hmm," a whine came from the shawl which was once again in motion. "God help the soul who has to depend on Norns like you."

Else hung her coat in the closet and went in and sat down in the rocking chair. Before long she heard Miss Hall and Miss Thomsen in the hallway. She quickly tiptoed over to the door and turned the key.

A moment later someone grabbed the door handle and tried to come in. Else listened, as apprehensively as if her life were at stake.

"Why is Mrs. Kant's door locked?" she heard Miss Thomsen ask.

"Because the superintendent has said Mrs. Kant is to have quiet," Anne replied.

Sweet Anne. She was so helpful.

છ

BUT LATER, when rounds had been made and Else had eaten supper, Miss Hall and Miss Thomsen brought bouquets of English daisies and violets from the garden and made sarcastic remarks about what an honor it was for Else to go walking with "the battle-ax." Else wished they would go away, and she had to struggle to keep from showing how oppressive she found their company. But when they had dragged her along and she was sitting in the red glow of Miss Hall's gas lamp, she decided they really weren't so bad after all. Her dread was mostly in anticipation. The love and trust of these two poor things moved her. Not for a second did they doubt that Else was just as glad to be with them as they were to be with her. And before she left they had promised they would absolutely, positively, go walking with her the next day. They would bring along baskets and fill them with flowers.

Chapter 24

"Well," the superintendent said when he came in one afternoon. "What's this I hear?" he scolded Else, pretending to be angry.

"I don't know what you mean," Else looked at him in astonishment.

"You were outdoors alone today."

"Oh that. I was walking with Miss Hall but then she wanted to pay a visit to the gatekeeper's wife and I walked around a half hour or so before turning back."

"Well," the superintendent said, with a good-natured smile. "If you hadn't warned us yourself that you wanted to escape, you could have gone walking alone every day."

"I didn't warn you. You asked me about it."

The superintendent picked up the newspaper Dr. Vibe sent Else every day; he leafed through it and started to talk about politics.

Else so thoroughly disagreed with him that she couldn't refrain from answering. And before she knew it, she was caught up in discussion. The superintendent argued from a staunchly conservative – in Else's opinion reactionary – point of view, but without being fanatical. Moreover, there was in the doctor's words and manner of speaking the serene humanity which had always had such a calming effect on Else.

"We are not going to see eye to eye," the superintendent said at last, bidding Else good night with a handshake. "But that's no reason for us to be enemies. Is it?"

"I will never be your enemy," was Else's reply.

"Oh, don't be so sure! If I keep you here long enough?"

"But you won't do that," Else said firmly. "Because there is no basis for that."

That evening Else was in Miss Hall's room sitting next to Miss Thomsen. Nurse Schrader had come by, as usual, and now Miss Hall was sitting up in bed.

"Tonight I wish to dance!" Miss Thomsen suddenly cried out, springing to her feet. In no time she had torn her dress off and was standing in her slip; then, unbuttoning her boots, she kicked them across the room, and lifting her slip between her thumb and index finger, started hopping around on the floor.

"No, you're doing it so unmusically!" Miss Hall cried. "Here, I'll show you." She was out of bed in a flash and started twirling around.

Else lay back on the sofa and laughed. In her short nightgown, with her plump body and those short, swollen legs, Miss Hall looked utterly and insanely comical. She was humming a tarantella, twirling around with heavy, though graceful movements while her feet stepped in time with the music.

Miss Thomsen was dancing too, a short distance away. She was moving like a wooden doll propelled by some internal mechanism, and eventually she knocked over a little table covered with a meticulous arrangement of empty soap boxes, Christmas cards with angel motifs, and gaily colored dancing ladies and knights made of papier-mâché.

"Dear God, my family, my beloved family!" Miss Hall called out, terror-stricken. "Fie, fie, my child."

"We can put it all back," Else said, getting to her feet. "Nothing was broken."

"Toss my family on the floor like that," Miss Hall went on reproachfully. "I can't imagine how you can be so thoughtless, my child."

Miss Thomsen helped Else gather up all the pieces and assemble them. "Miss Hall always carries on like this," she whispered. "But it's because she's not quite right upstairs."

At that moment the door opened and Anne walked in carrying Miss Hall's glass of chloral.

"Dear God have mercy!" Miss Hall cried, and in one or two ponderous leaps she was back in bed, pulling the white, fluffy coverlet over herself.

"Well, it looks like a party," Anne said, looking around. "That's quite a costume you are wearing, Miss Thomsen."

Miss Thomsen grabbed her clothes, quickly kissed Else good night, stuck her tongue out at Anne and ran out.

"You won't say anything, will you," Else said to Anne. "They haven't done anything, just had a little innocent fun."

"No, I wouldn't think of doing such a thing," Anne replied. "But we do have to keep up appearances. Now it's time for you to go to bed, Mrs. Kant. I'll be right there with your chloral."

Else went over and said good night to Miss Hall who threw her arms around her and pulled her down close. "I'm so very fond of you, Mrs. Kant," Miss Hall whispered, "and I'm so happy about my sweet little black children. I have seven of them." She pushed Else's face a little further away and, without releasing her grip, gave her a triumphant look and started to giggle. "Seven of them," she repeated, nodding.

"No you don't, Miss Hall," Else said seriously.

"No, I don't." Miss Hall laughed and gave a shudder that made the bed shake. "It's just a bunch of nonsense I can't keep from saying. I don't understand it myself." Suddenly she looked thoughtful.

"Yes you can. When summer comes and you're feeling better, then you'll be able to restrain yourself. Isn't that right?"

"Well almost," Miss Hall sighed. "But it doesn't last long. Two months. Hardly long enough. But can you fathom why I'm always compelled to say things I know are not true and do things I have absolutely no desire to do?" Miss Hall's lips quivered and her eyes filled with tears.

"You poor thing," Else said, kissing her. "As far as that goes, we are all poor things, in one way or another."

Chapter 25

Mrs. hein had come for a visit and now she was gone. Else sat red-eyed on the sofa, her arms folded.

Everything was flooding in on her. Talking with Mrs. Hein had somewhat altered her view of Knut's behavior toward her, and this new view was wrestling with the one forced upon her by the past months' suffering and her sense of having been abandoned.

Oh, the more she learned the truth about how Hieronimus had conducted himself, the more outrageous his behavior appeared.

So it was true that Hieronimus had denied Knut permission to visit her, and false that Knut had not wanted to see her. In addition, he had told Knut that Else felt so embittered toward him that a meeting would be futile and irresponsible. If he showed his face, she would make a terrible scene. Nothing else would come of it.

Hieronimus had cited her unwillingness to read the letters he had slashed open as further proof of her fury toward Knut. After she had expressly let Hieronimus know that she was much too fond of her husband to bear reading his letters when a third party – especially a third party like Hieronimus – had opened them!

And then, to top it off, Knut had given him the letters unsealed. So there had been absolutely no need for him to let Else know he had read them if he had wished to show her the slightest bit of consideration. But instead Hieronimus had first sealed them and then ripped them open so that Else would feel more keenly the humiliating control he had over her.

Moreover, Hieronimus had led Knut to believe that she was unquestionably insane and that her condition had deteriorated to the point that she was, finally, stark raving mad.

This information had taken Else's breath away. True enough, back in Ward Six Hieronimus had said yes when she asked if he thought she was insane. But still, to deliver this cruel and completely unnecessary message to her husband, who he must have known would consider it the worst calamity of his life? To say that her condition was deteriorating, that she had finally gone stark raving mad – this was the most blatant of blatant lies! Oh yes, Mr. Hieronimus was apparently not very particular about the truth when it came to someone like herself who had had the bad luck to step on his toes.

Furthermore, he had said that if it were to do any good, her stay at St. Jørgen's would have to last at least a year. A year! Why not two, or three or four? Or a lifetime? Why precisely one year?

And then there was the business about the ward; Else had expressed her indignation over this to Mrs. Hein. That too was Hieronimus: he had expressly told Knut that it made no sense to reserve her a private room – only the wealthiest people in the country stayed in private rooms. The ward was eminently suitable for his wife.

Else had been inside the ward one day and seen those huge rooms with the yellow wooden furniture and all those beds. All those beds!

So Hieronimus had wished to continue persecuting her, even after she had escaped from his clutches. The worse it was for her, the better.

Knut, Knut! How could he possibly have turned her over to strange places and strange people, sight unseen?

Because he had blindly believed in Hieronimus, of course. She had too. Otherwise she wouldn't have gone to him.

Oh well, what concern was Hieronimus to her now? There would be time enough to think about him once she was free and could write about him.

Now she only had to deal with the superintendent. Thank God. The superintendent would do her no harm and she could rest easy.

But still – she felt such an oppressive weight on her chest. To see at last how grossly a man could abuse his position – oh, this Hieronimus! Not only had he brought Else to the very brink of ruin, he had also done what he could to destroy her relationship with Knut.

⌘

THE SUPERINTENDENT made rounds that evening. He mentioned Mrs. Hein, said he was glad to have made her acquaintance, and then continued to make small talk.

Else waited for him to tell her that soon she would be free. When he didn't, she finally asked, "When will I be allowed to leave?"

"Are you starting that again?" the superintendent replied brusquely.

"Well, I have to, since you don't. Why in the world do you want to keep me here?"

"You really are impossible!" the superintendent exclaimed. "Quite unlike most people."

"Why should I be like most people?" Else cried.

"Your friend has been here to see you, and not a word to her about helping you get out of here."

"Why should I beg for something that is my right? If you are an honorable man, you'll let me go. I don't know that you are an honorable man, but I believe, I hope you are."

"Is that so?" the superintendent said scornfully.

"Well, what am I supposed to think, what am I supposed to believe!" Else burst out. "After what I've been through."

"Did you know Hieronimus has said you ought to stay here for a year?" the superintendent snarled angrily.

"Yes! And you obviously don't have the courage to stand up to Hieronimus, even when you know he's wrong!"

The superintendent's face changed color. He tightened his lips, narrowed his gaze at Else and said: "Now I understand Hieronimus's behavior toward you. And Mr. Kant, poor man, what a terrible cross he has to bear." He left abruptly without saying good night.

⌘

ELSE DID NOT SLEEP that night. Where was this going to end? She was supposed to have asked Mrs. Hein to help her leave this place! Whatever did the superintendent mean by that? In a case like this, when a person was locked up and presumably insane, surely it couldn't do any good to ask a casual visitor for help. This had to be one situation that was either/or.

The Norn came in with her dangling lantern and checked on Else.

"Can't you sleep, Mrs. Kant?" she whispered.

"No, I'm so upset," Else grasped the Norn's hand and raised herself up onto her elbow.

"For heaven's sake, why? There's nothing wrong with you, neither physically nor mentally."

"Only that I'm here," Else wept.

"Oh, you won't be for long, you'll see."

"Why do you say that? Have you heard that I'll be leaving soon?"

"No. But it wouldn't surprise me. Do you have little children at home?"

"Yes," Else sobbed.

"Then I can understand," the Norn whispered, gently stroking Else's arm. "Otherwise it must be very pleasant to be here. The patients are so well cared for."

Else dried her eyes and lay down on the pillow again.

"Good night, Mrs. Kant. Don't cry any more."

"No," Else said, nodding at the Norn.

But when the Norn was gone, Else started to cry again. She felt as if she were swimming in a pond with a muddy bottom, swimming and struggling to get to shore, repeatedly coming close, but always drifting out again. And when she no longer had the strength to swim, she would have to give up and sink, let the mud swallow her.

Now she was also at odds with the superintendent, who had been so kind to her. When he came tomorrow, she would surely feel his wrath.

❧

BUT WHEN the superintendent appeared during rounds the next morning, he was as sweet and friendly and cheerful as ever. No trace of any ill will was in evidence. Else was so touched and happy that she had to fight back tears, and as a result looked sulky and cross.

"Incidentally, Dr. Tvede was here the other day and he asked about you," the superintendent remarked at last.

Else gave him a quivering look. She couldn't say anything.

"He wanted to know my opinion. Whether I believed staying here was good for you, or not."

"What did you tell him?" Else asked and felt a chill run down her cheeks.

"I told him no! I said I thought it would be better for you to leave here."

Else was dumbfounded. In her inner soul she felt herself sink to her knees and thank the superintendent. This man had the power, had he wanted to use it or been blind enough to think it was justified, to keep her in here for years, exactly as the resident physician on Ward Six had said. This man had now pronounced her release.

"What did Tvede say?" Else's voice was low and muffled.

"He wanted to speak with your husband. But the question is, where shall we send you?"

"The Heins would be glad to have me," Else replied. "But I don't think I am fit to stay with friends. I feel much too much like a convalescent. I thought I might like to stay at St. Rudolf's Hospital in town, until I get my strength back."

The superintendent gave her a look which seemed to say: That might be an idea.

"Well, I'm going into town tomorrow and I'll talk to your husband. Good morning," the superintendent said amiably as he left.

Else sank down into the rocking chair and wept tears of joy. There was no doubt about it. If the superintendent had said she was insane and it was right to keep her there, Knut would have gone along. Oh Knut, Knut! Astonishment and anger at his behavior flared up in her as so often before.

But the superintendent – in actual fact, she owed this man more gratitude than any person in the world.

His behavior through all of this... Coming in here today, his usual kind self, after the words they'd exchanged last night. Suppose it had been Hieronimus!

In the afternoon Else took a walk with Miss Hall and Miss Thomsen. They picked flowers and tramped around, and Miss Hall sang and laughed and Miss Thomsen talked about the three relationships and Else felt exhausted by this, yet happy...

"You look so sweet and contented this evening," Nurse Schrader said when she came in to see Else later on. "The air is good for you. You really must go out every day."

"Yes," Else said, wondering if Nurse Schrader knew about Dr. Tvede's visit and what the superintendent had said.

"I'm having my ombre party next Thursday," Nurse Schrader continued. "Would you like to come?"

"Yes, thank you," Else forced herself to say. God willing, she would not be here next Thursday.

Chapter 26

THE NEXT DAY Else had another visitor. It was a young woman, a relative from abroad, who had been staying with Knut and Tage eight days and now had come to tell Else about the child.

Else listened to everything she said about Tage with a bleeding heart. It was like opening up a wound. And still she asked for more and more. She couldn't hear enough.

After a while the young woman started talking about Hieronimus. There were many stories about him and it was a fairly common assumption that he himself was insane, though he kept it under wraps. A number of his relatives were also peculiar, and his father had been an eccentric. Whenever he was working on his speeches for the national assembly, his wife always had to come and sit with him: "Surely you must understand that I can't sit here making up lies all by myself," he was supposed to have said.

"Well, well," Else replied. "That doesn't help me in the least, and to tell you the truth, I don't care much either."

Shortly afterwards the young woman left, and Else fell to musing about Hieronimus.

Insane, she thought, among other things. Well, that was a convenient explanation, of course. But much too crude. Moreover, it struck her as particularly repugnant, because it was the same explanation Hieronimus had seized on when he encountered aspects of her personality that he hadn't understood.

Looking for proof of a person's insanity in the bizarre behavior and peculiarities of a relative – one would have to be extremely careful about doing that. This was the kind of evidence Hieronimus cited to establish that someone was insane, the young woman had told her: Your father despised ministers, your mother was pietistic, your brother got divorced and married again, your sister committed suicide, your son is impossible. Ergo you are insane.

No, Hieronimus was simply a man with a terribly inflated opinion of himself. A man who believed in his own infallibility like Catholics believed in the miracles of the Virgin Mary. What difference did it make that he was respected for his theories and scientific research? What did theory and practice have to do with each other in a field like his? Clearly very little. His entire behavior toward Else had been dictated by an erroneous assumption born of his conceit. He had simply believed that a phenomenon like this – her unwillingness to humbly bow down to Professor Hieronimus – must be caused by insanity. When he had told Knut that she was "stark raving mad," he had surely spoken in good faith.

∾

THE NEXT DAY Else went to bed after she had finished her dinner. She didn't feel well – she had chills and was suffering from chest pains. She knew the superintendent had gone to town and that she wouldn't be seeing him that day.

An hour after Dr. Sejer had made rounds, however, the superintendent suddenly appeared at her bedside, and reported that he had spoken with Knut.

"Well, and what happened?"

"Well, I conveyed your wishes that you be sent to St. Rudolf's Hospital."

"He didn't object to that, did he?" Else asked.

"No. But perhaps I object."

Else looked at the superintendent, her eyes wide open. So tonight he felt like teasing her.

"Why would you object? You told me yourself what you said to Dr. Tvede."

"Yes, but I'm having second thoughts, nonetheless. You are such a strange creature that I'm having trouble convincing myself that you are completely normal. Now this, wanting to go to a hospital rather than going home!"

Else sat up in bed and answered him in much the same way as on earlier occasions. But she was so surprised and upset at this sudden reversal in the superintendent's reasoning, that her voice trembled and grew heated.

"And then there's your temper," the superintendent said. "That really isn't normal in a patient."

"Surely there are times when getting angry and having arguments isn't necessarily abnormal?" Else stammered, on the verge of tears from exhaustion and helplessness.

"I met the resident physician from Ward Six today," the superintendent continued gruffly. "He told me a number of things which indicate that you were an extremely difficult patient in there."

"What you're saying seems irrelevant to me. How can anything the resident physician may have said pertain to the matter at hand?"

"Well, I want to think this over very carefully before I let you go." The superintendent made a hasty departure and Else had another sleepless night.

၈

THE NEXT MORNING during rounds the superintendent brought Else a letter. He stayed for a couple of minutes and made casual conversation. His demeanor was unchanged, pleasant and friendly, and for that Else was grateful.

The letter was from Mrs. Hein. She wrote that Else could now rejoice. Her hour of suffering would soon be over. After Dr. Tvede's visit with the superintendent the other day they had decided that she could leave.

Else felt as if her body were suddenly released from the chains that bound and oppressed her. Taking a deep breath, she rose and paced the floor.

Then why had the superintendent behaved that way last night? To tease and torment her? But that was so unlike the superintendent – he was such a good, kind person.

Perhaps he really did have second thoughts after his conversation with Tvede. He had said something to that effect, after all. But how could he vacillate so wildly about a thing like this? And what grounds could he possibly have for second thoughts? She wasn't the slightest bit different now than when she first set foot in the hospital.

Well yes, physically she was weaker. Lately, she sometimes stayed in bed nearly all day, because she didn't have the strength to stay up. But that was natural, of course. The long imprisonment, the longing for her child and freedom, the insomnia that so persistently returned, and the nagging worry about how this would end – it was really a wonder that she was still in one piece.

But now she felt lighthearted. No matter what the superintendent meant by what he said last night, it couldn't be long now before she would be released. Mrs. Hein wasn't given to gossip and idle chatter. Least of all in a situation like this.

Right after dinner Miss Thomsen came in and asked Else to go down to the garden. But Else, curled up for a nap on the love seat, shook her head. She wanted to try to sleep a little.

Miss Thomsen stood there for some time repeating her request. Then she wanted to know if Else was quite sure she didn't want to go down to the garden; finally she begged Else to tell her why she didn't want to go.

Oh God, Else groaned silently as she continued to hold her ground.

At last Miss Thomsen left and Else lay down again. A little later the door opened again and Nurse Schrader stepped in. "Don't get up," she said, waving her hand. "I just wanted to look in on you."

But Else had already thrown the blanket off and was sitting up. She cheerfully asked Nurse Schrader to sit down, waiting expectantly to hear something about her imminent departure.

But when Nurse Schrader left Else ten minutes later, after the usual chat about this and that, she had given no sign, verbal or otherwise, that she knew anything. So she doesn't know either, Else said to herself. Otherwise she would surely have said something, just to please me. Whatever was the superintendent thinking?

∽

SHOULD SHE curl up on the love seat again and try to sleep? No, there wasn't any point now. The fact that Nurse Schrader clearly didn't know she was leaving had reawakened her anxiety.

Sitting down by the window, she took up her table runner and started to embroider.

Then Miss Hall appeared in her hat and coat and suggested they go for a walk. Miss Hall thought it was so much fun that the two of them had permission to take walks by themselves.

Why not? Else thought. Might as well do that as sit here brooding. She put her work away, fetched her coat and went outside with Miss Hall.

They walked past the large building with the enclosed garden where Else had stopped that day with Nurse Schrader and Dr. Vibe. Pretty, blond Madam Nilsen appeared like a shot, pressing up to the picket fence, waving at them.

Else headed toward the garden and Miss Hall, who was holding her arm, came along.

The garden paths were full of female figures whose sharp contours stood out against the clear, bluish sunlight. Most of them were wearing blue-checked cotton dresses. Some had hats or kerchiefs on their heads, others were bareheaded.

A strange confusion reigned inside. A couple of the women were rushing back and forth at full speed, eyes straight ahead, holding their hands on their stomachs under their aprons. Some were hopping around in circles and singing at the top of their lungs. Others were stationary, legs far apart, scolding and swearing and making threatening motions with their arms. Here and there along the sides of the paths figures sat curled up into balls, tongues hanging out of their mouths, eyes staring dully. The

321

large, blue-faced woman who looked like a pagoda was sitting on the same spot of lawn as the previous day, making her growling noises; her arms were crossed and her dangling hands never stopped moving.

"You aren't wearing your blue silk spencer today," Madam Nilsen said to Else. Her voice was gentle, her inflection calm and normal.

"No," Else said. "I'm wearing a different dress today."

"That one is pretty too," Madam Nilsen remarked. "But spencers were all the rage when I was young."

"What do you two bitches want!" screamed a voice from behind the fence, near Madam Nilsen. Else saw a coarse face with glaring green eyes and clenched fists poised to strike.

"You mustn't use that kind of language with ladies, Madam Sørensen," Madam Nilsen admonished without turning around or taking her eyes off Else. "These are two very fine and proper ladies. I've seen that one," she pointed at Miss Hall, "for many years."

"Yes, I recognize you, too," Miss Hall said.

The coarse face came closer and pressed up against the fence, the green eyes rolling and staring greedily.

"No, don't go," Madam Nilsen said when Else, frightened, pulled back. "I really must speak with you. I've been here for 137 years now. Don't you think it's about time that I got to go down to my daughters on the mountain?"

"Yes, I do."

"Will you help me?"

"Yes."

"God bless you." Madam Nilsen dried her eyes with the corner of her apron.

Miss Hall and Else walked on and turned the corner to a side of the picket fence that seemed to go on forever. Inside was yet another large building, set back, with a garden that was separated from the previous one by a high, solid board fence. There were only a few solitary women quietly walking around in this garden.

One of them came over to the fence right away and said hello to Miss Hall.

The woman was tall and slender and her face was pale and washed out, but not old. She was wearing a full-length, dark grey coat with wide lapels, dark grey gloves and a blue English felt hat.

"Isn't it awful," she complained to Miss Hall, tears rolling down her thin cheeks. "They're still keeping me here, locked up. How long will it be? Do you know, Miss Hall?"

"This is Mrs. Hamilton, wife of General Hamilton," Miss Hall told Else. "She has been here seventeen years."

"Yes, seventeen years," Mrs. Hamilton repeated. "It doesn't matter to me, but all my little children! They freeze in there at night. They freeze and whimper so I can't get to sleep." Her tears kept flowing, faster and faster, but her face was perfectly motionless as she cried.

"They are paper dolls she cuts out and keeps in her room," Miss Hall explained.

"How could you say such a thing, Miss Hall," Mrs. Hamilton reproached, tears streaming down her face. "You know very well that they are my own flesh and blood, and you know they must be freezing and suffering, out on that bare table at night."

"Put them in your bed then," Miss Hall said.

"I don't dare," cried Mrs. Hamilton. "I might crush them to death."

"Poor thing," Else said. "What agony it must be, believing they're her children."

"Yes, agony, don't you agree? And then to have the doctors act as if they are paper dolls. Oh God, I don't know what will become of me." Mrs. Hamilton's tears kept streaming down her motionless face.

"I've sent two appeals to the King," she went on, "but he hasn't answered me. How can a king, the father of his country, be so heartless?"

"You can't be sure that he's received them," Miss Hall said.

"If you get out of here," still crying, Mrs. Hamilton turned to Else, "won't you please go to the King and tell him everything? I'm sure he would help me then – that dear, good King."

"Calm down, now, Mrs. Hamilton," Miss Hall admonished.

"Answer me, lady. Will you go to the King for me?"

"Yes," Else said.

"I thank you, I thank you." Mrs. Hamilton curtsied deeply. "I'd get down on my knees, but the grass is wet."

"The poor thing," Else sighed as she looked at Mrs. Hamilton who continued curtsying through her tears.

"There must be a lot of people here," Else remarked, when she and Miss Hall left Mrs. Hamilton. "So many buildings."

"Yes," Miss Hall said. "And now they're putting up a whole lot of new ones, because there isn't enough room here." She pointed at a hill off in the distance where a whole complex of long, light-colored buildings loomed in the sunlight.

They walked on to the woods. Miss Hall had brought her basket along and wanted to fill it with flowers. She was constantly discovering tiny, nearly invisible plants of all shapes and colors. Else had to jump over ditches and reach high up on the hillside in order to get them. Miss Hall was so heavy and squat that she couldn't pick them herself.

On their way home they met Miss Thomsen who was with Maren and some of the patients; Miss Thomsen joined Else and Miss Hall immediately. She was visibly offended that Else had gone out, since she had refused to go walking in the garden. But even so, she slipped her arm through Else's and started in on her usual prattle. With Miss Hall on her other arm, Else felt like she was dragging lead weights.

&

WHEN THE SUPERINTENDENT came that evening, Else was taciturn, nearly speechless. Tensely she waited for him to say something about her departure.

While he engaged in small talk, the superintendent gave Else looks that were a mixture of surprise and vexation. It wasn't long before he said good night and left.

Else was overcome with despair. This uncertainty, this feeling of being tossed upon the waves, from hope to hopelessness, was almost worse than everything she'd been through.

Nor did Nurse Schrader, when she came on her evening rounds, say the words that Else was longing to hear.

She asked Anne to lock her door and put the key in her pocket. Tonight she couldn't possibly be with her "girlfriends."

Miss Hall and Miss Thomsen were both at her door time after time, asking to come in. But Else sat still as a mouse and didn't answer their whispered entreaties.

❧

"WHAT WAS in that letter you received from Mrs. Hein?" the superintendent asked. It was the next day during rounds and Else was sitting in Miss Hall's room with her work.

"You may read it, superintendent," Else said curtly and started to go fetch the letter.

"I don't care to do that," the superintendent answered. "If I wanted to read it, I could have opened it before you got it. Tell me what it said."

"You may read it," Else repeated. "You can't ask for more."

The superintendent spun around and walked out, an angry expression on his face.

"Shame on you, that was horrid." Nurse Schrader had come with the superintendent and as she was leaving, turned in the doorway and shook her finger at Else.

"That's the way to talk to them," Miss Hall laughed. "Never give them an inch."

"That's not it," Else said, collapsing into tears. "I'm just at my wits' end." She went back to her own room.

Immediately afterwards she heard a knock on her door. It was the porter with the newspaper. Else thanked him, but put the paper down without looking at it.

That afternoon Else went out with Nurse Schrader. They walked over toward the cemetery which was situated on slightly hilly terrain, with many flat, neglected grave sites. Some of them were attractive and well maintained, with crosses on which names and dates were written. Others had only an unpainted wooden cross with a number.

Some gloomy looking men were puttering around among the graves, pulling weeds, raking and sweeping up. Others were busy digging ditches that filled with muddy water and gave off a rotten stench. They solemnly paid their respects to Nurse Schrader, who, on the way out, brought Else to the grave of the previous superintendent. It was enclosed by an iron fence and a handsome monument had been erected.

Else read the inscriptions on the graves and was surprised that the people buried here had lived to be so old.

"That's because they live such healthy and regular lives here," Nurse Schrader said.

A thousand times better to rest here, buried in the earth, Else thought, than to remain in the asylum, amidst all that dead life, all that disconsolate misery.

Chapter 27

IT WAS SUNDAY. Dr. Sejer had made the rounds and Else had been walking in the garden with her "girlfriends."

After dinner she started a letter to Mrs. Hein. The scent of wild flowers and newly cut spruce boughs filled her room, and the fragrance of spring and trees in bud, which always before had quickened Else's heart and filled it with joy, now brought on a vague, stinging pain which she struggled in vain to suppress.

She wrote a despondent letter. If the superintendent had told Tvede that she ought not stay there any longer, he must have changed his mind later. She gave a detailed account of what had happened the past three or four days, quoted her conversations with the superintendent and asked that Mrs. Hein not visit her again. It only upset her to see someone from outside. There was nothing to do but to leave her to her fate. How long she would be able to hold out, she didn't know. She was clearly heading for destruction, one way or another. Mrs. Hein must promise to look after Tage, be a mother to him, etc.

"I am giving up the struggle and abandoning any hope of leaving this place," she wrote in conclusion. "You should do the same. As for the wisdom and insight of Danish psychiatrists – *kämpfen selbst die Götter umsonst.*"[14]

She had just finished the letter when Maren came in to change the water in her carafe. "Take this to the superintendent," Else said, and handed Maren the letter, unsealed, in accordance with rules she'd been given at the very beginning.

Then she went down to the garden. Miss Thomsen was out with the others, thank goodness, and Miss Hall was in bed with a cold today.

She had probably been down there for half an hour when Maren rushed out and said that rounds were under way and the superintendent had asked for her.

Else hurried toward the garden gate, but just then a second-story window opened and she heard the superintendent's voice call out, "Just stay where you are, Mrs. Kant. I'll come down to the garden."

The superintendent appeared a moment later. Else had never seen such an angry expression on his face.

"You have written a letter," he began. "May I ask, is the letter addressed to Mrs. Hein or to me?"

"What kind of a question is that? You can see it's to Mrs. Hein."

"It is an exceedingly impertinent letter. How could you permit yourself to write such a thing?"

"Is it impertinent to tell the truth?"

"Truth," the superintendent said. "Truth?" he repeated. "Haven't we done everything we could for you? And here you are, giving the impression that I want to drive you mad?"

"As long as you keep me here, can't I assume it's because you think I'm mad?" Else quickly moved past the superintendent, who had stopped in front of her in the middle of one of the paths. The superintendent followed her.

"Staying here could very well be to your benefit," he said. "If I let you out, be careful that the day doesn't come when you say, 'If I had only stayed at St. Jørgen's,' and ask to come back."

"Your concern for me truly exceeds all bounds," Else retorted contemptuously. "In any case, Superintendent, you can wait until that day comes around. If I come back, there will be time enough for you to gloat. Now I think the only logical course is to stick to the matter before us."

"Well, I don't know what's before us," the superintendent shot back angrily.

Else, who had walked on, with the superintendent directly behind her, whirled to face him, and said, "You'll never convince me that a man like you, with all your years of experience as a specialist in mental diseases –

a man who's not possessed by any kind of arrogant demon or megalo-mania – doesn't know, absolutely, positively know, that I am not insane."

"It depends entirely on how you define the word," the superintendent said in a threatening tone.

"Exactly," Else replied. "One of these days a professor might come along who was absolutely convinced that you, for example, were insane."

"What good fortune then, that I'm already at an insane asylum." There was a hint of a smile in the corners of the superintendent's eyes.

Else stood for a minute and looked at him. There was so much, so much she could cite as proof that she was not insane, so many arguments at her fingertips, but she hadn't the energy or the desire. It served no pur-pose. She had learned that lesson at an outrageously high price during this frightful time.

"Well, then there's nothing more to talk about," she said, turning and walking away.

"Oh yes there is!" The superintendent was right behind her. "I'm not sending this letter."

"All right, you're the one in charge," Else replied. "It really doesn't matter to me whether or not the letter gets there."

"Under any circumstances, I will add something to it," the superinten-dent went on, his voice slightly more conciliatory. "The choice is yours."

"Then I choose to not send the letter."

"As you please. Here you are." The superintendent took the letter out of his breast pocket and handed it to Else.

Else thanked him, said good-bye and quickly walked out of the garden and up to her room.

Chapter 28

"Well, mrs. kant, I hear you will be leaving soon."

Else, who had risen to greet Nurse Schrader, stared at her, speechless.

"The superintendent has ordered me to get your clothes together," Nurse Schrader continued. "Your stay here was a short one. You must be happy now."

Else put her arms around Nurse Schrader and cried into her shoulder.

"Do you see now that what I've been saying all along is true? The superintendent is a man you should trust completely. Not only the patients, but anyone who has anything to do with him."

"Yes," Else said, lifting her face and drying her eyes. "The superintendent is just the man he ought to be."

"And you've certainly not always been nice to him," Nurse Schrader went on. "A couple of times you've been downright horrid."

"Oh yes, Nurse Schrader. But you don't know what agony I've been through. You can be sure, however, that I will remember the superintendent with gratitude for the rest of my life. And you too, and Dr. Vibe and Sibylle and everyone."

"God grant that everything goes well for you now." Nurse Schrader took Else's hand and gave her a heartfelt look. "You've asked to go St. Rudolf's Hospital, I hear. Good night."

"Good night," Else said, giving her a kiss.

Else paced up and down her long, narrow room. She pushed the rocking chair up against the wall to have more space. She felt her soul fill with song. Whatever the future would bring, whatever she still had to go through – none of that mattered compared to this: she would have her freedom! She would once again be regarded as a human being and no longer belong to a caste for which society made no provisions. She heard talking out in the hallway and went out. Maren and Anne were there.

"I'll be leaving soon," she beamed.

"Well," Maren replied, without showing the least bit of surprise, and Anne, who was turning a dress inside out, remarked dryly, "We'll have more room then."

"Did you think this would happen, Maren?" Else asked. In her happiness she felt a need to continue the conversation.

"Yes," Maren said with her usual sweet smile. "Anne and I have said the whole time that we couldn't understand what Mrs. Kant was doing here." She and Anne exchanged glances.

"Oh yes, some of us also know a thing or two," Anne replied as she walked off with the dress she'd turned inside out.

Else opened Miss Hall's door. She had gotten into bed and Miss Thomsen was sitting on a chair under the red gas lamp reading aloud from the newspaper.

"Come in, come in," Miss Hall waved.

"We thought your door was locked," Miss Thomsen said. "They just do it to be mean, the scoundrels. Isn't that right, Mrs. Kant?"

Else went over to the bed and told Miss Hall that she was leaving.

Miss Hall sat upright, clapped her hands together and with a bereaved look exclaimed, "That's the worst news I've ever heard!"

"You've promised me all along that I wouldn't be here very long, Miss Hall."

"But such a short time." Miss Hall just stared straight ahead with a bereaved expression.

"What are you talking about?" Miss Thomsen asked, curiously looking from one to the other.

"Mrs. Kant is leaving, my child!"

Miss Thomsen's face grew white and her cheeks seemed to cave in.

Then Else had to tell them every detail about how she had heard the news, what happened beforehand, and assure them it really was true.

"They come and they go, one after the other!" Miss Thomsen burst out in despair, arms raised above her head. She fell to her knees with a thump, laid her face on the sofa and sobbed.

"There there, my child. There there, my child," Miss Hall said comfortingly. "Your time will come. Nothing endures forever in this world."

"I'll run away from here and go straight to the King," Miss Thomsen sobbed. "Then I'll see that their wickedness is punished. Straight to the King, straight to the King!"

Wearing her bed jacket and short chemise, Miss Hall got out of bed and, kneeling down beside Miss Thomsen, put her arms around her.

"Have faith in God, my child," she said softly. "Not the God the ministers tell lies about, but the Virgin Mary's Son, grand and pure, dripping with blood-red love for mankind's suffering children."

Miss Thomsen had lifted her face to look at Miss Hall's mouth as she spoke, and now, in a voice choked with tears, said querulously, "Don't give me that virginmarynonsense. I'm a believer, but you – you're worse than a Catholic."

"No, not Catholic," Miss Hall answered solemnly. "But the radiant Son, who is the sun, who is dripping with love, in Him I believe. He is our Redeemer and He is your only friend and savior, my child."

"Oh, what difference does it make, what difference does it make?" Still crying, Miss Thomsen shook her head from side to side. Then she freed herself from Miss Hall's arms and stood up.

Miss Hall crept back into bed and Else said good night.

"I have lots of things to talk to you about," Miss Thomsen whispered as she and Else left Miss Hall's room. "Important missions to confide." She wanted to follow Else into her room, but just at that moment Anne came along with the chloral and forbade it.

Chapter 29

"HERE YOU ARE," the superintendent said when he came the next morning. He laid an opened letter on the table in front of Else and she leaned forward and read.

It was a short letter to the superintendent from Knut in which he reported that there would not be an available room for Else at St. Rudolf's Hospital for five days.

"Well, are you satisfied now?" the superintendent asked.

Else thanked him.

"Well, you are now free to go wherever you please. If you would like to go to your friends, I will write to Mrs. Hein and ask her to come and get you tomorrow."

Else considered for a minute. No, she wasn't fit to be any place but a hospital as long as she felt so weak and frazzled.

"If you would let me stay here a few more days until there's a room at St. Rudolf's, I would prefer that," she answered.

"Exactly as you wish. Then I'll write to Mrs. Hein and say she should come – on Saturday?"

"Thank you very much."

"Not at all," the superintendent said coldly and left.

જી

THEY WERE strange days for Else, those five remaining days. A weary peace settled over her and she felt as if she were moving around enveloped in a pale yellow light, which faintly warmed her heart and occasionally emitted rays of hope. But behind the pale yellow light everything was shrouded in heavy, leaden clouds that assailed her with cold gusts of fear, despondency and dread. And in her heart of hearts she felt as though she had been stretched on the rack and subjected to all the arts of torture.

And how long the days were! She marked every hour as it passed, counting the hours left to wait.

Meanwhile, Miss Thomsen was constantly at her side. In the morning before Else got out of bed, in the afternoon and in the evening, always, always, every minute of the day she clung to her, chattering on and on in a feverish and agitated state Else had never before observed in her. Else was often nearly at her wits' end and had to muster all her strength to keep from screaming at the sight of Miss Thomsen, to keep from shouting, right to her face, that she had become an abominable torment. But the thought that these days would also pass and that she would soon be free, while poor Miss Thomsen had to stay behind, helped her put on a good face.

Only once during these five days did Else succeed in getting away from Miss Thomsen. One afternoon Nurse Schrader gave her permission to go to town with Miss Hall so she could buy small gifts for Maren and Anne and the Norn. For Else it was a festive occasion and she stretched the time out as long as possible.

Chapter 30

S<small>ATURDAY FINALLY CAME.</small>

"This is the last day I'll see you on rounds," the superintendent said when he arrived around eleven o'clock.

"Yes," Else said. "Thank God."

"Mrs. Hein should be here at one o'clock. You'll walk down to the station, I suppose. It's such a beautiful day."

Else nodded.

"Your things will be driven down so they're there when you arrive."

"Thank you very much."

"Well, I don't guess there's anything else, is there?"

"Yes, there is, superintendent," Else said. "I would like to ask you to give me a document certifying that I am not insane, and that I've never been insane during my stay here."

The superintendent looked at Else through narrowed eyes. "No, I won't do that. In my opinion you could be a completely different person from the one I've come to know."

Else was taken aback. "A completely different person – different in what way?"

"More agreeable, easier to get along with."

Else could barely restrain the impulse to smile. If the superintendent had been put in a madhouse and kept locked up for an indefinite length of time against his will, wouldn't he, too, be less agreeable and easy to get along with than when he was free as a bird?

"So you won't give me a certificate, superintendent?" she said after a moment's silence.

"No."

"All right," Else nodded and thought to herself, Good Lord, what do I care about this? After all her experiences with psychiatrists! But she had thought it was common practice to receive such a document when one was released from a madhouse.

∽

MRS. HEIN came at one o'clock and ten minutes later Else was dressed in her coat and had said good bye to Nurse Schrader and her "girlfriends."

When they came out to the corridor, Maren, Anne, and, to Else's delight, the Norn were there to say good-bye.

As Else walked past Mrs. Henderson's room she peeked in. Mrs. Henderson was marching in time, today as every day. She turned her back to the door.

Down at the entrance they met the superintendent. He shook hands with Mrs. Hein and Else and politely but coolly said good-bye.

Out on the road Else stopped and grasped Mrs. Hein's hand. She took a deep breath and said, "I can hardly conceive of the bliss of being free again."

"Yes, thank God," Mrs. Hein replied.

Then they walked on, side by side. Behind them lay St. Jørgen's Hospital with its gardens and fields and assorted buildings, and before them the open, dun-colored landscape and a low and hazy sky. Under the broad, gently sloping hills huddled the little town with the railway station that was their destination. The houses with their irregular shapes and the old cathedral were faintly visible through the spring haze. They met no one as they walked, and they both stared sorrowfully straight ahead.

Then a gentleman in a long overcoat, soft felt hat and brown leather gloves came toward them. He lifted his hat and looked as if he were going to stop. But Else turned her head away and walked more quickly. It was the same hospital employee, Knut's relative, whom she had seen through the carriage window the day she had driven up with the friendly old woman.

Else shuddered at the memory and suddenly felt how shy and timid she had become. Meeting acquaintances and friends now would be like running the gauntlet between curious, staring spectators.

"You look so sad," Mrs. Hein remarked. "I would think you'd be happy now."

"I am happy," Else replied. "But after everything I've experienced . . . I feel like my soul is naked and dripping with blood."

Mrs. Hein squeezed Else's hand silently and after a while said: "The superintendent at St. Jørgen's is nonetheless a very different man than Hieronimus, isn't he?"

Else just nodded. She couldn't answer. The gratitude she felt toward the superintendent of St. Jørgen's swelled up inside her, and her throat was choked with tears – just because he had acted honorably and done his duty. That's how degraded you became, when you stood powerless against the shame and misery of injustice.

"What do you think Hieronimus would say?" Else said when she had regained her composure. "After he recommended that I be locked up for at least a year. I've been here for twenty-six days now, the last five of my own free will."

"Oh, Hieronimus," Mrs. Hein replied. "Who cares about him now?"

Oh yes, Else thought. She cared about Hieronimus.

Notes

Professor Hieronimus

1. *The Children's Christmas Book (Børnenes Julebog)* was published each Christmas in Denmark from 1889 to 1959. The slim, inexpensive volumes were filled with stories, poems, and illustrations of an uplifting sort.

2. The resident physician was roughly equivalent to a chief resident in a modern hospital. As Vagn Lyhne explains, the Danish medical hierarchy formed a steep triangle of authority: the professor was alone at the top, with one or two resident physicians below him; next came a number of assistants (corresponding roughly to modern interns), followed by a group of students who had not yet passed their medical examinations. There was a similar hierarchy for the nurses, with the nursing supervisor at the top, the floor nurses below, and the nursing assistants at the bottom. The highest nurse was below the lowest physician. Patients had no authority at all.

3. *Berlingeren* refers to the oldest Danish daily newspaper, founded by Ernst Heinrich Berling in 1749. Its present name is *Berlinske Tidene*.

4. The "puerperal maniac" suffers from what we would now call postpartum psychosis. The acute depressions and manic states that developed after childbirth were often short-lived, but they could lead to infanticide.

5. "Who knows?"

6. Bertha von Suttner was born in Prague in 1843 and did most of her writing in Vienna. Her work was first translated into Danish in 1887: *En Eftersommer* followed in 1899 by *Ned med Vaabnene*. An ardent pacifist, she won the Nobel Peace Prize in 1905, the first woman to do so.

7. Madam From's name means Madam Pious in Danish.

339

St. Jørgen's

8. Else, like Amalie Skram, was a foreigner in Denmark. Amalie Skram was born in Bergen, Norway, in 1846 and moved to Copenhagen in 1884 when she married Erik Skram.

9. Miss Hall's ranting does appear in English in the original text. We have normalized the spelling, but not changed the passages in any other way.

10. "It is God's will that I perish."

11. In Nordic mythology the Norns were goddesses of destiny. The three foremost Norns, Fate, Being and Necessity, resided under one of the roots of the World Tree at a well whose name means fate or destiny. Each day the Norns would sprinkle the World Tree with water from the sacred well, nourishing and preserving it. It was believed that the destiny of men and gods, indeed, of all living beings, was determined by the Norns. There were many Norns, and every time a child was born a Norn was present to weave that child's destiny. Some Norns were good, others were evil, and so the lives of men and women were either blessed or cursed.

12. *René Mauperin* was a novel by Edmond and Jules de Goncourt, first published in 1864. Mrs. Edgren, a.k.a. Anne Charlotte Leffler (1849–1892), was a Swedish author. Like her contemporary Amalie Skram, she was an active participant in the current social debate and in her plays and fiction (she is best remembered for six volumes of novellas) she exposes society's hypocrisy and inequality from a woman's point of view.

13. The reference is probably to Bjørnstjerne Bjørnson, prominent Norwegian author and cultural figure, with whom Amalie Skram conducted a voluminous correspondence over a period of many years.

14. Else is quoting from Schiller's play *Jungfrau von Orleans*: "Even the gods battle in vain."

"To Look Truth Squarely in the Eye"*:
The Life of Amalie Skram

Katherine Hanson

WHEN AMALIE SKRAM was released from St. Hans Mental Hospital in the spring of 1894 and announced her intention to make her story public, concerned friends advised her to spare herself further grief and keep silent. But their words of caution served only to strengthen her resolve – the threat of scandal could neither frighten nor dissuade Amalie Skram, who, at the age of forty-seven, could look back over a lifetime of controversy. As a young wife and mother, she had rebelled against the pressures of family and church and demanded a divorce from an unhappy marriage. As a divorcée, she discovered she was the object of gossip and rumors and further challenged public opinion through her association with writers, artists and intellectuals. Her first novel, *Constance Ring*, was meant to provoke the bourgeoisie with its frank depiction of marriage and female sexuality, and yet she had not expected there would be so few who dared come to her defense. Later novels received much the same treatment in the press by critics who saw no reason to stop at attacking her books – Fru Skram was denounced as an immoral woman. The lack of understanding and sympathy saddened and discouraged her, but Amalie Skram was not silenced. Nor did she sway from her course – she believed fiction had an obligation to represent the world realistically and truthfully; in this, as in other areas of her life, she was uncompromising.

૪

* Letter from Amalie Skram to Professor Høffding, July 30, 1899.

AMALIE ALVER was born on August 22, 1846 in Bergen, Norway. Her parents were of modest means – her father was a shopkeeper – and they had five children, four sons and a daughter. Amalie was sent to the best grammar school in town, but the family income did not allow for a daughter to continue her schooling beyond that. At about the same time Amalie was confirmed in 1863, her father fell onto hard times and was forced to declare bankruptcy. Whether he was motivated by fear of creditors or desire to try his luck in the New World, Mons Alver left Norway suddenly and sailed to America.

Within a few months Amalie was engaged to Captain Bernt Ulrik August Müller, a man nine years her senior; they were married on October 3, 1864. Müller came from an established Norwegian family, one that had considerably more status and wealth than the Alvers. This was clearly an advantageous match that Amalie and her mother, given the financial uncertainty of their situation, could hardly afford to pass up. For his part, Müller got a young wife of exceptional beauty and intelligence.

Müller was a sea captain and soon after the wedding he and his bride set sail for Mexico and the West Indies. A born sailor, Amalie never got seasick and liked to walk the deck, even in stormy weather. She was equally fascinated by what she saw and experienced when the ship came into port. During the long hours at sea, she put her time to good use, reading literature, philosophy and religion, and teaching herself English, French and German.

The Müllers' first child, Jacob, was born in 1866 and a second son, Ludvig August, came in 1868. Amalie stayed at home in Bergen during these childbearing years, but in 1869 she and the boys joined Müller. For nearly two years the young family sailed to ports all over the world. In 1871 Müller brought his family back to Bergen and the years that followed were in many ways stormier than the ones at sea. On the one hand, Amalie enjoyed the social status granted her as Captain Müller's wife – with her striking appearance and personality, she was always the center of attention at parties. She was able to cultivate her interests in literature and the arts, even appearing in amateur theatre productions, but the more she became involved in these activities, the less interested she became in family life.

Her interest in the newest plays and novels brought her into contact with a group of radical intellectuals associated with the newspaper, *Bergens Tidende*, and her interaction with these journalists and writers undoubtedly kindled her desire to try her own hand at writing. She wrote a piece for the theatre entitled *Playing with Fire*, which, though never published or performed, hints at her later career. Her first publication, an unsigned review of J. P. Jacobsen's classic novel *Marie Grubbe*, was printed in *Bergens Tidende* February 17, 1877. In it she combines a sensitive appreciation and understanding of the novel with comments on new developments in contemporary literature and the ideas shaping those changes. She praises the novel's realism and the author's psychologically perceptive depiction of the main character, but she also voices a criticism: at one crucial point Jacobsen offers his readers a mere description of the heroine's undoing when he should have explained *how* and *why*. The modern reader expected no less from a serious and gifted writer.

In the meantime, the Müllers' marriage was on the rocks. According to Antonie Tiberg, Skram's first biographer, Amalie Müller sought a divorce because of her husband's infidelity, a situation very similar to the one she would later depict in *Constance Ring*. Family members rallied to her husband's side, urging her to abandon her demands for separation, and unnerving her with stories of the scandal she would bring upon herself and the possibility she would not get custody of her sons. She gave in to these pressures, but on the very night she had agreed to remain under her husband's roof, she suffered a severe nervous breakdown.

She entered Gaustad Mental Hospital in Kristiania (present-day Oslo) just before Christmas, 1877. Distance from her domestic problems seemed to have a calming effect and she was released after only two months. The doctor related her illness to a very unhappy marriage and he recommended that she not return to her husband. Fortunately, Amalie Müller had brothers to turn to and when she left Gaustad, she and her sons went to live first with her older brother for a few months and later with a younger brother for nearly three years. Her home was now a small town in eastern Norway, closer to the capital city, Kristiania, the country's cultural and intellectual center.

At first, Amalie Müller kept a low profile. She managed her brother's household and, sensitive to people's curiosity and gossip, chose not to be a part of the small town's social life. But if she was socially retiring she was not at all reluctant to enter the literary debate. She wrote articles and book reviews for newspapers and magazines, she translated books and articles. These writing and translating projects were ostensibly a means of earning money, but they were most valuable as a learning experience, both personally and professionally.

Amalie Müller could not have come upon the literary scene at a more opportune time. The 1870s and '80s saw a true flowering in Norwegian literature, with authors like Henrik Ibsen, Bjørnstjerne Bjørnson, Alexander Kielland and Arne Garborg making important contributions to the new realism. It was a period when social issues were debated on the stage and in novels, and when attitudes toward such cherished institutions as marriage and the church were openly challenged. In subject matter and style the current literature was particularly well-suited to Amalie Müller's temperament; she had a serious, at times brooding side to her personality, and the emotional trauma of her divorce and hospitalization was followed by an intense spiritual and moral crisis. Antonie Tiberg tells us Amalie had been deeply religious since her youth and had stayed in her marriage as long as she did because she believed it was her Christian duty. In the months and years following her separation from Müller, she examined the church and its teachings with critical eyes and, indeed, questioned the very tenets of her belief.

She was, in this period of self examination, clearly receptive to authors like feminist Camilla Collett and literature such as Ibsen's *A Doll House*. Her enthusiasm for the ideas propounded by Collett and Ibsen is reflected in two review articles published within a month of each other. A short review of Collett's collection of essays *Against the Current* appeared on December 31, 1879 and a lengthy article entitled "Reflections on *A Doll House*" was published on January 19, 1880. Both were signed "ie.", the signature Amalie Müller used until late in 1883. The anonymous "ie." praises Camilla Collett for criticizing prevailing assumptions and attitudes about women's moral and social status, but acknowledges the price Collett pays for it: "Naturally she is not what one would call popular, but that only underlines her solitary position and stature. She is one of those who is in the fore, blazing new trails, and it's an old story that these individuals open themselves to attack." In Collett's writings and in her example as an independent author Amalie Müller had found a mentor.

Collett's feminist arguments are evident in "Reflections on *A Doll House*," but beyond ideology one perceives a strong sense of identification between reviewer and protagonist. In a detailed analysis of Ibsen's drama, "ie." reveals a deeply felt sympathy with Nora's situation and an intimate understanding of her thoughts and emotions. Where other critics expressed shock and indignation over Nora's decision to abandon her family, "ie." praised Nora for the moral courage she showed in refusing to submit to patriarchal authority after her husband had destroyed her belief in him and in their marriage. The article concludes with what is tantamount to a warning to all those who have held women down by virtue of their authority: "When Woman awakens to full consciousness of her worth as an individual, when her eyes are opened to all the injustice committed against her throughout the ages, she will arm herself against the man to whom she was given as helpmate; she will break all the bonds and scale all the walls society and institutional authority have built around her. Her resistance will perhaps lead her far beyond the boundaries of reason . . ."

Contemporary literature brought to life issues that mattered deeply to Amalie Müller, and the process of writing reviews helped her define and articulate her own positions. In addition to writing articles for publication, she conducted an active correspondence. She was eager to discuss and argue, and lacking friends and colleagues close to home, she sought to establish a dialogue through letters. Many were sent to personal friends, of course, but she also corresponded with writers whom she had never met.

The author she most admired, and the one she would value most throughout her life, was Bjørnstjerne Bjørnson. In the winter of 1878 she got up her courage and sent him an essay she had written about his play *The King.* He was pleased with her essay, even arranged for its publication, and this was the start of a long correspondence. Bjørnson was a central figure in Norwegian literature in the 1870s and '80s, a popular author who believed he had an obligation to participate in the public debate by voicing his opinions on cultural, social and political issues. Amalie Müller felt particularly drawn to him because he wrote frankly about his own religious crisis, because he was an outspoken defendant of a woman's right to divorce, and because he was as passionate in his demand for truth and honesty in literature as she herself. She was no doubt flattered that he maintained a correspondence with her, and the criticism and encouragement he gave her must have meant a great deal. When he came to know her better and understand her precarious financial situation, he did what he could to find work for her. Efforts to find her a permanent position never materialized, but he did send writing and translation jobs her way.

By the summer of 1881 Amalie Müller had had enough of small town existence and moved to Kristiania. Her older brother had recently found work there and so was able to provide a home for Amalie and her sons. She was now ready to fully experience the intellectual life of the capital city. There were parties and social events, of course, but she also attended public lectures and met with people with whom she could discuss and debate the issues of the day. Her circle of friends included artists, writers and intellectuals, many of whom were associated with the new political left. She continued to review literature for the press, but she was also working on her own fiction, sending pieces to writer friends for their criticism and suggestions.

But the fact remained that she was a divorced woman and fair game for gossipmongers. At social gatherings much was made of her by men – she claimed she neither encouraged nor was interested in this. But as a handsome, impulsive and outspoken woman, who was also linked with the radical left, she was bound to draw attention to herself. Perhaps it was her failure to respond to male attention more positively that made the rumors so malicious; in 1883 a book titled *Modern Women* appeared and all of Kristiania could recognize that the main character was a caricature of Amalie Müller. Though deeply hurt and angered, she could take some comfort in the fact that so many of her friends took her side, publicly denouncing colleagues who wrote reviews of the novel, and refusing to contribute to newspapers and journals that published reviews.

Friends in Kristiania were not her only source of comfort these days. In August of '82 Bjørnson had thrown a huge party to celebrate his fiftieth birthday and he had invited people from all over Scandinavia. Amalie Müller was among the guests and, as usual, found herself surrounded by potential suitors, including the Danish critic and author Erik Skram. The festivities lasted for several days at Bjørnson's country estate, and when the party was over, Amalie and Erik Skram left together. He returned to his home in Copenhagen, she to hers in Kristiania, but Skram was not about to forget this spirited woman from the North and he sought to woo her with letters.

In the first letters from Amalie, sent that same summer and fall, ambivalence was written on every page. On the one hand she had clearly fallen for Skram – she calls him a "trollmand" and her "Pygmalion" and admits that if the relationship were to continue, it would "swallow her." That in itself was reason enough to break it off – how could she fulfill her responsibility to her boys if she were completely absorbed in an affair of the heart? More troubling, however, were her fears that by becoming involved she would no longer be her own master, but would lose all peace and quiet and open herself to pain and grief. Her hesitancy stems in part from a fear of being hurt; she writes that "Life has nearly scared the living daylights out of me" and as a consequence she has pulled back from the world into her shell. But she also believed she was so fundamentally different from the male species that it was best she had nothing at all to do with men. She seemed to have a sense of what she wanted to accomplish in life, and at the conclusion of one of her letters she vowed that, left alone, she would be industrious and productive.

Erik Skram was not discouraged. Letters from Copenhagen kept coming, and they were received and answered; his words evidently conquered her uncertainties. They sometimes exchanged two and three letters a week, letters in which they opened their hearts to each other, but in which they also discussed literature. Skram insisted that she send him the novel she was working on. When he had read it, he assured her it was good and

347

then told her how it could be better. Amalie learned a lot from Skram and in the process fell deeper and deeper in love. In the spring of 1884 she finally agreed to be his wife and live with him in Copenhagen. By this time her boys had started secondary school and it was agreed that they should stay in Kristiania and finish school.

The next ten years were the most creative and productive years of her life. She completed seven novels, two plays and numerous short stories. She wrote about what she knew best, what she herself had lived through: the experience of a young woman entering marriage quite innocently and unprepared; life aboard a sailing ship, on the open seas and in foreign, exotic ports; and the world of her childhood and youth – places and people from her native Bergen.

Erik Skram had challenged Amalie to create a female character that no man could, to look inward and chart all the secret rooms and dark corners of the feminine psyche and show what drove women to act as they did. This was during their correspondence, while she was working on *Constance Ring*. She took his advice to heart in that and three subsequent novels dealing with male-female relationships, marriage and the double standard (*Lucie*, *Fru Inés* and *Betrayed*). The women in these novels are complex and unadorned; their behavior is not always becoming nor are they always sympathetic characters. Amalie Skram addressed the issue of sexuality head on, but female fears and fantasies on this subject were taboo and the public responded to her portrayal of women with incredulity and shock.

The work Skram considered to be her most important, and without doubt her most ambitious project, was a four volume epic recounting the story of a family through several generations. *The People of Hellemyr* is set in the 1800s and opens on a harsh and unyielding plot of land on Norway's west coast. Here Sjur Gabriel and his wife Oline struggle to make a life for themselves and their children against overwhelming odds, and when the hardships and losses become more than they can bear, they turn to drink. Their children do not stay on the farm, but leave for nearby Bergen, and the saga of the succeeding generations is played out against the backdrop of this seaport and trading center. The second novel in the series takes place at sea and it is among the most authentic and colorful depictions of life on a sailing ship in Norwegian literature. But it was evidently too authentic for Skram's contemporaries who were used to more sanitized sea stories. In her recent study, *Amalie Skram: Danish Citizen, Norwegian Author*, Ragni Bjerkelund discusses the critical reception of Skram's tetrology, including sales figures, and she reports that neither reviews nor sales gave Skram much encouragement. Fru Skram offended her readers with a prose that was too realistic, details that were too graphic, depictions that were too honest. Even the language in her books was a barrier for some. With her uncanny ear for dialogue, Skram let her characters speak just as she had heard them – in dialect. This had not been done before and critics, especially the Danes, complained that they couldn't understand it. Skram's "marriage" novels are social commentary, but in *The People of Hellemyr* she did not set out to judge or condemn. Her objective was to tell the story of a family as truthfully and honestly as she could, and to do so in a way that would make readers understand her characters and share her compassion with them. She was bitterly disappointed in the public response.

In 1889, twenty years after the birth of her youngest son, Amalie gave birth to a baby daughter. Both parents adored their little girl, whom they nicknamed "Småen" (Little One), but for Amalie the demands of motherhood interfered with her writing, and juggling the conflicting roles wore her down to the point where she felt she could perform neither. Erik Skram was very supportive and kept the child with him for extended periods when she went off and tried to concentrate on her writing. But when she was separated from Småen, she worried about her and longed to see her. Her uncompleted novel, the final volume of *The People of Hellemyr*, was becoming an albatross around her neck.

In the summer of 1893 Amalie and Småen went to Bergen for a couple of months; perhaps seeing her old familiar haunts and breathing in the atmosphere of the city would be the inspiration she needed to finish her family saga. But in early September, plagued by difficulties and her own despondency she wrote the following to her husband:

I feel such piercing anguish when I write "September 2." September 2 and no further in my work. I think the suffering I've endured this summer which grows worse and worse every day, must have settled in my heart like a consuming disease. Oh God, this feeling of hopelessness is terrible! And the worry of always paying money out and earning nothing. And then I long to be home and long to be with you and long to be able to work. Never have things seemed as impossible as now. My brain is dull and empty and my heart is sick from suffering. But talking about it doesn't do any good, of course. The baby that was supposed to come is no more, my beloved! It's gone and I've had to stay in bed a couple days on account of that. I don't know what could have caused it – on the preceding days I didn't exert myself in the least, didn't even take a walk. It was just the burden of my usual melancholic state of mind. And Småen had kept me awake a couple of nights – well, she was awake for only a minute, but you understand.

Amalie and her daughter returned to Copenhagen soon thereafter, but her condition did not improve. She remained sleepless and depressed, worried about her daughter's health and unable to finish her novel. Finally, in February 1894 she agreed to seek the help of Dr. Knud Pontoppidan, a renowned nerve specialist and Professor of Psychiatry at the Copenhagen City Hospital. Skram looked forward to a short rest and the relief she had experienced in her earlier hospitalization at Gaustad. Instead, she found herself locked in a battle with her physician, a battle in which she felt powerless against the weight of medical authority. Skram had been on Ward Six for less than a month when Pontoppidan declared that she would be transferred to St. Hans Hospital, the state mental institution at Roskilde, for an indefinite length of time. She emerged after four weeks with one thought, to tell the world about her experiences.

WORKS CITED:

Bjerkelund, Ragni. *Amalie Skram: Dansk borger, Norsk forfatter.* Oslo: Aschehoug, 1990.

Tiberg, Antonie. *Amalie Skram som kunstner og menneske.* Kristiania: 1910.

Skram, Amalie. *Optimistisk Læsemaade. Amalie Skrams litteraturkritikk.* Intro-
duction by Irene Engelstad. Oslo: Gyldendal, 1987.

———. Letters. Det Kongelige Bibliotek, Copenhagen. Amalie Skram to
Erik Skram, August 16, 1882; September 6, 1882; September 2,
1893. Amalie Skram to Professor Høffding, July 30, 1899.

Amalie Skram's Asylum Novels

Judith Messick

IN A LETTER to Bjørnstjerne Bjørnson written shortly after her release from St. Hans Hospital, Amalie Skram gives several motives for writing about her experiences as a mental patient. Writing will help her cure the bitterness and anger she feels toward Dr. Knud Pontoppidan:

> I can see you shaking your dear beautiful head in skepticism, and I can well understand it, for who could believe that something as medieval as what happened to me could occur in the King's Copenhagen in 1894. But it's true just the same, and if you wait a minute you'll be convinced. I am so full of bitterness – you would understand if you knew the truth – that I can't breathe freely again until I've written an account of what happened and made it public.

Having herself experienced the "humiliations, insults, and torments" of being treated like a madwoman, Amalie Skram also writes to protect other people:

> It's more than bitterness at the unheard-of mistreatment I suffered that drives me to write; the possibility of saving just one fellow human being (in the same state I was) from falling into Pontoppidan's dreadful hands is justification enough."

Like Clarissa Lathrop and other authors of asylum narratives, Skram's novels expose a "secret institution" that lies within the legal framework of society. In *Professor Hieronimus* and *St. Jørgen's* Amalie Skram writes a blis-

tering attack on an aggressive and dehumanizing system of medical authority empowered to hold people against their will, strip them of adult
prerogatives, and label them indelibly. Else Kant, like her creator, fights
against the silencing effects of a repressive culture. The novels are thus in-
evitably about expression. Breaking through the masculine formulations
that confine her, Skram's heroine demonstrates the curative power of the
written word.

The physician in charge of Ward Six was a rising star in the newly
emerging field of psychiatry. Vagn Lyhne has described the contradic-
tions in Knud Pontoppidan's extraordinary career. A dominant figure in
Danish neurology, Dr. Knud Pontoppidan published articles on chronic
morphine addiction and diseases of the central nervous system. Like Sig-
mund Freud, S. Weir Mitchell, and other eminent neurologists of the
period, he had travelled to Paris, a center for early clinical work on hysteria, and was regarded as an innovative practitioner and theorist. Professor Pontoppidan's reforms of the psychiatric division of the Copenhagen
City Hospital included such humane measures as abolishing mechanical
restraints, initiating an open-door policy, and most significantly, intro-
ducing nurses rather than attendants into both male and female wards. In
treating nervous disorders Pontoppidan argued for the exercise of benevolent authority. The superintendent of a mental hospital must direct his
patients with an "iron hand [in] a glove of deep and genuine sympathy."
Patients in a mental hospital should feel themselves under an "energetic
will," Dr. Pontoppidan asserts.

Yet the professor's confident pronouncements sometimes reveal an uneasy mixture of compassion and hostility toward the female patients he
desires to cure. In a lecture on "Hypochondria: Factors in the Treatment
of the Functional Neuroses," Pontoppidan cautions his older colleagues
against a "false and exaggerated humanity that impedes a vigorous inter-
vention: There are hysterical and hypochondriacal patients who must be
handled like naughty children, and there is a call for mental orthopedia."
Particularly problematic is a class of "inveterate hysterics and neuras-
thenics whose diseased self love has usually been nourished in the home
and been permitted to go beyond all boundaries." Just as the physician

must vanquish selfishness and the lapse of duty to others, he must also guard against being manipulated by his female patients. In treating such patients the physician must "immediately, from the first instant, break down their opposition and their selfish pretensions and if necessary make himself respected by fiat." Pontoppidan's ominous phrases reveal the patriarchal assumptions that Amalie Skram describes so vividly in *Professor Hieronimus*. For the female artist, already at war with her domestic status, such assumptions were not easily borne.

Else Kant, Skram's thinly veiled surrogate, is trapped between the rival claims of her profession and marriage. Staring at her unfinished painting, Else feels unworthy in every way: a failed mother and a failed artist. In her exhaustion she hallucinates conflicting images of freedom and constraint, a procession of horses moving effortlessly through the claustrophobic spaces of her apartment. Frantic about her inability to order and depict what is in her heart, she agrees to enter Ward Six for a short rest and the relief of expressing her thoughts and feelings to Professor Hieronimus. But instead of the talking cure she anticipates, Else is searched and stripped by nurses, and confined to bed in a corridor of psychotic patients.

When she enters Ward Six, Else experiences the systematic mortification of self that the sociologist Erving Goffman describes in *Asylums*. The hospital admissions procedures signal her dispossession from her normal roles: attendants take away her clothing and possessions, confiscating her garters and cough medicine as potential weapons against herself. In the eyes of the authorities her identity has become suspect. As an inmate of a mental institution, her rebellion against the system is taken as a proof of illness. In what Goffman calls "looping" the institution generates a defensive response and uses that response as a target for further attack. Else's objections to her treatment become the confirmation that the professor's judgments are valid.

At first Else tries to believe in Professor Hieronimus. Surrounded by madness, she is suspicious of her emotions. Surely he is not as rigid and arbitrary as he seems. Surely a man who has dedicated his life to caring for unfortunate people can not be consciously persecuting her. These are "mad," paranoid thoughts, she realizes. Else tries to maintain "healthy" visions of her physician's goodness: "Her eyes filled with tears of longing, with kindly feelings toward this man who was so wise and so humane, whose life and powers were dedicated to the most unfortunate of his fellow creatures, people he helped more ways than he could know." But inescapably she sees the arbitrary nature of his authority and she struggles to resist it.

The battle between Else and Professor Hieronimus is a battle for the word. Whenever Else and the professor meet, Else names her suffering. At first she complains about conditions on the ward, the open doors, the noise of other patients, her inability to eat or sleep. She begs him to give her a new room, to let her see her husband. Gradually as she comes to realize that she cannot move him, her attacks become more personal. She accuses him of being cold and capricious, of committing "inhuman tortures." To Professor Hieronimus, Else's anger, growing as the days in the hospital pass, is evidence of her worsening condition. The challenges to his authority are signs of madness, not of health. As the diagnostician, the physician controls the word: sanity and insanity are defined by him. Hieronimus wants to silence her, to reduce her discourse to expressions of gratitude and humility. His goal is to reeducate Else and teach her the proper female role: "Above all you must learn to subordinate yourself," he tells her; "You have a great need to learn self-control." To Hieronimus, Else's artistic expression is a particular danger. In a climactic scene, the professor tells Else that he thinks she is mad, that her paintings show an "interest in the abnormal." Else represses her retort that his interest in the abnormal has given him the authority to label her. She labels him in return: he "belongs to the category of the executioner who delights in his work." Else's words strike at the heart of his identity. She questions his medical competence by challenging his diagnosis, questions his benevolence by accusing him of inhuman treatment. Marked by fear and suspicion on both sides, the battle of words between Else and Hieronimus is a battle to interpret and control their story.

Professor Hieronimus, as Skram presents him, is a satanic figure. Skram's choice of names is richly resonant. The name suggests both

Heaven and Hell: it is derived from the Greek *hieros*, holy, and *onoma*, name. Skram may also have been thinking of Hieronymus Bosch, whose infernal landscapes provide a visual image of the tormented souls on Ward Six. Presiding over the Hell of the asylum, Hieronimus tempts Else to destroy herself. Alternately ignoring her, speaking coldly, or bestowing favors in an arbitrary way, he tries to break her down. He opens her husband's letters, tells her Knut does not want to visit her, lies to her husband about her condition. After visiting the depressed and exhausted Else, he tells Knut that she is "clearly insane." "Her madness takes the form of an almost total inability to control her emotions. At times she's an absolute fury." This lack of discipline requires strict measures: commitment to St. Jørgen's Hospital for at least a year: "The first six months will pass under protest from your wife," Hieronimus assures Knut. "Then she will quiet down, and eventually leave the hospital with a grateful heart, quite cured ... And then you will have peace in your home as well." Hieronimus holds out the promise of a new and improved wife, with all the irritating barbs removed. The masculine allegiance between husband and physician is evident in every word of Hieronimus's diagnosis.

In an 1896 review of *Professor Hieronimus*, Bjørnstjerne Bjørnson described the professor as "one of those specialists in mental diseases who is all too apt to mistake rebelliousness for a sign of mental derangement." Bjørnson's observation about madness and rebellion has been echoed by Elaine Showalter and other feminist scholars, who accuse nineteenth-century physicians of confounding sanity with submission, medical judgments with cultural stereotypes. Carroll Smith-Rosenberg argues that the new specialists in mental illness were ambivalent toward the women they diagnosed as hysterical. By defining her mental symptoms as disease, the physician stigmatized the female patient, but he also legitimized her refusal to fill the expected female role. A patient who suffered from hysteria or neurasthenia could not be held responsible for fulfilling her obligations as a wife or mother; issuing such a diagnosis made the physician complicit in the woman's rebellion against the fathers and husbands with whom he normally would have identified. In this uneasy symbiosis, physicians and their female patients could all too easily become antagonists. Elaine

Showalter suggests that physicians felt helpless before their hysterical patients' baffling symptoms; they feared their patients were malingering or using their continued illness as an assertion of authority against them. Marked by anger on both sides, the therapeutic relationship could degenerate into a battle of wills: the psychiatrist's authority confronted by the patient's obdurate refusal to be "cured."

Locked in her battle with the professor, Else finds that writing helps control her fear and rage. She seizes every opportunity to write her story. In a letter to the professor, using the mildest expressions she can manage, she explains her expectations about her treatment: "Even if I really am insane, I can't understand why you, who are in authority over me, should make it your business to cause me as much pain and suffering as possible." Distancing himself from Else's argument, concealing outrage beneath aesthetic judgment, Professor Hieronimus objects to her style of expression: "The language you use is much too strong." Against the professor's orders, Else smuggles out a letter to her husband, "a cry for help from a soul in distress." The emotional benefits of writing are immediate: "For the first time since she arrived the crushing pain in her chest was gone." Once started, she continues to write on every scrap of paper she can find, unburdening herself of what could otherwise destroy her. In a final letter of protest before she leaves the hospital, Else angrily lists her objections, point by point. Promising that when she is released from St. Jørgen's she will make Professor Hieronimus answer for his treatment of her, she boldly signs herself, "Your sincere enemy, Else Kant."

Focused on her struggle with Professor Hieronimus, Else does not at first see her bond with the women who share her confinement. She is sane; the other patients are mad. Her initial relationship is with the nurses who comfort and advise her. Influenced by the nurses, Else gradually begins to turn her attention to the other female victims of marriage and maternity. Cast off by lovers and husbands, they represent all ages and conditions of womanhood: the senile grandmother, the sexually frustrated young wife, the "puerperal maniac," the alcoholic, the battered wife who swallows carbolic acid. In their madness they still cry for men to come and save them. Else, too, has expected men to save her: her hus-

358

band would come, her doctor would cure. But convinced her expectations have been in vain, she turns toward the women who share her confinement and begins to cure herself. She returns from her new room to the cells where she had lived before and brings tea to Mrs. Fog, talks to the puerperal maniac, advises Mrs. Syverts to be quiet. "It's a kind of diversion," she tells another patient; "Now they all know me and some of them smile when they see me." It is significant that Professor Hieronimus sneers at this female solidarity. As the weeks in the hospital pass, he maintains control of Else's body, but he no longer dominates her mind. When he transfers her to St. Jørgen's, Else leaves convinced of her sanity and with a new sense of self-respect. Ward Six has become more than a prison: "Here she had suffered, and fought, and won." More important than the battle with Hieronimus is the battle with internal demons: her dependence on Knut, her sense of abandonment, her impulse toward self-destruction.

Skram's asylum is thus an emblem of patriarchal power and female helplessness, yet the edifice also contains the seeds of its own subversion. The corridors are locked and access to freedom is under masculine control. The maladapted women, casualties of marriage and motherhood, live in their own isolated cells. But when the patients emerge from their cells, when they try to help each other, they transform the social structure. Madmen still rage on the floors below; the professor's veneer of rationality – which only partly conceals his fear and malice – still controls from above. But in the center of the hospital, the women quietly go about the work of sisterhood. Amalie Skram's contribution to feminist literature is not just her liberating anger, but also her healing vision of what Carroll Smith-Rosenberg has called the "female world of love and ritual." This vision of female solidarity becomes Skram's focus in *St. Jørgen's*.

At first glance, *St. Jørgen's* seems to follow the same pattern as *Professor Hieronimus*. Once again Else struggles to assert her sanity, fights to free herself from a coercive medical establishment. To some readers the novel has seemed regressive and repetitive, its primary justification being to move Else beyond the long arm of Hieronimus's authority. But freed of the dynamic presence of Hieronimus, Skram's attack on medical authority widens. The physical journey to St. Jørgen's prefigures her cognitive and emotional journey: *St. Jørgen's* begins with Else enclosed in the claustrophobic spaces of the carriage to which Hieronimus has consigned her. She feels her physician's presence "like an evil spirit, above, within and without." Throughout the journey to her new "prison" Else frets about Knut, expecting to see him at every turn. She worries about her son. As the journey progresses Else's perspective widens, she thinks less about her relationships with men and more about the old woman who accompanies her. She wonders about the submissive wife she sees at the inn. Her conversation with the old woman opens vistas of lives more terrible than her own – dead children, unfaithful husbands, extinguished hopes. Out of disappointments the old woman has fashioned a philosophy that sustains her: her work, her diversions, her usefulness. Enmeshed in a web of suffering, she has created a life with meaning. During Else's stay at St. Jørgen's she too struggles to find some meaning in her experiences. In her struggle, it is not the doctors but the community of women – nurses and patients – who point the way.

Gradually Else learns to see the other women in St. Jørgen's more clearly. Ragni Bjerkelund has noted the many instances in which Else spies on other patients, coolly observing their behavior from doorways. Skram exposes Else to criticism, just as she exposes Professor Hieronimus. She does not idealize Else's reactions to the other patients – she shows her boredom, frustration and fear. But Else's observations, unlike those of Professor Hieronimus, are increasingly driven by sympathy and fellow-feeling. As on Ward Six, the loving ministrations of the nurses nourish Else's spirit and teach her compassion for the women who share her confinement. Her companionship with Nurse Schrader is from the beginning a friendship of equals, for they share the bond of common tastes and interests. But Else only gradually learns to value the patients. Here Else meets no cultured women like the countess; she must look through the patients' forbidding surfaces to the thoughts and feelings below. Mrs. Hall, at first only a fearful voice spouting English curses through a wall, becomes an individual who tries to moderate her fury to gain Else's approval. Conquering her fear and aversion, Else grows to enjoy her walks with Mrs. Hall and Miss Thompson, her "girlfriends." She is moved by the love they feel for each other, by their capacity for joy and happiness. In her treatment of the other patients, Else becomes a model of compassionate care. The books she will write about Hieronimus will fight not only for herself but for the dignity of forgotten women.

At St. Jørgen's, authority wears a mask of benevolence. The superintendent of the asylum seems at first to be everything Professor Hieronimus is not. He overrides Hieronimus's orders and gives Else a comfortable private room; he delivers her mail unopened and allows her to choose her reading materials. Most importantly, he treats her kindly in spite of her continued complaints about Hieronimus. Yet in spite of his apparent respect for Else's autonomy, the superintendent also tries to silence her. His primary allegiance is not with his patient but with the men who have sent Else to him – her husband and physician. To the superintendent, Else's anger at her husband and Professor Hieronimus reveals a dangerously ungoverned spirit. The bond between the two physicians remains firm. The superintendent refuses to listen to Else's complaints and warns her against talking or writing about Hieronimus. The superintendent is infuriated by Else's letter to Mrs. Hein; it is partly the risk to his reputation that concerns him, but like Hieronimus, he also wants Else to show a proper female spirit. He wants to change the nature of her expression, to sweeten it, and make it less individual. His final diagnosis is equivocal: Else is "not normal." Although he releases her from the asylum, he refuses to write a declaration that she is sane.

But Else understands better than her physicians the curative effects of narrative. Throughout her stay at St. Jørgen's the thought of the book she will write sustains her. *St. Jørgen's* reflects Else's final understanding of her experience as a mental patient. It is only partly driven by her desire to unmask her physicians. Some of her continued anger toward Hieronimus is personal, the result of new disclosures by Mrs. Hein and the superintendent. Only at St. Jørgen's does she discover the extent to which he has meddled in her relationship with Knut, manipulating both of them for his purposes. But it is also the more general abuse of authority that infuriates her. There are rules for people who transgress the laws of society: "For people taken into custody by the police there was law and justice: interrogation, acquittal or conviction. But for her? She now belonged to a caste for which society made no provisions." Where are the legal protections against a physician's power, she wonders. What protects the citizen if definitions of insanity are entirely arbitrary: "What did it really mean to be insane? It was easy enough to call each other's quirks and more or less irritating peculiarities insanity, just like that. Who could prevent it?" Else recognizes the personal impact of being labelled a lunatic. She looks at the red numbers that mark her clothing and notes their "strangely annihilating effect." The social impact of psychiatric labelling is also destructive: "Once you've been labelled a lunatic, there's no pardon." Else understands what David Rosenhan has called "the stickiness of psycho-diagnostic labels."

By the end of her stay in St. Jørgen's, Else has come to understand the motives of her physicians. When a visitor reports rumors that Hieronimus himself has mental problems, Else refuses to label him insane. She looks for a more commonplace cause:

> His entire behavior toward Else had been dictated by an erroneous assumption born of his conceit. He had simply believed that a phenomenon like this – her unwillingness to humbly bow down to Professor Hieronimus – must be caused by insanity. When he had told Knut that she was "stark raving mad" he had surely spoken in good faith.

At the end of *St. Jørgen's*, Else still cares about Hieronimus, and she will write about him, but he is no longer satan or an executioner, merely a self-deluded physician whose unmasking has both a personal and social value to her. If her books are a testament to her sanity, they are also a warning to other women who might fall into Hieronimus's hands.

Amalie Skram accomplished the goal she described to Bjørnson: she unmasked the "petty pedagogical tyrant." But her asylum novels, however personal their origin, also illuminated the plight of mental patients in Denmark. Irene Engelstad, Vagn Lyhne, and most recently, Ragni Bjerkelund have assessed the impact of Skram's asylum novels. The publication of *Professor Hieronimus* and *St. Jørgen's* fueled a public debate in Denmark about the rights of patients and the unbridled authority of psychiatrists. At stake in what was called the "anti-psychiatry debate" of the 1890s was the issue of forcible detention and the individual's right to autonomy. Although in Amalie Skram's native Norway a law guaranteeing minimal legal rights to psychiatric patients had been passed in 1848, not until 1938 was such a law passed in Denmark. Danish mental patients were regarded as legally incompetent; if their relatives did not object, they could be hospitalized indefinitely. Amalie Skram had voluntarily admitted herself to the Copenhagen City Hospital, but she had been forcibly detained there on Dr. Pontoppidan's recommendation, and her husband had been denied permission to visit her. Having diagnosed her as insane, Pontoppidan could transfer her to St. Hans Hospital for an indefinite period. Skram's fury was due in part to her utter helplessness in this psychiatric context, dependent as she was on persuading the physicians at St. Hans of her sanity before she could be released from confinement. Else Kant asks the crucial question in *Professor Hieronimus*: "Does a man have a legal right to lock his wife in an insane asylum against her will, simply because he and a physician say she's insane? The resident physician answers, "Yes. And vice versa." Amalie Skram's asylum novels comprise a moving appeal for legal reform.

In 1897 Knud Pontoppidan resigned his position at the Copenhagen City Hospital, his reputation damaged by the publicity surrounding Skram's novels and several lawsuits by former patients charging unlawful detention. In the years that followed the anti-psychiatry debate, a number of improvements were made in Ward Six. The ward was no longer used as an emergency unit for poisonings and acute medical cases. Violent patients were no longer housed with those who were non-violent. In the furor that followed the publication of Skram's asylum novels, some of the policies that had caused her such misery on Ward Six were amended.

Skram's mental breakdown was rooted in a failure of expression, her inability to finish *The People of Hellemyr*; her asylum novels are both the evidence of and the means of her cure. They are verbal constructions about verbal constructions. As they portray Else's experiences as a mental patient, the novels depict a world in which only the physician's verbal formulations have the force of authority. When Else Kant enters Ward Six she enters a system in which the physician's judgments reign. But by writing *Professor Hieronimus* and *St. Jørgen's*, Skram assumes control of the word. Writing allows her to put her construction on events, to shape her personal experiences into a moving polemic for other, less expressive women. This battle of formulations doesn't end within the borders of Skram's books. As a professor of psychiatry and an author of medical articles, Knut Pontoppidan has also mastered the written word. In *Lamentations from Ward Six* (1897), he defends the profession of psychiatry, passing judgment on Skram's heroine as he has judged her creator. He clings to the image of benevolent healer: The physician should "stand in the eyes of the people as an apostle of humanity, an angel in a white coat." Pontoppidan decries a "conscienceless press" that has brought the medical profession, particularly specialists in mental diseases, into disrepute. Characteristically, he uses the metaphor of illness to describe opposition: The debate about the power of the physician is a "spiritual epidemic." Pontoppidan's defense also contains a sugar-coated critique of *Professor Hieronimus*:

> It is a splendid book – for those who are able to read it. It gives a realistic portrayal of the way an insane person's malicious bitterness distorts her vision and leads to twisted ideas. It's quite incorrect to believe that the central character has maintained her powers of observation intact, or that she presents "the complete truth to her readers." Quite the contrary. She is incapable of giving an objective account. To understand Mrs. Kant's condition, one must compare her to someone who is looking through a glass that is not just colored but also warped. She doesn't make an observation, she doesn't make a judgment without falsifying the result.

Dr. Pontoppidan's confidence in his diagnosis remains undiminished: He still equates resistance to his authority with insanity. Else Kant must be insane so that Amalie Skram's novel can be discredited. But by venturing into the realm of the literary, Pontoppidan has entered Skram's domain; his words no longer possess their diagnostic power. In a letter written to a friend in 1897, Skram picks up Pontoppidan's image of the distorting glass and reflects it back upon him:

> I have just read Pontoppidan's piece and it did not have the disturbing effect he intended. Too bad, I might add. The main impression one gets is a curious feeling of sympathy for him. Read it and you'll see. He calls me a brilliant example of the way an insane person sees through a warped and colored glass. My book is sheer lies, insane fabrications, and in a couple of places, flagrant lies. That he says so is understandable of course. What else could he say? I don't think the piece will improve his position. He whines and complains too much.

In this cool dismissal can be seen the distance Amalie Skram has traversed: a journey that began in illness, descended into anger and despair, and concluded in the self-administered cure of narrative.

WORKS CITED:

Anker, Øyvind, and Edvard Beyer. *"Og nu vil jeg tale ut" – "Men nu vil jeg også tale ud"*: *Brevvekslingen mellom Bjørnstjerne Bjørnson og Amalie Skram 1878–1904*. Oslo: Gyldendal, 1982.

Bjerkelund, Ragni. *Amalie Skram: Dansk borger, Norsk forfatter.* Oslo: Aschehoug, 1990.

Engelstad, Irene. *Amalie Skram: om seg selv.* Oslo: Norsk Bokklubben A/s, 1981.

———. *Sammenbrudd og gjennombrudd.* Oslo: Pax Forlag A/s, 1984.

Goffman, Erving. *Asylums: Essays on the Social Situation of Mental Patients and Other Inmates.* New York: Bantam, 1961.

Lathrop, Clarissa. *A Secret Institution.* New York: Bryant Publishing Company, 1890.

Lyhne, Vagn. *Experimentere som en gal – Psykiatriens sidste krise: Brun, Andreasen, Schimmelmann & Amalie Skram contre professor Pontoppidan.* Aarhus, 1981.

Pontoppidan, Knud. *6te Afdelings jammersminde.* Copenhagen: Linds, 1897.

Rosenhan, David L. "On Being Sane in Insane Places." *Science.* 19 Jan. 1973: 250–258.

Showalter, Elaine. *The Female Malady: Women, Madness and English Culture, 1830–1980.* New York: Pantheon, 1985.

Smith-Rosenberg, Carroll. "The Female World of Love and Ritual: Relations Between Women in Nineteenth-Century America." *Signs: A Journal of Women in Culture and Society.* 1 (Autumn 1975): 1–29.

———. "The Hysterical Woman: Sex Roles and Role Conflict in Nineteenth-Century America." *Social Research* 39 (1972): 652–678.

About the Translators

JUDITH MESSICK and Katherine Hanson have been working together for nearly ten years. Judith was a contributing translator to *An Everyday Story: Norwegian Women's Fiction* (Seal Press, 1984), which Katherine edited. They then collaborated on the translation of Amalie Skram's first novel, *Constance Ring*, also published by Seal Press, 1988. Judith Messick received her Ph.D. in English literature at the University of California, Santa Barbara. She has been a lecturer in the Writing Program at UCSB since 1985. Katherine Hanson received her Ph.D. in Scandinavian Languages and Literature at the University of Washington. She has taught Norwegian language and Scandinavian literature at a number of colleges and universities, most recently at St. Olaf College in Northfield, Minnesota.

Acknowledgments

A NUMBER of people have made this volume possible. We owe special thanks to Elisabeth Aasen for answering our many questions and making detailed and thoughtful comments on the text. Rochelle Wright also read the manuscript and provided a helpful and generous critique. Janet Rasmussen, Hanna-Marie Nordby, Elizabeth Witherell, Ursula Mahlendorf, Dunny Hassan and Hanne Gliese are among the numerous friends and colleagues who have helped us address specific problems in the text. Finally, we wish to thank our husbands, Michael Schick and David Messick, for their many contributions and their loving support.

The 1899 translation of *Professor Hieronimus*, by Alice Stronach and G.B. Jacoby, provided a window into turn-of-the-century language and values. It was illuminating, both for what it did and for what it didn't do. Throughout our work we have felt a bond with the original translators, who struggled to render Amalie Skram's prose into English.

This translation would not have been published without the generous support of the Norwegian Cultural Council and the National Endowment for the Humanities. The Institute for Social Science Information Technology at the University of Groningen provided valuable assistance in the final preparations of the manuscript. We also want to thank the Royal Library in Copenhagen for giving us access to Amalie Skram's correspondence. Finally, we owe a special debt to Barbara Wilson, the editor of Women in Translation, for her help and encouragement in every phase of the project.

Welcome to the World
of International Women's Writing

How Many Miles to Babylon by Doris Gercke. $8.95. ISBN: 1-879679-02-7. Hamburg police detective Bella Block needs a vacation. She thinks she'll find some rest in the countryside, but after only a few hours in the remote village of Roosbach, she realizes she has stumbled onto one of the most troubling cases of her career. The first of this popular German author's provocative thrillers to be translated into English.

Unmapped Territories: New Women's Fiction from Japan edited by Yukiko Tanaka. $10.95. ISBN: 1-879679-00-0. These stunning new stories by well-known and emerging writers chart a world of vanishing social and physical landmarks in a Japan both strange and familiar. With an insightful introduction by Tanaka on the literature and culture of the "era of women" in Japan.

Wild Card by Assumpta Margenat. $8.95. ISBN: 1-879679-04-3. Translated from the Catalan, this lively mystery is set in Andorra, a tiny country in the Pyrenees. Rocio is a supermarket clerk bored with her job and her sexist boss. One day she devises a scheme to get ahead in the world...

Two Women in One by Nawal el-Saadawi. $9.95. ISBN: 1-879679-01-9. One of this Egyptian feminist's most important novels, *Two Women in One* tells the story of Bahiah Shaheen, a well-behaved Cairo medical student – and her other side: rebellious, political and artistic.

ORIGINALLY ESTABLISHED in 1984 as an imprint of Seal Press, Women in Translation is now a nonprofit publishing company, dedicated to making women's writing from around the world available in English translation. We specialize in anthologies, mysteries and literary fiction. The books above may be ordered from us at 3131 Western Ave., Suite 410, Seattle, WA 98121. (Please include $2.00 postage and handling for the first book and $.50 for each additional book.) Write to us for a free catalog.